Dragons of Remini

Book Three
of
The Dragons of Nibiru

Lorna J. Carleton

Published by
Nibiru Press
9556 Winchester Road
Vernon, BC V1H 2E2

ISBN 978-1-7750440-8-6

First Edition December 2020

First Canadian Printing December 2020

Illustrations by Danielle Hebert
  with guest illustrators Brianne Robins,
  Katrin Hierl-Steinbauer and Jordyn Polowaniuk

Also by Lorna J. Carleton

The Dragons of Nibiru

Dragons of Earth

To Julie—
loved and missed.

CHAPTER 1

Suspension

Up. Slowly, slowly, up. From a deep, lightless fog of blank stupor, Jager rose to the edge of awareness.

Light. Dim light. Light from...somewhere. Just light. Pale.

Floating. Or...suspended? Not tied or chained or shackled or wired. Just...hanging.

Can't move. Paralyzed? Try moving—head, fingers, arms, legs, anything. Nothing. No response. Just sensation. Pain. A feeling of floating, like the free-fall of space.

Vision. A wall, maybe ten meters away. Shiny, gray, some whitish streaks. Like frost on rough-hewn rock. Cold. But you can't *see* cold, he thought. Just looks that way. Ice, maybe.

And then he found he could shift his gaze. His head, his eyes remained paralyzed, yet he could shift his perception. Scan leftward along the icy wall. Just more wall. And more. Like a circular chamber. Scan. More wall. And then Celine.

His heart leapt in a flash relief, then clenched in sick fear for her.

Emotion. No. No. Not now, he thought. Choke it back, choke it down. Assess. Analyze. As you were trained.

A few meters away, his soulmate hung suspended. Just as he seemed to be. Suspended inside some sort of thin, faintly shimmering capsule or bubble. A meter above the chamber floor. No evident physical restraints. Just hanging, limp, still, eyes closed. As though afloat in mid-air slumber.

Scan her. Assess. His heart leapt anew: Blood. A raw red streak, maybe two centimeters, from her cheekbone downward, toward the corner of the mouth. Her mouth. Her lips.

Memory burst sharp upon him. Her lips... Kissing. They had been kissing. Their first. After long, long years apart, their first.

Kissing. And then, abruptly, grabbed. Gripped tight in the all-numbing, eerie stasis of a transbeam field. But odd—unlike any 'beam he'd ever experienced.

And now they were here. Wherever "here" was. They would figure that out.

He called out to her, mentally.

Nothing. Not even a sense of presence. Blank.

No. *No*, he thought. Another wave of emotion. Forcing it down, he wrestled his attention back to solving their situation. Analyze. Walls that *appear* to be ice—but if they were ice, the ambient temperature wouldn't be this high. Two bodies suspended, paralyzed—but without physical restraints, and with no evidence of an anti-grav field.

Magic! Of course. And there lay the obvious solution: counter-magic. He hung for what seemed hours, conjuring. Unable to vocalize, he had to work silently to himself—always more difficult, for reasons he'd never understood. He cast spell after spell, seeking an incantation that would liberate them, all the while unsure if a spell cast without vocalization would work, and ever alert for any sign of her

 LORNA J. CARLETON

wakening. She looked so horribly vulnerable, dangling like a discarded rag doll. Worse, she was injured, maybe badly.

Without warning, a motion to his right caught his attention. A small, circular hole had appeared half-way up the wall. It opened rapidly outward, wider and wider, to reveal a vast cavern beyond. And, approaching like two angry swarms of glowing insects, came a pair of presences. Mesmerized, Jager watched them come, and quailed at the pure evil they emanated. Though they made no physical sound, the boy sensed they were conversing as they came. Then one seemed to sense Jager watching; it halted, the second followed suit, and they turned their hideous attention fully his way. Unprepared for the evil onslaught, the boy struggled to turn away, to avoid their malevolent "glare." But it was no use. With a mental wail of despair, he reeled back into black oblivion.

CHAPTER 2

Concerns and Reassurances

Fianna shrugged and scowled at her brother's desperate look. She knew his unspoken question all too well—he had already asked nearly a dozen times, in less than an hour. And no, she still had no idea how Joli was doing. How could she? She'd been right here with him since they arrived; if there had been any news at all, he'd have heard it too.

At least they were safe here, in the Mentors' hidden Mars outpost. She and her brother Ahimoth, his darling Joli, their old friend Vin, and Narco and Choy—the scarlet, two-headed Kerr Dragon.

Little more than an hour ago, the Mentor known as North had transbeamed them all from Earth to this refuge—from a mountainside in Vogelsberg, Germany, where they had just won a fierce battle with the unspeakably evil half-Rept criminal, Soader.

They had defeated and captured Soader, and consigned him to the infamous prison planet RPF113.

The young Dragon Joli had been gravely injured, but was now in the care of the Mentors: masters of healing, medical and magical.

Father Greer, an elder priest whose meek manner belied his immense power, had bid his young friends farewell and returned to the Vogelsberg caverns he called home.

Narco and Choy, released at last from Soader's hypnotic thrall, had been forgiven for the part they'd played—against their will and true gentle nature—in the conflict. Now the Mentors were arranging to transport them back to their native planet, Kerr. It would be the first time they would breathe the air of home since Soader had inveigled them into his evil service, decades ago.

Finally, the young Fleet Officer Jager and his sorceress soulmate Celine—Fianna's cherished Companion—had vanished mysteriously, mid-kiss, at the height of their victory celebration. Their friends guessed the pair must have worked some of their considerable magic to buy a bit of time alone.

The wounded Joli was not Fianna's only concern, nor her biggest. She couldn't help but worry about Celine. Where had she and Jager gone? Fianna had reluctantly agreed with the group's conjecture about a romantic escape, but in her Dragon's heart lay unspoken dread. She pushed aside the haunting image of the couple's abrupt disappearance, and—for what seemed the hundredth time—reached out mentally to her Companion, in their long-accustomed mode of communication. And again she despaired at the stark silence in reply.

The white Dragon groaned. The severed link with Celine could mean only one of two things: either the girl was behind telepathic shielding, or.... Fianna shuddered, unable to complete the thought. To escape her dread, she rose, stamped her feet and flapped her great wings. It pained her greatly to do so, thanks to her fresh battle wounds, but she was glad

of the pain and wished for more: it distracted her thoughts. And she considered the pain fair, just and deserved. *If only I had been stronger and braver,* she thought. *It is my fault dear Celine is gone. I am responsible for her and for Jager. I failed them!*

Hearing his sister's thoughts, Ahimoth interrupted. "Sister. Sister! Please do not torture yourself."

"Oh! I am sorry if my reflections have disturbed you, brother."

"My dearest Fianna, you are not to blame for what may have happened to your friends. Like the others, I do think it likely they left us of their own choice, but admit I share your doubts. If they *were* taken against their wills, the forces involved must be powerful indeed—yet until we know more, there is nothing we can do. And I know of no way to learn more. We must be strong, and trust in our young friends' abilities and skills. Whatever the cause of their absence, we will be reunited. Of this I am certain. The ancient prophecies do not lie. Celine is the 'Moon' of Nibiru's legends, and Jager the 'Hunter.' They have great works yet to perform, and perform them they will. Have faith, dear sister."

Her worries quieted for the moment, Fianna nodded. "Thank you, my brother. Again you show that you will one day be a great king to our people. You think like a leader, and your counsel is wise. Our parents would be proud." She sighed, then went on. "You are right, the prophecies do not lie; we will see my Companion again. Yet still I have fear. I do not feel complete without her by my side, or at the least in my mind."

"I understand. Believe me, I truly do," said Ahimoth. "Imprisoned on Earth for so many years, separated from you and from our parents, unable to breathe the air of

Nibiru, I understand your anguish. But please, do not fret so. I am here. As are Vin and Joli. The Mentors are here, no doubt willing to help in any way they can—perhaps in ways we cannot imagine. We will all be together once more."

"Again I thank you, brother. I am ashamed of my weakness. Please, forgive me," Fianna replied. "I have been selfish; instead I should concentrate on what I *can* do, here and now. On the constructive, the positive—at the least, thoughts and deeds of support for our injured friends. Joli and Vin need us."

Still, lingering feelings of shame haunted the white princess. Somehow, some way, she thought, it must be her fault that Celine and Jager were missing, and that Joli lay injured nearby. It was a stretch to blame herself for Vin's wounds— the legacy of long years in Soader's cruel cavern prison—but she managed even that bit of self-punishment.

Seeing he had not yet relieved her brooding, Ahimoth interrupted her thoughts once more. "I wonder how many new hatchlings there are now, back on Nibiru," he mused. "It is incredible what you and Celine achieved, reversing the Brothers' hex upon our people. A miracle! New births at last, after centuries with but few, few hatchings! You should be so proud of yourself. My pride in you knows no limit."

Fianna began a reply, but cut herself short when a Mentor appeared at their chamber entrance: North. The Dragons turned their attention to her, hoping for news of Joli.

"Have you news for us?" asked Ahimoth.

"I do," replied the graceful being.

"Oh!" cried Fianna. "But may we call Vin to join us, before you relay it?"

"Of course, Fianna."

Fianna nodded at Ahimoth, who dashed past the Mentor and down the corridor to fetch his old friend. Soon the black Dragon returned, the blue right behind him. They settled next to Fianna; all three gave North their complete attention, hoping against hope that her news would be good. Their tails twitched in anticipation, white, blue and black.

Ahimoth could not contain himself. "Our Joli—how is she?"

"Dear Prince," replied the Mentor with a nod, "Joli is resting comfortably. She will be fine, near fully recovered, within a few days."

The Dragons heaved sighs of happy relief; the atmosphere brightened at once. In truth, their worries had been exaggerated—Joli's wounds had been severe, but not life-threatening for a young Dragon in good health. It was their awful, indelible memories of Joli's previous-life body, battered, burnt and lifeless after a horrible accident, that had amplified their present anguish.

"When can we see her?" asked Ahimoth, standing tall.

"In fact, by sometime early tomorrow, she is likely to come to see *you*," North replied. "By no means fully recovered, but able to move about. And encouraged to do so, as part of the recovery process."

"Wonderful!" said Ahimoth. "I cannot begin to thank you enough."

"You are welcome," said the Mentor. "Until then, I suggest you all get some rest." She bowed and turned to leave.

"Oh, North, please," Fianna said, "is there news of Celine and Jager? And West—where is West?"

"I am sorry, but no, Princess, we have no news or word from your friends, nor from West. Please do not worry yourselves, though. For I am certain that soon we shall know more. And no matter the hour, I will bring you any news at once."

"Thank you, thank you," said the three. The Mentor nodded, then departed as gracefully as she had arrived.

"Well, at least we know a bit more," sighed Fianna. "And I do trust that the Mentors will keep their word." She rose, plodded across the chamber and slumped onto the bed of fresh, aromatic straw the Mentors had provided. Other races might think such accommodations crude, but to the Nibiruans it was a taste of home, a comforting touch of tradition. "I am exhausted; I could sleep for days. Perhaps I shall. And perhaps Celine will be back at my side when I wake."

"Perhaps she shall," agreed Ahimoth, "perhaps she shall." He and Vin exchanged a look of fond concern for their beautiful companion. Vin gave a little bow, wordlessly requesting his prince's leave to retire. Ahimoth smiled and nodded, and the blue Dragon slipped out into the corridor, heading for his chamber.

Ahimoth made his way to his own chamber and bed of straw, carefully curled his tail about him and fell fast asleep in moments.

The young princess, however, lay long awake, pondering the last few days. Elated to have reunited with her parents, brother and old friends after painful years apart, she still felt desperately alone. Her Companion was gone, and she knew neither where nor why. Why must life be so strange, so painful, so confusing, she thought. She shifted about, seeking a more comfortable arrangement of her graceful form. Finally, she rested her muzzle on her finely scaled forelegs, wrapped her tail all around her, and fell into fitful slumber.

CHAPTER 3

Spirit Trap

Far across the universe, the Mentor, West, was having difficulties of her own. Suspended in the mercilessly intense energy field of a spirit trap, she faced her captor: the being known as Byrne.

Byrne was one of a small group of evil entities, twisted outcasts from a great and powerful race long since departed to another universe. Byrne and his fellows—known as the Lords among those few who were aware of their existence—shared a single, insidious goal: total subjugation of all life in this universe, and in several others beyond.

Byrne had captured West roughly two days past, judged in Earth time, shortly before battle was joined between the Rept-Human Soader, and Celine, Fianna and their compatriots. He had brought the Mentor here, light-years from Earth, thrown her onto the spirit trap, and begun a vicious interrogation that continued even now.

The spirit trap itself was diabolical. Its physical manifestation was a vertical shaft of blue-white energy, about three meters high—as if a short segment of flaming lightning bolt had been captured and frozen in space. Any being coming in contact with the shaft was held fast—trapped. But the infernal device did not simply pin a being in place. It turned that being's own force back against it. That is, when a captive spirit made any effort to escape, the device captured that effort's energy and re-channeled it to amplify the shaft's own holding power. The harder a captive struggled, the stronger the shaft's grip grew.

Byrne sought to tear from West the secrets of Nibiru and its Dragon race. He knew that somehow all life in the Phoenix Universe—the universe of Earth and Nibiru—depended upon them. To succeed in their quest for total dominance, the Lords must pierce the barriers protecting the mystic planet and either enslave or exterminate its peaceful inhabitants.

From the way the Mentors guided and protected the young Humans known as Celine and Jager, Byrne and his brethren had deduced that the two must also play crucial roles. This was why the Lords had influenced their own minions, the Barbdews brothers, to pursue the pair. Neither the Barbdews nor the underlings they themselves employed suspected the true reason for the young Humans' importance. Nor did Kurucz and Bsrn, the beings Byrne had ordered to capture and interrogate them when the Brothers had failed.

The evil pair had snatched Celine and Jager from Earth a few days ago, just after their battle with Soader. The Humans were now imprisoned in an ice cavern on Byrne's remote planetoid. At Byrne's direction, Kurucz and Bsrn sought to extract whatever information Celine and Jager had regarding Nibiru and its Dragons, about their own roles in the Mentors' plans, and about the Mentors as well.

"So you see, my lovely Mentor," sneered Byrne to his captive, "*your* ages-long coddling and grooming of the two

Humans has betrayed them. If you hadn't been so painfully obvious about it, we'd never have known of their existence, much less their importance to you."

Neither being now inhabited a body, though both could and did, when it served their purposes. At present, West manifested as a gently swirling cluster of scintillating golden particles. Byrne's manifestation was in violent contrast: a swarm of deep violet and sickly yellow-green particles—like a wicked bruise on the fair skin of the universe—snapping and flashing in jarringly erratic spasms.

Because ordinary physical force would have no hurtful or persuasive effect on the Mentor, Byrne had been pummeling West with spiritual energies—energies native to a universe outside and "above" (for want of a better term) the Phoenix Universe from which he'd snatched her. To inhabitants of that universe, the forces he employed would be viewed as magical.

"I've no idea what could be so terribly important about those pathetic little creatures, but you shall soon enlighten me," said Byrne. "Oh my, yes. And meanwhile, my servants will extract whatever useful information the Humans have. The little darlings will be stripped of their knowledge, and then of their useless lives." And with that he slammed the Mentor with another searing blast of other-worldly energy.

West had not known Byrne's minions had captured the youngsters, but knew his threat to kill them was an idle one. He dared not allow them to die—nor even be seriously harmed. Byrne was unfathomably evil, but far, far from stupid. He would realize that if the young Humans perished, he would lose access to the power he suspected they held.

Even Celine and Jager had only the vaguest notion of the roles they were to play in safeguarding their universe. Nor did they have any truly important information for Kurucz and Bsrn to extract. Their interrogation would be horrible, but they were tough and supremely resilient. They would survive it unharmed, and no crucial secrets would be revealed. Still, West was determined to escape Byrne's trap and rescue the pair, to spare them as much torment as possible. And she knew precisely how and when she would do it.

West showed no sign of succumbing to his battering, so Byrne cut short the onslaught and stormed off, furious. West knew that when he returned, her tormenter would redouble his efforts, and perhaps draw near to the limits of her endurance. The time had come.

First, West uttered the final phrases of an incantation she had been chanting for some time, in preparation for this moment. The spell complete, a tiny "capsule" appeared before her, undetectable and impenetrable by anyone but herself. Next she duplicated her being, creating a quasi-West, indistinguishable from her true self—yet false, and perishable. Finally, she moved into the secret capsule, leaving her quasi-self behind. Much as Jager had once done, following her careful tutelage, to outsmart the hateful Soader.

Byrne returned, his fuming rage replaced by deadly resolve. West saw the monster's energy field intensify, preparing for an overwhelming blow. Her quasi-self quailed—the first fear Byrne had perceived from his captive. He emitted a rumbling growl of self-satisfaction, and unleashed an unspeakable blast of other-universe force.

The glowing, golden particles that marked West's presence flickered, then went dark. Moments later they faded from existence in a pale wisp of inert vapor.

Byrne gloated. Though he had not torn from her the information he sought, there were others he could capture

and torment to gain it. Meanwhile, he had eliminated a major impediment to his devilish plans. He deactivated the restraint field that had held the Mentor, and departed.

WEST—THE TRUE WEST—watched from within her secret capsule. Seeing that Byrne was convinced of victory and ignorant of her deception, she vanished—bound for Celine and Jager's icy prison, faster than the speed of thought.

CHAPTER 4

Darkness and Light

Byrne's underlings, Kurucz and Bsrn, made their way toward the ice cave where their Human captives hung helpless.

"So," said Bsrn, "we snapped them up like the boss ordered. And we've been bashing away at them ever since, but they sure don't have much to say." The deep green, spark-like particles of his physical manifestation churned and glinted.

"Yeah," replied the ochre-and-gray swarm that was Kurucz. "And they are not what I expected at all. Weak little things. Pathetic."

"Right," said Bsrn. "I thought they'd be brute warrior types who'd fight back like beasties. Or maybe overstuffed ruling-class gasbags, decked in fancy outfits and jewels. Or even giants, or Dragons, or *something* worthwhile. But a couple pale Humans, not even fully grown? Huh. Typical of the pathetic scum you see on Earth, though. And they've got the endurance of a damned gnat—we barely get started on 'em and they black out. But who are we to argue? We obey our orders and keep old Byrnzee the Awful as close to happy as we can."

"Amen to that," said Kurucz. "But watch what you say. He could be listening."

"Yeah, true. Well, let's hope they're conscious again so we can get back to work. We've got to get something out of them soon, or Byrne's gonna incinerate us."

"Or worse," said Kurucz. "Let's get to it."

Advancing toward the ice cave, the pair stopped short. "Someone's coming," said Bsrn.

"Yeah, I heard it too," said Kurucz. "We expecting visitors? An inspection?"

"Nothing I know of. Let's see what this is about. Maybe some intruders we can slaughter outright—none of this cursed 'careful, careful, keep them alive and functional' crap." The two entities vanished from physical view.

Jager woke. Damn! he thought. Still hanging here. Still paralyzed, though his attention and perception remained free. And there was Celine, just as he'd seen her last. Same position, still unconscious, still unresponsive to his mental call. Hells, he couldn't even be sure his calls were going *anywhere*. The faint "mental echo" he associated with menting was absent; and had been since they'd arrived here. Maybe he was being blocked altogether. He tried to reach West; utter silence. Nothing I can do about it, he thought. He scanned Celine again, hoping for any change. Her breathing was shallow but steady; a good sign, but no change there. Ah! The facial wound no longer bled. At least there was that.

His attention shot to the wall to his right. The same circular aperture he'd seen earlier had appeared, and now irised out from floor to cave-roof. Ohhhh no, he thought. Those entities again, with their incessant questions—and the pain.

But it wasn't Kurucz and Bsrn he saw swarming down the corridor toward his prison. It was a gang of people—Repts, Greys, Humans—including a Human he recognized, in a hover-chair: Scabbage.

The crowd jostled its way into the ice cave. First in were a half-dozen Rept and Grey guards, who took up positions around the perimeter. Then came Scabbage in his hover-chair, followed by a pair of grossly obese Repts, so similar in appearance that Jager guessed they must be twins. Indeed they were: Lancaster and Dodd Barbdews, widely known as the Brothers. Finally, a few Greys scurried in to take up positions close to Scabbage and the Brothers, ready to respond to their masters' whims.

The three had been arguing and berating each other nonstop since Jager first caught sight of them. They were still at it, so engrossed they didn't notice Bsrn and Kurucz streaming down the corridor and straight into the chamber. At once the foul entities took over the noisy harangue session, to the great surprise of their Rept targets.

"Scabbage! What in all the bloody, bloody hells do you think you're doing here?" Bsrn demanded. "And you Barbdews vermin—Xenu's name, you have a hell of a nerve showing up here after losing the Jager Human. And you couldn't even manage to grab the damn female. You can thank whatever you pray to that we managed to snag them. It may—*may*—save your worthless lives from Byrne's oh-so-righteous wrath!"

The Brothers' baleful looks of contrition were as nearly genuine as such arrogant souls could manage. Scabbage just gaped, trembling so hard his hover-chair rattled.

Lancaster was quick to recover his composure and launch a deft blame-shift. "Lord Byrne's wrath would be righteous indeed, and well deserved," he offered. "Especially after Scabbage here put his trademark irresponsible idiocy on grand display, trusting the matter to Soader. *That* half-Rept fool took the boy to Earth, of all places, and promptly lost him—*and* the girl—in an epic fail of a battle."

"Hmm. Is that so?" queried Kurucz.

"Quite," answered Dodd. "*We* dealt with the half-breed, though," he lied, taking credit for what Jager had done. "Extracted from his body and dispatched to RPF113, where he'll trouble us no more."

"Exactly so," said Lancaster. "We apologize most profoundly for being slow to tend to the Humans once Soader was out of the way. You can imagine our consternation when the little rats vanished, just as we were about to ensnare them! We recognized your transbeam's signature frequency, though, which laid our concerns to rest. We knew the pair were now in the best of possible hands—yours— to be dealt with precisely as Byrne intended."

"Mmm," acknowledged Bsrn, though neither he nor Kurucz seemed entirely convinced.

"And now, with your permission, of course, we will deal with the High Chancellor here," said Dodd. "Severely."

"*Most* severely," agreed Lancaster, turning to Scabbage and glowering his darkest glower.

"Very well," began Kurucz, her ochre-gray manifestation flaring, "but hear me well..."

From far down the stony corridor, a blinding flash of purest white radiance cut short the entity's threat. With a cry, Kurucz and Bsrn vanished. The Brothers, Scabbage and their entourage stood frozen in awe and terror.

The flash's bright-white pinpoint source advanced toward

the ice prison, expanding as it came and resolving into an achingly beautiful shimmer of white, gold and silver, intertwined and revolving at a steady, near-hypnotic pace.

With a desperate screech, Dodd grabbed for the comm pickup at his lapel. "Get us out of here!" he cried. Moments later, the Barbdews, Scabbage and their entire entourage faded from view in the swirl of a transbeam field. Only Jager and Celine remained, still in paralyzed suspension.

As the radiance entered the chamber, Jager felt a gentle, welcome warmth envelope him. Feeling returned to his face, then his neck, and on down to his extremities. Discovering he could move again, he gave a cry of joyful relief. He saw the bubble that had enclosed him vanish, then felt his body ease downward toward the cave floor.

His feet touched down and he attempted to stand, but his legs wobbled too badly; he slumped to the floor. Leaning forward as best he could, he began rubbing his legs to restore circulation.

The brilliant entity drew near to him. Suddenly, his pains became bearable, and all vital bodily functions resumed. Amazing, he thought. Clearly, he would still need medical attention, but at least he could operate freely for the moment. With a fervent "Thank you," he bowed toward the shimmering presence that floated before him.

"You are most certainly welcome, Jager," came a familiar voice, both audible and mental.

"*West!*" he cried out in wonder. "*West?*"

"Yes, my dear. It is I."

"But..."

"I have changed, yes. Changed in what you perceive and in what I may achieve, but not in who or what I *am*. I have been freed from layers of limitation. Advanced toward ultimate Truth."

Jager could only stare in wonder.

"Now let us free our dear Celine," said the Mentor.

"Uh... Oh! Yes! Yes, please!" said Jager, and he rushed to where Celine still hung within her force bubble, unconscious. In a few moments, the girl's body began to gently descend. Jager caught her as she dropped, eased her to the floor and held her body against his, softly calling to her mentally.

Thinking he felt the girl stir, he held her slightly away and gazed hopefully at her precious face, still pale and silent. He called to her again, but no response came. He fought back the fear welling within him.

Now West's manifestation swelled in brilliance until the whole chamber was filled with swirling light and color. And for Jager, the surging fear was banished, leaving only peace in its place.

The shimmering luminance quieted, subsiding slightly. Jager rocked his soulmate gently, whispering her name.

And then, to his joy, her impossibly beautiful green eyes opened to him. Slowly at first, then popping wider in loving recognition.

"Jager!" she breathed.

"Yes, love. Yes."

Neither spoke again for a long while. Warmth, comfort and peace washed over them, suffused with memories of lifetimes past—lifetimes together, lifetimes apart; moments of challenge and struggle; failings and victories large and small; moments of passion and joy.

The Mentor stayed silently by, sharing their rapture for

a long moment. Then she called out to her sister-Mentor, North, requesting that she come quickly with a jump-drive ship. North replied at once, and West resumed her over-watch of the happy pair.

With a sigh, a soft chuckle and a mischievous smile, Celine finally broke the silence. "So, wow! That was one heck of a first kiss!"

Jager smiled. She was back. And she was going to be okay. They would both be okay.

With a start, Celine noticed the brilliant entity hover-ing nearby—she recognized the being at once, but her eyes went wide with amazement at West's new form. "West!" she called out.

For a fleeting moment, the being flashed a bright yellow gold; a manifestation Celine had once decided was Mentor laughter.

"Celine!" came West's reply. "I am so very pleased to see you safe, and united with young Jager at last."

While the three waited for North's arrival, West briefed the young Humans on what had transpired since they'd last been in touch, and the couple briefed her in turn.

At length North arrived, brought Celine and Jager aboard, and jump-shifted the vessel back to the Mentor outpost on Mars. From orbit, she transbeamed the couple to the out-post's spacious Common Room—straight into the joyful company of their Dragon friends: Fianna, Ahimoth, Vin and Joli. The celebration was long, loud and loving.

CHAPTER 5

Reunion and Restoration

When the joyful reunion had run its course, West—who had joined the party a few minutes after it began—announced that the time had come to tend to Celine and Jager's physical and spiritual well-being, after their recent traumas. North was to oversee their care and treatment.

The Dragons agreed at once, wished their young friends well, and commended them to the Mentors' care. North thanked West and the Dragons; then, with the aid of three other Mentors, she prepared to escort the pair to the outpost's medical facilities. Because of Celine's more serious injuries, one of the Mentors stood beside her, asked her to relax, then raised her body—without physical contact—from the floor. The Mentor urged the girl to lay her body back slowly; Celine complied, and soon floated, horizontal, a meter in the air. Jager moved to the girl's side and took her hand, and the little entourage moved off down the wide corridor.

When Celine and Jager had departed, the Dragons turned to West; she now animated a lithe, female humanoid body, nearly identical to those "worn" by her fellow Mentors, and similarly draped in shimmering white, gold and silver cloth.

"How ever did you find them, West?" queried Fianna.

"I will be glad to tell you the tale, though I hope you will forgive me if I delay the account somewhat. I am fatigued, and must rest. And I think it best that we wait until Celine and Jager can be present, too, so all may hear at once."

"Of course," said Fianna. "Please accept my apologies. I did not mean to seem demanding. You were missing as well, and no doubt had trials of your own!"

"Thank you, Fianna. No apology is needed, though. Your concern for your Companion is entirely understandable."

Fianna bowed her head in acknowledgement, but turned to look anxiously down the corridor where Celine had just been taken.

"Celine is in the best of hands, Princess," reassured West. "She will soon be well, as will Jager; they will rejoin you, refreshed and restored."

Abruptly the Mentor became distant, as if listening to a voice only she could perceive.

Presently she returned her attention to the gathered Dragons. "I am sorry," she said. "I must leave you now. I shall return as soon as I may."

Now the body the Mentor wore appeared to contract and reduce in size, seeming to recede and recede into the distance until it vanished from sight. The phenomenon appeared the same to all the Dragons, even though each saw it from a different angle; it was as though the body had slipped away to another dimension. And that was not far from the truth.

"Well!" said Fianna.

"Well indeed," said Ahimoth; he shook his ebon head in wonder.

"I think we should all take this opportunity to refresh and rest," he said. "I am certain the Mentors will alert us when we may see Celine and Jager again."

The others agreed, and all headed toward their quarters.

In the treatment room, Celine and Jager sat hand in hand on an examination table, gazing lovingly into each other's eyes. Utterly caught up in the moment, they basked in the deliciously new experience of physical closeness, after so many years of only mental contact and communion. They scarcely noticed the three Mentors moving about the room, preparing for the treatments soon to begin.

"You know, girl, you're even more beautiful than I ever imagined," said Jager. "And that's saying a *lot*. I'm a universe-class imaginer."

Unaccustomed to such admiration, Celine groped for a reply, embarrassed at the flush she felt racing up her fair cheeks. "Um...I...uh...thank you!" she managed. "You're awfully good to look at too."

She groaned to herself, now even more embarrassed at what seemed a painfully pathetic reply.

"Well, thank *you*, my precious pumpkin!" said Jager, beaming. Celine couldn't help but laugh at the pet name Jager had so recently bestowed, spoken aloud for the first time. Jager laughed right along with her, but they quickly lapsed back into their dreamily adoring gaze-fest. The busy Mentors paused and smiled, pleased at the happy normalcy of the young people's communion.

The preparations complete, one of the Mentors departed the room; the other two stood quietly near the entrance.

Soon, West's sisters North and South entered, with warm greetings for Celine and Jager and a nod to their fellow Mentors.

North asked Celine to lie down on the table where the couple sat. Jager gave her hand a squeeze and hopped off, his eyes never leaving hers.

"You need treatment too, young friend," said South. "Please follow Celine's fine example, and take your place on that table behind you." The young man nodded and complied. Easing himself down on the smooth, lightly padded surface, he laced his hands behind his head and smiled, as though his recent imprisonment and brutal interrogation had been nothing out of the ordinary.

With the assistance of the Mentors who had prepared the room, North and South set to work on their young charges, with both medical treatments and magical incantations. North tended to Celine while South worked upon Jager.

South finished first, satisfied with Jager's treatment after about half an hour's steady work. Leaving the young man to rest quietly, she joined North in tending Celine's graver hurts. Another half-hour passed before they stepped away from the girl's table, their ministrations complete. "We are finished, young friends," North announced.

"Thank you, thank you," said Jager and Celine, in unison—then laughed at this recurring sign of their intimate bond. It would become a regular part of their lives together, of which they'd never tire.

Thanks to the Mentors' care, both were greatly relieved in body and spirit, but their bodies cried out for sleep, long and deep. Sensing this, North and South helped the pair off their tables, then led them toward the quarters readied for them,

one room for each, with comfortable beds.

When they reached the rooms, North said, "Though I am certain there is much you wish to share, I counsel you to refrain for now; sleep is my prescription."

Both voiced agreement, but with ever so slight a begrudging edge. Being so close was still a novel and heady experience, and they wanted all the togetherness they could get. The Mentors watched as they entered their rooms, lay down on their beds, and mented each other good night and sweet dreams.

"But please, before we sleep," Jager began after a pause, "couldn't we just…" North smiled a patient smile, raised a graceful hand—and the two fell at once into deep and dreamless slumber.

CHAPTER 6

Incommunicado

Late the following morning, Celine awoke to a faint clicking sound. Rising up on one elbow, she looked toward the sound's source. And there was Jager: seated at a small desk, typing something into a computer terminal.

Sensing her eyes upon him, Jager turned and smiled as bright as sunrise. "Hey! Good morning, sleepyhead! At least I think it's still morning. We slept a *long* time."

"Well, we must have needed it," she replied. "Funny, though—I don't remember falling asleep."

"Neither do I. We were probably more exhausted than we realized. How ya feeling now, though?"

"A little groggy yet," she said, stretching carefully. "Ooo. And sore in spots. Lots of spots, to be honest. But overall, I'd have to say *much* better. You?"

"Great. Better than I would ever have thought, after the working-over those two whatever-they-weres gave me. The Mentors are the best healers ever." His smile took a sheepish turn; "Hey, I hope you don't mind me slipping into your room while you slept. It's only been a little while. Wanted to be here when you woke."

"No worries!" she replied. "Really, I'm glad you're here. Sounds like you're in better shape than I am, too—cheers!" They both giggled, nervous at the newness of such intimacy.

Jager shook off his hesitance, rose, and crossed to her bedside. She climbed from the bed, beaming, and met him in a fervent, silent embrace—and then an even more fervent kiss.

After a long while that seemed far too brief, Celine leaned away, flushed—but no longer from embarrassment. "Mmmm," she purred. "More of that would be heavenly, but really—I should let my parents know I'm okay."

"There you go, being practical again," Jager grinned. "You're right, though. And we should contact Major Hadgkiss."

"Right! As far as he knows, you're just plain AWOL, pleasure-cruising around the sector with some floozie!"

They laughed, then walked arm in arm to the desk. "The major first," said Jager. "I know you're anxious to reach your parents, but he may have news we should know before we talk to them."

"Right again," agreed Celine. Jager seated her in the desk's only chair; standing beside her, he gave the comm link Major Hadgkiss's contact code. The device responded at once: Unavailable.

"Hm," he shrugged, and tried three more codes—including one only he knew, a special phrase he and Dino had established for emergency use. The response was the same. Unavailable. Nothing, nothing, and perplexing, frustrating, nothing. He felt a twinge of anxiety. Celine felt more than a twinge.

"Okay, so he's out of range or under cover or unable to answer for some good reason," said Celine. "Let's try Dad."

She fed in her father's code, and back came the reply: Unavailable. She tried all the other codes she knew—his office, his assigned driver and more. No response. Nearly desperate, she tried to reach her mother. Same response: *no response*. And her sister, whom she never called if she could possibly avoid it: no reply. Now her anxiety had keyed up to full volume. Jager put his arm round her shoulders, felt her tremble.

"All right. This is not good," he said, "and it's impossible, on the face of it. They can't *all* be unavailable. But there's got to be a simple explanation. Maybe the Mentors have this place totally shielded right now. Should have thought of that in the first place. Look, let's ask West. She'll know, and she'll know what to do."

"Right," said Celine, only slightly relieved. "She'll know. She has to."

Celine called out mentally to the Mentor.

To her enormous relief, West replied at once. "Yes, Celine. I hear you. Is Jager there with you?"

"Yes, he is."

"Excellent. May I join you?"

"Oh, yes! Please!" mented Celine. "We're in my room."

Jager smiled. "See? Everything's going to be okay."

Celine sighed. "I hope so. I can't take much more of this."

Within a minute, the door opened and West glided in, emanating calm reassurance. "Please, what troubles you, child?"

"Oh, thank you for coming," began Celine. "It's my family. We can't reach them. Just now, Jager and I tried to reach my parents and my sister. Major Hadgkiss, too. We couldn't connect with them at all. The only response was 'unavailable.' That just can't be—not for all of them, not all at once. So we thought maybe the communication system is down here, or that there's some sort of shielding, or a lockdown, or...I don't know! Can you tell us?"

"Not with certainty, Celine. We are always on alert here to some degree, but the shields are in mid-intensity mode. You should be able to make contact on the channels you two can access. This is unusual. But just a moment, please." She went silent, her attention clearly elsewhere. After less than a minute, she returned to them. "Thank you for your patience. I have someone looking into the matter," she explained, reassuring. "I am quite certain we will remedy the problem soon."

"Of course," said Celine, still deeply worried. "But, do you know anything about my family, or Dino? I just wanted to say hello and tell them we're safe, but now this!"

"I have no news of them, dear. I will inquire, though, and tell you at once whatever I learn."

"Thank you, West! I know you will, and..." Celine stopped, seeing West go suddenly distant once again. "Oh, no," she said, and waited, fidgeting.

"I must leave you," said the Mentor, moments later. And without a further word, she vanished.

Celine collapsed into the chair before the desk, a heap of helpless anguish.

"Mm," said Jager, "this is the second time West's disappeared since we arrived. Something drastic must be happening. And we're just stuck here in the dark. Now out of touch, too."

"It's awful!" said Celine. Unable to contain her emotions

any longer, she broke down and wept.

Jager tried to think of some appropriate words of comfort, but none came. Unavailable, he thought. So he did the only thing he could.

He held her close.

CHAPTER 7

Explanations and Revelations

After a while, Celine collected herself. "All right. I'll be okay," she said to Jager, who still held her.

"Of course you will," he said, with a confident smile. Celine returned it, though with a shade less assurance.

"Now I think we'd better go see about something to eat," said Jager. "What is it, lunchtime?"

Before Celine could answer, a knock came at the chamber door.

"I'll get it," said Jager. "You just take it easy." He crossed to the door; "Who's there?"

"Message, sir. For you and Celine." The voice was small and high, like a Human child's.

Jager called for the door to open, and there stood a dark-skinned, red-haired Human girl who looked to be no older than twelve. She nodded a greeting and held out a small hand computer. Jager accepted the device and thanked her. She blushed, bowed, then rushed off with just a hint of a giggle. Jager grinned at the retreating figure, wondering if she could be a fellow Earther. It had been more than a year since he'd talked with anyone from his homeworld. Smiling still, he secured the door and rejoined Celine.

"I wonder what this is about," she said, as Jager powered on the hand-held and called up the message.

"It's from North," he said. "She says we've medical appointments scheduled an hour from now. Suggests we contact Fianna and ask her and the others to join us for a meal when we're done there. Says the medical stuff should take an hour, maybe a little less. Then we can eat!"

"Food! Yes!" exclaimed Celine. "I'm famished. Never imagined I could feel so hungry."

"Same here," laughed Jager. "I've lost track of when I last ate anything. I know we were given nutrients yesterday in Medical, but that doesn't count for much. I'm still so hungry, I could—as we used to say on Earth—eat a horse."

"Me too...I think," said Celine. She'd seen plenty of animals on her visits to Earth, but wasn't sure which of them, if any, were horses. But the concept was clear enough. And she loved Jager's little eartherisms. "I'll talk with Fianna right away. She hasn't mented me since yesterday, and I've totally neglected her. The dear thing is probably dying to talk, but doesn't want to disturb my rest. I'll let her know I'm fine and set up the meal."

"Perfect," Jager replied. "And while you two chat, I'll finish up my research." Celine raised an inquiring eyebrow. "I'm going through everything I can find on the Volac Forces. Looks like our recent distinguished hosts were pretty high up in their organization; Bsrn and Kurucz, they're called, though I'm probably not pronouncing that right. We're already somewhat familiar with the Brothers, and of course His Perverted Insanity, High Chancellor Scabbage, but I'm learning more about them, too." He grew serious. "I've got to get my head around these people. Who they are, what drives them. They're sick, they're evil, but they are not stupid." Celine nodded. She had felt this sort of intensity in him before, but this was the first time she been physically present to see it. She felt a fresh surge of loving admiration.

"So, go ahead and chat with Fianna," Jager said. "But you might want to freshen up first. All that medical attention yesterday didn't include a bath, which is why I grabbed a shower before sneaking over here. I needed it! And I hope you'll forgive me for saying so, but you're not entirely, uh, springtime fresh, if you know what I mean."

"Oh!! How rude!" she flared; then laughed and lunged forward, meaning to swat him for his insolence. "Ow!" she cried with a grimace, gingerly folding an arm against protesting ribs. "I guess I'm not quite up to that sort of thing yet. Hmph! You get away with your insults this time, but watch it, Ensign—watch it!" They shared a laugh, and Jager held her carefully. With a happy sigh, she kissed him on the chin, excused herself and headed for the hygiene chamber. Jager watched her go, then returned to his research.

After a shower and all-over assessment of her physical state, Celine returned to the main chamber, eased herself onto the sofa and called out to Fianna.

"Oh, Celine!" came the Dragon's mental cry; then a jumbled torrent of Dragon-thought and emotion cascaded into the girl's mind.

Though there hadn't been a sound, Jager caught a hint of the mental tumult; he turned momentarily from his work to smile at his soulmate. Odd, he thought—her thoughts resonated quite differently with him now. Perhaps it had something to do with their new physical proximity, a major change from their long-accustomed multi-light-year separation. No matter; it was new and it was pleasant and he liked it. But much to his surprise, tears welled up and threatened to spill—so deeply was he touched by the warmth, love and affection between the girl and her Dragon companion.

"Oh, Little One!" cried Fianna again, "Are you all right? When can I see you? Is Jager okay? Oh, how I have *missed* you! I was so, so worried. Tell me, tell me, are you going to be okay?!"

Celine laughed, and so did Jager. It was as though a gigantic, maternal mountain bear had wrapped her in a hug-frenzy of epic proportions.

Sensing the Humans' amusement, Fianna turned off the flood and began laughing too. "Oh, I am sorry, Little One! I did not mean to overwhelm you. It is simply that I..."

"No worries, dear friend!" said Celine. "I understand completely. I'd have done exactly the same, if it had been you who'd disappeared without a word, and then required a Mentor rescue!" The Dragon relaxed a bit, but the outpouring of relief and affection continued unabated.

"And yes, yes," Celine went on, "I'm fine, just fine. Battered and bruised, but the Mentors have tended to that, and I'll be back in fighting trim in no time. Jager's okay too. He came through in better shape than I."

A fresh mental flood of relief from her friend nearly knocked Celine off the sofa.

"Now, look," she continued: "I *have* to see you! And I will, and soon. But first the Mentors insist on having another go at us in Medical. After that, let's meet in the refectory, okay? Jager and I are *starving*." She laughed at Jager, who pretended to be fainting from hunger across the room.

"Starving is humorous??" asked Fianna, perplexed.

"No, no—I'm just laughing at Jager; he's goofing around over here, when he ought to be working." She shot the young ensign a stern look of mock disapproval. He saluted with a grin and turned back to his research.

"Ah. I see," replied the Dragon. "Very well, then! When shall we meet?"

"Hm...let's say two hours from right now. That should give the magnificent Mentor medical magicians time to work their morning miracles."

"Wonderful!" said Fianna. "Although the thought of waiting so very long pains me terribly, it will all be worth it in the end." And with a final flood of fond relief, the Dragon's mental voice went still.

Happy at her reconnection with the Dragon, Celine considered what the day ahead might hold. Then, suddenly, she sensed an approaching presence. "Jager—West is coming!" The young man looked up from his computer terminal, first at Celine, then toward the door. There came a knock; Celine called, "Please come in!" and the Mentor entered, animating the same body in which they had last seen her.

"West!" exclaimed Celine, standing as quickly as she dared. A sudden sense of foreboding gripped her heart. "Is something wrong?"

"No, my dear. But the time has come for you to learn of certain matters." She motioned for Jager to join Celine on the sofa, then positioned the chair he'd vacated to face them. She seated herself, smoothed her gown, and addressed her young charges.

"I will come directly to the point. Before your recent capture, you sensed increasing disturbances in this sector of the cosmos. There were times I alluded to such developments, but did not offer specifics. I appreciate your patience and restraint in not pressing me for details—at the time, I could not have provided any, in good conscience. That time has passed; now I shall explain, and also request your help."

Celine took Jager's hand in hers, and slid closer to his side. Neither spoke. Both sensed this was a moment the Mentors had led them toward since their earliest memories in this life. Their recent capture by Volac agents had been the final trigger to what now must happen, for the sake of all that was good.

Thanks to West's counsel through the years, both understood they had crucial roles to play in sweeping events soon to come, though they knew almost nothing of the details. They were aware they possessed attributes and abilities that set them apart from other Humans, but not how they would use these gifts to assist the Mentors. Or why the Mentors, clearly more advanced and powerful beings than they, would even *need* their aid in the struggle with the evil forces arrayed against them. Both sensed they were on the brink of expanding their understanding—and responsibilities—a hundredfold.

"As you have learned in your studies and life experiences," West began, "there are two fundamental types of individuals and groups in our universe. There are those such as ourselves whom we think of as good, and those we consider evil.

"Let us first examine the forces of life and light. There have long been good and just individuals, groups, and entire civilizations in our worlds. In general, they have sought happiness, freedom, peace and enlightenment for all. They have acted independently or in cooperation, as seemed best, within their own social structures and upon their own worlds. And as races and civilizations have spread to new territories and encountered other peoples, they have formed new alliances and groups to promote common goals and aspirations.

"And then there have been darker elements: individuals, groups and, more rarely, civilizations focused solely on their own perceived gain. They have sought to dominate, subjugate and control others to satisfy a twisted lust for wealth, power, and satisfaction of their perverted, destructive desires. In a word, they are evil.

"These two types of individuals and groups have been in conflict, to one degree or another and with ever-varying outcomes, throughout all known history.

"On the side of the good, you may have heard mention of the Aadya Coalition. The Coalition is a collection of peoples who believe in sound ethics and morals—that is, systems and rules of conduct that promote and protect a free, happy, healthy, prosperous and creative existence for all. Their codes of conduct include confronting and deterring individuals and groups who would harm others or inhibit their lives and liberties.

"Many in the Coalition have achieved greatly advanced levels of understanding and skill, both technological and spiritual. For such beings, the Coalition's codes include the duty to protect those who are less knowledgeable and skilled, guiding and nurturing them toward greater understanding and ability.

"All but a very few races in the known sectors of this galaxy are represented in the Coalition. We Mentors are among them; in fact, though there are those, such as the Ancients, who are wiser and more powerful than we, Mentors were instrumental in forming the Coalition. Many Human groups are included as well, such as the brotherhood of priests you encountered on Earth, Celine. Though many Repts are evil, and some Greys aren't often much better, both races are represented in the Coalition. Other sentient peoples play active roles as well.

"At the same time, relatively small factions within many races do not subscribe to Coalition beliefs and codes. Some such factions are in a more or less fragile state of tolerant co-existence with the Coalition; others stand actively opposed.

"The only sizable and significant faction opposed to Aadya beliefs and codes is a group currently known as the Volac Forces. Composed of groups from many races and worlds, on the whole they embody the sort of evil intentions I described earlier.

"The Forces intend to gain dominion over all the known portion of our galaxy, and then to extend their influence to new regions beyond. They seek control of every world, every race, every living individual—and all of their resources, physical and otherwise. For centuries the Volacs—in keeping with the demonic nature of their very name—have worked tirelessly to infiltrate nearly every race and government, with varying degrees of success. They are well aware that to achieve their ultimate aims, they must destroy the Aadya Coalition, by whatever means necessary. They will stop at nothing—nothing—to do this.

"A consortium of terribly potent beings known as the Lords sits at the top of the Volac Forces power structure. One of the Lords, the entity Byrne, was responsible for your recent capture. He acted through two minions, Bsrn and Kurucz. The Brothers, with whom you have also had some experience, are members of the Rept race, subverted by the Forces. Enslaved, to be more accurate, though the poor twisted creatures are far too self-absorbed to recognize it."

"Excuse me, West, but may I ask a question?" said Celine.

"Of course. What do you wish to know?"

"You explained that most sentient races belong to the Aadya Coalition, and you gave several examples. You didn't mention Dragons, though. Are they part of the Coalition, too?"

"An excellent question, Celine," West replied. "And the answer is no—the Dragon race takes no active part in the Coalition's work. The Dragons are unique, as I will explain in due time. There are a few more factors to cover before I come to that."

"Oh! All right," said Celine. "Thank you for explaining. Please do continue."

"You are welcome, child," said West, "and I shall. First, there is the matter of the Galactic Omniplanetary Democratum—the dominant governing system in the sectors that include your own homeworlds. The Democratum, or 'G.O.D,' as some megalomaniac managed to persuade one and all to call it, began as a force for good. And in large measure it remains so, though it has been under persistent, insidious assault by the Volac Forces for at least two centuries. The Forces are masters of the long game, as patient and persistent as they are evil. You can see their influence in the lofty positions some of their operatives have attained. High Chancellor Scabbage is a prime example. High Chancellor Jin is another Volac puppet, though he is only vaguely aware he acts almost entirely at their behest. He believes instead that he cleverly, cunningly, and above all justifiably acts in his own interests.

"The Democratum's fine Space Fleet has long been a

target for infiltration as well, though the great majority of its line officers and crews are honorable, staunchly loyal to the Fleet's founding principles.

"The Democratum has not yet directly involved itself in the growing conflict between the Aadya Coalition and the Volac Forces. It is our hope, in the Coalition, that enough of their original goodness remains—especially in their command structure—that if and when they do become embroiled in the war, it will be on our side.

"And now, as promised, I will further explain the Dragon race and their singular role. In essence, the fate of our universe depends utterly upon the Dragons and their well-being—particularly the Dragons of Nibiru. The reasons for this are rather complex, but simply put, if the Dragons are safe, the universe is safe; evil—including the evil of the Volac Forces—cannot prevail here. The Volac masters know this. It is why they strive continually to gain access to Nibiru. They wish to penetrate the spiritual shield that surrounds the planet, and so gain free access to the immense power that resides there. In fact, they captured and interrogated the two of you in hopes of gaining any kernel of information or insight that might allow them to penetrate that shield.

"But to return to the Dragons themselves: these noble beings are only partially aware of the evil forces seeking to invade, overwhelm and subvert them—to turn their spiritual power to the Volacs' evil purposes. They sense the need to protect themselves, but not the magnitude of what they must protect themselves *against*. They are not fully cognizant of their own universal importance, nor even aware of the Coalition's existence, as such. And yet, though the Dragons are not *part* of the Coalition, protecting them is perhaps the most important reason for its very existence.

Jordyn Polowaniuk - age 10

"In a way, the Dragons could be likened to innocent children. They are more important to the future life of the universe than they realize. They are the key to the future, much like the children of any race.

"I promise you that at some future time, I will reveal further details of the Dragons' nature, and of their influence and power. At present, I have related all that I may, but for one final detail: If your Dragon friends—those here with you on this station—were to learn what I have just told you, they would feel compelled to return to Nibiru, to relay the information to others, out of a natural desire to protect their families and their homeworld. This could have disastrous consequences, wholly unintended. In brief, through their actions and revelations, they could inadvertently lead the Volac masters to the information they seek. Information which would give the evil ones access to Nibiru, and so to the ultimate dominion they desire.

"Further, and even more pressing, should the Dragons make any attempt to return to Nibiru at this time, they would be placing themselves in more direct but equally grave danger."

"Oh. I think I see why," said Celine.

"Please, share your insight," prompted West. Jager nodded, eager to hear.

"It's simple. Just in the last few weeks, the tube-chute has been used a lot. I don't know *how* many times. And there's been a lot of Dragon and Dragon-related activity on Earth—battles and chases and abductions and comings and goings. So if the Volac people wanted to capture or kill any of us, they would be sure to monitor Earth like a cat at a mouse hole. The Loch Ness area in particular, since that's where the entrance to the tube-chute appears. So that's the *last* place the Dragons should go—and it's exactly where they would *have* to go, to access the tube-chute and travel to Nibiru."

"Most excellent, child, and keenly perceptive. That is precisely the reason," confirmed West.

Jager smiled, fairly glowing with pride in his soulmate.

"Thank you," said Celine, struggling to seem matter-of-fact. "It's obvious, though, isn't it?"

"Yes, it could be considered obvious," said West, "but only to one with a sharp, clear mind and a broad grasp of situations and motivations."

"Exactly so," Jager concurred.

Celine could barely contain the impulse to wriggle like a puppy at the Mentor's praise, and Jager's earnest approval.

"But again I must caution you," said West, "not to reveal what I have told you to the Dragons. There will come a time when you may explain it to them —and a time when they may return to Nibiru, of course. I will tell you when that time has arrived. Meanwhile, I hope that you both understand this, and that you will abide by my warning."

"Yes, of course," said Celine.

"Certainly," agreed Jager.

Celine sighed, her brow furrowed.

"What troubles you, Celine?" asked West.

"I'm worried," she replied. "It's just that I find it harder and harder to keep anything from Fianna. I'm worried that I'll slip up and inadvertently reveal it, or even just a part of it. Or that Fianna will sense that there's something I'm not saying, and either be silently hurt, or try to get me to tell her everything. Either way, it would be awful. Yet I *do* understand why it is best that I not tell her, at least not now—not until you tell me it's okay."

"Ahhh," said the Mentor. "I understand, my dear. And so I will teach you how to avoid such a dangerously unfortunate occurrence. Jager is familiar with the technique; in fact, it was not long ago that he put it to most clever and effective use."

"Oh! What is it?" asked Celine. Jager smiled, guessing what West referred to.

"It is a method of establishing a compartment within your mind, where you may safeguard any thoughts or emotions or information you wish. No one but you may penetrate such a compartment, nor learn what lies within."

Jager nodded, and patted Celine on the shoulder. "She's right," he said. "It's a wonderful tool. But I promise: I don't have one to keep anything from you!"

Celine chuckled, "You'd better not!" She turned her attention back to the Mentor. "Yes, please! Please show me how to do this."

For the next several minutes, West explained the technique and coached Celine through the process. When the girl had mastered the skill, she safely stored what West had told them about the Dragons and their importance.

"Wonderful!" Celine exclaimed. "You can scarcely imagine what a relief it is, knowing I won't accidentally endanger our dear friends—or the whole universe! I can never thank you enough."

"Ah, but as always, your bright existence is thanks enough, and more than enough, child," West replied.

Celine bowed her head, speechless with gratitude and love for this radiant being.

CHAPTER 8

Feast and Foreboding

When West had gone, Celine and Jager continued their studies and research. Soon the time came to visit Medical for the day's checkup and treatment, and the two headed off down the corridor, hand in hand.

The Mentor healers did their work with care and efficiency. In less than an hour, Celine and Jager thanked the gentle beings and left the facility, feeling restored and refreshed. Though it would be a few days at least before their hurts were fully mended, they felt the worst was well behind them. Now their attention turned to another pressing need: Food!

They hurried toward the refectory, anxious to rejoin their Dragon friends and enjoy a big meal together.

Celine considered making their arrival a surprise by hiding thoughts of their approach from Fianna, using the skill West had just taught her—but then thought better of it. Because of their intimate mental and spiritual connection, Fianna ordinarily sensed her Companion's impending arrival. It was too likely the Dragon would think it quite odd to be surprised at a sudden, unanticipated appearance, especially at such an eagerly awaited meeting. And if Fianna were to inquire about the oddity, it would put the girl in a most uncomfortable position.

And so it was that Fianna was the first to be aware of the couple's approach—and it was she who trumpeted an exuberant greeting, the very instant they arrived at the refectory entrance.

Fianna rushed to her Companion and enwrapped the girl in her great, snowy wings. Celine reached up and around the Dragon's neck and hugged hard and long. The others looked on, silent, respectful of the happy reunion.

At length, the two stepped apart, and the whole assembly broke into joyful celebration, with greetings and embracings and nuzzlings and cheery chatter.

When the hubbub subsided, the *formal* greetings and introductions began. Dragons are a notoriously proper lot, and good manners dictated Celine must greet each of them individually.

Next, because Jager had never been formally introduced to any of her dear Dragon friends, she presented him to each one in turn. First, Princess Fianna; next, Fianna's brother Ahimoth, Heir Apparent to the Nibiru Throne. And finally, Joli and Vin, long-time friends of the royal siblings.

Jager wore the broadest of smiles through the entire ceremony, delighted and deeply impressed with these magnificent people. Still, he managed to maintain just enough serious decorum to properly honor the occasion.

"Oh, Celine," said Fianna, when the formalities had concluded, "never will I permit anyone to kidnap you again; *never.*"

"I surely hope not," said the girl, serious. "And you can be sure I will hold you to your word!" She laughed, and everyone

else laughed with her—Fianna included.

Jager piped up: "Look, I hate to cut short the celebration, but please—I'm *starving!*"

"So am I!" shouted Celine, and the whole party converged on the feast their Mentor guests had prepared. For the Humans, there were comfort foods from their native worlds, along with a few gourmet delicacies.

For the Dragons—whose tastes were, by tradition, much simpler—there were barrels of fine fish: their favorite fare by far, arrived fresh from Earth within the hour.

Everyone dug in heartily, chatting all the while. In all the excitement, they hardly noticed they were overeating. They wouldn't realize it until it was too late, but they'd hardly mind. Especially Celine and Jager, who hadn't had a real meal in many a day. Though Vin had been nourished well since his arrival at the outpost, he attacked the meal as though afraid it would be his last. It was a habit he'd developed during his long captivity—when Soader had often starved him for weeks at a time, just to watch him suffer.

As the meal went on, it was increasingly evident that Vin and Fianna were growing quite fond of each other. Jager didn't hesitate to tease them about it, and the Humans were surprised to discover that Dragons blushed! Fianna's white cheeks bloomed a charming pink. Thanks to his basic blue coloration, Vin's blush was a handsome purple.

When all had eaten their fill, the friends cleared away the dishes and empty barrels, then settled down to talk some more. Most, having put away considerably more than just their fill, groaned at their bulging bellies' plight—but that didn't for a moment hinder their cheerful chatter.

It wasn't long, though, before the conversation grew

serious. The joyful reunion had given them a brief respite from the grim realities that loomed outside the Mentors' Martian haven. War threatened, like a mass of black and roiling cloud over all the worlds they knew.

Though life on their homeworld, Nibiru, was largely insulated against direct involvement in the conflict, the Dragons were in no way blind to the matter. In fact, the Dragons as a people were more aware of the gathering darkness than almost any of the sector's other races, at least in a general sense. Their simple, almost primitive lifestyle and society belied the fact that they were quite highly advanced, spiritually. Even more advanced, in some respects, than the powerful Mentors. The Dragons perceived more of the magical and spiritual forces at work in the cosmos—for good and for evil alike—than one might ever suspect. Until one came to know them well and deeply.

It was the Dragon race's very advancement that placed them squarely at the center of the war that now brewed at an ever more frightening rate. Yet it was their long, sacred tradition to stand apart from such conflicts. They kept their own counsel, allowing other races to clash and clash again, ultimately to work out their fates and fortunes. The Dragons stood by, circumspect, as they had for eons: guardians of the sacred spiritual framework that made all life possible.

CHAPTER 9

Companionship

A while after the friends' conversation had taken a serious turn, it struck Jager that the gathering began as a joyful one. This isn't quite right, he thought.

"Hey," the young man said, "I know everything isn't stardust and rainbows in the world, but do we need to be so serious so soon?" Everyone turned to him with looks of concern or puzzlement, as if to say a big, collective, "Huh?"

"Look," Jager went on, "I'll be the first to admit some things are not looking very bright and hopeful right now. And nobody wants a war. Nobody! But at least we can see it coming, and we're free to do something about it. We've also got a wealth of amazing resources, and they're increasing. West seems to have become more powerful than ever, and Celine is learning more and more magic, and the Dragons on Nibiru are making a big comeback, too."

"Hm. Quite true," admitted Fianna. "I am still worried, though."

"Well, to be honest, so am I," said Jager. "But surely we can make at least a little more time for happy fellowship. Tomorrow is soon enough for councils and plans."

Joli brightened. "Jager is right, is he not? We were having a lovely party. And, by the Ancients, we needed one!"

"And deserved one, I would say, after all we have experienced," put in Fianna. "Ha!"

"And all we have *accomplished*," added Ahimoth, with a proud snort and a ruffle of wings.

"Very well then, Jager!" said Vin. "Since you have so wisely steered our reunion back to a happier course, it is only right that you be allowed to choose our next topic of conversation."

"Yes! Yes," they all chimed in.

"Fair enough!" Jager said, and sat a few moments, thoughtful. "Ah! There *is* something I've never fully understood, and this would be a great time to remedy that. It's Companions. The whole subject of Companions. I understand the linking between Dragon and Companion—at least to the degree anyone could, without experiencing it. But as far as I know, Humans aren't native to Nibiru, or any of the other worlds Dragons call home. And I've never heard anything about any Humans living on Nibiru today. So, what's the story?"

"Excellent questions, Jager," said Fianna, "And quite an appropriate subject for this time and this company. I would be happy to explain it, but my esteemed brother here has always been a more dedicated student of history than I. Perhaps he would be willing to tell the tale." She turned to Ahimoth and cocked her head to one side, inquiring.

The black Dragon gave smile and a short huff; "Thank you, sister. I would be delighted and honored to relate this episode of our history." He stretched elaborately, spread his wings wide as the chamber would permit, then settled, looked pensive, and cleared his throat to begin.

Celine laughed to herself, and mented to Jager: "He looks

like an Academy professor, about to deliver a lecture!"

"Ha! You're right," he replied silently, without seeming to take his attention off Ahimoth. "Now, no talking in class, young lady, or you'll be sent to the headmaster."

Celine barely suppressed the urge to chuckle aloud, but maintained a suitably fascinated expression. She wasn't just pretending, though—she had never heard the whole story herself, and she was a Companion!

Scanning the group to ensure all were properly attentive, Ahimoth began. "First, Fianna is correct; I have been in love with the history and lore of our people since I was scarcely more than a hatchling, hearing tales in the Nursery. Yet I count myself no great expert; and so I beg my three fellows, Fianna, Joli and Vin, to interject their own comments and insights at any time. And I ask that you correct me, should I state anything one of you knows to be inaccurate, or at variance with our history as you have learned it."

With nods and words, his Dragon friends agreed.

"Very well," said Ahimoth. "I shall begin."

"The tale begins centuries ago. A Human spaceship, traveling from the planet Mu on a mission now lost to history, suffered a catastrophic failure of one of its vital systems. The crew made a heroic effort to repair the ship, but to no avail. The vessel was within days—maybe hours—of breaking up and spilling them all into the deadly vacuum. They scanned the void around them, hoping to find, by some miracle, a habitable planet they might reach before the ship perished. They were overjoyed to detect just such a planet, only slightly off their current flight path: Nibiru.

"As you know," Ahimoth continued, "today our homeworld is surrounded by an impenetrable shield, obscuring it from detection and preventing any approach or landing on its surface. At the time of this event, however, the shield did not yet exist. The desperate captain and crew changed course and limped toward Nibiru, praying they could make landfall in time.

"Their prayers were answered. The ship came to ground, but in so jarring a fashion that it was clear she would never rise again. Sadly, three of her crew perished in the disaster.

"The survivors emerged from the wreckage, shaken, battered, but grateful to be alive—only to discover what seemed a horrible new calamity: Their ruined vessel was surrounded by Dragons.

"At first, the Humans were terrified. In all their travels, they had never encountered such creatures. And although Dragons figured in some of their ancient stories, they had always considered them purely mythical. Worse, most of the old lore did not describe Dragons as benign—far from it. The Humans' fears were soon quieted, though. The Dragons made no hostile move; they merely gazed with interest upon their unexpected visitors, clearly curious. And, to the Humans' great surprise, the creatures *spoke*. They talked among themselves, in the common language used among nearly all spacefaring planets!

"The Human captain, a native of Mu known as Malek, stepped forward and addressed the nearest Dragons. 'Greetings! I am Malek, leader of our group. Our vessel was damaged in flight, forcing us to land here with almost no control. We sincerely hope we have not injured any of your people, or caused serious damage or distress.'

"A large, brown-hued Dragon took a step forward and replied. 'I am Morgon, an elder of our people,' he said, his voice deep, mellow and measured. 'We are deeply sorry for

your plight, and assure you no harm was done us in your arrival. Thank you for your kind concern, in such a trying time.'

"The Dragons took Captain Malek and a few of her officers to appear before their king, Alexem. The ship had crashed not far down the valley from Dragon Hall (which was already well established in those ancient days), so the journey was not a long one. King Alexem heard the spacefarers' story, then welcomed them to his kingdom and homeworld. He offered whatever help he and his people might be able to provide. Malek and her officers expressed their deepest gratitude.

"The Humans assessed their wrecked ship, hoping they could restore it, but it was no use. Between the original failure and the damage sustained in the crash, the vessel and nearly all its advanced equipment were beyond repair. Even the best of repair facilities would have written it off as scrap.

"The Dragons could offer little help with salvage work. Though rich in culture and spiritual power, Nibiru's society was simple and rustic. And so the Humans found themselves well and truly marooned. They had no means of return to their own worlds, nor even a way to call for Human help.

"The Dragons reasoned that the Humans' arrival was not a random-chance event; rather, it must be a manifestation of the vast and mysterious spiritual powers which guided the life of the universe. They viewed it as their sacred responsibility to welcome the little band and make them feel at home. They supplied the castaways with food, helped them find suitable places to live, showed them where they could hunt, gather and cultivate the planet's bounty, and advised them on how to deal with the few potential threats in their new environment. In short, they welcomed the newcomers with open wings, set them on the path to self-sufficiency, and even invited them to take part in many of their rituals and celebrations.

"In less than a decade, the Humans were well settled and happy in their new planetary home. During that time, they had also formed close bonds with the Dragons and become contributing members of their society. Still, the Dragons kept to themselves in several respects," Ahimoth explained. "Such is the nature of our race."

"Some twelve years after the Humans' arrival, the first Dragon and Companion bond was formed. The first Companion was Captain Malek—still the leader of the Human community—who bonded with King Alexem. I am not at liberty to discuss the details of that event; suffice it to say that the possibility of such a bond, and the means of forging it, were discovered almost by accident. The wise among the Dragons knew, however, that it was no accident at all. No, it was the powers guiding all life, at work once again.

"Dragons and Humans alike rejoiced in the miracle of Companionship and its fabulous potential for good. They viewed it as a bond, not just between one Dragon and one Human, but between their two races.

"New Companionships soon followed, and so began a long and beautiful tradition. Many are the tales of the exploits of Dragon-Companion pairs: resolving weighty problems, defending the peoples of Nibiru against threats both native and alien, creating artistic works to the delight and inspiration of their peoples, and applying their shared wisdom and skills to enhance the lives of all.

"More than a century after that first Companionship was formed, the evil Barbdews brothers appeared on Nibiru.

 LORNA J. CARLETON

They came with an army of their minions to steal the Dragons' legendary treasure. The Brothers wanted the vast riches for their material value, which was beyond counting.

"The Dragons had no interest in that sort of value, however. They had no need of it, and in fact regarded such 'value' as misplaced, and a threat to their peace and happiness. No, the Dragons had amassed their vast treasure—and guarded it with their lives and honor—for quite a different reason; one which I shall be glad to explain at another time.

"The struggle with the Brothers and their horde was long and brutal. During the course of it, the Barbdews learned of the phenomenon of Companionship, and witnessed the power Companion pairs could wield. They reasoned, in their sick and twisted way, that if they could become Companions themselves—bonded with Nibiru Dragons—a clear path to Nibiru's total subjugation would be theirs—along with all of the Dragons' fabulous treasure.

"They captured three Dragons, including an elder Dragon shaman, and demanded to be made Companions. But after they drugged the shaman, extracted from him the bond's secrets, and attempted a bonding, they learned an awful truth: Because they were Repts, there was no way they could become Companions. The process simply did not work. Worse, it nearly killed Lancaster, the Brother who first attempted it.

"The Brothers were furious, and vowed to crush the Dragon race in payment for thwarting their plans—as though the Dragons had done it deliberately! They lead their cruel minions on a killing spree, decimating the Dragon population and utterly destroying the Humans who'd come to call Nibiru their home.

"The Brothers personally hunted down and slaughtered

every living Dragon-Human Companion pair. Or so the wicked creatures thought."

"Do you mean some escaped?" asked Celine. "I'm sorry to interrupt, but..."

"Ah, I will come to that presently," said Ahimoth, "I promise you." And he returned to his account.

"Rather than wiping out every last Dragon, the Brothers hatched a cruel new plan. They would allow a few hundred Dragons to survive, to mourn the loss of the rest of their race, and to eke out what existence they could on their devastated planet. Then, as their ultimate stroke of evil, the Brothers cast a spell upon the hapless survivors. A spell they had discovered in a pair of ancient grimoires, stolen in a bloody raid some years before."

"Oh! Was that the egg spell?" asked Jager, unable to contain himself.

"Precisely," replied the black Dragon. "Though the survivors would live out their long, long Dragon lives, few of their precious eggs would ever hatch. They were doomed to watch, helpless, as their numbers dwindled, until at last the Nibiru Dragon race would vanish forever."

"Unspeakable," whispered Joli, weeping. She had heard the story before, but it had lost none of its horror—even though the Brothers' curse had at last been broken.

"As I implied just earlier," continued Ahimoth, "one Companionship pair survived: Princess Linglu's father— Fianna's great-grandfather—and his Companion.

"The pair had been in total seclusion when the Repts' rampage began; they emerged only in time to witness the last hours of the slaughter. Though their immediate impulse was to join the battle at once, they recognized such action would

be futile. Though torn with anguish, they wisely remained hidden, biding their time. Their survival and presence were known to only a few of the surviving Dragons, who kept them secret and safe.

"Ultimately, the hideous Brothers were tricked into leaving the planet—a worthy tale on its own, but one for another day. As soon as the wicked ones were gone, the Dragons invoked the most powerful magic in all their long history, enveloping their stricken homeworld in an impenetrable and obscuring shield. The planet was now inaccessible to the Brothers, and to everyone else as well, regardless of race or intent. Even the most powerful—the Mentors, for example, and the supremely evil Lords, were shut out entirely by the potent spell. The only way on or off the planet was via a cosmic wormhole, known as the tube-chute. And the only way to enter its passage was through portals known as vortexes: one on Nibiru, one on the planet Earth, and a few others whose locations were known to but a handful of Dragons.

"As you may well have surmised, there is much more to the tale, and you might wish to explore it further someday. For the present, though, have I answered your question, Jager?"

"Yes," said Jager. "Yes indeed—better than I could ever have hoped for. I am honored you would share it with me."

CHAPTER 10

Omaja Awakens

With Ahimoth's account concluded, everyone relaxed and chatted amiably. Those who'd feasted a bit too enthusiastically hoped their over-indulged bellies would be more comfortable before it came time to retire.

"...And the most amazing part," said Celine, in the midst of recounting her first days on Nibiru, "was when Fianna..." She stopped short, her attention suddenly drawn to the refectory's wide entryway. "West!" she cried, elated. "Please, come join us!"

The Mentor crossed to stand among the group. "How wonderful to see you all together and at peace. I do hope the provisions were to your liking."

"Yes!" "Oh, indeed." "Wonderful!" came a flurry of delighted replies.

"Good, good. You have endured much, these recent days. Your rest and revelry are well deserved."

"Our thanks to you, and to all the Mentors," said Fianna, and the others chimed in their agreement.

"You are surely welcome, all of you," West replied. "And

now, may I ask a favor?"

"Certainly," said Ahimoth. "What can we do for you?"

"Permit me to borrow young Celine and Jager, for but a little while."

The pair exchanged a look—what could this be about? West had already briefed them twice in the short time they'd been here.

The Dragons agreed at once, and the Humans stood, ready to go wherever West might lead them. But first, Celine dashed to Fianna and gave her a quick but mighty hug. "Sleep well! Talk soon," she said, and hurried back to Jager's side. West turned and made her way out of the refectory, then turned down the long corridor; Celine and Jager followed close behind.

Ahimoth rose, gave a gusty yawn and stretched his great neck and forelegs. "It has been a wonderful celebration," he said, "but now I am ready for a good, solid sleep. I bid you all a pleasant evening." He bowed to each of the others and made his exit.

"I agree with Ahimoth," said Joli. "Time to curl up in some fresh, soft straw."

"Mm, yes," said Vin.

"Well, then! We are all in accord," said Fianna. They bid each other good night and sound rest, and took their leave until morning.

As Celine, Jager and West made their way toward Celine's room, West spoke only of inconsequentials. The Humans took this as a cue to reserve weightier discussions for the security of their quarters. The Mentors' outpost was as safe and secure as any place might be, but in light of recent events, extra caution seemed prudent.

Once in Celine's quarters, West motioned for them to be seated on a small sofa. Celine felt a chill of anxiety, and struggled to remain calm. Sensing the girl's unease, Jager gave her a reassuring smile and took her hand.

"I am sorry to take you from your friends," West began, "but I felt you would wish to know what I have learned."

"Yes, please," said Celine, as bravely as she could manage.

"Celine, I know you have been worried at your inability to reach your parents or Major Hadgkiss, so I asked some of my fellows to learn what they could of their whereabouts. No one has been able to locate them, or to learn anything of their status or condition, beyond the fact that neither Commander Zulak nor Major Hadgkiss have been in communication with Fleet for many days.

"Ohhh," moaned Celine, her eyes filling with tears. Jager put an arm across her shoulders and held her close.

"Our scouts now search for all of them," West continued. "The moment I receive any word, be assured I will inform you, no matter the time or circumstances. They will be found, there is no doubt. And should they be in need of assistance, they shall have it without delay." The Mentor paused, her attention momentarily elsewhere.

"I must leave you now, to attend to another urgent matter. Be calm, be brave. All will be well." And with that, she departed—in as close to a hurry as they had ever seen her.

The girl leaned into Jager and cried, long and hard. He knew grief bottled up too long could foster depression and illness, so he comforted his young love as best he could and waited out the storm. At last she grew quiet, and the two fell asleep right where they sat.

Waking shortly before the evening meal, they freshened up and made their way to the refectory; there they found their Dragon friends already gathered for dinner. Sensing Celine's disquiet, the Dragons did not pry, but kept their conversation light and optimistic. Jager did as well, and his gift for raising others' spirits soon had Celine laughing at jokes, and even enjoying a spirited game. When at last they all retired, her grief and worry seemed almost forgotten.

Hours later, Celine was torn from a deep sleep by a siren's strident blare. She screamed, slamming her hands over her ears in a vain attempt to escape the terrible din. "What's *happening?!* Stop it! STOP IT!!" she wailed. The siren's shriek was frightening enough all on its own, but it triggered long-buried memories of an awful trauma in her most recent previous life. Mental images flashed in horrible clarity: vicious raiders laying waste to the small town where she'd lived with her family. Her breath coming in ragged gasps as she raced to escape the murderous band; the sound of her own terrified screams and those of the maimed and dying; the roar of the flames.

Hearing her mental anguish, Fianna and Jager responded at once.

"I am here! I am coming to you," called the Dragon.

"On my way!" called Jager, racing toward her chamber. He crashed through the door to find her huddled beside the bed, gasping; a look of pure horror distorted her features almost beyond recognition. It was a look he would never forget. "Celine! I'm here! I'm here, my dear," he said, as gently as he could. He held out his arms, inviting her to come to him— but careful not to advance, wary of aggravating her trapped-in-the-past mental trauma.

Suddenly, her wide-eyed terror turned to recognition. "Oh! Jager!!" she cried, then leapt up and ran into his arms. He held her tight and rocked gently, soothing her with words of comfort.

Fianna arrived in the corridor outside. Her body too large to enter, she called to her Companion. "I am here, Celine! You are safe! You are safe!"

The girl eased her hold on Jager and called back, "Fianna! I'm okay. I'm coming!" Jager let her go. She raced out to the great white Dragon, wrapping her arms around the snow-white neck in a fierce hug. Fianna hummed softly, a sort of cooing rumble, to reassure her precious friend. Jager joined them, with a smile and a nod to Fianna and a firm hand on Celine's trembling shoulder.

Soon the girl regained her composure. "That was terrible!" she said. "I don't know what came over me! But the sirens—what's happening?"

"I do not know, dear one," said Fianna.

"I'll find out," said Jager, and he called out mentally to their Mentor hosts. "West! North! Anyone! What's happening? What's the emergency?"

The sirens abruptly went still; the sudden silence was almost palpable.

"West is not present," came North's mental voice to all three. "Please proceed at once to the transbeam chamber. I will direct the other Dragons to join you there with all speed. I repeat, proceed..." A violent thump resounded through the surrounding rock; the corridor shook. "Proceed at once to the transbeam chamber," North repeated.

"Understood!" called Jager. "Let's go!" he urged the others, and all three hurried toward the transbeam facility.

They had gone only a dozen meters when Celine halted. "Wait!" she shouted. Fianna and Jager stopped short.

"What? What is it?" asked Jager.

"Our things," she said. "My bodypack, my spell books—I can't leave without them. And Fianna's saddle and saddlebags; we *have* to go get them."

"She's right," said Jager to Fianna. "Some of those things are priceless, and it won't take us long to grab them. You go ahead to the transbeam room. Let the Mentors 'beam you wherever they're sending us. We'll join you right away."

Horrified, Fianna looked from Jager to Celine and back, imploring.

"It's okay, Fianna," said Celine. "We'll be okay, and we'll be right behind you. I promise. *I promise.*"

Reassured, but only slightly, the Dragon agreed. "Be safe, Little One! Be safe and be swift." She turned and rushed on down the corridor.

"Thank you," Celine said to Jager with a quick smile. "Let's go!" They raced back to Celine's room; the girl snatched up the few belongings she'd set out by her bed, slipped them into her bodypack and nodded to Jager. They dashed back out to the corridor and made for Jager's chamber. He grabbed his hefty Fleet duffle and made a quick scan for any loose items; then they ran for the storage room where Fianna's saddle and saddlebags were stowed.

"Celine, Jager," came North's mental voice, calm but insistent, "please proceed to the transbeam chamber at once." Another concussion rocked the outpost.

"We're coming," replied Celine, "but we cannot leave without Fianna's saddle and bags. We're getting them now."

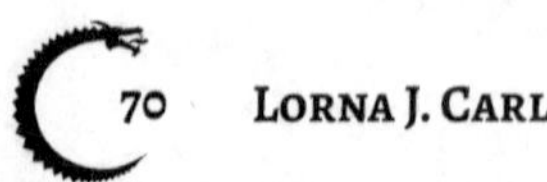

"Very well. But with all haste."

"Roger that," said Jager. "We'll be there!" And on they ran, dodging occasional piles of fallen debris. They came to a lift that would take them to the storage level. It was open. They rushed in; "Storage," Jager commanded. The doors slid shut and the lift shot downward. As they descended, the pair leaned against the walls, catching their breaths. And then Celine was struck by a puzzling idea. The saddle and bags are precious, she thought, but they could be replaced. So what are we doing? But no. No. We *must* bring them, she insisted to no one but herself. I'm not sure why, but I know we must.

The lift came to rest and opened. They rushed out and to the right, down the corridor to the storage facility, some thirty meters away. They entered, and Celine led the way to the area where she'd stowed the items they sought.

"Here they are!" she announced, pointing to Fianna's sturdy but elegantly wrought saddle, and the matching bags beside it. "Would you mind if I carried the bags, while you take the saddle? I think you'll be able to manage it better than I would."

"Sure," Jager replied. "Just what I was going to suggest. Here, I'll get the bags down for you." He grabbed the bags and handed them to her, one at a time. "Now the saddle," he said, and reached up to get a grip on it.

"Whoa!" cried Celine, pointing at the saddle. "What's happening?"

Strapped along one side of the saddle was a staff, about a meter and a half in length: the staff she had discovered in a poorly lit corner of Fianna's Nibiru cave, hidden in a recess where the rocky wall and floor met. Though sturdy and graceful in form, the staff had not been particularly striking to look at. Now that had changed. Dramatically. The instant Jager's hands had touched the saddle, the staff had begun to glow—and to hum with a mellow, pure tone.

"It's never done *that* before," muttered Celine.

"Hmm," mused Jager, gazing at the staff. After a moment, he pulled the saddle from the shelf, set it on the floor, untied the leather straps that secured the staff, then took a step backward.

Celine gasped, expecting the staff to clatter to the floor. It didn't. Her hand flew to her open mouth, a look of utter surprise on her face. The staff hung suspended, still alongside the saddle but no longer restrained or in contact with it. It remained where it was for a moment; then its humming shifted a half-tone higher. It moved slowly upward, then straight toward Jager. Rotating as it went, it slowed to a stop hanging vertically, within easy reach of Jager's left hand. Its silvery glow popped momentarily brighter, as if to prompt the young man.

Jager regarded the staff closely for a moment, then reached his left hand toward it. The staff advanced toward the open hand; when it made contact, he clasped it firmly. Again its glow intensified momentarily, and it let out a single high, pure note, like a chime of purest silver. At the same time, a line of clear, shining crystals, each about the size of a grape or cherry, appeared along its length, seven on each side.

Celine looked on, entranced.

Jager examined the staff more closely; he felt a pleasant energy coursing through his body. A sense of calm, peaceful power perfused his entire being.

"What...?" Celine began, mesmerized by the aura that now surrounded her soulmate and suffused all the space around

them.

"This is Omaja, the Staff of Malek," Jager explained.

"Why...?" said Celine; she noticed his voice had taken on a mystic tone, to match his distant, intense expression.

"It has found me. Or we have found one another. It is pleased—and so it sings for the eyes and the ears and the soul, as you perceive.

"But we must go—at once!" he said, ending the magical moment.

"Oh! Yeah!" said Celine, startled and a bit embarrassed. She picked up the saddlebags and slung them over her shoulder, ready to go.

Jager released the staff; it remained hanging motionless before him. He shifted his duffle to hang across his back, lifted the saddle with his right hand and held out his open left. Omaja leapt to his grasp, and he led the way back to the waiting lift. Celine followed close behind, still amazed at what had just transpired.

When they reached the transbeam station, they found a line of outpost personnel waiting; a group on the platform vanished just as the pair entered the room. North greeted them and motioned toward the platform. "Please, step up— you must go at once." A distant concussion shook the walls and floor, punctuating the Mentor's urgency.

Embarrassed to be rushed to the head of the line this way, Celine flashed a look and helpless shrug to the waiting crew, as if to say, "So sorry!"

The pair stepped up, clutched tighter their belongings and nodded to North. The Mentor activated the 'beam, and the young Humans vanished.

Private Investigation

"Remain off Fleet lines," ordered Hadgkiss. "No communication, cloaking up full."

"Aye, sir," Madda replied, settling the ship into the partial shelter of an overhanging cliff.

Madda and Dino had brought *King Hammurabi* to one of the remotest areas on Hadgkiss's home planet, Erra. They came to rest at the foot of a long, winding escarpment that towered over an arid, lifeless plain. Lifeless, that is, except for the bodiless souls who wandered there. Most were troubled but benign; a fair percentage were demented and vicious enough that Errans shunned the region entirely. No one had yet discovered a way to rid the area of the troublesome beings—compassionately or otherwise—so it remained an utterly forsaken wasteland.

"We're down and secure, sir," announced Madda. "No one would think of looking for us here." Though still confined to a hover-chair after a recent injury in action, and despite their eerie surroundings, the Chameleon Rept acted as though their circumstances were perfectly normal. Her calm efficiency was a comfort to her troubled friend and commanding officer.

"Thank you, Lieutenant," the major replied. "So, as discussed, we've got several things to accomplish. Hopefully, we can get them all done from right here, without interference or interruption."

"Or detection, mm?" added Madda.

"Exactly. The number of adverse 'coincidences' of the kind we've seen lately means infiltration, pure and simple. So for now we trust no one. Not until we know who killed Commander Zulak and Admiral Stock. And who kidnapped Celine and Jager. Almost surely a connection there, but we won't assume so. We look, and we find what we find."

Madda nodded agreement. "How shall we approach this? We didn't have a chance to discuss that in any detail."

"What I've got in mind is splitting up—each of us tackling a different part of the whole situation, with regular breaks to debrief, compare notes and decide what to do next."

"I'm aboard with that," agreed Madda.

"Good. I'll start with the earliest of the recent incidents—Admiral Stock's murder. Meanwhile, I'd like you to dig into this Piccolo person. Who is he, really? Why did he send himself down to Scobee's surface right after 'beaming Rafael, and what was his part in the commander's murder? Working for Soader, or the Brothers, or what? You know what we're after. And if anyone can find the answers, it's you."

"Thank you. I should be able to do all that from right here, and without leaving any traces of the search."

"All right. I'm going to go search Stock's office to see what I can learn. The Fleet Police have been over the scene already, but they're included in the 'anybody' I don't trust right now."

"Mm," said Madda. "What's your plan for accessing the old man's offices?"

"Ah! You're going to love this. I'll be right back," said Dino, and he left the bridge. Returning a minute later, he held up what looked like a typical Fleet space-work suit, minus a helmet and with a larger-than-usual systems pack on its back.

"And what might this be?" asked Madda, smiling. She knew how the major loved mysteries, almost as much as high-tech, special-duty gadgetry.

"Nothing terribly special," said Dino, nonchalant. "Just a standard-issue transbeam suit."

"A *what?*" asked Madda.

"Oh, you heard me. A transbeam suit."

"Yes, I heard you, but I have no idea what you mean. Never heard of such a thing. If it's a suit you wear when being transbeamed, okay—but so what? And I don't think that's what you mean at all, is it?"

"Perceptive, Lieutenant. Perceptive. And correct," said the major, grinning. "It's just what its name suggests. A suit that 'beam-transports itself and its wearer, without the wearer having to be present at a ship-, station- or planet-based transbeam unit."

"Oh! What an asset! If it works," said the lieutenant, her mind racing with possibilities.

"An asset for certain," agreed Dino, "and yes, it works. It's just become available—on an unbelievably limited basis— in the past month. So limited that you are looking at one of only four in existence. And you have just become the fifteenth person who even knows of its existence at all. Fifteen, not counting the Mentors who suggested the technology to a tiny handful of Fleet command and tech people. And, thanks to the Mentors, two of the four existing units are aboard this ship. That was part of their agreement with Fleet. I hope that everyone who knows about these things is completely loyal, but I suspect the Mentors made quite sure of that before they passed on the tech.”

“I am duly amazed,” said Madda. “How does it work?”

“That I don’t know, exactly,” said Hadgkiss. “I was only told that the suit somehow links itself, on demand, to the nearest standard ’beam unit, and causes that unit to transport it to the location the user specifies. There’s no participation by personnel at the standard unit’s location. All record of the ’beaming can also be blocked, at the user’s discretion.”

“I am beyond impressed,” said Madda.

“Rightfully so,” said Dino. “Now, I’m going to put this one on and show you how to use it. And then you’re going to put on *King’s* second suit. And you’re going to keep it on, just like I’ll stay in mine, until we’ve gotten to the bottom of a few things. Who knows when they might come in life-savingly handy.”

“At the risk of seeming terribly unprofessional, I’m thrilled,” said Madda. “And I believe it’s a wise course of action, considering what we’re diving into.”

“Exactly,” said Dino, with a chuckle. “Now, let me show you how to operate it.” He donned the suit and demonstrated the use of the small control panel integrated into its left sleeve.

“You can control it using the keypad on the panel, but you can also pre-set it. You key in the code for the transbeam unit you want the suit to use, or set it to find the nearest one automatically. Then you put in the coordinates for the

location you'll want to be 'beamed to. Once that's done, you can activate it in either of two ways. First, you can tap right here—he pointed to one of the control panel's buttons—or you can pre-set a command word or phrase, and just speak that when you want to be 'beamed." He demonstrated how to set up a voice command.

"What a beautiful piece of work," said Madda. "Where is the second suit? I'll go put it on right now, and get it set up. You know how I am about advance preps."

"Oh, yes," said Dino. "You'll find the suit back in the starboard storage bay, bin forty-seven. Why don't you grab it now and try it on before I take off?"

"Aye-aye!" said Madda, and she headed aft to retrieve the suit. She returned shortly and donned it. "Fits perfectly. You'd think the Mentors knew who would be wearing it," she said.

"Hm. Wouldn't be surprised," said Dino. "Now you show *me* how to use it, as though you were teaching a newbie."

Madda demonstrated the procedure and various options; both were satisfied she would be able to use the device, should the need arise.

"Ah," said Dino. "One more thing to show you. The control panel has a fully secure communications function, too, in case you don't want to use your regular comm pickup." He showed her how the system worked, and demonstrated by sending her a message: "Good hunting!"

She opened the incoming message, laughed, and tapped in a reply: "And good hunting to you!"

"Excellent," said the major. "All right. Best of luck in your investigation. I'm leaving—going to Stock's office, as we discussed. Call if you need anything, or find something world-shattering. I've set my panel for silent notification, so no worries about alerting anyone to my presence."

"Roger that," said Madda. "And as soon as you leave, I'm pre-setting the suit to take me to wherever *your* suit is. I can imagine a scenario or two where you might need a hand, in a big hurry. I'll pre-set a voice command, too."

"Very good," agreed Dino. "When that's done, send me your voice activation code; *I* can imagine a scenario or two where I might need to activate it for you, remotely!"

Madda laughed. "Aye-aye, sir. Good thinking. Good luck!"

"And good luck to you," he replied, then tapped at his control panel for a few moments. With a nod to Madda, he gave one last tap and vanished in a much, much smaller and faster version of the familiar transbeam energy pattern— almost as if he'd simply winked out of existence.

Madda was taken aback. "Whoa!" she said aloud, "That is some *impressive* technology."

In seconds, the transbeam deposited Hadgkiss in the small vestibule and waiting area just outside the late Admiral Stock's office at Fleet Headquarters. Suit functions perfectly, he thought. Brilliant.

Moments after he arrived, a tiny, inaudible vibration from the suit's control panel heralded an incoming message from Madda. He opened the message and made a mental note of the voice activation code she'd chosen: "Rafael." With a grim smile, he returned his attention to the admiral's outer office.

The place was deserted and dark; an orange-and-black Fleet Police crime scene sash crossed and re-crossed the vestibule's glass-paneled outer door. Scanning the space carefully as he went, he made his way to and through the inner office door. The office was a complete shambles; clearly, it had been ransacked, and by people who knew what they were doing. What could they have been after?

Stock's fine old officer's chair lay toppled behind his broad desk. About three meters away was a smaller armchair, also on its side. One of its arms was blood-stained, as were several spots on the carpet close by. And, square in the middle of a blotch of dried blood, lay an earring. Dino's stomach clenched at the sight. It was one of Stock's wife's favorites, presented by the admiral at a birthday celebration some years before.

Damn them to the deepest hells, he thought. This could explain the admiral's odd behavior during their last video conversation. His captors must have had his wife there, and forced him to watch her be tortured until he agreed to repeat only what they dictated.

Dino fought down his fury and resumed careful inspection of the scene. He had just slid open one of the admiral's desk drawers when there came a sharp chirp from the comm pickup at his lapel. Damn! he thought. Should have switched that to silent, too. He tapped the device to accept the connection, whispered "Hadgkiss," and heard…nothing. Then came a dull thud, and a cry of pain—in a Chameleon Rept's distinctive voice tones.

All caution forgotten, he bellowed: *"Madda!"*

CHAPTER 12

A Joyful Discovery

Emerging from the transbeam field, Celine was delighted to find Fianna waiting to greet them. She leapt off the platform, dropped the saddlebags and rushed to meet her dear friend.

"Oh, Little One," the Dragon gasped, with a loving nuzzle.

After a long moment's silent embrace, Celine stepped back. "I'm *so* happy to see you! And the others—is everyone here and safe?"

"Yes, we are all here. South directed us to go to the refectory to wait for you, but I insisted on being here when you arrived. We are all in fine shape. Except for my nerves! I know the time was not long, but with all that was occurring back on Mars, I was impossibly worried for you."

"Well, I'm safe, but I surely wonder what was going on back there," said Celine. "Sounded like an attack."

"It must have been," said Jager. "At first I thought it might be some sort of volcanic event, but those concussions were too sharp, and there were none of the typical aftershocks. But here we are. It would be nice to know where 'here' is, but North never said where they were sending us. Look, let's get out of the way, though—we're blocking traffic. And all this gear is getting heavy!"

"Oh...right!" said Celine, realizing they were squarely in the way of a group of outpost staff, just arrived on the platform. She grabbed the saddlebags, and the three hurried out of the bay.

"Follow me," called Fianna, and she headed down the corridor toward the station's refectory.

"You two go on in," said Jager when they reached the refectory entrance. "I'm going to go find South or one of the other Mentors and get some answers." He set down the leather saddle and unslung his duffle, but hung onto his newly acquired staff.

"Okay," said Celine, and she gave him a quick peck on the cheek before he moved on down the corridor.

Vin, Joli and Ahimoth gave Celine a warm greeting, and asked where Jager was.

"He's gone to find out what happened back on Mars, and ask where we are now. But do any of you already know?" All four moved their forewings forward and slightly up, in the Dragon equivalent of a shrug.

"We are as mystified as you," said Ahimoth. "South was present when we arrived, but left the transbeam chamber before we could even step down from the platform."

"Jager will find out," said Fianna. "Let us be patient, and rest while we may. I have no idea what will happen next."

"I suppose that's a good idea," said Celine, "though I don't know if I'm going to be able to rest much; I'm awfully keyed up." They all settled down to wait, talking quietly from time to time. Celine busied herself inspecting Fianna's saddle, looking for anything that might need tightening or repair.

She came across the loose straps that had held the staff Jager now carried; thoughtful, she re-tied them neatly.

Less than half an hour later, Jager returned. All the Dragons greeted him, and Celine gave him a quick hug. "What did you find out?" she asked.

"As I think everyone already guessed, the Mars outpost was attacked. It must have been some element of the Volac Forces, but I've no idea how they managed to find the place. The Mentors' security is awfully tight.

"Oh—you might have noticed a strange sort of jump or flicker when we were 'beamed here. That was because West had us 'beamed twice—once to an intermediate station, then on to this one, with the 'beam signatures scrambled to make it impossible for anyone to track where we ended up. Or as near as impossible as could be managed."

"And what is our current location?" asked Ahimoth.

"Another Mentor outpost, but I don't know where it is. South said West would be here soon to brief us; maybe she can tell us where we are, but I won't be at all surprised if she doesn't. That's just good security. What we don't know, we can't divulge, willingly or otherwise."

"Ah. That would indeed be prudent," said Ahimoth. Joli, Vin and Fianna nodded agreement.

Just then, West entered the refectory. On seeing the staff Jager bore, she paused almost imperceptibly. The reaction was not lost on Jager, though. Nor on Celine.

"Welcome, friends," the Mentor began. "I am sorry for your abrupt displacement, but I believe you understand the necessity."

"Yes." "Certainly." "Of course," came their agreements.

"Can you tell us what happened, and where we are?" asked Celine.

"As Jager has learned, our Mars outpost was attacked. His conjecture that the attackers were of the Volac Forces is correct, though we do not yet know their exact identity, nor how they discovered our location. Most important, they do not appear to have tracked any of us to this outpost. Our security measures have been escalated to keep it that way. For example, you may remember that on your first visit to our Mars outpost, we discovered and removed from Celine's body a hidden locator chip—which we assume Soader placed there. We subsequently programmed outpost security systems to detect and disable any locators not our own, whenever anyone entered or left the outpost.

"I should like to brief you further, but I must leave at once to tend to related matters. I hope you will forgive me."

South entered the refectory, followed by East. "Ah. Here are my sisters," said West. "They will see you to the quarters we have prepared for you. And as we learn more about the attack and attackers, they will brief you. Soon we will examine new courses of action, and consult with you before any decisions are made. Now I must go. I thank you for your understanding and cooperation." She turned and left the refectory.

"Celine and Jager, I will take you to your quarters," said South. "Dragons, East will lead you to yours—they are in a different part of the station, where you can be accommodated more comfortably."

"Thank you!" said Fianna, "That is most considerate. Sometimes our bodies present challenges, in places built by smaller races."

"Yes, thank you," said Celine to the Mentor. She addressed the Dragons: "Once we're settled, there are things we should all discuss. Perhaps we could meet back here in a little while. Say, an hour? What do you all think?" The Dragons agreed, and the groups headed off in opposite directions, their Mentor escorts in the lead.

Celine sensed some upset in Fianna, so she mented to her. "What's troubling you, Fianna?"

"I am frightened, my Companion. It troubled me deeply to leave the Mars station without you. I feared I might never see you again, or that something horrible might befall you. I could not bear either. I wish all of this were over!"

"So do I, so do I. But I know we will come through it. Just as we have before. And better."

"I must trust that you are right. Your faith is a great comfort. Thank you."

"You're welcome, Fianna," Celine replied, and sent her friend a warming mental burst of deepest care and love.

As they followed their Mentor guide, Jager spoke. "West said you might be able to brief us further. Is there anything you can tell us?"

"Yes, we have learned a bit more since your earlier queries, but I would prefer to wait until we reach your rooms to say more."

"Understood," said Jager, and the three walked on in silence.

"Here we are," said South, stopping before a pair of doors, on opposite sides of the corridor. She pointed to the one on their right. "This room will be yours, Jager. And this will be yours, Celine. Let us go in, and I will tell you what I can." She opened the door and held it while her charges carried in their burdens.

"If you wish, Celine, I will call someone to take Fianna's saddle and bags to a secure place for storage, until it is time for you to move on."

"Thank you for the kind offer," the girl replied, "but I'd rather keep them right here with me. Especially after what happened on Mars. We nearly lost them."

"As you wish," said the Mentor. "I understand completely."

"Thank you for your willingness to tell us more," began Jager. "I realize my questions may put you in a difficult position. But I suspect a great deal of what's going on involves Celine and me quite directly, so we have a responsibility to stay informed."

"Quite so," said South. "Young as you are, others might regard you as children, and so withhold information they would otherwise reveal. Be assured that we do not view you in that way. We consider you able and responsible partners. Indeed, the parts we foresee you will play are essential to our quest. Our mutual quest."

"Thank you," said Jager.

"We appreciate that, and we take our responsibilities seriously," added Celine.

"Excellent," said the Mentor. "And now, here is the most current intelligence I have. As you have already learned, the attack on Mars came from the Volac Forces. Shortly before the assault, orbiting sensors warned of an attempt to probe the outpost. Though our shielding and defenses went to highest alert at once, the response was not adequate to avert the attack. We were, however, able to evacuate before our enemies could disrupt our transbeams, or penetrate deeply enough to harm any of our people.

"Further, it is evident our transbeam security measures were successful—as West mentioned briefly, the Volacs have not traced us to this location. In fact, they have mounted a major assault upon a false outpost situated far, far from any of our actual sanctuaries. Eventually they will discover that the frenzied communications emanating from the false facility are deceptions, just as are the scenes of devastation and death their imaging equipment displays. They are expending enormous effort to crush the non-existent life out of a sizable mass of stone, and some well-protected electronics.

"In short, they have been thwarted, and we are safe and secure here."

"Good news, good news," said Jager. "And where are we located, if I may ask?"

"You may certainly ask. However, as I am certain you can understand, protocols prohibit me from revealing that openly. Not just yet."

"I do understand," Jager said. "I'm still intensely curious, but I've been through enough security training and drills to know how to sit on my curiosity. For now, at least."

"That goes for me, too," said Celine. "But we'll behave ourselves, don't worry. And I'm sure if the time comes we really do need to know, you'll tell us."

"Exactly so," said South. "And now I will take my leave. Do not hesitate to call, should there be anything you require." The graceful Mentor dipped her head and departed.

"Listen, why don't I stow my duffle in my room," said Jager, "then come back here so we can talk. There's still half an hour before we're supposed to meet Fianna and the others."

"Good idea," replied Celine. "I'm going to freshen up just a little, too."

A few minutes later, the couple collapsed on the room's comfortable sofa. "Okay," said Jager, "let's review where we stand."

"Well, to start, I owe you an apology," said Celine. "That's where *I* stand."

"An apology? What for?"

"For being such a totally hysterical child."

"What? When did you do anything like that?"

"You know. Back on Mars. When the sirens went off." She rolled her eyes and sighed. "I don't know. It was like I wasn't myself, or wasn't really *there*, or…or…something. It was awful! I was *so* embarrassed. I still am. And ashamed. Look, I promise nothing like that will ever happen again. Never." She hung her head.

Jager laid aside his staff, drew her close, gently lifted her chin and looked lovingly into her wide, bewildered eyes. "Celine, you don't have to apologize for such a thing. Ever. You are the bravest person I've ever known; you've faced things that would overwhelm almost anyone else.

"*I* don't think you were acting like a hysterical child. It was clear you were in the grip of something out of the past. Some terrifying incident, maybe when you were just an infant, maybe long before. No matter, though—whatever it was, it's not *here*, and it's not *now*. If it comes up again, or you think of what it might be and want to talk about it, please, please do. But don't ever worry that I would think one tiny nano-bit less of you for such a thing." He kissed her on the forehead and smiled. "Okay, pumpkin?"

She sighed in relief, and ventured an uncertain smile. "Okay."

She thought for a moment. Her smile grew. "Yeah. Yes.

Totally okay. Thank you." She reached up, pulled his lips down to hers, and kissed him long and lavishly.

"Whoa!" Jager said, when she let him up for air at last. "We should have these little talks more often!"

"Okay, but *not* for the same sort of reason," she said with a laugh.

"Agreed! So, we were going to review where we stand."

"Mm-hm," she said, "but tell me: Do you realize you just picked up that staff again? And that, except for our little encounter just now, I don't think you've let go of it since we arrived on this station?"

"Oh. Hm! No, actually—I didn't realize that. I hadn't even thought about it, but I guess you're right." He regarded the staff with fresh interest. "Funny, it seems to be completely natural to have it. Almost as if it were part of me—a fifth limb or something."

"Well, maybe it *is* a part of you. Or meant to be. I'm sure you'll agree there's no way it's just a coincidence that you have it. Things like this do not just happen. They are caused."

"True, true," mused Jager. "How did you say you came to have it?"

"I didn't say, but I will now. I discovered it in Fianna's cave, back on Nibiru. It was hidden at the base of the cave's farthest rear wall. I brought it out and examined it. I couldn't have explained why, but I knew I should hang onto it. Must have been one of those 'little inner voice' things that happen once in a while. Anyway, I secured it to the saddle, and never gave it much of a thought after that."

"Well, if you run into that little inner voice again, please thank it for me."

Celine laughed. "Yes, sir!"

Jager, you are *so* amazing, she thought to herself. Somehow you stay so cheerful and positive, no matter how rough things get.

Now he examined the staff closely, running a hand up and down its smooth, red-oak surface. "Do you know what this is, girl? And what it can do?"

"Well, yes. It's a staff. A pretty one, with crystals that appear and disappear. And it floats and shines and sings. Seems quite attached to you, so it has excellent taste—in my humble opinion, that is. It's magical, clearly. But that's all I know. Why? Do you know more?"

"Oh, yes. Yes I do. Only because I did a little research, though. You'd have found it too, if you'd had a chance to look."

"Thanks. So would you now please *tell* me what you know, before I grab it and whack you with it?"

"Okay, okay. No need for violence. This is, in fact, the Staff of Malek!"

"Yesssssss, I know, silly. You told me that before. Staff of Malek. Wonderful. So...??" She was intrigued by his excitement, curious to know what lay behind it.

"I'm sorry. I'm just so excited. This means so much. It can *solve* so much."

"Cheers! Go on, please! *What* does it mean? *What* can it solve?"

"Okay. I'm really sorry. So, you found it in Fianna's cave. Before it was Fianna's, that cave belonged to an earlier princess—Linglu, right?"

"Right. You *have* been doing your homework."

"Yes, I have. So, if it was in Linglu's cave, and she wouldn't have had a use for it—staves being Human things, of little interest to Dragons—it stands to reason it belonged to her Human Companion: Schimpel."

"That makes sense," said Celine. "But you said it was the Staff of Malek."

"Correct. And who was Malek? As Ahimoth recently explained, she was the *first* Companion. Companion to Alexem, King of the Nibiru Dragons."

"Ah. So it must have been passed down to Schimpel, then," said Celine.

"Precisely."

"Hm! And you say it's named Omaja, right?"

"Correct."

"It really is a lovely name. Sounds almost mystical. Do you know if it has a meaning?"

"Yes," he replied, "it means 'the result of spiritual unity.' That's from an old Earth language called Sanskrit. It's funny—so many of the Dragons' names for things seem to come from Earth languages. You've told me how much they used to enjoy spending time there; they must dearly love the place. Or they used to, anyway. Too bad it's gotten so crazy and messed up they can't safely visit much anymore."

"That's for sure," said Celine. "Maybe someday we can change that. So, 'Omaja' means 'the result of spiritual unity,' eh? The name sounds even lovelier when you know what's behind it."

"Quite true," said Jager. "Here's something else. Probably the most important thing I learned. Among many other wonderful things, Omaja is said to be integral to one extremely important invocation and ceremony. The ceremony has never been used, but I can't imagine a more timely occasion to perform it than right now. You see, its purpose is to unleash the incalculable power the Ancients invested in another artifact: Nibiru's Cynth Pedestal, which you've mentioned to me several times. To be more accurate, the ceremony unleashes the power of *two* artifacts: the Cynth Pedestal, and its twin, the Talyth Pedestal, located on the planet Pax—another ancient Dragon Homeworld.

"When the ceremony is complete, an impenetrable barrier or shield is established. A shield nearly identical to the one that surrounds, obscures and protects Nibiru. The difference is, this shield would extend across light-years and light-years of space, all the way from Nibiru to Pax. It would obscure and safeguard both planets, and the several Dragon Homeworlds that lie between."

"Oh!" Celine exclaimed. "And West told us how important the Dragons are to life in our universe. So, if all the Dragons are safe and free to flourish and prosper, all other living things have a far better chance to do the same!"

"Right again, my beauty." Jager beamed with admiration. How wonderful this young woman was. And how very, very lucky he was to be with her. "Omaja has come to me, now," he continued. "I can learn how to wield him. Perhaps the Mentors can help me there. Meanwhile, *you* can get access to the Ancients' most important books, *The Book of Atlantis* and *The Book of Mu*—and you know how to unlock and employ all the power that lies in their spells, invocations, incantations, rites and ceremonies. Together, we can stop Scabbage. We can stop the Brothers. We can root out the corruption that's been poisoning the Fleet and even the government. Now I think I understand why the Mentors have given you and

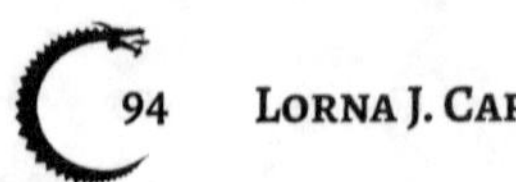

me so much care, attention and help all our lives. And discipline—that's quite a gift all on its own."

On a sudden impulse, Jager leapt up, pulled a surprised and delighted Celine to her feet, and whirled her about the room in a dance of wonder and elation. Omaja—held fast in his hand the entire time—began to glow; his crystals appeared, shining and sparkling, showering the walls with a whirl of pure, white points of light. And to complete the moment, the staff sang, with an infectious rhythm and enchanting melody of pure, voice-like tones.

The couple danced and laughed, danced and laughed, until at last they collapsed upon the sofa, thoroughly out of breath.

After only a minute's rest, Jager leapt to his feet with a gasp and a cry. "The Dragons! We're supposed to meet them—and we have exactly one minute to get there!"

They burst from the room and dashed down the corridor.

CHAPTER 13

Compromised

The massive boot struck again—square on the brace cradling the hip Madda had broken only days earlier. She yelped, louder than before. Lying face-down on *King Hammurabi's* operations deck, pinned by the heavy arms that had wrenched her from her hover-chair, she couldn't see her attacker. But the grossly obese Repts commanding him were visible enough: the Barbdews.

"You're a traitor to your race, you know," Dodd growled. "And here's what your treason earns you. Look at it!" He shoved a hand-computer down where she could see it. "This is a live stream. It's your precious Pleiadean friends. Right where you left them, along with your shipmates. Safely hidden away on Headley. 'Safely hidden.' *Har!*"

Madda gasped at the images on the screen. There was Remi, hunkered down against a wall, arms wrapped around her daughter. The women looked wildly about, like cornered animals—terrified, desperate for escape where none was possible. Again and again the image shook violently, to the sound of heavy explosions. With every new concussion the women cowered, arms over their heads to fend off the showers of rubble and debris raining down from above.

"NO! Stop it!" screamed Madda. "Call them off! Stop the attack!" she begged. "I'll do whatever you want—*anything*—just call it off. Please. Please." Under any other circumstances, Madda would never have resorted to begging. Now it was a calculated gamble. The Brothers were sectors-wide criminals; she'd studied them closely, and knew the twisted pleasure they took in seeing their victims grovel and beg for mercy.

"Ohhhh," cooed Dodd, "Did you hear that, dear brother? She'll do *anything*."

"Indeed I did," said Lancaster. "But really, do you think we should believe her? 'Anything' is rather broad. Hmmm. And I do have my doubts about her sincerity."

"Ah. True. I'm afraid I must agree," said Dodd. A fresh barrage could be heard over the hand unit, followed by screams of terror.

"No! No! Please! I swear to you. Anything you want..." Madda begged anew, then broke down into hysterical sobs. *"Please!!"*

"Disgusting," Lancaster opined. "A discredit to our noble Rept race."

"Mm, quite so," Dodd agreed. "And a vile traitor, too. Perhaps we should do the wretch a favor and put her out of her misery."

"Indeed," Lancaster replied. "And out of *our* misery. I honestly don't know how much more of her wailing I can stomach."

"STOP IT! Please, please, I BEG you!!" Madda screamed, then collapsed into wracking sobs.

"Well now, Lieutenant," said Dodd, "perhaps there *is* something you could do for us after all."

"Oh, come now, Dodd," said Lancaster. "Please let's not debase ourselves by capitulating to her pathetic display."

"I understand, brother," Dodd replied. "One does have standards one must maintain. But hear me out. You may find my proposal interesting."

"Very well," said Lancaster. "One must keep an open mind as well, I suppose. What is it you propose?"

Madda kept up her lugubrious display, hoping the degenerate pair would get to the point; time was clearly running out for her people on Headley.

"Simply this: If our traitorous guest here were to call her precious Major Hadgkiss, and convince him to negotiate with us, well, that might be worth a pause in the attack."

"Mmm! Now, that is a splendid idea," said Lancaster. "I agree. You there!" he addressed Madda, "You heard brother Dodd. We'll call off the attack—just for the moment, mind you—and release your arm so you can reach your comm pickup and call Hadgkiss. *If* you persuade him to negotiate with us, we'll spare the Headley bunker and your people there. If he gives us what we want, we'll pull back our attack force altogether. If he should refuse, well, I don't think we need to explain what will happen. Do you think you can pause your disgusting whimper-fest long enough to do that? Hm?"

Madda feigned grateful surprise. "Oh! Thank you! Thank you! Yes! I'll do it! *Yes!*" she groveled, sick at her own performance but playing it to the hilt.

"Splendid. Splendid," said Dodd.

Lancaster spoke quietly into the comm pickup at his

collar. Releasing the device, he addressed Madda. "There! The attack is on hold. Show her, brother." Dodd pushed his hand-computer toward the lieutenant. It showed Mia and Remi still huddled together, but now they looked about hopefully. They were surrounded by piles of debris, but the explosions had ceased and the drifting dust was settling.

"You see? Our word is as good as ever," said Dodd. "Now it's time to honor *your* end of the bargain." He turned to the brutish Rept who'd been holding her down. "Guard, release one of her arms. But first give her a little reminder of what's to come if she tries anything sly."

"Yes, yes. That's a capital idea, old boy," cheered Lancaster. "And guard, once she's made contact with the esteemed major, give her another—stiff enough that he'll hear we mean business."

Dodd raised his scaley snout high and clapped politely at his brother's suggestion. "Hear, hear!"

Perfect, thought Madda. "Oh, thank you! Thank you!" she gushed.

At a nod from Lancaster, the Rept guard gave her a brutal kick to the ribs; she gasped in pain. The guard released her right arm. She reached up and activated her comm pickup. "Major Hadgkiss," she said, prompting the device to connect with the major's pickup. There was a pause, and Madda braced herself for the guard's next assault. The Brothers leered, relishing her capitulation and anticipating her pain.

"Hadgkiss," came a barely audible whisper through her pickup.

The guard lashed out with an even harder kick, catching Madda on the injured hip once more. She'd meant to amplify her response, to ensure Dino got a clear idea of her

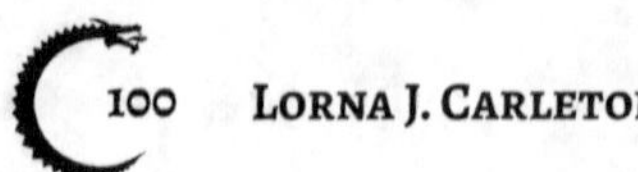

situation—but there was no need to exaggerate; the blow hurt like all hells and a blast of Dragon fire. "OHHHHHHHHH!" she half groaned, half wailed.

Hadgkiss got the message, loud and agonizingly clear. *"Madda!"*

Madda fought down a wave of nausea and quickly composed herself. "H-hello, old friend."

Dino was on the alert at once. Though they were certainly old friends, Madda had never once addressed him that way. Something was up, but he played along. "Hello; good to hear from you. But what the hells happened to you just now? You okay?"

"What? Oh, yes," she managed a wry chuckle. "Not used to this new *jump*suit yet; hover-chair rammed my poor hip into a console while I was busy trying to find my comm pickup. It's not oriented the same as on the old suits. I'll be okay, though. But did you learn anything interesting while you were out and about?"

Now Dino was certain something was amiss. "Out and about" was a phrase he couldn't even have imagined Madda using. He assumed she was in trouble, being held captive or monitored. Her emphasis on the "jump" in "jumpsuit" meant she was still wearing the transbeam suit. Good to know.

Dodd scowled and gestured impatiently for her to speed things up.

"No, nothing unexpected here, L-T" said Dino. Madda caught the major's signal at once: though "L-T" was common slang for "lieutenant" among Fleet spacers, he had never addressed her that way. Good; he'd gotten her message.

"Well, that's good to know," Madda replied conversationally. "Were you able to..."

"Blast!" barked Dodd. "Enough of your damned nonsense!" He ripped the comm pickup off her collar. "Major Hadgkiss! Or should I say *Captain Hadgkiss*—now that you've inherited Commander Zulak's hulk of a ship? Miss your old pal, do you?"

Dino's head reeled. The Brothers! He'd recognize their voices anywhere, after what they'd done to his wife and son. How in all the universe had they found the *King?* Let alone boarding her! She was as secure as any ship could be—he'd been sure of it. "What do you want, Barbdews?" he growled.

"Mmm. Touchy, aren't we?" said Dodd. "No matter. We were just having a lovely conversation with your minion here, traitor to her race though she is. Discussing whether we might reconsider our bombardment of your not-so-secret bunker on Headley. You know—the one where Zulak's widow and child were attempting to hide? Along with some of your esteemed shipmates? You really *should* look into whoever suggested the place. In any case, we graciously forestalled its annihilation for a moment so we could have this little talk."

Dino's shock tripled. Headley compromised too? He'd figure that out later. Right now, he and Madda had to get to the bunker and haul everyone out of there. He shouted loud enough for Madda to hear, even though Dodd still held her pickup: "Madda—GO!"

Madda let out a blood-curdling Rept battle cry at the top of her very capable lungs. Startled, the guard who held her loosened his grip—just enough for Madda to slip from his grasp and roll across the deck, screaming all the while. The Brothers added to the din, bellowing curses and orders at the hapless guard.

Madda scrambled under a console, ignoring the stabbing

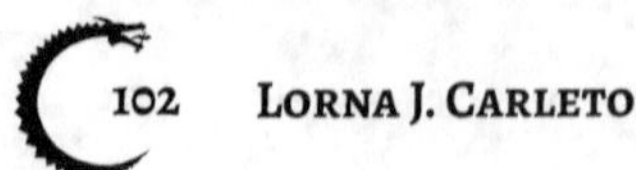

pain in her injured hip. Out of the guard's reach for the moment, she screamed something new: **"RAFAEL!"**

The transbeam suit did its work. In less than a second, it accessed *King's* transbeam unit, fed it her pre-set coordinates, and activated the device.

Dodd, Lancaster and the guard all stared, mouths agape. Madda was gone. Vanished.

CHAPTER 14

A Curse Reversed

"**W**hat in all the forty-seven hells??" roared Dodd.

"What have you **done?**" bellowed Lancaster at the guard who'd been holding Madda.

His only response was an open-mouthed stare at the furious Repts. He was just as bewildered as they. Despite her injuries, Madda had slipped from his grasp and crawled under a console—and then she was gone.

"Where did she go? How?" screamed Dodd at the guard. "There must be a hidden escape hatch under there. Find it! Follow her!"

The guard leapt to obey, banging about and tearing open panels under the console where Madda had just been.

"There's nothing, sir," he said. "Just standard decking and panels with the usual conduits and feed lines behind 'em."

Furious, Dodd lashed out, aiming a kick at the Rept's ribs—but he was so overweight and out of shape that the only damage was to the underling's pride. The guard squelched a growl and jumped back a meter or so, well out of range if Dodd should try again.

"Idiot! Inept fool!" shouted Lancaster.

Dodd turned dramatically round to glare at his twin brother. "What did you just call me?"

"No, you inept idiot! I was talking to *him!*" He jabbed a pudgy digit toward the guard.

"Oh," replied Dodd, mollified. "Well, you got that right." He turned to the guard. "*Why* did you let her go? And where *is* she?"

Used to such idiocies—and knowing what was good for him—the guard apologized profusely, explained he had no idea where Madda had gone, and swore he'd never do such a thing again—all while backing out of the ops deck and down the main passageway.

"Well, see that you don't!" yelled Lancaster after him, "Or you'll be busted to sanitation duty so fast your head will spin!"

"Right!" confirmed Dodd, though by now the guard was gone. "Now get out of our sight!"

"And here's what *you* get for just standing there and letting her escape," snarled Lancaster at a Grey orderly who'd 'beamed aboard with them. He shoved so hard the poor wretch flipped over a railing and landed in a groaning heap. Lancaster smiled, admiring his fine work in the service of justice.

"You know, brother Dodd," he said, "the bitch can't have escaped like that on her own. She had to have help. And there's no one else aboard, so it had to have been one of our crew that helped her; *Morrighan's* crew. Some traitorous bastard must have 'beamed her out of here."

"I do believe you're right," said Dodd. "And that 'Rafael!' she screeched must have been code to tell her conspirator to

'beam her."

"Precisely," agreed Lancaster. "And now we're faced with the tedious duty of finding out who the traitor is."

"Or traitors!" added Dodd.

"Or traitors—quite so," agreed Lancaster. "Well," he sighed, "a leader's work is never done; we best return to the ship and ferret out the traitor."

"Or traitors!" added Dodd.

"Or traitors. Yes," said Lancaster. "Let's get on with it."

"Lunch first though, of course," said Dodd.

"Goes without saying," answered Lancaster. "You, there!" he shouted at the Grey orderly, who'd just regained his feet. "Call the ship and have them 'beam us out of here."

When the Brothers arrived on *Queen Morrighan's* transbeam platform, each promptly collapsed, writhing in pain.

"Ohhhhhhh!" moaned Dodd, clutching his midsection. "Help! Ohhhh! I'm dying!"

The crewperson manning the transbeam console rushed to Dodd's side and tried to assist.

Lancaster lay nearby, curled up in an agonized ball and wailing piteously. Hearing the commotion, a passing crewmember dashed into the transbeam bay, took in the scene, and hurried to Lancaster's side. Lancaster couldn't answer his queries, so all he could do was grip the big Rept's shoulder and try to reassure him.

After a minute, the Brothers' agonies subsided, and the anxious crewmembers helped them to their feet.

"What was *that?*" groaned Dodd.

"Maybe the transbeam is mis-calibrated," said Lancaster.

"Or maybe it's the work of the damned conspirators," said Dodd.

"Mmm. Quite possible," agreed Lancaster. "Are you all right now?"

"I suppose," said Dodd, "but I have to admit, I've been having a lot of this sort of trouble lately. Pains out of nowhere, sometimes quite severe. And just this morning I was suddenly unable to breathe. Thought I was going to suffocate right where I stood. Heart palpitations, too."

"I know exactly what you mean," said Lancaster. "The very same sorts of things have been happening to me. For a week now!"

"My guess would be poisoning," mused Dodd, "all part of that conspiracy, no doubt."

"Ordinarily I would agree," said Lancaster, "but no poison should have any effect on us. Nor should anything else, for that matter. Not while we're under the witch's protection. Her potions and spells should make us immune to such vile and vicious attempts upon our noble persons."

"Mmm. True. Quite true," agreed Dodd. "But here is something further to consider: What if the witch has been subverted? What if old Villa is *part* of the vast conspiracy against us?"

"Ahhhhh," said Lancaster. "That would explain much. Most everything, in fact."

"Yes, it would. And so I propose we pay the miserable hag a visit as the first step in our investigation. After all, restoring ourselves to full function is of paramount importance. And if she is indeed behind our recent afflictions, nothing we do to anyone on this ship will remedy the matter."

"True, true, and most astute, brother," said Lancaster,

nodding sagely. "And then we can resume our campaign against the Dragons."

"Indeed," said Dodd. "And here is one further consideration: We can't afford to be in anything less than top form at this time. Not while we're involved with scoundrels like Kurucz and Bsrn. They've been acting more strangely than usual of late, and I don't trust them. For one thing, they could feed the boss vicious lies about us—and if he believed them…well, nothing could save us if Byrne wanted us out of the picture."

"True," said Lancaster. "We're resolved, then. We jump-shift for Yeske and see to old Villa."

Dodd nodded. "After lunch, of course."

"Goes without saying," agreed his brother.

Hours later, their lavish lunch completed, the Brothers ordered the ship to Yeske. On arrival, they decided to take one of *Morrighan's* shuttles to the planet's surface. They had no interest in risking the transbeam again. Not after their latest awful experience, and certainly not while there were conspirators aboard.

The crew who heard about it wondered why in hells anyone would choose a slow, bumpy shuttle ride over a fast, safe transbeaming. But the Brothers were the Brothers, and no one had any slightest interest in questioning their orders. Much less their random whims, which were as senseless as they were frequent.

The shuttle departed the great ship and made the transit to Yeske's surface without incident. The moment the little ship touched down, though, the Brothers were once again overcome, this time worse than before and complete with bloody, convulsive vomiting. The shuttle crew's attempts to assist their dreaded superiors were futile; they decided to get out of the way and hope the attack would pass. Or—a brighter prospect—end in the deaths of the vile pair.

When the agonizing spasms subsided and they'd cleaned themselves up, the Brothers limped down the gangway. They had landed in, and mostly destroyed, a well-tended field of young crops. They trampled the few undamaged rows on their way to a tidy but tiny hut at the field's edge. As they drew near the hut, an old crone emerged, her dark, wrinkled face a mask of stern resolve. It was the witch, Villa, and she relished the prospect of transforming whoever had ruined her crops into beetle grubs. Three plump hens and a pair of ducks scurried into the yard and looked on, hopeful. They'd seen this sort of scenario play out before, and they were eager for a nice lunch.

When Villa saw who approached, and their wretched condition, she could barely hold back a cry of satisfaction. She'd had an inkling this might be coming, and she had been right.

"Greetings, Barbdews," she said. "What brings you to my humble home this day? How may I help you?"

"Don't...ohhhhhhh!" began Lancaster. "You...you're... uhhhhhh..."

"Yes! We're on to you, you b...ohhh, ow!" croaked Dodd.

"I'm sorry, but I'm having a bit of trouble understanding," said Villa. "Could you say that again? Are you in some sort of distress?" She fought down a laugh.

"Don't play g-games with us, witch," managed Lancaster. "You're supposed to be protecting us, but look! We're suffering horribly. Horribly."

"H-he's right," said Dodd, "and we *are* on to you. *You* are part of a conspiracy. We know it. A wicked, treacherous

conspiracy. Admit it, you filthy, traitorous, ungrateful hag!"

"I'm so sorry to hear you aren't feeling quite your best, but I assure you I've done nothing that would cause such a calamity." She had to turn away and clamp a hand over her mouth to suppress a gleeful cackle.

"Well, *someone* is certainly doing this," said Lancaster, interrupting himself twice with racking coughs. "And *you* are supposed to be protecting us. Therefore, I order you to stop whatever this is. This instant."

"Right," grunted Dodd, now barely audible. "Do w-what he s-said."

And with that, both Repts collapsed. They convulsed, retched and coughed up great globs of bloody mucus. "F-f-fix...us..." they pleaded.

"Ah, well. I'm afraid I can't do that for you, boys. The truth is, you've done this to yourselves. Oh, yes. To yourselves. And, just as I warned you when you started it all, there is nothing I can do to stop it now. Nothing anyone can do. Too bad for you."

"What? What are you talking about?" gasped Lancaster.

"Oh, I see your memory needs refreshing. Very well. Do you remember when, many, *many* long years ago, the two of you forced me to assist you in casting a hex on the Nibiru Dragons? You had stolen the books of the Ancients—*The Book of Atlantis* and *The Book of Mu*, eh? Yes? Though the noble Dragons had never done you the slightest harm, you hexed their living eggs so none would hatch. Nor would scarcely any new eggs they laid from that day forth.

"I warned you—oh, yes, warned you most severely—that there would be dire consequences for you, should anyone ever reverse that spell. But you sneered and spat at me, and insisted I was only trying to trick you. You were utterly certain no one could, or ever would, reverse your precious spell. Ever. Then you redoubled the threats you'd used to force my compliance to your demands. And I have never forgiven myself for the part I played.

"Well, I don't know who did it or how, but it is clear that your wicked spell—your utter-evil perversion of the Ancient's sacred magic—*has* been broken at last. And it was broken sometime in the recent past. I sensed such a thing might have happened, and hoped against hope that my intuition was true. Because that beautiful Dragon race never deserved what you'd done to them.

"So! By whatever agency, your evil work is reversed. And here you are. But not here for much longer! Oh, no—not for much longer."

The Brothers cursed at her weakly, then turned to each other. "We've got to get to a transfer station, fast," said Lancaster, "and get new bodies. These are shot. Planet 444 has a station, and Soader has plenty of bodies in stock. Probably crap quality, but they'll have to do for the moment. We can get better ones later."

A muttered "Right" was all Dodd could eke out in reply.

They crawled painfully toward the waiting shuttle. Villa followed, enjoying the show and speculating on just how far they'd get.

They reached the gangway, where the shuttle's three Grey crewmembers stood waiting.

"Help...us," pleaded Dodd.

The Greys moved to help, but then stopped. No, no more help. No more groveling. Because it was obvious their vile, abusive bosses were at death's door.

Villa let out a cackle and danced a little dance. She knew that the moment the Barbdews expired, she would be free. Free to leave this dreary planet where they'd imprisoned her for centuries. Free to take a fresh new form, beautiful and lively as she once had been.

"Damn you all to hells," said Lancaster to the Greys. "I order you to return us to the ship, and jump for the transfer station at Planet 444. Or its moon. You know where I mean." His body convulsed in another bout of violent coughing and retching.

"You heard him," said Dodd. "Do it. Now. Or I'll…" And he, too was overwhelmed by a coughing fit.

The Greys stood fast.

"You see?" said Villa. "They won't help you. No one will help you now. It's just one more way you're reaping what you've sown so long. There's no time for help now, anyway. If you somehow survived the journey to a transfer station, you would have no chance whatsoever of successful transfers. No, those bodies you've abused so long are going to die. Die. Dead. And when they're dead, the black, shriveled cinders you have for souls will be sucked up to the nearest transfer station, where you'll be plopped into whatever body is available." She cackled anew, imagining her tormentors implanted in primitive, clam-like bodies like those found on Ian Ru or BetPet V.

There came a sizzling, popping sound and a horrible stench. Villa and the Greys watched as the Brothers' bodies shriveled, curled, crackled and shattered, dissolving at last into gray-green dust. Their souls would drift off now, powerless, to be caught up by a transfer station's soul-seeking mechanisms.

The Greys sighed. They were free, but it would take time to get used to the concept. They bowed to Villa, then turned and re-entered the shuttle for the flight back to *Queen Morrighan*.

Villa let out a long, lusty laugh, danced a few joyful turns and then headed for her hut. Seeing her chickens and ducks still waiting hopefully, she stopped for a moment. "I'm sorry, my dears. No grubs for lunch today. But that's a good thing, in truth. If I'd transformed those two, you'd have turned them down flat. You're too savvy to gobble such as they. Come along now, and I'll treat you to some tasty grain."

CHAPTER 15

Betrayed

The transbeam suit functioned perfectly. Madda arrived, practically at Dino's feet, in a rapid flash of transbeam energy. She clutched at her injured hip, now battered twice by the Brothers' guard. Hadgkiss leapt to ease her into a more comfortable position.

"Thank you," she said. "I'll be okay—but we've got to get to Headley. *Now.*"

He nodded; without a word, he flipped up the cover of his suit's control panel and tapped in a string of coordinates. Then he took her arm, opened her suit's panel and tapped in the same string.

"Ready?" he asked.

"Aye, Captain," she said with a determined smile. "Let's roll!" She poised a finger over the suit's activation button.

He returned her smile, and counted down: "Three, two, one, GO."

Both activated their suits. Moments later, they appeared on Headley, in a corridor intersection less than twenty meters from the shallow alcove where Remi and Mia crouched. The place was still quiet; the Brothers hadn't yet ordered the attackers to resume their assault. Dino threw Madda's arm over his shoulder and helped her to her feet. Together they moved down the corridor to Remi and Mia.

"Dino!" Remi cried, amazed. Mia just stared at him, wide-eyed and mouth agape.

"Are you hurt? Either of you?" Hadgkiss demanded.

"No, no—we're okay. But, how...?"

"No time," said Dino. "Attack's stopped for the moment. Follow us!"

So commanding was Hadgkiss's intention, the women were on their feet in an instant and without a word. The major moved off down the corridor, still supporting Madda, the Zulak women at their heels.

They came to an auxiliary command center and rushed in. "Safer here for the moment," Dino said, "it's reinforced. Remi, where's Hyatt?"

"He went to the exercise room before this all started," she replied. Mia nodded. "Oh!" Remi gasped, "He could be injured!" Mia was still, but tears welled in her eyes, then spilled down her cheeks. Hadgkiss could see she had fallen away from terror and was nearing emotional overwhelm. He had to get her out of here fast, before she collapsed into complete apathy, unable to help herself and a danger to all of them.

"You're right Remi, but we'll find him. Right now, please take care of Mia. Talk to her, get her to respond—to talk *with* you. I'll get some help, and then we'll find Hyatt and get out of here." Remi nodded and turned to her weeping daughter, just as a new barrage began.

"Damn!" said Dino. He tapped his comm pickup,

connecting with *Queen Asherah's* bridge.

"Jessup here," came the reply.

"Jessup, this is Hadgkiss. On Headley, with Madda and the Zulaks. Base under attack—Barbdews. Jump-shift here at once. On arrival, you, Doyle and Deggers 'beam to my location. Peggers to take the con and repel attackers, then assume overwatch."

"Aye, Captain. Jessup out."

Now the major contacted the woman in charge of the Headley base. "Chief, Captain Hadgkiss of *Queen Asherah* here. The ship is on its way to repel your attackers, but you must evacuate your staff the moment the way is clear. *Asherah* will cover you. Understood?"

"Yes, sir. I'll initiate our evac drill at once. Thank you, sir."

The bombardment abruptly ceased. Good, thought Dino. *Queen* must be here. Come on, Jessup—where are you?

Moments later, he had his answer: Jessup, Doyle and Deggers transbeamed in. Hadgkiss wasted no time with greetings. "Deggers, Hyatt should be in the exercise facility. Get on that terminal behind you and call up the base plans; go to him and report back. Leave the plans open on the monitor. We may need them."

"Aye!" said Deggers, and turned to his task.

"Doyle," Dino continued, "open that second terminal. Call up the base equipment inventory, see if they have a hover-chair. If so, find it, bring it back and strap Madda in. If there isn't one, come up with some way to get her mobile. She's not going anywhere on that hip, but best if we don't have to carry her." Doyle snapped a quick salute and went to work.

"Jessup—there's a light gunship in a hidden hangar, far north end of the complex. Entrance looks like a raw rock wall, veined with white quartz. Access panel is where two veins cross, a meter to left of the wall's center. You'll see it. Tap the cross four times; panel will open. Passcode is ANCIENTS. Prep the ship for launch, set for random deep-space jump. We'll join you shortly."

"Aye, sir!" said Jessup, and he was gone at a dead run.

Moments later, Doyle returned with a hover-chair. "Perfect," said Dino. "All right, set Madda up, then get to the ship as fast as you can—Madda will brief you on what I'm talking about. Madda, you've studied the layout here—do you know the way to the far north end?"

"Aye, Captain."

"Good. We'll meet you there. Go!"

Dino's comm pickup chirped. "Hadgkiss," he answered.

"Deggers, Captain. Found the boy. Exercise room. Injured. I've done what I can here—need to get him to a medical bay, fast." Hadgkiss saw Mia flinch at the doctor's last phrase. Rough, he thought, but at least she responds.

"Understood, Doc," Dino replied. "Prepare to move him. We'll be there shortly. Is there anything we should bring along?"

"No, sir, just please come as fast as you can."

"That we will." Dino closed the pickup's connection and scanned the base plan the doctor had left open. He spotted the exercise facility, and the route to get there.

"All right," Dino said to Remi and Mia, "We're going to the exercise place. Follow me, and stay close." Remi nodded. Mia raised her eyes, her look vaguely pleading. Dino moved off

down the corridor with the women following.

They reached the gym. "Wait out here," Dino told Remi and Mia. He didn't want to make things worse for them, if Hyatt was badly injured. He entered; the doctor stood beside an exercise mat where Hyatt lay unconscious amid a pile of fallen rock. The doctor had hastily tried to clean himself up so as not to alarm the women, but his clothes and hands still bore spots and spatters of the young man's blood. He'd covered his patient with a couple of towels, doing his best to hide the severely mangled left leg, but his head and face still showed. There was a nasty gash on the left cheek; his face was deathly pale.

"Okay. Not good. Let's use the mat as a stretcher. The ship we're headed for is small, but it has a pull-out bed, and a decent med kit." Deggers nodded.

"Mia, Remi, we're coming out, carrying Hyatt. We're going straight to the ship that will take us out of here. The doctor will care for Hyatt there. Let us go past, then follow close behind. It's not too far."

"Got it," said Remi. Mia said nothing, but nodded in response to a searching look from her mother.

Dino and Deggers emerged from the exercise room, carrying Hyatt on the mat between them, stretcher-fashion. The doctor had used another towel to cover the worst of the young man's head and face wounds, but there was no hiding his awful pallor. Both Remi and Mia blanched at the sight.

"Let's go, let's go," urged Hadgkiss, and he headed on down the corridor at the quickest pace he and Doc could manage without jostling Hyatt too badly. Remi followed, leading her daughter by the hand.

Dino led the desperate procession through a series of

corridors, up a steep ramp to a level closer to Headley's surface, and down a final, short corridor to the base's northernmost end. The last people through the hidden doorway had closed it behind them. Good, Dino thought. Keeping security tight.

"Okay, Doc—we'll have to set him down for a moment. Easy. On three. One, two, three." They lowered Hyatt to the floor. Deggers remained kneeling at the boy's feet, ready to lift him again as soon as the major returned. Just as he'd described to Jessup, Dino tapped the spot where two thick white quartz veins crossed. A small access panel popped out and opened, and he entered the codeword, ANCIENTS. The massive false wall split down its center and slid silently open, revealing a short passageway and a ramp leading into the waiting ship. He nodded to Deggers, crouched in front of the improvised stretcher, grabbed its corners and counted: "One, two, three." The men lifted the mat and Dino led off down the passageway, up the ramp and into the vessel. "This is *Spitfire*," he announced as Remi led Mia through the hatchway. "Welcome aboard. Doc, the bed and med kit are forward of this hatch—to our right." They moved up the narrow passageway, careful not to jolt or jar their patient.

"Here," said Dino, when they came to a small alcove. They lowered Hyatt to the deck and Hadgkiss opened out the narrow bed—little more than a well-padded shelf—then helped Deggers lift the young man and position him. Dino took two steps farther down the passage, opened a storage compartment and drew out a bulky medical bag, then a portable monitor and life-support unit. He set them down beside the doctor. "Here you go, Doc. Call me if you need anything at all."

"Aye, sir," Deggers responded, and went straight to work.

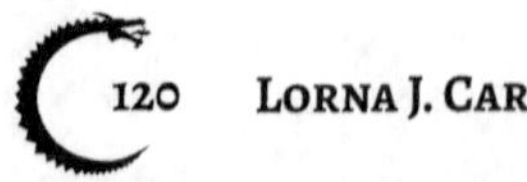

"Is he...will he...?" queried Mia, her face a cloud of anguish.

Deggers looked up at her, his manner as reassuring as he could muster; inside, he was wracked with doubt. "I'll do all I can, my dear. He's had a rough time, but he's a remarkably strong young man."

"Uhh..." muttered Mia, her worries undiminished.

Dino spoke up: "Remi, Mia, follow me forward. We have to leave this base fast, but there's something I want to do first." He moved on up the passageway toward the ops deck.

"Captain," Jessup, Doyle and Madda greeted him. "Ladies," they said as Remi and Mia followed Dino into the now-crowded space.

"Gentlemen, Madda," Hadgkiss acknowledged, with a nod to his trusted officers and long-time friends. "Before we launch, Doyle, make a sweep of the ship. Fast as you can, but thorough. I know the whole base has been swept before, but the Barbdews didn't just find it by magic. There must be a bug somewhere, and it *could* be aboard with us here. We can't risk leaving until we know we won't be tracked and followed."

"Aye, sir," said Doyle. He grabbed a scanning device from an overhead locker, activated it and began a careful sweep, first of the whole ops deck, then on down the passageway aft.

"Remi, Mia, he'll be back in a few minutes—she's a small ship." He pointed to a pair of flight couches—deeply padded, form-fitting chairs—and asked them to be seated. "Once Doyle's completed his scan, I'll help you strap in, and then we'll fly straight out of here."

Remi moved to comply, guiding Mia. In moments they were both settled in.

Hadgkiss, Madda and Jessup conferred quietly until Doyle returned, minutes later. "The ship's clean, sir, but I believe I've found how they located the base."

"Good work, Doyle; how?"

"I'm afraid it's our guests here," the man replied, indicating Remi and Mia. They're carrying embedded locator chips."

Remi gasped. Mia's eyes widened.

"Well. That could explain a lot," said Dino.

"Yes it could, sir," replied Doyle. "Good thing you checked before we left."

"Roger that," said the major. "Can you show the doctor exactly where the chips are?"

"Aye, sir."

"Good. Go explain the situation, and ask him to come up here the moment he can safely leave Ensign Hyatt."

Doyle acknowledged and headed aft.

"Jessup, once we've disposed of those chips, are we ready for space?"

"Aye, sir. Engines warmed, course laid in and the random jump you ordered programmed and ready."

Doyle and Deggers hurried onto the ops deck, the doctor carrying a small instrument kit and field dressings.

"Show him, Doyle," said Dino. "Ladies, I apologize for the unforgivable circumstances, but we've got to have those chips out at once."

"*Not* a problem, Major," said Remi. "Please, doctor—let's get this over with!"

Doyle stepped forward; he moved the scanner over Remi's

body, eyes on its readout. "Here, Doc," he said, pointing to a spot on the woman's back.

"Thank you. Ma'am, would you please undo your garment and expose your upper back? The chip is just below your right shoulder blade." Remi hurried to comply. "Thank you, ma'am," said the doctor. "First I'll apply a bit of local anesthetic; it will control any bleeding, too—though there won't be much of that at all. Once it's had a few seconds to take effect, I'll remove the chip."

"Go to it," said Remi. "And hey, Doc, that's enough of the 'ma'am' business. We've known each other for years."

"Yes ma'...sorry—Remi," replied Deggers. "Here we go." In less than thirty seconds, he held the tiny chip in his gloved hand, and Remi was re-fastening her tunic.

"What a relief! Thank you. How could it ever have gotten there?" she asked.

"Judging from the type of chip, I'd say Soader put it there, when he had you and the younger lady captive."

"Oh! Of course!" said Remi. "Makes me sick to even think about it. And Mia has one too?"

"I'm afraid so," said Deggers, but we'll remedy that right now. He turned to Mia and was surprised to find she'd already exposed her shoulder and upper back. "Well! Thank you, Mia," he said. "Doyle, would you confirm the location?"

Doyle moved in with his scanner, watching its readout. He nodded and pointed to a spot on the girl's back, almost identical to the place her mother's chip had been.

"Thank you Doyle," said Deggers. "Ready, Mia?"

"Yes, doctor," she said, surprising the others with the calm firmness of her reply.

Deggers soon had the vile device in hand; Mia dressed and settled back into her flight couch.

"Take the blasted things aft, smash them, toss them out the hatch and secure it," ordered Dino. "Then strap in and report. Doc, go secure your patient for launch, and strap yourself in too. Report up when you're ready. Jessup, prepare for launch!"

Doyle raced aft, chips in hand. The ship hummed as its engines built up toward launch-ready power. Dino helped Mia strap herself into the flight couch while Remi—a veteran of many space voyages—secured herself. Dino double-checked her straps and gave her a quick smile and a thumbs-up.

"Secured for launch, Captain!" came Doyle's voice from down the passageway.

"Doc and patient secured!" called Deggers.

"Mr. Jessup, take us..." began the major—but he was cut off mid-command. A heavy shock rocked the cavern and tiny ship; falling rock and rubble battered her hull from above.

CHAPTER 16

Bunker to Bunker

The tremor passed; the fall of rock and dust tailed off. Jessup turned to his captain.

"Status?" asked Hadgkiss.

Jessup scanned his monitors, punched several contacts. "Damage negligible, Captain. Still secure for space. But the hangar doors don't respond to our controls. They must have been damaged in the attack."

"Damn. All right. Hold on a moment." He released his restraints, leapt to the co-pilot's station next to Jessup's and hastily strapped in while Jessup activated the station's monitors and controls. Dino took a moment to familiarize himself with the setup, then concentrated on the weapons control module and adjusted several settings. "Okay. No time for niceties," he said. "I'm going to blow the hangar doors; get ready—the moment the way is clear, blast us out of here. I'll be on the weapons and scanning for hostiles as we emerge—we don't know what caused that last tremor; may have to fight our way off-planet."

"Understood," said Jessup. "You'll have flight-control override if you need it for evasive action."

"Roger that," said Hadgkiss. "Now, you've got about two hundred meters of straight-line access tunnel ahead. Exit is open but well camouflaged. Tunnel's spacious, but keep her centered."

"Aye!" said Jessup. He tapped at his controls. "Okay. Standing by."

"All hands, brace for detonation, then launch," Hadgkiss called out. He punched the fire control contact for *Spitfire's* forward blast cannon. The weapon roared; the forward view panel went instantly black, filtering against the blinding flash, then returned to normal view. Before them was a wide, smoking aperture where the hangar's massive doors had been. Jessup and Dino scanned their monitors; they had expected to see at least a glimmer of daylight from the access tunnel's far end, but there was nothing but blackness.

Hadgkiss scanned his monitors. "Got it," he said. "Sensors show rubble blocking the tunnel, one-hundred thirty meters up. Take us up a hundred meters and hold. We'll handle the obstruction just like the doors."

"Aye-aye. One hundred meters." The ship's forward floodlights flashed to life; *Spitfire* rose from her berth and hummed slowly forward, out of the rubble-strewn hangar and up the long tunnel. "One hundred meters," said Jessup, easing the ship to a halt.

The major adjusted his fire controls. "Fire in the hole!" he shouted, and punched the firing contact. The forward cannon roared again; the main view panel dimmed, then refreshed—and a shaft of dust-laden daylight streamed down to greet them.

"All clear, Captain," said Jessup, eager.

"Take us out!" said Dino. *Spitfire* darted forward, burst

from the tunnel's hidden exit and burned hard for open space.

"Looks like we're all clear," said Dino. "Sensors show no hostiles."

Less than a minute later, Hadgkiss's panel indicated they had cleared Headley's atmosphere. "Make your jump, Lieutenant," he ordered.

"Aye, Captain. Attention all hands—brace for jump-shift." He tapped a contact; the ship answered with a bone-deep hum and eerie vibration.

And then they were in deep space, uncounted light-years from Headley.

"Random jump complete, Captain," reported Jessup. "All systems nominal. We're free and clear here.

"Thank you, Lieutenant," said Dino. "I've got your next co-ordinates." He passed the pilot a small paper card; on it were groups of figures, written in Dino's neat, crisp hand.

"Paper?" Jessup asked, puzzled.

"Security."

"Ah," Jessup acknowledged. He rapidly punched the fig-ures into his control module, then checked and rechecked them against the card for accuracy. "Course laid in, Captain," he said. "But, where are we going?"

"Your guess is as good as mine," said Dino. "We'll know when we get there. I hope."

The coordinates Hadgkiss had just relayed came from a similar slip of paper Rafael had handed him, weeks before. "Admiral Stock gave me these," Zulak had explained. "He wanted you and me to have them, in case of dire emergen-cy. No further specifics. So, now you have them. Let's hope they're never needed. I've memorized them. Do the same, then incinerate the paper." Dino had done so, right then and there.

"Doc," Dino called over his comm pickup, "We're going to make another jump. Is the ensign up to it, or should we hold off for a bit?"

"Just a moment, Captain," came the medic's reply. He examined the young officer, checked his monitors, then administered an injection. "He's stable for the moment. Stable enough for one jump."

"Thank you, Doc. If all goes well, one's all we'll need," Hadgkiss replied. "Madda, you okay?"

"Aye, Captain. Well enough. But it's making me crazy just to sit here doing *nothing*."

"Understood," said Dino. "Jessup, make the jump."

"Aye, Captain. All hands, brace for jump-shift!" he called, and engaged the drive. Again the ship hummed, vibrated, and leapt across another wide expanse of the void.

With a thunderous blast of violently displaced atmosphere, the ship burst into normal space, fifty meters above a broad, grassy meadow.

"Damn!" shouted Jessup. "A damned *planetside* jump?! Good thing those coordinates were accurate, or that could have been the end of us. *And* a lot of this place, too."

"Roger that!" said Hadgkiss, shaken but quick to regain his composure. "Everyone all right?" he called out.

Each of the others answered up; all were unharmed, but Remi and Mia were mystified at the pilot's reaction to the event. Only Dino, Madda and Deggers understood—and shared—Jessup's shock. Planetside jump-shifts were strictly forbidden by Fleet regulations—and common sense—because of their enormous potential for disastrous consequences. They had all just had a close brush with death.

Jessup ran a fast damage assessment; satisfied all was well, he brought *Spitfire* to rest on the grassy surface.

A warm, yellow sun hung high in the sky above. Or appeared to. A quick scan of his sensor readouts showed Dino the "sun" was a massive light-orb. The "sky" was the roof of a vast cavern, hundreds of meters high; the planet's true surface was more than a thousand meters higher still.

The cavern was a close cousin of the underground cave system housing Soader's former base on Earth, beneath the mountains of New Mexico. A small world within a world. But what world? Dino wondered. "Jessup," he said, "find out what planet this is, but passive sensors only. We don't want to attract any attention. I'm heading aft. Ladies, you are welcome to secure from space. Uh...that is, you can undo your restraint belts. Sorry for the spacer jargon. Just not used to having civilians aboard."

"Oh, heavens. No worries, Dino," said Remi.

"Thanks. You can get up and stretch if you like, but I'd prefer you remain at your flight couches for now. Oh—you can hit the head...uh...use the facilities, if you need to." He pointed to the tiny restroom's door. The women nodded understanding. "Okay. I'll be back shortly."

Hadgkiss made his way down the narrow passage to the alcove where Deggers was bent over his patient, re-tightening a tourniquet mid-way down the young ensign's left thigh. He sighed and turned to the captain. His hands and arms were thick with blood. His face and tunic were smeared with it. His close-cropped hair was wet with sweat; trickles ran down his face and neck. The man's expression told Dino all he needed to know.

"I see," said Hadgkiss. "Do you need help?"

"There's barely room for me to work here solo, but yes—I could use an extra pair of hands here. Can you spare Jessup? He's had plenty of med training, and field experience too."

"I'll send him right back. Keep me posted; if you need anything at all, sing out."

"Aye, sir," said Deggers, his face still a mask of grim concern. "Oh, would you also let him know the first thing we'll need is some sort of lighting rig? The light here is awful—makes this kind of work absolute hell."

"Will do," said Hadgkiss. "And thank you, Doc. I know you'll do everything you can. The ensign's lucky you're here."

With a brief, grateful smile, the medico turned back to his patient.

Dino headed back toward the ops deck but paused halfway there. I hope that boy makes it, he thought. Losing him would be terrible in any case, but he's supposed to marry soon. And I don't think Remi and Mia could take another loss, so soon after Rafael. Hells, I don't know if *I* could. And to make it all worse, Celine is missing, too.

He reached for the medallion on the chain round his neck; holding it tight, he whispered a few words for Hyatt, Remi, Mia and his own lost wife and son. That done, he composed himself, called up his confidence, and moved on forward to ops.

Remi and Mia looked up when the major entered. Each woman's face was a study in mixed emotions—anxiety, pleading, hope, and despair kept barely at bay. Hadgkiss gave them what he hoped was a confident and reassuring but conservative smile. "The doctor has assessed Hyatt's injuries. As I'm certain you've guessed, some are quite serious. But Doc reiterated that Hyatt is young and strong, and he's kept himself in top condition—all significant positives. I'll add that the ensign is in the best possible hands."

"Can we see him?" asked Mia.

"No, not just yet. The doctor is still working. I'm sending Jessup back to assist him, though. That should speed the process. I promise you, as soon as Doc says he's ready for visitors, you'll be the first to know."

"Okay," said Mia, crestfallen. A tear spilled down her cheek, and she stifled a sob. Remi rose from her couch, put an arm around her daughter and whispered words of comfort and hope. Still, the trickle of tears became a steady stream.

Dino watched for a moment, silent, then crossed the ops deck to Jessup. Quietly, he relayed the doctor's requests for better lighting and direct assistance, and sent the man on his way.

He turned to his next concern: Madda. It was less than an hour since she'd escaped battering and beating at the hands of the Brothers and their thugs. "All right, Madda. Your turn at last. Your patience has been beyond commendable. Deggers will check you over and patch you up as soon as he's able, but is there anything I can do for you right now?"

"As a matter of fact, Captain, there is. It may not seem strictly according to regulations, but..."

"Oh, come on. Out with it. What can I do?"

"Well, the Mentors outfitted this ship, correct?"

"That's right. So?"

"It's just that when we were prepping *King*—also a Mentor vessel—for our first mission, I noticed the ship's stores included a selection of special beverages. Alcoholic beverages, to be precise. Including—I was surprised to note—quite a fine bottle of...well, call it whiskey, from one of the Rept homeworlds. It occurred to me that the Mentors may have provisioned this vessel similarly."

"Are you trying to tell me you want a *drink*, Lieutenant?"

"Yes!" blurted Madda.

"I mean, yes, sir. Strictly for medicinal purposes, sir. You see, sir, Rept physiology is such that certain alcohols actually do have *quite* potent restorative properties, when administered in moderation..."

"Ohhhh. I see. I see," said Dino. "'Administered.' Yes. I do see." A flick of a smile escaped his best effort at solemnity. Madda caught it at once.

"I am quite serious, sir! A few sips...well, maybe a smallish glass, should be most efficacious in making the *wait* for the doctor pass more comfortably. Medicinally speaking, that is."

"Hmm. Very well, then," said Dino, still struggling not to laugh. He hadn't missed her ever-so-slight emphasis on "wait."

"I would be glad to check the stores myself," the major continued, "but since you know exactly the item in question, perhaps it would be best if you were to seek it out yourself. And then you could 'administer' the, um...treatment, as well."

Madda straightened in her hover-chair. "Aye-aye, sir. As you wish, sir. Permission to proceed, sir?"

"Granted," Hadgkiss replied, "but please return soon. I have a task for you."

"Aye, sir," she replied, and steered her chair down the passageway aft. Dino smiled after his junior officer and old friend.

After a quick sensor scan of the surrounding area, the major returned to the tiny improvised medical bay. Jessup had set up a temporary lighting rig, and he and the doctor were huddled together, working on Hyatt's badly mangled left leg.

"Hold that right there," Deggers said to Jessup. "I'll be just a minute. The doctor straightened up, did a quick stretch to ease his wearied back and arms, and addressed his captain. "We've done all we can for the leg," he explained. "I'm afraid there's no way to save it, though. Not in a situation like this. If the boy's to make it at all, it has to come off."

Dino nodded. "Understood. That's too bad. I'm sure Hyatt will bear up to it all right, but Mia will be horrified. I'd be horrified, too, if I hadn't been through limb losses of my own." He raised his bionic arms and flexed their powerful hands. "I trust they'll set him up with a new leg, just as good as these. Right?"

"Most definitely," said Deggers. "He'll scarcely miss the original."

"All right. How is he otherwise?"

"Assorted lacerations and abrasions, a couple of minor fractures, and some nasty bruising. Nothing we can't handle. My only concern is how he'll respond to the amputation. He's young and strong, as I've said, but response to such massive trauma can be unpredictable. Assuming it goes well, we'll tend to the other injuries, then set him up with intravenous fluids, antibiotics and so on. Then it will be a matter of time and rest. I recommend we set up a rotation, so someone is always with him until he's in the clear."

"Understood and agreed," said Dino. "Carry on, then. If anyone can bring him through—especially in conditions like these—it's you two."

"Thanks for your confidence, sir. We'll do our best to live up to it." He lifted the laser scalpel he'd been preparing to use when Dino arrived. "I'll keep you briefed." Dino nodded, and Deggers returned to his grim task.

Hadgkiss returned to the ops deck. Remi and Mia looked up from their couches, anxious. He reassured them that Deggers and Jessup were making good progress, and were confident Hyatt would recover. He made no mention of amputation.

Dino had just settled into the pilot's flight couch when Madda returned. "Well?" he asked.

"Feeling much better, sir," said Madda, with a flicker of a smile.

"Glad to hear it," he replied. "Now let's go over the task I mentioned. Position yourself here next to the co-pilot's station, and swing the console and monitors around so you can use them."

When Madda was set up to work, he continued. "I want you to do a thorough scan of this cavern-world. Primarily for security purposes, but also to give us an idea of what we've got. How extensive it is, resources, any inhabitants, any structures, routes to the surface and so on. Find out what you can about the surface, too—what sort of world it is."

"Understood. This should be interesting. I'll do a rapid preliminary scan and summarize that for you, then take a more in-depth look."

"Excellent. Carry on, then—and call me if you run into

anything I should know about right away."

Madda went straight to work. Her rapid scan found nothing alarming or unusual. The initial sensor scan complete, she sent out four aerial survey drones for a more detailed assessment. The cavern was of the usual type the Mentors and others had constructed over the centuries, on various planets and for various purposes. It had its own well-established ecosystem, including a self-sustaining power source for the artificial sun that gave it light and warmth. There was a system of streams and small lakes and an abundance of plant and animal life. Less than a kilometer from their landing spot, she discovered a collection of tidy buildings. They appeared to be cabins or cottages, though there was no sign they were currently inhabited.

Her survey complete, Madda called Hadgkiss to report her results. As he re-entered the ops deck, he caught Madda's eye and, with a questioning look, motioned toward Remi and Mia, napping in their flight couches. Madda understood his unspoken question at once, and nodded: yes, it would be fine for them to hear her report, too.

Dino approached the women and softly spoke their names; they woke, stretched and rubbed the sleep from their eyes.

"Oh! Dino," said Remi.

"Is there any news?" asked Mia.

"Hyatt is resting," he replied. "Dr. Deggers says he should be okay. They have him hooked up for intravenous fluids and medicines, but Doc says he won't need any of that much longer. I'm guessing he'll allow visitors before too long."

"Oh, good," said Remi. "I was so worried!"

"I still am," said Mia, "but if the doctor says he'll be okay, I guess that's good."

"It is, it is," said Dino, still not ready to mention the young man's missing leg. "Look, I'm sorry to wake you like this, but Madda has completed a survey of this place where we've landed, complete with video capture. She's about to brief me, and I thought you two might want to take part."

"Yes!" said Remi. Mia only nodded, still fragile after the trauma of recent events.

"Good!" said Dino. "Go ahead over to her station. We'll start in a minute or two." He tapped his comm pickup. "Doc, can you spare Jessup for a little while?"

"I can," Deggers replied. "Hyatt is resting well, and we've just finished putting our little micro med bay in order."

"Excellent. I've had Madda run a survey of our temporary home here. She's about to brief us, so please send Jessup forward. You're welcome to listen in, if you like. And she can probably stream the images she's gathered to your hand-held."

"That would be good. Thanks. I do want to stay here with the ensign for the time being."

"I figured as much," said Dino. "We'll begin as soon as Jessup arrives, and you're all linked up for the images."

"Roger that," said the doctor.

Madda addressed the group. "To begin, we are on—or rather, beneath—the planet Remini. The surface is normal enough, and so is this under-world. We can breathe the atmosphere and drink the water." She went on to present all she had learned, keeping the statistical and scientific details to a minimum, for the sake of their civilian guests. When she came to the images of the nearby buildings, one and all noticed Mia's mood and interest brighten.

"Little houses," she said. "They're cute. Like country cottages. And there's even a garden, and some animals grazing; see them there, on the right of the screen?"

The others' relief was instant and enormous. The girl was coming back to life.

"Oh, yes—I see them! They look like goats," said Remi.

"I think you're right!" said Mia. "Uncle Dino, Madda says they aren't far away. Can we go there? Can we stay there?"

Dino chuckled; his relief may have been greater than anyone's. "That is exactly the plan, Mia. Shall we go have a look right now?"

"Yes, please," she replied, with the first smile anyone had seen grace her young face in days.

CHAPTER 17

A New Bond

Celine and Jager barreled down the corridor toward the refectory, where they were overdue for a meal with their Dragon friends. They were about to turn into the passage that would take them the last hundred meters to their destination when Jager suddenly slowed to a walk, then stopped. Celine noticed he had fallen behind; she stopped and turned to find out what had happened. There was Jager, a few meters away, staring at nothing and wearing an odd, far-off look.

"Vin?" he said.

"What? Did you just say 'Vin?'" asked Celine, baffled.

He was momentarily startled, then came to himself. "Huh? Oh! Sorry. It's just...I... Just a moment." His vacant look returned; Celine recognized it—he was menting with someone.

"It's Vin!" he said, incredulous.

"Vin? You mean *our* Vin? You're *menting* with him?" asked Celine, twice as incredulous.

"Yes! Yes! I don't know how, but yes. We were running like crazy just now, and suddenly I *heard* him. His mental voice or whatever it's called. You know what I mean. I heard his thoughts, so I spoke his name; mented it at the same time, I guess. And he answered! I don't know who was more surprised, him or me, but we could ment. Just like you and I, or with the Mentors. He's there in the refectory right now, with the others staring at him like he's lost his marbles."

"Marbles?" asked Celine.

"Sorry. More Earth talk. Means…oh, I'll explain later. Means they think he's gone nuts. Gone crazy, I mean."

"Oh! Well are you sure *you* haven't?" teased Celine.

He laughed. "No! No—I mean *yes*, I'm sure! I could hear him, plain as day. And he could hear me. We talked! Mented!"

"My!" she replied, eyes wide. "But, how can that be? I thought a Human could only ment with a Dragon if they were linked as Companions, or a Companion's mate."

"Exactly. That's what doesn't add up. How could Vin and I…" he tailed off, frowning in thought. "Oh! I know! It's Omaja!"

"The staff? What do you mean?"

"It was in the records I studied. The staff can somehow choose or designate a Dragon-Companion pair, and then help them become aware of each other by menting. And then it guides them to come together—meet up somewhere, if they're far apart. Omaja must be telling Vin and me we're meant to be joined…" He went silent, in complete awe at the idea.

Celine was equally awestruck, but re-found her voice first. "That's wonderful! But, will you? Do you want to? I mean, it's nice that the staff thinks you should, but it's really up to you and Vin. No one—and no thing, I suppose—can *make* you link. From all I've learned, it has to be your free choice."

"Oh! But, well, of course! Yes! If Vin wants to, that is. What could possibly be more amazing?! I've never mentioned it, but...well, I've often been a little envious of the wonderful closeness you and Fianna share. Not jealous, really, but almost." The faintest of blushes rose in his cheeks.

Celine could see he felt sheepish, a trifle embarrassed. "Oh, but that's sweet," she said, reassuring. "I understand completely—I'm sure I'd feel the same, if it were the other way around. And after all these years you and I have been in each other's heads, so to speak—menting all the time—I know you too well to believe you'd ever be truly jealous. You're way bigger and better than that."

Now he blushed in earnest. "Oh! I..." He stood speechless for a few moments, gazing at her; then he gently set Omaja down, stepped forward, wrapped the girl in his arms and hugged for all he was worth. "Thank you, pumpkin. Thank you." She hugged him right back, and just as hard.

The pair embraced for a few seconds longer before Celine jumped back. "Hey! We've done it again! We're supposed to be at the refectory by now. Let's go!" he shook his head and laughed, snatched up the staff and sprinted on down the corridor, Celine matching him stride for stride with her long, lean legs.

The young Humans burst into the refectory. There stood the four Dragons, lined up to greet them. "Welcome!" boomed Ahimoth.

Before anyone else could speak, Vin stepped forward. "Forgive me, Ahimoth, Fianna, but I must ask: Jager, did we just...?"

"Yes, my friend. Yes we did," Jager replied.

"You just what?" asked Fianna, puzzled.

"We mented, Fianna. Impossible though it might sound, Vin and I communicated mentally—just as though I were his Companion."

All four Dragons dropped their jaws and ruffled their wings in astonishment. With great effort, Celine suppressed a burst of laughter; they looked *so* silly like that, for such proud, majestic beings.

"How can that be?" asked Fianna.

Jager held Omaja aloft, beaming.

"Oh!" Fianna exclaimed. "Celine, isn't that the staff you found, hidden at the back of my cave-home?"

"The very same, Fianna. And do you know what it turns out to be?"

"Ohhhhh…" said the Dragon.

Ahimoth's craggy eyebrows shot up; he, too, had guessed what the answer must be.

"If you are guessing it's Omaja, The Staff of Malek, you are quite correct," said Celine proudly.

"Ohhhh…" said Fianna again. "But I…it was…I never… ohhhhhh."

The white Dragon stared at the seemingly simple object Jager bore. "I feel so foolish," she went on. "Something so powerfully precious was right there in my home. A priceless treasure of all my people. Right *there.*"

"Please don't feel foolish," said Jager. He lowered the staff's tip to the ground and continued. "Omaja seems to have a mind of his own. There he rested, hidden in your cave, looking for all the world like a cast-off bit of junk, through all the years since Princess Linglu's Companion Schimpel last held him. My guess—and it's an educated guess, since I've been doing a lot of study lately—is that Omaja was waiting for the right moment to reveal himself, and the right person to reveal himself *to*."

"That would be me, apparently," said Celine. "I happened on the staff weeks ago, while tidying up the cave-home one day. If you'd never seen it, Fianna, it must have been revealing itself to me!

"Thinking it might be useful someday," she continued, "we picked it up, dusted it off, secured it to Fianna's saddle, and promptly forgot about it. It's been through a lot with us. I hope it enjoyed sharing our adventures! But I truly believe Omaja *intended* for me to find him, and to bring him along with us and keep him safe."

Jager picked up the story. "Now, remember yesterday, when we were leaving the Mars base? Celine and I ran off to retrieve the saddle and saddlebags. Well, when I lifted the saddle down from the shelf, there was Omaja, neatly tied to its side, practically staring me in the face. And then he revealed himself and came to me—on his own, mind you, floating through the air—and he *sang* to me."

"Omaja has chosen you, then," said Ahimoth, reverence in his voice. The other Dragons gasped in wonder.

"I believe that is true, yes," said Jager, lifting the staff again and gazing at it in admiration.

"It is certain this is true," intoned Fianna, solemn. "There can be no other explanation. There can be no doubt. You, Jager, are now the Holder of the Staff of Malek. You are a power to be reckoned with. You are a being to be respected. And you are charged with great responsibilities. This you already know, though—am I not correct?"

"Yes, I know this," answered Jager. "It is an awesome

burden. I believe I have but a faint grasp of just how broad and weighty those responsibilities are, but I am proud and honored to bear them. And I humbly call upon the Ancients to guide me in doing so."

Vin spoke up. "And, if I understand correctly, the staff has also chosen Jager to join with me as my Companion."

"That appears to be so, Vin," said Fianna. Ahimoth nodded his agreement.

"Then it is I who am honored as well, to have been so chosen. And if Jager agrees, I shall be honored to bond with him in this way."

"Oh, I agree, I assure you!" said Jager. "It's almost too much to take in all at once, but I agree. But, what must we do?"

"Hmmm," mused Fianna. "Tradition dictates that a Dragon and Human who are to bond must wait at least a year to do so, from the date of their first meeting."

"So, we'll have to wait a whole *year?*" said Jager. "But, we can already ment. And I have a notion Omaja chose us to bond sooner than that."

"I do understand," said Fianna. "And I cannot escape the feeling that such a delay would be...incorrect."

As if in response to the Dragon's words, the staff in Jager's hand emitted a flash of light, purest white. No one failed to notice, and none had any thought the event was a coincidence.

"Ah," said Ahimoth. "White. Pure white. The color of truth. I believe your feeling is confirmed, my wise sister."

"Indeed," said Fianna. "This must be an exception to the tradition. Understandable, under the circumstances."

"Excellent," cried Vin. "Let us proceed, then." He approached Fianna and bowed deeply. Not with the familiar Dragon bow of respect and greeting, but a more formal, ceremonial gesture. First he extended a foreleg and bowed his neck and head in a graceful downward arc, in the usual manner. But then he spread his great wings and brought them forward, together and downward before him, their tips crossing just a few centimeters from the ground. He paused for a moment, then stood tall and folded his wings.

"Princess Fianna," he began, his words solemn and measured, "I humbly request your leave to join with this Human, Jager, as Dragon and Companion."

"Vin Druk Malbaz, Dragon of Nibiru," said Fianna, "I hereby grant your request. And hear well: I charge both you and your Companion with eternal vigilance and protection of our heritage, our home, and our people. On the morrow, we shall complete this bonding in solemn ceremony and joyful celebration."

Vin bowed again, the customary bow. "Thank you, my Princess!" He turned to Jager. "I am honored by this opportunity, my soon-to-be Companion. My name, Vin Druk Malbaz, means 'conquering thunder Dragon.' Yours, as I understand it, means 'hunter' in a language of your world. I say that together we shall hunt down and conquer in thunder those who would threaten our worlds—and all good peoples, wherever they may reside."

"I, too, am deeply honored, Vin. And I second your declaration. Together, we shall care for and defend our planets and our peoples, and act together to make a universe where all those of good intent may flourish and prosper." He bowed to Vin, and the Dragon returned the gesture.

Then Vin stepped forward and enwrapped the young man

in his great, blue-hued wings—Jager's first Dragon hug.

"Well, all this changes my plans for the day. And for to-morrow, too!" joked Jager.

All present cried out in celebration. Celine and Fianna were the most touched of all, for they knew what wonderful closeness and shared joy lay ahead for the pair.

The cheers that followed filled the refectory and racketed down the corridors. Soon station staff began appearing at the door, wondering what it was all about. Though few were familiar with Dragons or Companions, their guests' joy was infectious—and a welcome, welcome relief from the grim realities of a war growing ever nearer. And when they heard there was to be a ceremony and a celebration, they eagerly offered their help to make it all a grand success.

Celine and Fianna took them up on their offers at once, and an impromptu, high-speed planning session ensued. Dragon and Companion listed items they'd need, staff ran off to round them up, Jager and the rest of the Dragons made suggestions and took on various tasks. All in all, it was a purposeful frenzy of fun.

North, who also joined in the activities, glowed with ap-proval. The tremendous positive energies and emotions generated by the event—and those sure to arise in the next day's ceremony and festivities—were the best possible med-icine for her Human and Dragon guests, and for all the sta-tion's personnel. She knew well that such energies were, and always would be, more powerful by far than the dark evil of ruined entities like Byrne, Scabbage and their minions.

By evening, nearly everything was ready for the next day's events. Celine and Fianna still had plenty of work ahead, though. Celine to master the rite that would seal Vin and

Jager's bond; Fianna to rehearse and re-rehearse (and re-re-rehearse) the part she would play. It was well past midnight when the two were satisfied with their readiness, and gratefully settled down for a few hours' sleep.

Next morning, Celine and Jager rose early and headed for the refectory. They decided against anything more than a hot cup of teala for breakfast; they were much too excited to eat. They were soon joined by the Dragons, who agreed with their decision. "Just a single fish is plenty for me," said Ahimoth. "We shall feast heartily when the ceremony is done!"

"Exactly," agreed Jager, eyeing the filled and covered trays the staff had laid out for the feasting—and the empty platters arrayed beside them, soon to be piled high.

Their abbreviated breakfast complete, Celine led the way to the large meeting hall where the ceremony was to take place. When all were assembled, she and Fianna explained how events would proceed. Then they showed each member of their little party where he or she should stand at the ceremony's start, and did a walk-through of the whole process for those with active roles. After a few times though, all were satisfied they knew their parts. Even Celine and Fianna, with the most elaborate roles in the proceedings, felt confident.

"Okay!" shouted Celine, "We're ready!"

"We are not meant to start for another half hour," Joli pointed out. "And none of the station staff have arrived yet. I say we should just take the time to relax and enjoy each other's company. After all, some of us have only just recently met—and who knows when we will have another such opportunity, in these troubling times?"

Everyone agreed, and they all settled down to chat. All but

Celine, who took the time to review the placement of all the physical elements of the ceremony.

She had obtained permission to make a ceremonial fire, as long she kept its smoke to a bare minimum, and placed it where the air circulation system could draw in the smoke and carry it away for filtration. She re-checked the location and the set of the fire; everything was in order. When the time came, she'd only need to throw a spark from her incant-baton, and a perfect little blaze would spring up in moments.

At Celine's request, two of the station maintenance people had gathered twenty-two oval-shaped rocks from the planet's surface, then helped her arrange them to form a wide three-quarter ring at the appropriate spot, to define the ceremonial circle. She, Jager and Vin would be inside its boundary throughout the ceremony. A half-meter ring of smaller stones had been set at the center: the fire circle.

Close to the fire circle rested a small wooden chest, its ornately carved lid closed and clasped. Celine unfastened the clasp, opened the chest, and inspected the contents: forty-four candles, half of them white, the rest a rich royal blue.

Her checks complete, Celine rejoined the group—just in time for Ahimoth to announce, "I believe it is time for all to take their places. The ceremony is meant to begin in twelve minutes." And so they did, just as several Mentors and all the station staff who were not on duty began arriving. Joli, who would play no active part in the ceremony, greeted the guests and helped them find places from which to view the proceedings.

When the guests were all present and settled, Ahimoth looked to Celine. She scanned the whole scene one last time, assuring herself that everything was in readiness. Turning back to Ahimoth, she nodded.

The great black Dragon drew himself up as high as the chamber would permit, stretched forth his long neck, and trumpeted: a clear, pure tone of such marvelous timbre that most everyone present—and many who were still at their posts in the farthest reaches of the station—were gripped by a chill of excitement and joy.

"We begin!" announced Fianna, and she recited the invocation prescribed by centuries-old tradition.

Next, Celine, incant-baton in one hand, bodypack in the other, walked sedately into the center of the arc of stones and stood beside the small fire circle. She laid her bodypack aside, then turned toward the watching crowd.

"Welcome!" she cried, then bowed: first to Fianna and Ahimoth, then to the assembled guests. She turned to the fire circle beside her, held her incant-baton high, then swept it sharply downward toward the fire-set: a neat, conical arrangement of dry sticks, laced with aromatic oils and herbs. A long, white spark leapt from the wand, and the wood flashed into flame.

The warrior-witch now turned to Jager, who stood waiting outside the ceremonial circle. She pointed to a spot on her left, on the far side of the now-crackling fire. Jager bowed, strode to the place she'd indicated, then bowed again: first to Celine, then, turning, to Fianna and Ahimoth. He remained facing the regal Dragons, beaming with excitement and anticipation.

Now Celine turned toward Vin, who also stood outside the ring. The ritual steps were repeated, Vin proceeding to Celine's right and across the circle from Jager.

When Vin had completed his bow to Fianna and Ahimoth,

Celine raised the incant-baton. "Attend!" she commanded. Jager and Vin turned back toward her, bowed deeply, then stood straight and proud.

Celine nodded to each, then extended her arms toward them, hands open, palms upward. She held the position for several moments, then turned her palms downward.

Jager and Vin turned to face each other, then advanced slowly forward, coming to a stop with their faces no more than half a meter apart. Jager knelt, one knee on the ground, his hands resting on the other. Vin lowered his great body to the ground, wings tucked tightly along his glistening blue flanks. He laid his head on the ground, just in front of Jager and facing the young man.

When the two were in position, Celine knelt, took up her bodypack and began carefully, ceremoniously drawing forth an assortment of objects and arranging them neatly on the floor beside her. She chanted softly all the while.

She opened the wooden chest lying near her and drew out a candle. With her ceremonial knife—its grip intricately carved in the form of a Dragon—she carved a five-pointed star in the candle's waxen side. Two of the points she shaped with folded ends, like a dog's floppy ears. She repeated the process with the rest of the candles, and closed the chest that had held them. Now she took up a white candle, held its base to the fire for a few moments to soften it, then carried it to one of the oval rocks at the boundary of the ceremonial circle and pushed the base firmly against the top of the rock. The soft wax shaped itself to the stony surface and anchored the candle in place. Then she repeated the process with a blue candle, fixing it to the top of the same rock, a few centimeters from the white one. She did the same with all the remaining candles, affixing one of each color on all the twenty-two encircling rocks: white, blue, white, blue.

Next, she poured liquids from two vials into a small pewter cauldron, then added a cachet of fragrant herbs and placed the cauldron at the base of the fire, where it warmed without burning. A heady scent of mint, herbs and rare oils soon wafted upward and outward to the farthest corners of the chamber.

This series of steps complete, she took up two satchels of salt and walked to where Jager and Vin still waited. Beginning at the point where the two were face to face, she walked backwards around the pair, sprinkling a thin trail of white salt crystals as she went, until she'd completely encompassed the young man and Dragon in a long oval of white. Throughout the process she chanted rhythmically, to rid her mind of worldly worries and welcome the energy of the universe to flow freely through her.

Her first circuit complete, she made another pass around the pair, this time traveling in the opposite direction and sprinkling blue salt. When she'd returned to her starting point, she paused, laid down the now-empty salt satchels, stood tall, raised her arms high, and began a new chant, clear and resonant:

Gods and Goddesses of the light

Please bless my friends

The left, the right

Protect them now

And to the end,

Safe, together

Forever true friends

Onto Vin's muzzle and into Jager's left hand she placed red amethysts, to enhance their psychic abilities, intuition, spirituality, strength and inner peace. Into Jager's right hand she placed a bright red-purple agate to bolster strength and courage. She placed a matching stone beside the red amethyst on Vin's muzzle. Next, she walked at a carefully measured pace along the arc of stones, lighting every candle as she went, and chanting in low tones. She returned to the waiting pair and began yet another quiet chant as she anointed Jager's hands, then Vin's muzzle, with a blend of fragrant oils.

She took two steps back from Jager and Vin, and three steps to her right, so the fire's light shone full upon the pair. Throwing her arms up high and wide, she chanted loud and clear, so all present could hear:

Mother Dragon of the light

Father Dragon of the night

Bless our comrade

And his friend,

Bless their linking

To the end

Their intentions are good

Their intentions are strong

Unite these souls

Bind them life-long

Unite their hearts

Fulfill desires

Protect their union

'Til breath expires
Unite them now
And to the end
Safe, together
Forever true friends

After a brief pause, she began the chant again, beckoning those watching to join in. More and more added their voices and hearts to the invocation, until all took part; some loudly, some soft, all intent on the words and their meaning. Nine times the chant rang out; then Celine held out her hands for quiet, and a hush filled the room.

After a long moment's pause, Celine began her final chant, alone:

Gods and Goddesses of the light
Guide our friends through day and night
Guide them safe, hear my song
Guide them now, and all life long
Guide them together
Guide them apart
Guide them home
Guide them afar
Bless their union
Sanctify their names
Support their families
And sever all chains

Keep them safe

Their souls to blend

Bless my Hunter

And his Conqueror friend,

Thunderer, Hunter

Until the end

When she'd completed this ultimate invocation three times through, Celine drew out her incant-baton, and with a flick and a flourish, sent a vibrant bundle of brilliantly colored energy bolts arcing into the fire's center. Its flames exploded at once into a rainbow of sparks and sparkles, which roiled up to the very top of the chamber, then settled harmlessly upon the awestruck assembly.

When the shimmering shower had subsided, Celine advanced to Jager and Vin; she reclaimed the gems she had given them, then seated herself facing the arc of stones that marked the ceremonial circle. Their candles, white and blue, were nearly spent. The sorceress watched in silent contemplation until the last of them sputtered and went out. Jager, Vin and all the witnesses watched with her.

Celine rose, took up a satchel from beside the fire circle, and carefully collected the waxy remnants of all forty-four candles. This task complete, she tucked the satchel into her bodypack, and followed it with the now-cooled cauldron and the various bottles, vials and other items she'd employed in the ceremony.

At last, she closed the pack and stood to face the gathering. "It is done!" she cried—and one and all cheered their

loudest.

Jager and Vin leapt up and embraced, the young man's arms wrapped about the great blue neck as the Dragon's wings encircled him.

Into the early evening the joyful feasting, dancing and singing went on. And none were more joyful than Jager and Vin.

New Light

Their satisfying breakfast complete, Celine and Jager let their companion-Dragons know it was time to head for Celine's quarters.

"Lots of study and practice for me," said Celine, "and unless I miss my guess, Jager's nose will be glued to his computer screen for the second day in a row."

"Not glued, dearest," Jager joked. "There's no way I'll miss out on the chance to gaze at your loveliness now and then."

"And you had better not miss any chances to follow your newest routine," said Vin. "Checking in with me throughout the day!" All four had a good laugh.

The Dragons wished their beloved Companions a productive day, and reminded them to be on time for the evening meal—or they would find a couple of impatient Dragons at their door.

The pair arrived at Celine's room and settled in. Celine took a seat at her desk, looked over the grimoires piled there, selected the second one in the stack and spread it open before her.

Jager sat at the desk they'd moved in from his own room, and woke up his computer terminal and hand-held. The devices had been his near-constant companions the day before; today would be no different.

Before he began reading, Jager addressed Celine: "Still nothing from West?"

"No, nothing yet. But I still promise to tell you if she contacts me, or responds. As long as you promise the same!"

"You bet, sweet cheeks," he replied. "Well, here I go!"

Both dove into their studies: Celine expanding her knowledge and repertoire of magical methods and lore, Jager his ever-widening search for more information about the enemies they faced. He remembered everything he read in perfect detail, but still used his hand-held to make notes of key points. The act of note-taking was simple enough, but it helped him keep the vast quantities of data he absorbed ordered and organized. And more than once, it had sparked insights into relationships between bits of information.

After about an hour of intensive work, Jager turned from his screens to look at Celine. Sensing his attention upon her, she looked up.

"Hello!" he smiled. "At a good point to take a little break?"

"Almost! I was just thinking about having one, actually. Let me go over this spell one more time, though—a few minutes should do it."

"It's a deal," he said, and turned back to his computers to neaten up some notes.

"Okay!" called Celine. "Done for now. Whew—I'm learning a lot. Some of it seems a bit obscure, but who knows when something like that will be exactly what I need?"

"That's my wise and clever girl," he replied.

"You're sweet," she smiled. "So, break time! Was there anything particular you wanted to do?"

"Yes! Something I read here reminded me I have a present for you. I'd forgotten all about it, with all the recent excitement. Anyway, here it is." He reached into a utility pouch he'd brought from his room and took out what looked like a small, round, furry creature.

"Oh! What's that? Where did it come from?" she asked, examining it and petting its silky brown fur.

"Believe it or not, I've had it since I left Earth. My parents gave me one just like it when I was a little guy. It was my favorite. Years later—after the Mentors introduced us and we'd been menting for quite a while, I spotted this one in a shop. I bought it and tucked it away, promising myself I'd give it to you when we finally met in person. It was one of the few possessions I brought with me when Major Hadgkiss moved our family from Earth to Erra."

"It's cute!" she said. "But I'm still not sure what it is. Does it bite?"

"Oh, only if I tell it to."

She cuffed him playfully. "And it's for me?"

"For you, and you alone, my dear." Knowing its story, she looked at the fuzzy thing in a whole new light. "Here—I'll show you how it works." He turned it over and clicked a switch on the toy's belly. "There! Now say something."

"There! Now say something," said the creature, before Celine could even open her mouth.

"Hey! That was you!" she exclaimed, and laughed merrily.

"Hey! That was you!" echoed the toy, then laughed just as

she had, note for note.

"Exactly!" said Jager.

"Exactly!" said the creature.

"That's so cute," said Celine, "but let's stop it before it makes us crazy!"

"That's so cute," began the creature, but it went silent when Jager flicked its switch.

"You've kept it with you ever since Earth?"

"Yup. Good thing my shipmates didn't know, or I'd never have heard the end of it. Anyway, I guess it seems sort of silly with all that's gone on, but it reminded me of happy times, and I *did* get it just for you. So it's yours. That is, if you want it."

"*Want* it? Of course I want it. It's my first gift from you, and it's impossibly sweet. A treasure!" She reached up and kissed him soundly, then hugged him tight. Stepping back a bit, she was surprised to see a tear in his eye. "Hey, are you okay?"

"Yeah. Sure. It's just that I held onto that little creature through all that time you were missing. Sometimes it seemed like the only thing that kept me going—*knowing* I'd find you and give it to you at last." Now Jager's single tear had company: more of his own, and trickles of Celine's as well. They hugged again, happy.

"Well!" said Celine, wiping at her eyes with a sleeve. "We'd better get back to work here."

"Quite right, my practical girl," said Jager. "Oh! But first I should check in with Vin." He did so, and Celine took the opportunity to do the same with Fianna.

Their Companionable duties fulfilled, they returned to

their desks and their tasks, refreshed and recharged.

While Celine learned and practiced a new incantation, Jager studied more about their enemies. Chief among them were the Lords—Byrne and the few powerful but incorrigibly wicked beings like him. Then there were the various groups that tended toward evil, but whose power and reach were inferior to the Lords' in varying degrees. The Lords had searched out such people and groups, and formed them into the black amalgamation known as the Volac Forces. A foolishly arrogant few had refused the Lords' overtures and commands, and would not become minions. They had become, instead, extinct. Typically in ways too hideous to describe.

The Galactic Omniplanetary Democratum—G.O.D.—had originally been a sensible and benevolent multi-sector governing body, presiding over a thriving civilization of more than a hundred planets and peoples. The Lords and their Volac Forces had steadily, stealthily infiltrated G.O.D.'s ranks, though, perverting the once-healthy organization with criminality, corruption and discord. As but one aspect of this, the government had, thousands of years ago, begun using the remote and relatively backward planet Earth as an experimental station and a breeding ground for bodies. For reasons not quite fully understood, Human bodies from Earth were ideal for the transfer of souls from their original host bodies—of almost any race—to new ones. The practice of soul transfer had become increasingly necessary as the fertility rate among some of the Democratum's chief races declined. G.O.D. had instituted a regular harvest of Earther bodies, sending fleets of ships to round up the choicest bodies and carry them off to a system of transfer stations to await implantation of their new occupants.

G.O.D. had also learned, early on, that while individuals

among Earth's natives could rise to relatively high states of spiritual advancement—by far the cream of the crop for body transfers—the planet's population as a whole had an unfortunate but pervasive tendency to fall into corruption, intolerance, and violence; violence to the point of genocide, attempted or accomplished.

Little did G.O.D. realize that the Lords and their minions were behind all these hateful, sub-animal proclivities. Over the millennia, the Democratum had made several attempts to curb such tendencies among the Earthers by sending out wise teachers, skilled at enlightening masses of people and leading them to peaceful, loving, harmonious lives— individual to individual, family to family, and ultimately society to society. But it seemed the Lords' evil intentions always won out, sooner or later.

This was why a vast fleet of transports was on its way to Earth right now, and with some urgency. G.O.D. wanted to take in a bountiful harvest as soon as possible, fearing that the Earthers had grown dangerously close to a new, world-wide outbreak of conflict and slaughter. And with the destructive capabilities they had developed in the past century or so, such a conflict could spell the end of Human life on the planet. Which would be the end of the richest known source of precious transfer bodies. Worse, it would be the end of a race with tremendous potential for peace, prosperity, creativity and beauty.

The Mentors and the rest of the Aadya Coalition they had helped establish objected to any harvest at all, no matter the reason. They correctly suspected G.O.D.'s need for soul transfer—their own failing ability to reproduce bodies of their own—also had its roots in the insidious works of the Lords and their Volac Forces. The Coalition's ultimate goal was to rid the civilized universes of the Volac Forces—beginning with this, the Phoenix Universe, then reaching out to and decontaminating the others. But that was a longer-term strategy. For the present, they had plans in play to block the impending harvest. Fortunately, the harvest fleet now en-route to Earth had no jump-shift capabilities. The Aadyas hoped this would give them just enough time to achieve their objective.

As Jager learned all this, Celine studied diligently away, learning each new spell, invocation, rite and ceremony perfectly. Her spirits rose with each item she mastered. And with every advance in competence, so advanced her confidence, courage, and sense of peace with herself and the universe.

During a brief breather, she casually called out to West. To her surprise, this time the Mentor replied.

"Greetings, my dear. I see you have been studying most diligently. I commend you! Ah, and Jager is studying deeply too, in his own way." She opened the mental conversation to the young man. "Greetings, Jager. I have just commended Celine for her diligence in study, and now I must commend you as well. Admirable work, both of you."

"Thank you!" said the two, in unison.

"I am sorry to have been so neglectful of you these past few days," said West. "I have, however, a bit of time to meet with you now. May I join you?"

"You certainly may!" they said.

"Excellent. I shall be with you presently." Moments later, a gentle knock came at the chamber door.

"Come in, come in," the pair called, cheerily. West entered; both were struck at once by her appearance. The physical body she animated was as lovely and graceful as ever, but the energy the Mentor emanated carried clear evidence of stress and fatigue. West had been working extremely hard, it was plain. Even such an ethereal, powerful being required time for rest and restoration, and clearly she had had scarce little of either in recent days—if not weeks.

"So, my children, what news have you for me?"

Jager smiled at Celine, then turned to the desk beside him and took up the staff he'd left resting against it. He held it out toward the Mentor, beaming. "This would be the best news we have, I think," he said.

The faint glow that always surrounded the Mentor flicked brighter; its hue warmed to the bright yellow-gold Celine knew meant pleasure, approval, and at times, light-hearted amusement.

"And what is this?" she inquired, though she knew the answer well.

"This," announced Jager, "is Omaja—the Staff of Malek."

"So it is," said the Mentor, "so it is. I suspected as much when I saw it in your possession some days ago. I said nothing, wishing you time to discover its name and nature, had you not already done so. And are you aware of what it is, and what it means about you, who hold it now?"

"Yes," said Jager. "But I sense there may be more to it than I'm yet aware of. Would you enlighten me?"

"Certainly. But first please allow me to congratulate you." Jager sensed Vin joining the conversation, mentally. "I see that you have become Companion to the noble Dragon, Vin. This is cause for great joy. Jager, Vin, may your union be long and fruitful."

"Our deepest thanks," said Jager.

"Indeed," echoed Vin.

"And now to continue," said West. Sensing the subject matter no longer pertained to him directly, Vin quietly left the conference.

"As you have already learned, the instrument you hold is Omaja, the Staff of Malek. It was passed down from Malek to its most recent Holder, Schimpel—Companion to Princess Linglu. May I ask how you came to have it?"

Celine spoke up. "I found it in Fianna's cave-home on Nibiru, half-hidden. I secured it to her saddle, and we've had it with us since."

Jager took up the story. "A few days ago, when North was about to beam us here from the Mars outpost, we rushed to where Fianna's saddle and bags were stored. When I reached to take the saddle off the shelf, the staff revealed itself. I did some studying, and discovered what it must be. I haven't yet had time to learn its use, but I know it holds enormous power. I also understand that its choosing me as its Holder confers equally enormous responsibilities."

"Most excellent," affirmed the Mentor. "You have studied well. And now I will further enlighten you, as you have requested. Most significant and portentous of all, please understand that Omaja has not simply chosen you. He has revealed himself to you because he recognizes who you are."

"Oh," said Jager, a bit puzzled. "Um...who am I, then?"

"You, Jager Cornwallis, are a Regent of Pax. Rightful ruler of that planet. Or, as I believe you will come to discover, rightful *co*-ruler."

Then, to Jager and Celine's utter astonishment, the Mentor bowed to Jager, her yellow-gold aura growing momentarily more intense. She straightened again and regarded her two young charges. "My dears, you may wish to close your mouths," she said, with another faint surge of her aura. "It is a simple fact. And it is also a fact that I am honored to be in your presence, good Regent."

"Wait—*you* are honored to be in *my* presence?" said Jager. "You're...you're a *Mentor*."

"That is correct. And may we Mentors, as a force, serve you, your homeworld and this universe well, just as you and your people serve *our* kind, and all others of good will. And now each of you is Companion to a Dragon of Nibiru—another portent of great promise."

"Okay," said Jager, "but there's got to be something I'm still missing here."

"Me, too," said Celine. "What does all this mean? I know Mentors don't kid, so this isn't a joke. But...I don't know...is it some sort of test or something?"

"No, my dear," said West, placing her body's slender hands on the girl's shoulders. It is all part of a puzzle of which you both are integral parts. It is why you are soulmates, and why we Mentors have been intimately involved in your current lives—and many lifetimes before."

"Oh," said Celine, taken somewhat aback.

"It is why we separated you physically, centuries ago, and have kept you apart. We were and are sorry to have done so—sorry because separation can be hard and troubling—but we did it because we believed it necessary for your own safety, and that of your people and homeworld.

"It is why each of you had the Dream, known as the Dream of Atlantis.

"Now that Omaja has found you, our power to accomplish what we must is greatly enhanced.

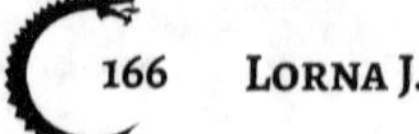

"And now I am sorry, but my time with you grows short. I shall be glad to answer any immediate questions you might have, though, before I depart."

Celine felt inadequate to the sort of responsibilities West seemed to imply they must assume; that the Mentor overestimated her capabilities. "I have to tell you I feel inadequate to all it seems we'll be called upon to do," she said, "but you seem quite confident. So I'll trust in what you say. But what now? What must we do next?"

"First," said West, "you must return to your homeworld." The Mentor abruptly went silent and gazed off into space.

Menting with someone, thought Celine. I hope she doesn't disappear again.

West continued: "I will return later to discuss matters further. But for now, as I have said, you must return to your homeworld. When you have reached your final destination, you will know what you must do there."

"Thank you," said Celine. "I have one last question, though. You speak of *our* homeworld. But Jager is from Earth and I'm from a moon near the Mu system."

"It is true that those are the worlds of your present lifetime's birth. However, Jager, as you both now know, is of the line of the Regents of Pax. Pax is his true homeworld. And, though you were born in this lifetime on the moon you mentioned, that place is not your true h..."

"Pax!" blurted Celine. "Pax is *my* homeworld too. That's right, isn't it?" Then she blushed, realizing she had rudely interrupted the Mentor.

"Quite correct," said West, unperturbed. "You are both, in essence, natives of that world."

"I'm amazed," said Celine, frowning in thought as she

considered what this new revelation implied.

"That's both of us, then," said Jager, "we're both amazed, I mean."

"Wait, though," said Celine, addressing the Mentor, "I don't understand. From all the history and lore I've studied, natives of Pax are...well, they're considered almost super-beings. More advanced than the old Atlanteans, and peoples from Mu and other worlds. And you're saying Jager and I come from Pax. So..."

"Once again, you are correct," said West, and again her yellow-gold aura swelled in intensity. Then, suddenly, she took a step back. "I am sorry, my dears, but I must leave you at once. You know what you must do." She crossed to the chamber door and departed.

"Well!" said Jager. "That was a lot to take in. In fact, it's going to be a while before I can get my head around it."

"That's two of us," agreed Celine. "Anyway, we know we're supposed to go to Pax. And at some point, we'll discover why."

"Right. Maybe we'll get lucky and West or one of the other Mentors will give us a hint before we leave. In any case, we'd better tell the Dragons, and get our gear together."

Celine smiled at her beloved soulmate. No matter what happened, Jager always made her feel safe and secure.

Jager mented Vin while Celine reached out to Fianna, asking that the Dragons meet them in the refectory. "I will gather the others," said Fianna, "and we will be on our way at once."

A Leap of Faith

The group had nearly finished a hearty breakfast. "For a remote outpost, these people surely do serve some good food," said Jager.

"True!" agreed Joli, downing one last tasty mackerel.

"Dragons, you know what Jager and I will be up to today," said Celine, but what about you?"

Before anyone could answer, North entered the refectory, followed by two of the outpost's staff—one Human, one Arcturian. The Human carried a handsome black saddle, hand-made in fine leather and set with satin-finished tungsten alloy fittings. His Arcturian station-mate carried a matching set of saddlebags.

"Jager and Vin," announced North, "we wish to present you with these items, as a token of our love and congratulations. May they serve you well, and may you serve all life in their use."

The blue Dragon and his Companion bowed, expressed their gratitude, and assured the Mentor that they would be proud and honored to use the magnificent equipment to the noblest of purposes. The staff carefully set their burdens down on a banquet table and everyone gathered round for a closer look. The assembled friends admired the beautiful pieces, with showers of praise for the fine craftsmanship they so artfully displayed.

"May we try them?" asked Jager and Vin, in perfect unison. Realizing what they'd done, they looked at one another in mild surprise. Fianna and Celine exchanged a look, too—they had been doing the very same thing since the earliest days of their Companionhood.

"I've seen *that* phenomenon before!" Jager exclaimed, turning to Fianna and Celine. "You two do it all the time!"

"I like it!" said Vin.

"Well, I think you can expect a lot more of it," said Celine. "Fianna and I have become used to it, but it absolutely never gets old."

"Fine with me," said Jager. "But North, may we try these out?"

"You certainly may," said North, "though trying them *on* may be all you are able to accomplish under current circumstances. I do not believe this station will accommodate much flying about." The whole group laughed.

I don't know that I've ever heard a Mentor make a joke before, thought Celine. She looked at Jager, who seemed to be thinking the same. She raised her eyebrows and puckered her lips, as if to say, "Well, how about *that?*" Jager grinned in reply.

Fianna showed Vin how to position himself to accept the saddle, and the moves he'd need to make to help Jager place it. Meanwhile, the two station staff members recorded the proceedings in video and still image-capture.

Jager lifted the substantial saddle and Celine explained

  LORNA J. CARLETON

how to work with Vin to maneuver it into the proper position. With only a few fumbles and re-tries, Jager and Vin succeeded in positioning the saddle, right where it belonged. Next, Celine and Fianna coached the pair through the steps of adjusting the various cinches and straps, and then tightening them down for maximum security and comfort for both Human and Dragon. Finally, they added the saddlebags to complete the process.

"Climb aboard, my friend!" called Vin.

"Aye-aye!" said Jager. With surprising grace, he clambered straight up and into the saddle, settling into flight position without a hitch—to the resounding cheers of everyone present, Vin loudest of all.

"Remarkably smooth, for your first time!" said Celine.

"Indeed," agreed Fianna. "As I believe you Earthers would say, bravo!"

Jager beamed from ear to ear, and Vin let out a trumpet that nearly deafened his new Companion.

"Now, you're sure to want to make some fine adjustments once you begin flying together," explained Celine, "but it won't take long before you have everything set just right, and the drill of mounting up the saddle and bags down pat. I hope we'll be there when you make your first flight!"

"Thanks!" said Jager and Vin—in unison once again.

"It's almost too wonderful to conceive," said Jager. "*Flying* together. Back when I was a little kid, if someone had told me I'd one day fly with a Dragon, I'd have laughed at them."

"I absolutely promise you'll love it, too," said Celine. Fianna nodded her hearty agreement.

"And *I* would have laughed, had anyone told me I would

one day have a Companion," added Vin. "It is as though a fantastic dream has come true."

"Will you teach us how to fly?" Jager asked Celine and Fianna.

"Certainly," said both.

"It would be ideal if your first lessons could take place on Nibiru," said Celine, "but that might not be feasible. We'll see."

"No matter what, though," added Fianna, "you must travel to Nibiru one day, to receive instruction and coaching in the finer points from Orgon himself. There is no finer instructor than Orgon the Wise; not in all the universe."

After one last image-capture of the whole happy group, Jager climbed down from the saddle, carefully removed saddle and bags, and bowed to Vin in thanks for the privilege. Then both thanked North and the station staff once again for their splendid gifts.

Jager and Celine took leave of their Dragon friends, retiring to their improvised academy in Celine's quarters. The Dragons remained in the refectory, enjoying each other's company and trading stories of their lives and adventures on Nibiru and Earth. Though they had been friends since their youths, many, many of the intervening years had been spent far removed from one another. There was plenty of catching up to do, and it afforded them a welcome relief from concerns about what might lie ahead.

That night, an awful nightmare assailed Celine's rest. Legions of smartly uniformed Seeyorg troops marched on city after city, town after town. They touted the lofty purposes of their "missions," promising peace and prosperity—but ultimately delivering only destitution and despair.

And wherever they went, they carried away scores of young people as "recruits"—fresh meat for their rapacious, self-righteous ranks. One of their squads had come to little Celine's village; terrified, she saw and heard them advancing down her street, approaching her house, then clamoring at her door as her defenseless family cowered...

And then she woke with a shriek and sprang bolt upright. In moments, she realized where she was, and that it had all been a too-vivid dream. She was bathed in a cold sweat nonetheless, and shaken to her core.

She slipped from her bed, turned up the lights and splashed her face with cool water at the room's tidy wash station. Well, she thought, that was about as nasty a dream as I've ever had.

The emotional trauma had passed, but now she was wide awake. Still too upset to continue her own studies properly, she sat instead at Jager's station, activated his computer terminal, and began a search for information about her birth world and birth family. There was scarce little to be found—the people of Mu and the worlds and moons near to it had hidden their existence long ago, and scrubbed most records in every sector's archives. No matter, she thought. The Mentors have told me the most important details.

She felt mildly sleepy, but wasn't yet ready to risk another encounter with the night demons of her dreams. Instead, she decided to pursue a new topic of research: Father Greer. She loved the venerable old priest, but realized she knew little of his background. And why would such a wise being and potent sorcerer be tucked away in a mountain cavern? And on Earth, of all places? Could *he* be from the Mu region too? Or Pax? She scolded herself for the silly thoughts, but realized the longing for true family—people of her same lineage, *living* people—haunted her. She felt driven to discover where she rightfully belonged.

It took nearly an hour of persistent, clever, insightful search—and several trips down twisting pathways to nowhere—to find any information at all about the elderly sage. At last, her efforts were rewarded: an obscure treatise on the order of which Greer was a part. He and his fellows were the last of a long line, charged by the Ancients to protect and preserve the Atlantean records and treasures. She learned more about the order, but could find nothing new about the man himself, or his origin. Unsatisfied, but fairly certain she'd exhausted the resources this open network could offer, she switched off the device, stretched, and headed back to bed. After a minute or two between the cool, crisp sheets, she fell soundly asleep—restful, dreamless sleep.

------ ❦ ------

"CELINE, MY SLEEPYHEAD!" came Fianna's mental voice, "Will you not join us for a meal?"

"Mmm...Fianna? Good morning, I think. Is it morning?"

"I am sorry, but no, silly creature. It is mid-day; I called to you earlier, but you were so deeply asleep I thought it best to let you rest. Our kind hosts have served your favorite lunch, though, and I did not want you to miss out. If you are quick, there *may* be some left when you arrive."

"Oh, no!" Celine joked. "There *may* be? You're beginning to sound like Jager!" They both laughed. "Okay, though. Give me a few minutes. I'll be there. Thank you!"

"You are welcome, Little One. But do hurry. There is not too much left, and you know how your Jager can eat."

"I sure do!" she replied, then swung out of bed, rubbed the sleep from her eyes and hurried through her morning

routine.

The friends shared an enjoyable meal, with much of the conversation devoted to highlights of the Dragons' experiences during their long years of separation. As the meal went on, Celine couldn't help but notice something was subtly changed about Fianna's tone and behavior. She had first noticed the phenomenon the day before. Today it was a bit more pronounced, but she still couldn't quite put her finger on what it was—much less the reason behind it. She was about to take the matter up with the white Dragon during a lull in the conversation, when a distraction drove it completely from her mind.

Jager had challenged Vin and Ahimoth to prove who was the best juggler: each was to juggle three melons, and whoever kept them aloft longest would win Jager's last savory meat pie.

The two imposing creatures looked utterly incongruous, leaning back on their haunches, scowling with intense concentration, tossing and catching the plump, greenish-yellow fruits with amazing dexterity. At last Ahimoth bobbled one of his melons and it plopped to the floor. Vin caught his three and placed them on a table with a flourish and a bow. Everyone laughed and cheered as Jager presented the prize. The Dragon downed it in a single gulp, then bowed to his worthy opponent.

As Celine and Jager returned to their quarters after lunch, the girl mented Fianna an apology for spending so little private time with her lately. Fianna thanked her for her thoughtfulness, and assured her there were no hard feelings whatsoever. Secretly, though, the Dragon was relieved. The truth was, she'd been spending more and more time with Vin, and felt ever so slightly self-conscious and guilty over it.

She'd lost none of her love or devotion for her Companion, but Vin was such a charming, fascinating fellow...

When dinner drew to a close that evening, Celine and Jager announced they had an important briefing for the Dragons. West had advised them they must travel to Pax at the earliest opportunity, and they had made preparations to depart that evening. Celine explained that they did not know why West had urged the trip, but that she'd assured them all would be revealed in its time. They promised to stay safe, and to return as quickly as they could. From what West had told them, their best guess was that it would be a matter of a day or two.

The Dragons expressed mixed feelings about their friends going off on their own, and eagerly offered to come along. The Humans voiced sincere appreciation, but declined the generous offer; the Mentor had made it clear they must go alone. After an emotional round of goodbyes and good-luck wishes, the pair headed for their quarters.

They had just reached Celine's room when she turned to Jager and gripped his shoulders. "Look," she said, serious, "I know this will sound strange, maybe impulsive, but before we go to Pax, we've got to go to Mu."

"Oh. All right," said Jager. "I trust this isn't just a whim or an impulse—that's not how you are—but can you tell me why?"

"That's the problem. I don't really *know* why. Just that it's terribly important. It's one of those sudden total-certainty things I get every once in a while. The kind I've told you about."

"I guessed it must be," said Jager, "and that's good enough for me. North will probably be surprised, but I'm sure she'll

go along with it. I think she and West have learned to trust your perceptions and intuitions. And with what West just told us about who we are and where we come from, I begin to understand why."

"That was my thought exactly," said Celine. "Thanks for understanding. Okay. Let's get our gear and talk to North."

In minutes, the two were ready. Celine with her bodypack, Jager with a borrowed bodypack and the precious staff. Together they called to North, who answered at once.

"We are ready to go to Pax, as West advised," they said.

"Very good," the Mentor replied. "Let us meet at the transbeam station."

North was already at the station when Celine and Jager arrived. "Welcome," she said. "There is a jump-drive equipped frigate in orbit; it also has full cloaking capability, to assure a safe, secure passage. We will transbeam to the ship, and then I will pilot you to your destination. The ship is un-crewed, but no crew will be necessary for what we have planned."

"Perfect," said Jager. At North's direction, the staff member manning the transbeam unit sent them to the waiting vessel.

Making their way to the ship's ops deck, Celine broached the subject of her new plans. "North, I know this is not what we discussed, and West knows nothing about it, but we want to visit Mu before going to Pax."

"That *is* quite a change, my child. May I know why you wish to do this?"

"To be honest, I'm not entirely certain myself. Last night, the idea just came over me. And not just as an idle thought, but an urgent necessity. I do not even know what we will do when we get there, but am certain I will know it when we've arrived. It is a sort of calm certainty I've had several times in the past. I've told West about these incidents, and she seemed to understand."

"Ah. I am sure she did; I understand as well, Celine. And I will be glad to accommodate you in this."

"Thank you, North. I imagined you would."

"I foresee a small difficulty, however," said the Mentor.

"What's that?" asked Celine and Jager at once.

"Mu, as you know, is impenetrably cloaked, and its exact location has been obliterated from all records."

"Mmm. Right," said Celine. "But I think I have a solution. I'm able to perceive the planet, despite the cloaking. Perhaps because it's the homeworld of my birth parents, and I was born in that region too. I don't know *how*, but I do know where. Anyway, here's what I propose: I will guide you to the planet's vicinity. Close enough for 'beaming. If you will take us there—cloaked, of course—I'll then tell you some coordinates, verbally. You send us to that location, then obliterate all record of the action from the ship's systems. I would also suggest you compartment them in your mind, as West has taught Jager and I to do. Wall them off so no one will ever know they're there, let alone be able to find them."

"My!" said North. "This is a most excellent plan."

"Thank you," said Celine.

"I'll have to compartment them too," said Jager, "since I'll hear you say them."

"Oh! Good thinking, Ensign," said Celine. "Now, once we're on Mu, it's possible we'll need to travel from place to place, at greater distances than we'll easily be able to manage. If that proves to be the case, I will ment you coordinates so you can

'beam us to our destination or destinations. And then follow the same security steps, of course. When we've finished our business on the planet—whatever that turns out to be—I'll contact you to bring us back to the ship. Then we can go on to Pax, just as originally planned."

"Thorough and well thought out," said North. "I must commend you."

"Thanks!" said Celine, proud of herself. "Shall we go, then?"

"Yes we shall," said North. "If you will give me the first set of coordinates, we may be on our way."

The three settled into flight couches, and Celine—after a few moments' concentration—supplied North with a set of coordinates. North prepped the ship for jump-shift, entered the coordinates, activated the drive, and there they were: within transbeam range of the point in space where Celine was certain her parents' homeworld lay. And, just as expected, the ship's sensors, viewscreens and viewports showed nothing. Nothing but raw, frigid void, spangled with far-distant stars.

"This is it!" said Celine. "Can't see it, but I know it's right there."

Jager shook his head. I'm sure she's got this right, he thought, but it still gives me the shivers.

"Okay," said Celine, "let's go to the transbeam bay for the next step." When they arrived she closed her eyes, and after another moment of concentration, spoke to the Mentor. "North, I'm going to tell you the coordinates now, out loud. Ready?"

"I am," North replied. The young woman reeled off a string of numbers, and the Mentor entered them into the transbeam's controls. "Coordinates entered. Ready to activate," she said.

Jager and Celine stepped up onto the transbeam platform, exchanged a look, then turned back to North and nodded.

The Mentor activated the unit, sending her young charges on their way. She had full confidence in Celine's plan, but couldn't escape the faintest of fears: Had she just transported the pair straight into the cruel, cold vacuum of open space?

CHAPTER 20

A Message and a Meeting

Jager let out a sigh of relief. "We made it."

"Of course we did," said Celine. She smiled, surveying the spot where the transbeam had deposited them: a broad, grassy meadow, surrounded by trees. Generally taller than the trees she grew up with on Erra, or those she'd encountered on most other planets she'd visited, their broad leaves were also a deeper green than she was used to. The planet's sun shone high in the sky, a trifle larger and redder than Erra's.

"So this is Mu, eh?" said Jager.

"Unless I got the coordinates wrong, yes," Celine replied. "But the fact that we couldn't see the planet from space—and we *are* standing on a planet—makes me pretty sure this is Mu."

"Cheers," said Jager, impressed. "Now what?"

"Well, first we'd better let North know we've arrived safely. Just a moment..." She mented North with the news. "She says, 'Well done,' and thanks us for checking in. She didn't say it, but I think she was just the tiniest bit worried."

"So was I, to be honest," Jager admitted. "I've never 'beamed to a place I couldn't even see—and neither could the sensors. What next, then?"

"Now we have to find out where we're supposed to go, and what we're supposed to do."

"Those would be good things to know, yes. How do we find out?"

"Hmm. I have a hunch about that. First let's go over under the trees," she said, pointing, "and get out of the sun."

"All right. You're in charge here. Lead on!"

They walked across the meadow through the rustling, knee-high grass, taking care not to trample occasional patches of white, daisy-like flowers with brilliant blue centers. When they reached the shade of the forest canopy, Celine pointed to a large log surrounded by dry leaves and bright yellow-green ferns. "That will do."

"Whatever you say, O Leader!" kidded Jager. "But, do for what?"

"I, sir, am going to take a nap. Sort of."

"Splendid!" said Jager, playing along. "And while you're napping, fairies will come and whisper in your ear with everything we need to know. I get it."

"No, silly. But actually not too far off. I really am going to lie down here." She took off her bodypack, opened it up, dug around a bit and pulled out a tightly rolled sheet of silvery film. She unrolled and unfolded it, then spread it out on the ground beside the log.

"A space blanket!" laughed Jager.

"A what?"

"A space blanket. That's what they used to call those on

Earth. The material was originally developed for use in our early space explorations. Extremely light-weight, but very efficient at reflecting light and heat. Someone got the bright idea of selling sheets of it for campers and hikers and others to use as insulating blankets, in case of emergencies."

"Oh! Well, this isn't an emergency, and I don't need any insulation, so I'm just going to use it as a blanket. A Mu blanket. Okay?"

"Oh, absolutely. As I said, you're in charge here. Are you really going to take a nap, though?"

"No, though it will look like I am. You can take one, if you want. This might take a little while."

"Mm. What might?"

"I'm going to do something I've been practicing ever since I first discovered I could do it, back in Father Greer's tunnels. I'll explain the details later, but if I do it right, we should end up knowing what we need to know."

"Oh! All right then. I'll be quiet and let you get to work." He sat down with his back against the log, propped Omaja beside him and took in the scenery.

Celine sat in the middle of the shiny blanket, then stretched out on her back with her rolled-up tunic for a pillow. She closed her eyes and cleared her mind. Not thinking, not wondering, not waiting. Simply being.

After a short while, a mental image appeared: a rolled-up scroll of what seemed to be fairly heavy paper, or perhaps parchment. Ah—so my hunch was right, she thought.

The scroll was some twenty centimeters long and two in diameter. Not a physical object, but a complete mental mock-up, in three dimensions. Or is it four dimensions? Or more? she wondered—then quelled the stray thoughts and refocused on the mock-up.

Someone, somewhere, had sent her this, she knew. That had been her hunch: someone would attempt to reach out to her in this way, and tell her what to do next. She responded with an outpouring of gratitude. Almost at once, a sense or concept of *completeness* came over her, signaling her grateful acknowledgement had been received.

Now she more carefully considered the object, pervading and exploring its entire form until she was suddenly, calmly certain she had fully duplicated this thought-thing her unknown benefactor had sent—including the sender's emotions and perceptics at the moment of its creation. The instant she duplicated the thought-message, the scroll winked into physical being, a meter above her head.

Jager, who just happened to have turned his idle gaze Celine's way a moment before, was startled to see the object appear, suspended above her.

"Celine," he said, gently so as not to unsettle her, "if you're awake, I think you might want to see this."

She slowly opened her eyes and turned her head to look at him, a faint, far-away smile on her lips. Jager calmly pointed to the scroll, still floating above her.

"Oh, good," she said, and sat up to pluck the scroll from the air, as though all this were as normal and natural as moonrise.

"Hm!" said Jager. "You don't seem surprised to see that."

"Surprised? No. I put it there. Or helped someone put it there, really. Let's see what it says."

Jager shook his head in puzzlement. "Uh, sure. Okay."

She unrolled the scroll. Hand-written in graceful script

was a single word, possibly a name, followed by a string of numbers: coordinates.

"Perfect!" said Celine. "This is where we need to go. I'll tell North."

"Right," said Jager.

Celine called to the Mentor and explained she had a new set of coordinates for her, and asked if she would transbeam them both to the new location. North agreed, then entered the coordinates into her transbeam console as Celine read them off. She activated the machine, the Humans were transported, and her console confirmed the transbeam cycle was complete; presumably, the pair had reached their destination. North deleted the coordinates and all record of the event from the ship's memory. Finally, she comparted and buried every mental trace of it; no one would ever even suspect she'd had the experience.

When the transbeam's familiar sparkling energy cloud had cleared, Jager and Celine found themselves high on a mountainside. Below them and far into the distance sprawled a vast cityscape. Most of its buildings were no more than eight or ten stories high, but here and there a tall, graceful group of structures soared toward the sky; Jager estimated some rose two hundred stories or more. The city's airlanes and surface roads were alive with traffic, and a busy air-travel hub could be seen far to their left; eastward, Celine guessed.

The two were still taking in the scene when they heard footsteps approaching. They turned toward the sound to see a slender, elderly man, his face alight with a kindly smile.

"Father Greer!" Celine cried, and she ran to embrace the ancient priest. "It was you who sent the message, then."

"Yes, my dear. And my compliments to you for receiving

it, and understanding it so well. Your skills grow apace, I see."

"Thank you, Father," she replied, secretly thrilled at such warm approval from so wise and skilled a sorcerer.

"Greetings, Father," said Jager, with a quick bow. "It's a pleasure to see you again."

The priest smiled and returned the bow. "The pleasure is mutual, my son. Now, if you both will follow me, we should be getting out of the open. Mu is well shielded, as you know, but the Volac Forces grow wilier and more resourceful by the day. It is prudent to be careful."

He turned and headed down the narrow path he'd come by, cut into the side of the mountain; Celine and Jager fell in behind him. They had gone less than fifty meters when the priest stopped and turned to face the mountainside. The spot looked no different than any other they'd passed. He raised his hands toward the rocky face and spoke a few quiet words; a portal appeared, its twin doors opening inward with a soft sigh.

Inside, Celine and Jager could see a short landing, then the beginning of a shallow stairway. They could see only a few meters into the opening—no light came from inside. Father Greer led the way into the mountain, the doors closing behind the group as soon as Jager passed them. The instant the doors clicked together, a pleasant yellow-white light filled the landing and stairway. Strange, Jager thought, the light doesn't seem to come *from* anything, or from anywhere in particular. It's just...there!

They descended the stair for what seemed like a hundred meters. The stairs ended, and the stairway tunnel gave out into a wide anteroom, with seven doorways ranged along its walls. Four of the doors were closed; the remaining three stood open. The priest led them through one of the open ones, down a short hallway and into a neat, comfortable living area. The space was modestly furnished with simple chairs and benches, and a table large enough to seat half a dozen people. A fire burned on a hearth set into one wall, with a kitchen beside it, rustic but tidy. There were two doorways, their doors standing open, in the opposite wall.

"Welcome to my Muian home," said Father Greer. "May I offer you some refreshment?"

Before either of his guests could answer, West entered through one of the open doorways.

Celine and Jager stood speechless, astonished.

"West!" said Celine at last.

"Hello," she said, "and welcome to you both."

Celine ran to the Mentor's arms. "It's so good to see you again. I have to admit, I've been worried about you. We rarely hear from you, and you've seemed… 'stressed' is the word, I suppose."

"My energies have been taxed of late, it is true," West replied, "but you need not be concerned. I am doing important work, and not without success. And that is a good thing. But here you are, and here is Jager; another good thing."

"Yes," said the girl, "We are on our way to Pax, as you advised—but somehow I knew we must come to Mu first. Did you put that idea in my head, as a guidance?"

"No, Celine, I did not. I do not know the source of the idea, but I would suggest that its genus may well have been your own growing intuition; your knowing."

"Hm! I guess that could be. It *did* feel like something I

came up with myself, but I wasn't sure. I don't suppose it matters now—for better or worse, I'm here. I'd say better, since we get to see Father Greer again, and you!"

"You are correct," said West. "You are here now; that is the result. The product. And that is what matters. I do hope you are growing more confident in the validity of your own perceptions, knowings and conclusions, though."

"I am, yes. Thank you."

"You are due another commendation as well," said West. "I speak of your reception of Father Greer's message, and your bringing it into physical form so that you might interpret it. These actions bespeak a remarkable level of ability and skill; I am pleased and proud."

"And so am I," added Jager. "She's a marvel."

Celine blushed at all the praise from people she valued so highly. "Thank you again, West," she said, "and thank *you*, too," she said to Jager, stepping to his side and planting a quick kiss on his cheek. "But shouldn't we get on with whatever it is we're here for?"

"Yes, practical one, I think we should," said Jager. "First we should find out what that *is*, though, eh? West, could you and Father Greer help us with that?"

"Of course," said West. "But as too often happens these days, I must depart, to attend to other pressing matters. I shall leave you in my brother's able care; he will show you all you need to see."

"Your...your brother?" said Celine. "Father Greer is your *brother*?"

"Why yes, my dear. I am sorry; I thought you knew this. But then, I have never mentioned it specifically, have I?"

"Well, no, but now I know it," said Celine. "And it surely explains a lot!"

"Very good," said West. "And now I shall take my leave. I will see you again soon." And with that, she left the chamber.

"Here we are, then," said Celine. "What can you tell us, Father Greer?"

"I shall be happy to tell you, and soon," said the priest. "But first, you must sit and enjoy some teala."

Jager, eager for action, barely suppressed an objection to what seemed a needless delay.

Celine felt a hint of impatience too, but pushed the feeling aside. In her time with him on Earth, she had seen the importance of simple rituals in the elder's daily life. She respected his rituals as she respected the being himself.

"Thank you, Father. That would be wonderful. A little relaxation would do us a world of good, I think." She glanced at Jager and saw that he had caught her unspoken hint to cooperate. Good, she thought. We'll get to the action soon enough.

The pair seated themselves near the fire and fell into idle chat with the priest as he prepared the teala.

"Father, I notice you're not wearing your translator today, as you have in the past," said Celine. "But now I understand you probably only wore it for appearance's sake."

"That is correct," said Father Greer, with a smile. "And now your teala is ready." He ladled the aromatic brew into two clay cups, added a sprinkle of sweet spice from a little pot on the sideboard, and presented them with the steaming cups. "I hope you enjoy it."

Each took a cup and a cautious sip.

"Mmmm," said Celine. "Delicious as always. Father Greer makes the best teala on any planet," she explained to Jager.

"Well, I'm not much of a teala drinker," he replied, "but this has to be the best I've ever tasted." He took another sip. "I can't quite tell what's in it, but it's quite soothing. I can feel my entire body sort of 'letting go.' Almost magical."

"Oh," said Celine. "Magical. Mm, that's...that's..."

Father Greer gently took the cup from her hands, then took Jager's as well and set them on the sideboard. The young man and woman were silent now, nodding as they sat. The old priest went to Celine and gently lowered her to the floor, placing a cushion under her head. Then he did the same with Jager. In moments, both fell deeply asleep.

Grand Tour

Moments after closing their eyes in sleep, both Celine and Jager fell into a dream—a dream in which both were present, each conscious of the other. They seemed to be floating, weightless, in a dark and empty space. Despite the darkness, they could see one another clearly.

"What's happening?" asked Jager.

"I suspect we're dreaming," Celine said. "Something like this happened once before, when I was staying with Father Greer on Earth. He offered me a cup of teala, I took a drink, and next thing I knew, I was asleep—and dreaming, in a place just like this. If this *is* a place, really."

"Oh, it is a place, to be sure," came Father Greer's voice. Celine and Jager turned toward the sound; there was the priest, floating just beside them. "It is a place, but not in the sense to which we are accustomed. It is a place outside of normal space."

"And you brought us here?" asked Jager.

"Yes, young man. I have brought you here to show you things that are important to yourselves and to your cause— or which may become so. I will also present things that may come to pass, or may not, depending on what you and others do."

"Thank you, Father," said Celine.

"Yes, thank you," said Jager. "Celine has told me of your wisdom and helpfulness. I see she did not exaggerate."

"You are welcome, both of you," said the priest. "And now let us begin." He held out an open hand and with a sweeping gesture, pointed to the nothingness behind him. Suddenly, they found themselves on a metal platform, suspended high above a green and rolling landscape. Looking around them, they could see a few patches of white cloud, at their altitude or a bit higher. The sun was high and to their left. To their right and low toward the horizon were a pair of silver-white moons, one large, one about a third its size, only faintly visible in the bright daylight.

"Oh! The moons!" exclaimed Celine. "I know them. We're on Erra!"

"Yes!" said Jager. "Or above it, at least."

"You are correct," confirmed Father Greer. "Or rather, that is the proper location of the scene you see around you. In fact, we have not left the physical vicinity of Mu. This scene's purpose is to lend context to the first thing I wished to show you." He waved a hand, and a round, broad console-table rose out of the platform's floor. The brightness of the Erran scene around them dimmed, and a high-definition holographic projection appeared above the console. There was Celine's adoptive father, Rafael Zulak, deep in conversation with Dino Hadgkiss.

"Father!" said Celine. "I haven't seen him in…so, so long." As the man talked, he casually brushed a crystal pendant at his neck: the crystal Celine had given him years before. Tears

welled in her eyes. How she missed him! How she longed to hear his voice.

"This image is from a few weeks past," said the priest. "I know how deeply you miss your father, Celine. And you, Jager, your uncle the major. We do not know their current location. We believe this is because they have taken your family, Celine, to a safe and secure place. That we have not located them is testament to the security of the location they chose."

Celine could only nod, still near overcome with emotion.

"And of course we will give you word at once, should we learn anything new," added Greer. "But for now, there is much more I would show you—to add to your knowledge and understanding of where our universe stands at this moment, to clarify your own places and roles within it, and to provide a glimpse of possible futures to come."

Celine straightened, took a moment to look all around her and reorient to the present, then smiled at the elder priest. "Thank you, Father. I'm ready."

"As am I!" said Jager.

"Excellent," said Father Greer. "Let us proceed."

He led them on a grand tour of the most significant sectors and worlds that made up their far-flung civilization. Each new locale appeared around them, as though they were there—just as the scene above Erra had. The priest showed them pivotal events of the past and significant circumstances in the present. In each case, he pointed out the key individuals, factions and sub-factions involved: primarily, the Aadya Coalition and its constituent groups, and the Volac Forces and theirs.

One of the past events he presented held particular

interest for the young Humans. The scene was Nibiru, centuries before. They witnessed a grand ceremony whose primary participants were the Dragon-King Alexem and the young Human Malek, bearer of Omaja. The priest briefly recounted their union as the first Dragon-Companion pair, and the highlights of their exploits in defense of their worlds and people. He also pointed out the interesting significance of their names, in light of the roles they played. Malek meant "angel," while Alexem meant "defender of the race."

"Quite appropriate, wouldn't you say?" he asked the young witch and wizard. The pair had to agree—and they came away with new insights into how their own Companionships could influence events in the present and future.

Finally, Father Greer provided glimpses of how the future might look, should major events go first in one way, then in possible others.

At last, he brought Celine and Jager back to the dark emptiness from which their journey had begun. "That completes our tour, my friends," he announced.

"Thank you, Father," said Celine. "I don't think I've ever seen and learned so much in such a short time."

"That goes for me, too," said Jager. "It's like a year of university, all in one...morning?" He laughed. "I don't even know what time of day it is anymore!"

"You are both quite welcome, as always," said Father Greer. "Now, have either of you any questions?"

"Mmm. Not I," said Celine. "There was so much to take in! I think it's going to take me a while to digest it."

"My thoughts exactly," agreed Jager. "If we do think of questions later, once we've had a chance to consider it all, may we ask you?"

"Of course, my son. Of course." He held a bony finger up before them, catching their attention. "And now," he said, in a gentle but commanding tone, "awaken."

And they found themselves in the priest's comfortable quarters, just as they had left them...but with no vaguest idea how long they had been "gone."

"Well. That was an experience!" said Jager. "Thanks again, Father."

"Yes!" said Celine.

With a warm smile, the priest regarded each of them in turn. "Now I have something I believe you will enjoy."

He went to the sideboard, pulled open a drawer, and drew out a pair of small boxes—one pale in color, one darker, each bound with a bit of twine. He handed the lighter box to Celine, and the darker one to Jager.

Jager and Celine exchanged a look. "You first, m'lady," said Jager.

Celine smiled at the gallantry, then carefully untied the twine and opened the box. "Oh!" she said, in wonder and surprise. "Oh, *oh*."

For the second time that day, her eyes filled with tears; this time tears of grateful joy. Inside the box, nestled in a bed of fluffy fiber, were two medallions. They were perfect duplicates of the ones she had buried in the loamy soil of Nibiru as part of the magical rite that had broken a centuries-old hex upon the Nibiru Dragon race. One was a five-pointed star of auburn-hued cherrywood, polished to a satiny sheen. The second was in the form of a Dragon and Companion, intricately carved in pure white ivory-wood. She took the star medallion from the box and examined it closely, then did the same with the ivory-wood carving. "Amazing," she said aloud. "They're exactly the same as..." she stopped, struck by a sudden thought. "Father, are these...?"

"No, my Celine. They are not the ones you employed so skillfully that night on Nibiru. Those rest beneath the soil there still, in the Glade of Linglu. These are as close to perfect duplicates as we could manage, though. I hope you will treasure them as you did the originals."

"Oh, I will! They're beautiful—and they mean so much to me. Thank you!"

"You are most welcome, brave sorceress." He turned to Jager. "And now, would you care to open yours?"

"Sure!" He untied the twine and removed the box's lid. There lay a cherrywood star medallion, perfect twin to Celine's. And beside it, a Dragon-and-Companion medallion. But, instead of ivory-white, this was carved from the most beautiful lapis lazuli Jager had ever seen.

"These are gorgeous, Father. I can't thank you enough." He lifted the medallions by their fine silver chains and inspected them closely. "Such craftsmanship," he commented. "I'll treasure them always."

"You are welcome, my son. And both of you should know that we have embedded a tiny locator chip in each medallion—though we hope never to have need of their use."

"Wonderful," said Celine.

"Yes. Perfect," agreed Jager.

"Now," continued the priest, "I believe your original mission was to visit the planet Pax, at my sister's rather urgent suggestion. Is that not so?"

"Yes, that's correct," said Celine. "Should we go there now?"

"That would be wise, yes," said Father Greer. "And, if you will permit it, I should like to make the journey with you."

"Of course," said Jager. "We would be honored by your company."

"Very well, then. What arrangements had you made for travel?"

"I just have to call North," said Celine. "She's waiting with the ship that brought us here." She called to the Mentor.

"Yes, Celine. I am here, and ready to transport you to Pax. However, I shall need coordinates from which to beam you aboard, even if you are still at the location to which I sent you. I have neither memory nor record of its coordinates."

"Ah. Right," said Celine. "We're in a different location now; I'll give you the new coordinates. Same procedure as before. Oh—and Father Greer will accompany us."

"Splendid," said the Mentor. "It will be most pleasant to see my brother again—we have not met in the physical plane for quite some time."

"Your brother? Oh! That's right. If Father Greer is West's brother, he would be yours as well. Hadn't thought of that. Here are the coordinates, then." She mented the coordinates for their location.

"Thank you, Celine. Are you all there, and prepared to be transbeamed?"

"All here and standing by."

"Thank you. Activating now."

Seconds later, the three travelers appeared on the Mentor ship's transbeam platform.

"Welcome aboard," said North. "I must ask that you please remain where you are for the moment."

She worked at the console, deleting the coordinates she'd just used, and obliterating them from all ship's records. Then she straightened and looked inward as she compartmented and locked away all memory of what had just transpired.

"There. It is done," she announced. "And a special welcome to you, my brother."

"Thank you, dear sister. It is a pleasure to be in your presence again." He made a quick bow, which she returned.

"And now shall I take you all on to Pax?" she asked.

"Absolutely. Please," said both Jager and Celine.

The party proceeded to the bridge, where North had already prepared and pre-programmed the ship for the jump-shift to Pax.

"Please ready yourselves," she said, indicating the flight couches they should use. Then she settled into the captain's couch and turned to a console to verify all was in readiness for the near-instantaneous journey.

Celine, Jager and Father Greer strapped themselves into their couches and braced for the sometimes-unsettling experience of a jump-shift.

"Is everyone secured and ready?" North asked.

"Ready," each replied.

"Very well," said North. "Initiating jump-shift."

"We have arrived," North announced, moments later.

There on the main viewscreen hung the planet Pax, much like Earth and Erra in appearance, despite its different configuration of continents and oceans.

"Well, here we are," said Jager, rising from his flight couch, "*at* the planet. But where exactly are we going *on* the planet?"

"If I may, I should like to suggest an initial destination," said Greer.

"Yes, please, Father," said Celine. "West didn't give us any details, but said we would know where to go, once we reached the planet. Perhaps she knew you'd be with us!"

The priest smiled in reply, then spoke quietly to North.

"Ah. Certainly," she said. "One moment. She tapped coordinates into the pilot's console; the ship moved off toward the far side of the planet, currently in darkness. "Here we are," she announced, a few minutes later. "As you see, it is currently night on this side of the planet. It has also entered its winter season, so I shall provide you with warm cloaks before sending you down—we'll collect those on our way to the transbeam bay. Now, if you would accompany me..."

When Celine, Jager and Father Greer were in their positions on the transbeam platform, North addressed them. "Once I have sent you down to the surface, I will remain here, in case you require transbeam transport from one location to another. However, I may at any time be called to return to the outpost, to attend to urgent business. Should this occur, I will contact you before leaving so that we may coordinate our actions."

"Thank you, North," said Celine, we'll try to keep you briefed on our progress, too." And with that, the Mentor activated the transbeam.

The three arrived in darkness and bitter cold. Snow fell thick about them, and the wind whistled through the branches of winter-barren trees, barely visible. Before the little group was a rustic cottage, its fenced garden-yard blanketed in new-fallen snow. A faint light shone weakly from the cottage windows.

"Ah! Perfect," said Greer. "Please follow me, my friends."

They approached the door, and the old man tapped gently—three times, then two; then he made a soft hoot, like a distant owl.

There was a pause, and the door opened with scarcely a sound. Peering out from the dimly lit interior were two large, round, yellow, cat-like eyes.

CHAPTER 22

Cats and Satchels

"Greetings, Irena," said Father Greer. "And how are you, this lovely evening?"

The door swung half-open. "Thaddeus! I am well, thank you. How fare you, old friend?"

There stood a tall, lithe cat-person—a Lyran, native to one of the several planets circling stars in the constellation Lyra. Her short, thick, glossy fur was cinnamon orange, with buttercream markings above each eye and around her upright ears. She was a bit taller than the average Human adult, but another striking feature distinguished her from the typical feline: a lush, silky mane framed her lovely face and cascaded to her shoulders. In contrast to her exotic appearance, she wore a simple house dress of a woven, white, linen-like fiber, with a blue-and-silver kitchen apron tied about her slender waist.

"Quite well, thank you," replied Greer, with a hint of a bow. "And I dare say I speak for all of us in that. May we trouble you for a bit of your time?"

"Well, of course you may, Thaddeus. Come in, all of you, come in!" She stepped back, opened the door wide and beckoned them in, her bootless paws silent on the smooth plank floor. When the travelers had entered, she closed the door behind them. As it clicked shut, Celine and Jager were startled by what seemed to be a shifting of the space around them. Looking about, they realized that what had seemed a tiny cottage when viewed from outside was in fact comfortably spacious within. Not large or ostentatious, but far from the cramped, close dwelling they had expected.

Father Greer noticed their quizzical looks. "Magical, eh my friends?" he said, with a cheerful wink.

Both nodded, realizing he was being quite literal. "Magical, yes!" said Celine. And she thought she caught the faintest of giggles from their feline host.

"Welcome to my humble home, friends," said Irena. She held out a forepaw to Father Greer; with another slight bow, he placed his hand on top of the offered paw and squeezed it gently. Irena purred and returned his bow. "And now you must introduce me to your fellow travelers!" she said, with a warm smile for Celine and Jager.

"It will be my pleasure. Irena, allow me to present Celine."

"Celine, then. I am enchanted to meet you," said Irena, offering her paw. Just as Father Greer had done, Celine bowed, extended her hand and gently squeezed the paw. She hoped this was proper form for a first meeting; she concluded it must be close enough, since Irena responded with an answering bow and a gratifying purr.

"Enchanted is the perfect choice of words, Irena," said the priest. "Celine is an accomplished sorceress—a protégé of my dear sister West, in fact."

"Oh, my!" said the Lyran. "This is high praise indeed, Celine, from one so skilled as Thaddeus."

"Yes it is," said Celine, blushing. "Thank you, Father Greer."

"And now who is *this* handsome young gentleperson?" asked Irena, with a nod toward Jager.

"Ah!" said Greer. "Allow me to present Ensign Jager."

"Ensign Jager! I am so pleased to make your acquaintance. Enchanted, in fact, whether you be sorcerer or no." Again she extended her paw.

The two followed the greeting ritual, complete with Lyran purr; then Jager replied: "I am enchanted as well, Irena, and I thank you for your kindness."

"Jager, too, is skilled in the ways of magic," said Father Greer.

"Though nowhere near as proficient as Celine," Jager added. "She is truly a marvel." Celine blushed two shades darker.

"Well, then!" said Irena, "It is not often I am honored with the presence of three such skillful persons. A day to be remembered! I am afraid that my own magical skills are somewhat limited. My friends tell me I am a sorceress in the kitchen, though; and at the risk of seeming over-proud, I am inclined to agree. I confess I love the products of my efforts at least as much as they. And, as it happens, my latest creations are cooling in the kitchen this very moment. Would you all please join me for some fresh biscuits, and perhaps a cup of teala?"

"Mm, yes!" "Oh, that would be wonderful." "Yes, please!" the travelers agreed. Irena led them down a short hallway to her bright and cozy kitchen, the buttercream tip of her long, orange tail twitching cheerily as she went. A sleek, black cat—of the usual housecat size—joined the procession, trotting along behind.

Though the aroma of their hostess's new-baked biscuits was heavenly, Celine felt a conflicted twinge. She doubted that a casual chat over teala and biscuits was what West had had in mind when she'd urged them to visit Pax as soon as they could.

"Please do not be concerned, Celine," came Father Greer's mental voice. "All is as it should be here, and our time well spent. I assure you, too, that you do not want to miss Irena's biscuits!"

Irena purred almost merrily as she led the little group into the kitchen, past a vast, three-tiered oven, and seated them at a capacious, round wooden table. Neither Celine nor Jager had ever seen anything quite like it; the table itself could rotate, as could its chairs.

Chatting all the while, the Lyran served them fresh biscuits with butter and jam, accompanied by steaming mugs of the most satisfying teala Celine and Jager had ever tasted. She brought her own teala and biscuit, seated herself between Jager and Father Greer, and the four embarked on a pleasant conversation. As they talked, Celine couldn't help noticing Irena's several glances at Jager's staff, which he'd rested against his chair. Were those looks of curiosity, Celine thought, or awe, or both?

A short while into the cheery party, the black cat—whom Irena had introduced as Freddie—leapt up on the remaining empty chair, planted his paws on the table edge, gazed intently at Irena and mewed once, politely.

"Well, certainly you may join us, Freddie," said Irena. "Please forgive my forgetting to invite you." She rose, went to the kitchen area, and returned to place a saucer of cream before the cat, complete with a bit of biscuit awash at its center. Freddie looked up at his mistress, mewed as if to say "thank you," and lapped contentedly at the cream. The others resumed their chat.

When he finished his last sip of teala, Father Greer addressed the Lyran. "Irena, that was absolutely delicious. As always! But now I am sorry to say that my young friends and I must travel on."

"I understand, dear friend," said Irena. "May I wrap some biscuits for you to take along?"

"That would be wonderful, thank you!" said the priest. "And may I make a request? I wonder if I might have the satchel I left with you, on a visit quite some time ago. I suspect these young people may have good use for what it holds."

"Certainly," replied Irena, brushing a stray strand of mane from her face. "The satchel is still here, safely tucked away. Excuse me for just a moment—I shall fetch it for you." She left the room; Freddie hopped down from his chair and trotted after her. Soon the Lyran returned and handed Father Greer a large, deep-brown leather satchel, filled to its limits.

"Ah," said the priest, hoisting the heavy bag to his shoulder. "Thank you so much for watching it these many years."

"One moment, now, while I wrap your biscuits." She returned to the kitchen, coming back a minute or two later with a neat cloth packet, tied up with green twine. She handed the packet to Celine; "There you are!" she said. "I hope you enjoy them."

"I'm absolutely certain we will," the girl replied.

"Yes, and thank you," said Jager.

"And now, we must be on our way," said the priest. He bowed to their hostess; Celine and Jager followed suit.

"You are more than welcome, Thaddeus. As are you, Celine

 Lorna J. Carleton

and Jager—welcome at any time. It was a distinct pleasure to meet you both, and I look forward to our next encounter."

The priest led the way through Irena's garden and out to the road that passed it by. Remembering their earlier surprise, Celine and Jager looked back at the cottage. Yes, it really *did* look tiny from the outside. Far too small to enclose the comfortable spaces they'd just visited. And yet, they had seen what they had seen.

Their cloaks wrapped tight about them against the chill, the three made their way down the road a few hundred meters, then Father Greer motioned for his charges to follow him off the road and onto a small path, through a copse of trees and into a clearing. "This will do," he announced, coming to a halt. "Celine, would you please call to North, and ask that she transbeam us to these coordinates?" He reeled off a string of numbers.

Celine relayed his request, and reported that North would transport them in a few minutes. While they waited, Celine addressed Father Greer. "My guess is that Irena is from Lyra, Father; is that right?"

"Quite right," said the priest. "She and many of her people fled to Pax at the time of the Seeyorg Invasion. Though some returned to the Lyran planets once the invaders had been banished, many found Pax greatly to their liking, and remained. She and other Lyrans here have assisted me a number of times. And you may count on them to assist you as well, should you ever find yourself in need."

"Thank you. That's good to know," said Celine. "Ah! North says she's ready to 'beam us. Here we go!"

The transbeam did its work, and the trio found themselves in an alley between two stone buildings, several stories high.

They were close enough to the alley's end that they could see it opened onto a broad circular plaza, paved with smooth stones. At its center stood a graceful pedestal of stone. Its height and shape seemed familiar to Celine—and then she realized it could be the twin of the Cynth Pedestal, in Nibiru's Dragon Hall.

"This way, my friends," said Father Greer, and he stepped off toward the plaza. From behind him came a gasp of surprise; he turned to see Jager and Celine staring at Omaja, held high in Jager's left hand. The staff was glowing with pulsing, bluish light. As they watched, it began a low hum, pulsing in rhythm with the blue glow.

"Do you know what this is about, Father?" Jager asked. The Mentor-priest only smiled, and gestured toward the plaza. The pedestal at its center was glowing and humming, just like the staff, their rhythms perfectly synchronous.

"Oh!" cried Celine. "And this one *is* just like the one on Nibiru!"

"Then it must be the Talyth Pedestal!" said Jager.

"Precisely, my son," said Father Greer. "Now, is suggest you pass your hand over the staff's head, like this—he held up a fist to represent Omaja's head, and passed his other hand above it slowly. "As you do so, calmly intend the concept, 'be calm.'"

Jager did as the priest had suggested. The staff ceased its activity at once, as did the pedestal in the plaza's center.

"Very good," said Father Greer. "And interesting, eh?" Again, his young friends glimpsed an almost mischievous twinkle in the old man's eyes. "Now, let's be on our way. We don't want to draw attention to ourselves, after that little display. Certain observers might make a connection we'd rather they didn't; not just now." He led them out of the alley, then diagonally to their right, cutting across the plaza.

"What...?" said Jager, and then he laughed aloud. Beyond the plaza's edge and a tall black iron fence rose a huge, stone castle. Three turreted towers looked down over the plaza, and uniformed guards could be seen in each, silently scanning the scene below.

"What's funny?" asked Celine.

"That castle. It's perfect. Like it came straight from a kid's storybook on Earth."

"One wonders where those storybook artists got the concept, no?" asked Father Greer. And *there* was that twinkle again. "But come, we must be on our way." He led them on across the plaza and into a roadway, perhaps three times the width of the alley where they'd arrived. It was lined with shops and market stalls—all buttoned up for the night—as well as stone houses, most two to four stories in height. Off to the left and above all the buildings could be seen the massive castle.

They continued on down the roadway until Father Greer stopped before one of the dwellings. A few stairs lead up to a gray wooden door. "Here we are!" the old man said. Mounting the steps, he tapped out the same code-pattern he had used at Irena's cottage, then made the same owl-hoot.

After a pause, the door opened a few centimeters. And, just as before, a pair of round, yellow cat's eyes peered out. "Why, Thaddeus Greer!" came a silky, feminine voice, clearly pleased. The door opened wide and a tall, dark Lyran stepped into full view. She was more heavily built than Irena, but no less graceful. Her thick fur and wild mane were black as space.

"Greetings, Nora. Please forgive our arrival with no fore-warning. May we beg a few moments of your time?"

"Beg? Ha! You always were a bit on the silly side, Thaddeus, for all your grave wisdom. You needn't beg for my time—it is yours always, as you know quite well. Come in! Let me meet your friends!"

When all had entered and Nora closed her door behind them, Celine and Jager once again experienced the strange expansion of space they'd encountered at Irena's home. Hm! How useful this could be, thought Celine. Perhaps all their houses are this way; I'll have to learn how they do it!

The visitors went through the same ritual of greeting and welcome they'd practiced just a short time before. And once again they were treated to delightful fresh biscuits, out-standing teala and sparkling conversation. They were joined by the true proprietor of the establishment—at least in her own estimation: a cinnamon-orange housecat named Yasu. She was strikingly similar in appearance to their earlier host, Irena, Celine noticed, though on a smaller scale. She even had the same buttercream markings on ears, face and tail tip. And, just like Freddie, she proved to be a connoisseur of fine cream. With a bit of biscuit, naturally.

As the visit drew to a close, Father Greer inquired after a certain satchel he had once left in Nora's care. She retrieved it from its safe storage and happily handed it over to her old friend. This one was just as capacious and heavy as the satchel Father Greer already carried, and Celine and Jager wondered how the old fellow was going to manage two. Jager offered to carry one or both of the satchels; after all, the priest seemed to be carrying them on their behalf, so it seemed only fair that he share the burden.

Father Greer thanked him for the kind offer, but declined.

He set the two heavy bags side by side on the floor, passed his gnarled hands above them and muttered something neither Celine nor Jager could quite make out. "There," he said. "That should do." He lifted the satchels, one in each hand, and slung them over his shoulders—as though they were as light as Nora's fluffy biscuits.

"Okay," said Jager, "there's a spell I need to learn!" They laughed, then thanked their hostess warmly, bid her goodbye and returned to the roadway from which they'd come.

"That was pleasant! Thank you, Father," said Celine. "What lovely people these Lyrans are."

"They *are* delightful, aren't they?" replied the priest. "And such earnest and trustworthy folk as well."

"Um, will you be telling us what's in the mysterious satchels anytime soon?" asked Jager. "You've got me wondering!"

The old man laughed. "Yes, yes—all in due time, my young friend."

"Is this what West wanted us to do here on Pax?" asked Celine. "I mean, did she send us to collect the satchels, knowing you would meet and help us?"

"No, my dear. They are important, as you will learn, but not so important as the quest she has in mind for you. We will be coming to that shortly. But first, there is one more friend I would like you to meet."

"Oh! All right. But I hope there won't be more teala and biscuits involved. I don't know how much more I can hold!"

"That goes for me, too," said Jager. "Though I'm famous for consuming mass quantities, as long as the food's good. And those Lyran biscuits are way beyond just good."

"I do understand," said Father Greer. "I hope you'll bear

with me and with our generous hostesses just a while longer."

"Ohhhhh. Well, okay," said Celine, gently cradling her belly in both hands.

"Thank you," chuckled the priest. "Let us proceed, then." With the twin satchels bouncing lightly on his shoulders, he led them back up the road toward the plaza, then down a narrower side street to their right. It was lined on both sides by two- and three-story buildings of various colors, materials and styles. At last they emerged from the street into a wide boulevard, paved with bricks in stately, colored designs. Across the boulevard and behind its tall iron fence stood the castle they'd seen earlier. "Ah. We've arrived," declared Father Greer.

"We're going in *there?*" asked Celine and Jager, in surprised unison.

"Certainly. It's the most important place on Pax," the priest explained. "Now, Celine, would you be so good as to relay the following coordinates to North?" He recited a new set of coordinates, which Celine promptly relayed.

"North says she's been expecting our call," said the girl. "If we're ready, she'll transport us right now."

"Excellent," said Father Greer. "Are you both ready?"

The pair nodded, and Celine mented North.

With the transbeam process complete, the trio found themselves standing against a whitewashed stone wall, looking out across a bustling kitchen; to their left was a simple dining area furnished with long tables and benches, its far wall lined with a long, continuous sideboard. Several people of different races sat in small groups, conversing as they ate. It looked for all the worlds like the servant's dining area in an old English manor.

"Oh, no!" said Celine, half joking. "A kitchen. More food! I knew it!" Jager groaned.

"Patience, friends, please," Father Greer mock-admonished. "Ah! Here comes our hostess."

Another Lyran! thought Celine. Despite their apparent tendency to overfeed their guests, she had taken quite a liking to these gentle, vivacious people.

"Dora! So good of you to make time for us," said Father Greer.

Dora was a bit shorter and rounder than their previous hostesses, but graceful nonetheless. Her gray fur was shorter, too, and marked in a pattern Jager remembered being called "tabby."

"Please, please, follow me—I've reserved a side room for our use," she purred, and led them along a passageway to a small chamber, furnished with a low sideboard, a round table and five stout stools.

Over the next three-quarters of an hour, the whole chat-over-teala-and-biscuits scenario played out once again. The biscuits were just as fresh and delicious, the teala just as remarkable, and the visit from the pet housecat just as predictable. Celine and Jager had complained of being overfed, but in truth the biscuits were so delicious that they didn't mind a bit.

"The food is amazing—again," mented Celine to Jager.

"It surely is," he replied. "I might just not be able to eat again for a day or two."

Their repeat repast at an end, Father Greer asked after the satchel he'd left with Dora. She'd apparently had advance notice of the travelers' impending visit, because she had tucked the item in question into the room's little sideboard before their arrival. After exchanging thanks and parting sentiments, Father Greer—now shepherding three bulky but nearly weightless satchels—led his young charges back to the spot where they'd arrived.

"Where should I tell North to send us now?" asked Celine.

"This time we won't be needing North's assistance," said the priest. "We shall proceed on foot. Please follow me, stay close, and make as little sound as possible." The pair nodded understanding, and they were off: down a corridor, through a low doorway, up a dimly lit flight of stairs, down another dim passage, on and on. Celine and Jager were amazed at the intricate network of passages and stairs; they correctly guessed it must extend throughout the vast palace. Now and then Father Greer would pause, hand to chin, reviewing in his mind where they had been and where they ought to go next.

After what seemed like an hour of this, the priest halted in front of a nondescript wooden door. From beyond the door could be heard the sound of voices, high and low, loud and soft, near and distant, engaged in what seemed to be a serious discussion or debate.

Father Greer held up his hand for attention. "Beyond this door lies the Great Chamber of the Paxian Parliament. As you can hear, the assembly is in session. Therefore we must enter most quietly. There will be seats to our right as we enter, along the chamber's rear wall. It is one of the visitors' galleries, in a balcony above the main floor. It is not unusual for visitors to attend; our presence will most likely go un-noticed, so long as we are respectful and unobtrusive. Hear well now: you may see or hear things that are quite surpris-ing, even shocking. I warn you of this now, so that you may prepare yourselves against creating a disturbance with your reactions. Do you understand?"

"Yes, Father," said Jager.

"I do," said Celine. "And I thank you for the warning."

"Excellent," said the priest. "Again, we shall enter quietly and take seats in the gallery to our right." He regarded their young faces, eager and intrigued. With a smile and a nod, he opened the door and turned to his right.

Celine and Jager followed, all their attention on the priest and their immediate surroundings so as not to stumble or take a wrong turn. They came to a row of straight-backed wooden chairs; Father Greer moved down the row and seated himself in the third seat. Celine and Jager followed and gingerly seated themselves, hoping the chairs wouldn't creak. Jager brought Omaja's pointed tip silently to rest on the floor beside him, but maintained a firm grip on the fine-grained shaft.

Settled in at last, the two Humans turned their attention to the great chamber below. The back walls spanned the width of the room in a great, sweeping arc. The floor sloped from the back of the room toward the front, descending in a series of broad, curving tiers. Running the width of each tier was a continuous bench of dark wood, its seat and back set with thick running cushions, upholstered in rich, crimson leather. Men and women were seated through much of the chamber; most were Human, but a few other races were represented as well.

At the chamber's front—at the focus of all the curving benches—rose a high dais. Ranged across its front at floor level were a dozen desks, facing out toward the ranks of benches; each was occupied by a clerk or officer of the assembly.

Above, at the center of the dais, was a large chair, simple but elegant in design and beautifully finished.

And there upon the Great Chair, clearly presiding over the grand assembly, sat...Jager.

An Unexpected Reunion

Celine barely managed to keep from leaping to her feet. The man seated on the dais was clearly, clearly Jager. Even from a distance, his features were unmistakable. And in his left hand, its tip resting on the dais floor, was Omaja.

But Jager hadn't left her side. So...*how?*

Sitting beside her, Jager simply stared.

Father Greer quietly observed the two, amused—but ready to step in, should either prove unable to maintain their restraint.

The second Jager—or whoever that was on the dais—listened intently to a tall, distinguished-looking person, addressing the assembly from her place in the chamber's curved benches. No one had noticed the visitors who'd just arrived in the gallery; business went on as usual.

It was Omaja that gave them away. The staff, still in Jager's firm grip, began to glow and hum. "Jager—calm the staff!" said Father Greer, in the most commanding whisper he could muster.

But it was too late. The staff held by the young man on

the dais had also begun to glow and hum. Startled, the man stood, held his staff at arm's length, examined it closely for a moment, then turned to look directly at Jager.

Jager stood, raised Omaja slightly, and returned the man's steely look. By now, all eyes in the assembly chamber were also upon their mysterious visitor.

"Greetings," said Jager—the one in the visitor's gallery. Omaja's glow intensified as he spoke, though its humming ceased. "I am called Jager—The Hunter, of the planet known as Earth." Omaja's head momentarily flashed bright white, and it gave out a loud, pure tone like the peal of a perfect bell. "And this," Jager continued, "is Omaja—the Staff of Malek."

The assembled dignitaries stared, dumbfounded, as did Celine. Father Greer smiled. *Very good, very good,* he thought. *Carry on.*

"Welcome, Jager," said the man on the dais. "I am called Jaecar—The Hunter, of this world known as Pax." His own staff flashed as Omaja had, then rang just as loud and purely, its tone a perfect match. "And may I present Zulema—the staff of my ancestors."

Jaecar turned to address the Assembly: "My good colleagues, I hope you will pardon me, but I wish to call for a recess until tomorrow. As you can see, we are presented with an unusual circumstance, to which I must attend."

All present called out their assent. "I thank you for your forbearance," said Jaecar. "This session of the Assembly is hereby declared in recess until tomorrow, at the usual time of commencement."

The assembly-persons rose and made their ways toward the exits, talking animatedly as they went and with many a glance toward the mysterious visitors.

Jaecar turned again to face his guests. "And now, would you three join me here on the dais?" he called. "Father Thaddeus, I believe you know the way, yes?"

Celine and Jager swung round to look at the priest beside them, mouths wide. "'*Father Thaddeus?*'" said Jager.

"Why, yes," said the old man. "That is what young Jaecar has called me since he first acquired speech." There again was that elusive twinkle in the priest-Mentor's eye. "I have mentored him these many years, you see."

"Well, I see *now*," said Jager. "And as of this moment, I shall cease being surprised at *anything*."

"That's two of us," chimed in Celine, shaking her head.

Father Greer led the two out of the visitors' gallery and, by a series of passages, stairs and doorways, down to the dais.

Jaecar bowed politely to Father Greer and to Jager; then he turned to Celine. "And who is this *lovely* young lady?" he asked, with a warm smile of unabashed interest.

Father Greer began to answer, but Jager cut in at once. "This lovely young lady," he said, "is Celine, Companion to Fianna, Dragon Princess of Nibiru. And my fiancé." His peremptory warning was equally unabashed.

Celine blushed; it was the first time she'd heard Jager refer to her that way—or take that tone with anyone.

"Ah! A Dragon Companion!" said Jaecar, with a gallant bow. "I am pleased and honored to meet you, Celine." Clearly his interest hadn't waned, but Jager said nothing further; he had no doubt of Celine's love and loyalty.

"Now that we've been introduced," Jaecar went on, "why don't we retire to someplace more comfortable, and become better acquainted? Follow me, if you would." He led his visitors through a door at the back of the dais, down a corridor and into a reception room where an elegant table had been set for teala. "Have a seat, friends, have a seat," said their host.

When they'd all been seated, a pair of servants entered through a side door and began serving teala. And, to Celine and Jager's quickly concealed dismay, biscuits.

"So, Father Greer," said Jager, "it seems you know more about Jaecar and me than we know ourselves. Would you fill us in on some of the more important details? For instance, I'm guessing we're related." He glanced at Jaecar, still struck by their uncanny resemblance. "Quite closely related! Is that the case?"

"It is indeed," admitted the priest. "In fact, though you were born of different women, you are twin brothers. You see, you were conceived as identical twins here on Pax. Your father led the planetary government; your mother was a charming, highly educated woman, and a world-renowned musician. Quite early on, we—certain Mentors—carefully separated you. Without your mother or father's knowledge, I'm afraid, though neither was harmed in any way. They were never even aware your mother had carried twins.

"Jaecar was born here on Pax. Jager, you were carried to term by the woman you knew as your mother, on Earth. Your parents—your biological parents—were murdered less than two years after your births, in a vicious raid by a faction of the Volac Forces. Jaecar escaped unharmed, thanks to heroic action by his nanny at the time, secretly an agent of ours."

Jaecar took up the story. "I was brought up by loving people, and groomed from my earliest days to assume leadership of Pax's government, if I proved willing, capable and suited to the role. Such parent-to-child succession is customary here, though the custom is by no means unthinkingly adhered to.

"My education included much about the Aadya Coalition and the Volac Forces who oppose them. I also studied extensively of Pax's history and legends, and respected prophesies about the planet's future. As well as Pax's place in the larger society populating our little corner of the galaxy. I assumed the leadership nearly two years ago."

"And his performance has been most commendable," said the priest. "Some say outstanding, and they are well supported by facts, figures, and the observable happiness and prosperity of Pax's people and institutions."

Jager and Celine took a few moments to consider all they had heard. It was staggering, but they had become rather used to momentous revelations.

"Thank you—both of you," said Jager. "That clarifies so much. And of course it raises many new questions. But now I believe I see why West advised us to come here. She meant for me to encounter you, Jaecar, and Zulema. I was to reunite with my twin, and Omaja with his."

"Precisely so," said Father Greer. "And what might you speculate would make such a double reunion important?"

"Well, West mentioned how crucial it is to protect the Dragons and their planets. And she explained that the two pedestals, one on Nibiru and the other here on Pax, were built, in part, to generate a shield between the two planets. A shield to safeguard both, and all the Dragon Homeworlds in between. She also said that without Omaja here," he raised the oakwood staff, "the Cynth Pedestal on Nibiru could not be activated to create the shield. That means I have to be on Nibiru for the activation. With all that in mind, I'm guessing that Zulema's power is necessary to activate the pedestal here. And since Jaecar is Zulema's Holder, he must be a crucial element in the whole puzzle too."

"Well reasoned, my son," said Father Greer. He smiled at the two young men. "You are correct. I should add that you will each have quite active and pivotal roles in the events that will follow, but safeguarding the Dragon worlds and their peoples is of paramount importance."

"Thank you, Father," said Jager. And then he had a sudden thought. "One other thing. Jaecar, what is your official position here—your title as leader of the government?"

"I am called Regent of Pax," Jaecar replied.

Celine gasped, realizing why Jager had asked.

"Well! That clarifies something West very recently told Celine and me."

"What was that, if I may ask?" said Jaecar.

"Certainly you may ask, brother!" Jager laughed. "Simply this: West explained that Celine and I are both Paxians by lineage. Then she surprised us by addressing me as a Regent of Pax—a rightful ruler of this planet—then added, 'Or rightful *co*-ruler.' I had no idea what she meant, and I was too astonished by all she'd said to even ask about it. But now it's clear."

Now it was Jaecar's turn to laugh. "That would be correct! You and I are twin brothers; therefore, by ancient Paxian law, we may rule together if we are suited and willing to do so. And believe me, you would be most welcome to share the job. The work and the responsibilities are daunting; quite a handful, even for me!"

"Now there's a mind-bending concept," said Jager. "However, judging from what we have seen of this fair planet and its peaceful, prosperous places and people, it seems you have things well in hand. I believe my training and talents are best invested elsewhere, for the greater good of all.

"I do recognize my responsibility to our people, though. Should you ever find yourself in urgent need of my assistance, may I trust you'll not hesitate to call on me?"

"You may, my brother," Jaecar replied. He was silent for a moment, pensive. "And how strange it seems to say those words, 'my brother.' Strange, but how uplifting!" He stood, laid Zulema aside, and approached his newfound brother. Jager rose to meet his twin, and the two came together in a hearty and heartfelt embrace.

When at last they parted, Celine saw the young men's eyes were wet with tears—saw this through deeply moved tears of her own. Father Greer looked on, fairly glowing with emotion and pride.

"So," said Jager, collecting himself, "now we're aware of each other. Our staves are aware of each other. And on our way here, Omaja made a connection with the Talyth Pedestal—which I take to be a good sign."

"Indeed it is," said Father Greer.

"All right. So we seem to be all set. I'm just not sure what we're all set *for*. Can you tell us what we should do next, Father?"

"Though other events and necessities may intervene, you and Celine must ultimately travel to Nibiru, along with Fianna and the other Nibiruans. There you must perform the shield-creation ceremony."

"Okay," said Jager. "That's pretty straightforward. Though I do understand that making it happen may not turn out to be quite so straightforward. That's okay, as long as we know where we're headed, and why."

"Exactly so," agreed Father Greer.

"Yes!" said Jaecar. "We are not only similar in appearance, my brother. We think along the same lines, and both have a penchant for action. Direct action. Quite admirable, don't you think?"

Jager laughed. "Quite!" he said. "Quite admirable indeed."

"And quite insufferable," said Celine. "Oi!" And they all shared a laugh.

"I suppose we should take our leave now," said Jager.

"Yes, we should," said the priest. "We thank you for making time for us, Regent, and for your kind hospitality."

Celine and Jager echoed his sentiments, and they all rose, preparing to depart.

Jaecar embraced his brother once again, then held out his hand toward Celine. She placed her hand in his, and he kissed it lightly. His earlier unabashed interest had changed—replaced by profound respect, and an almost proprietary pride in their connection through his new-found brother.

The group was headed for the door when Jager stopped. "Just a moment," he said. "Forgive me, Father Greer, but there's one last thing I'd like to know before we go."

"What might that be?" said the priest-Mentor.

"Well, Nibiru is a Dragon Homeworld," said Jager. "And we're meant to connect it to Pax, to shield both planets. Correct?"

"Yes, and the rest of the Dragon Homeworlds."

"Right," said Jager. "So, that would seem to imply that *Pax* is a Dragon Homeworld, too. Isn't that so?"

"Quite so, yes," said Father Greer. Celine stood listening,

mildly puzzled. She hadn't thought of this.

Jager went on. "Okay. But I haven't seen any sign of Dragons since we arrived on Pax. And I don't recall anyone mentioning them. Nor were there any present in the Assembly today."

"An astute observation, my son," said Father Greer. "The complete answer to your question is rather a lengthy one, I'm afraid." Jaecar nodded knowingly. "Too long to answer properly at present. However, I shall be pleased to answer it to your full satisfaction at some not-too-distant time, if that is quite all right with you. I believe you will find the account worth waiting for."

"Oh, yes," agreed Jaecar.

"Hm! All right, then," said Jager. "I'll have to set it firmly aside in my mind, though. I'm suddenly very, very interested!"

"Me, too," said Celine. "Soon, Father. Please!"

"Of course, my students," promised the priest. "And now, let us be off."

Jaecar accompanied his guests to the palace's main gate, where they exchanged fond farewells. Father Greer led the two young people down the long stairway to the plaza below, and then along a wide roadway lined with stately buildings. They hadn't gone far when they came to a low door, set into an otherwise blank wall. The priest came to a halt, then knocked on the little door in the same code pattern he'd used on their visits with the Lyrans.

This can't be another of the cat people's places, thought Celine. That door is nowhere near tall enough.

She was right. The door opened about half-way, but the light was too low to see who was inside. "Ah! Thaddeus," came a deep, gruff voice. "The others told me you'd be coming." Father Greer motioned for Celine and Jager to wait. "I'll be no more than a minute," he said. He entered the building, and the door closed behind him. True to his word, he emerged little more than half a minute later—with yet another bulging satchel added to the collection jostling on his shoulder. "Thank you so much," he said to the unseen person inside. "And please relay my greetings to your wife."

"I shall, I shall," said the deep voice. "She will be sorry to have missed you. Take care, now. Be safe and be strong." The priest gave a shallow bow, and the door closed.

"There! My business is concluded," said Greer to Celine and Jager. "Thank you for your patience. And now, Celine, would you please communicate with sister North? It is time for us to leave."

"Sure, Father," she said, and called out to the Mentor.

In less than an hour, Father Greer was safely back in his home on Mu, and Celine and Jager were once again among their dear Dragon friends at the Mentors' safe outpost.

CHAPTER 24

Resolutions and Plans

Ahimoth knocked politely on the door to his sister's quarters. "Fianna?" he called quietly, so as not to disturb her if she were sleeping.

"Ahimoth!" came Fianna's voice from within. The door opened wide. "Come in, brother, come in!"

"Thank you," he said, ducking low to enter; even the large doorways to the Dragons' quarters were a trifle low for someone of his heroic size.

"Have you heard from Celine?" he inquired.

"No, I have heard nothing since they left for Pax," she said. "I am certain they will be fine, though; West would not have sent them into harm's way. And after all, the planet's very name means 'peace.'"

"True!" said Ahimoth. "I had not thought of that. Another name from an ancient Earth language, yes?"

"Exactly so," said Fianna. "Or perhaps the ancient Earthers borrowed the word from the even-more-ancient Paxians."

"Ahhh. I had not thought of *that*, either," said Ahimoth with a nod. "History is a fascinating thing, is it not?"

"It surely is," Fianna agreed. "Especially when one begins exploring beyond the history of one's homeworld. But I sense you have not come to talk of history; am I right?"

"As usual, yes," smiled Ahimoth. "I wish to discuss something that has been on my mind. A matter that will become quite important when we return to Nibiru."

"Oh! What might that be?"

"It concerns our dear parents, and the future of our homeworld. To be specific, the matter of who shall assume the Nibiru throne when our father passes, or wishes to step down."

"Ah. That subject has crossed my mind as well, though I must admit I have pushed it aside more than once. What are your thoughts on the subject?"

"As the eldest," said Ahimoth, "the role of king would ordinarily devolve upon me."

"That is true," said Fianna, "but do I detect a feeling that circumstances are not ordinary?"

"You do," said Ahimoth with a deep Dragon's chuckle. "In my early youth—as would be expected—I was groomed toward eventual succession. Then, as you know, Vin and I recklessly traveled to Earth in hopes of recovering Joli's departed spirit, and I was imprisoned by Soader for long, long years. I know that in my absence, you were trained to assume the throne, should I fail to return. But now I am free. And from comments our parents made when we were all reunited, it is clear they expect to pass their rule on to me."

"I understand," said Fianna, "and you needn't fear—I have no pressing desire to rule, and will be proud beyond words to see you upon the throne one day."

"Thank you, sister," said Ahimoth, "that is most gracious

of you, typically so. But please hear me out."

"Of course."

"The fact is," explained Ahimoth, "I do not wish to rule our world."

Surprised, Fianna tipped her head to one side. Had she heard her brother correctly? "You do not?"

"No. And for several reasons. First, and most important, I believe you to be far better suited to rule. Your temperament, your insight into people and problems, your sense of justice and honor, your feel for striking a balance between tradition and progress—all are more finely tuned than my own."

"Why, thank you, Ahimoth—you are most kind. But please do not disparage yourself; not on my account, nor for any reason, ever."

Ahimoth smiled. "Ah, but I meant no self-negation, Fianna. I might have done so in my more foolish youth, but no longer. I know well my many strengths and capabilities. And my limitations, too. I know that I *could* rule. It is simply that I sense my strengths would be better invested in other ways, and to greater effect.

"I would also point out that you have, by your miraculous work with your dear Companion, earned the undying love, respect and gratitude of our people. There is no one in all the worlds they would follow more willingly, nor with greater joy and confidence.

"Mind you, I would never wish the weight of rule upon you against your will or your good conscience. But I believe in my heart that your reign would be to the greatest good for Nibiru, the Dragon race as a whole, and the broader community of peoples and worlds." He bowed deeply.

Fianna considered her brother's words for a time, head bowed and in silence. At last, she spoke.

"I cannot but respect what you say, brother. And I must agree, though not without reluctance. Rule is a weighty undertaking, as you say, but one we both were born and bred to. And, considering all you have observed, I believe it would be for the best. I charge you though, here and now: I will need and expect your help!"

"Excellent. I thank you, dear sister. I am happy you agree, and pledge to support you always, to the full extent of my powers. There is one last thing I would add: I believe this is the will of the Ancestors."

"Again I must agree," said Fianna. "I have heard their voices, though I have been hesitant to heed them. So! You and I are agreed, but now we face another question: Will our parents accept our judgement?"

"A cogent point!" said Ahimoth. "But I think that if we present our reasoning carefully, they will agree, support our decision, and proclaim it far and wide."

"I believe so, too," agreed Fianna. "It is the presentation that will surely be our challenge. I think it would be best if you were to broach the subject, though with me at your side, so we may plead our case together."

"Agreed!" said Ahimoth, and the two embraced, both resolved and relieved.

Ahimoth spoke: "Now I think we should ask Joli and Vin to join us in the refectory, and brief them on our decision."

"A fine plan," agreed Fianna. She called their friends over the room's intercom unit, and the two headed for the refectory.

After all exchanged greetings, Ahimoth said, "Vin, Joli,

we have made a rather important decision. We would like to share it with you.”

“It must be important indeed, to be announced this way,” said Vin. “Please tell us, old friend!”

“After careful consideration, Fianna and I have concluded it is in the best interests of our homeworld and our people that—when the time comes—it should be Fianna who assumes the throne of Nibiru, not I.”

“Oh!” said Joli.

“That *is* a momentous decision,” said Vin. “And quite unexpected. May I ask how you reached it?”

Vin and Joli listened closely as the royal siblings explained their reasoning. “That makes perfect sense,” said Vin. “I have every confidence the king and queen will agree, and support your choice gladly.”

“I have been long away from Nibiru,” said Joli, “and have had little association with our gracious rulers, but I cannot imagine they would fault your logic. Nor would the planet’s good Dragon-folk.”

“Thank you,” said Fianna. “Your confidence is greatly appreciated.”

“Yes!” agreed Ahimoth. “Appreciated, and encouraging, too. I only hope that we may return to Nibiru soon, to present the matter to our parents.”

“Mm, yes. That is another matter of concern,” said Fianna. “For the Mentors—West in particular, have told Celine that we Dragons must not be allowed to return to Nibiru at this time.”

The other Dragons were shocked. “Is this so?” asked Ahimoth. “How did you come to learn it?”

"Yes, I am afraid it is so," replied Fianna. "Celine is not aware that I know. I learned it when I inadvertently perceived, within her mind, a conversation she and Jager had had with West. I respect West's judgement, and yet it is imperative we return to our world. With the violence of war approaching, we must activate the Cynth Pedestal on Nibiru and its sister pedestal, known as Talyth, upon Pax. As you may know, the activated pedestals will extend the protective shield that now safeguards our world against detection and invasion. The shielding will then reach from Nibiru all the way to Pax, enveloping and protecting both—and all the intervening Dragon Homeworlds. Only with the shield in place can our worlds be secure against the ravages of war."

"But, do the *Mentors* not know this?" asked Ahimoth, incredulous.

"It would seem that they do not," answered Fianna. "For if they did, I cannot imagine why West would warn against our return to Nibiru."

"Perhaps we should explain it to West," suggested Vin. "That is, tell her of the power of the pedestals, and the fact that you and your Companion must be present on Nibiru to activate them."

"I have considered doing so," said Fianna, "but that would violate a decision and rule laid down long ago among the Dragon Wise: that the existence and power of the pedestals not be mentioned, ever, to anyone outside our race. Outsiders' knowledge of this secret could lead to efforts— overt, covert or both—to destroy the pedestals, and so expose our worlds to disaster. Still, current circumstances are dire in the extreme; perhaps it is time we confide in the Mentors, and seek their aid in securing our homes."

"Perhaps so," agreed Ahimoth. "But, as I am certain you

are painfully aware, it is not a decision to be made lightly."

"Indeed so," said Fianna. "I have been wrestling with it for some time now, unbeknownst to anyone, even my Companion. I know she detects an unnamed concern in me from time to time, but she has not inquired about it. In any case, it is a matter I shall resolve soon. The urgency of the situation forces me to do so. And I promise to inform you of my decision.

"This brings me to a further matter regarding the pedestals," she continued. "One that affects you quite intimately, dear Vin."

The scales at the sides of Ahimoth's great ebon head fanned slightly, in the Dragon equivalent of raised eyebrows. What could she mean? he thought.

"How is that, Princess?" asked Vin, mystified.

"Forgive me, for it is somewhat uncomfortable to broach this here, with others present; even others so dear. As we have discussed, to activate the Cynth Pedestal and link it to the Talyth Pedestal upon Pax, I must be present, accompanied by my Companion."

"Yes, yes, as you have mentioned," said Vin, wondering at her hesitance and barely able to restrain impatience.

"Well, as you may recall, the ancient prophesies say a bit more on the matter. To be specific, they foretell that the pedestal will be activated and the protective link forged by a Nibiru princess...with her faithful *husband* at her side."

Seized by an emotion he couldn't quite name, somewhere between fear and jubilant anticipation, Vin replied: "No, Princess, I cannot say I recall that particular detail. But then, I was never as deep a student of the lore as you; I do not doubt what you say."

"Well, then, you see, it seems...it seems that...with circumstances as they now stand, you see, that...that the prophesies are telling us that...that you and I must be wed."

"Oh. Oh!! I...I see. Yes. Yes, indeed," said Vin. The mysterious emotion that gripped him resolved into pure joy, yet he fought to maintain a semblance of composure and decorum. "Well, then, I...I..." Vin blushed, the handsome blue of his face shading toward lavender.

Fianna and Vin did not see it, but Ahimoth and Joli were grinning as broadly as ever Dragons could grin—fairly bursting with joy at what was transpiring before them, and amusement at their friends' touching discomfiture.

"Yes, dear Vin?" said Fianna.

"Well, it is simply that I...I believe that I have demonstrated my affections for you, you see, though perhaps not their full depth. In truth, I have been restraining myself out of respect, and sincere desire not to add to your concerns during these troubling, eventful days."

By now the blue Dragon was blushing near to plum-purple. "But, to be completely open with you, O Princess, there is nothing in all the universes I could ever desire more fervently than to be...than to become...than to, ahhh...to *wed* with you."

Fianna had blushed a lovely pale pink. "I...I must admit, dear Vin, that I have been struggling to keep my own affections—for you, that is—in check, out of consideration for the gravity of the recent events you cite, and as a matter of proper decorum. So, I...then...well...that is, are you, then, asking my assent to a wedding between us?"

"Yes!!" blurted Vin. "That is, yes, indeed, that is my humble request, Princess Fianna. Would you have me as your husband?"

"Oh, Vin. Yes. Yes. A score of yeses, and another score of scores thereafter."

The two stood speechless, gazing at each other.

Ahimoth could restrain himself no longer. "Oh, please! Go on, Vin! She said *yes!* Kiss her, Dragon! Kiss her!"

"Yes, yes, kiss her *now!* And soundly!" cried Joli.

Suddenly aware they were not alone in the universe, Vin and Fianna turned to look at their friends, their faces wreathed in blushing smiles. Then they turned back to one another, and fell together in a deep Dragon embrace and kiss.

Ahimoth and Joli cheered them on, flared their wings and hopped foot to foot in joyful celebration.

At last the couple relaxed their embrace and drew apart to catch their breaths. And, as if on cue, Celine and Jager appeared, transbeamed to the chamber by North. Ever after, Celine suspected the Mentor had timed their arrival deliberately.

"What...?" said Celine, taking in the surprising scene.

"Ohhhhh!" said Jager. "Are you two...?"

"Yes, they are, good Jager. Yes they are!" said Ahimoth.

Joli flared her wings again and let out a happy whoop.

"I see!" said Jager.

"Wonderful!" said Celine, and she rushed to embrace Fianna.

When the Dragons had welcomed their friends, and proper greetings and congratulations had been exchanged all around, Celine and Jager gave a detailed account of their adventures on Mu and Pax. Meeting Father Greer; West's visit and the revelation that she was Father Greer's sister; their meetings with the charming Lyrans on Pax—and their desire to stay away from teala and biscuits for a few days at least; their encounter with the Talyth Pedestal, and, finally, their meeting with Jager's twin brother, Jaecar, and his counterpart to Jager's staff.

When Jager had finished describing Jaecar's staff, Fianna's eyes popped wide. "Oh!" she exclaimed. "The staves! Jager and Jaecar! I completely forgot!"

"What did you forget, sister?" asked Ahimoth, thoroughly enjoying the cavalcade of happy surprises.

"A while ago, I explained the prophesy about the Cynth Pedestal's activation by a Nibiru Princess and her Companion, with her husband at her side. Well, I omitted an important detail."

"What was that?" asked Jager and Vin, in unison.

"The prophesy *also* specifies that her husband's Companion shall be there as well, wielding the Staff of Malek."

"Ahhhhh. I see now," said Ahimoth. "So, Vin and Jager must be present at the Cynth Pedestal for the activation ceremony. At least, I assume there will be a proper ceremony, yes?"

"Do not be silly, brother," said Fianna. "We are Dragons. Of course there will be a ceremony. My dear Celine shall perform it. I shall take part, as shall Vin and Jager—Jager with Omaja in hand."

"Just as I thought," said Ahimoth. "And may I also assume that Jager's brother—with his own staff in hand—shall also take part, upon far Pax?"

"Just so," said Fianna. "Just so. Though it seems a pity

Jaecar is not Companion to a Dragon."

"Yes," said Celine. "I wondered about that—about Dragons on Pax, that is—and asked Father Greer about it. He promised to explain sometime. Now I'm even more curious."

"I am quite curious too," said Fianna; the other Dragons nodded. "But, for the present, there is another matter we must confront," she went on. "A rather more troublesome matter. Celine, I must admit to you that I recently perceived, in your mind, a past conversation between you and West. One in which she warned that you must not permit we Dragons to return to Nibiru. I have no doubt whatever that she had only our very best interests in mind, and the interests of all. Mentors do take the broadest and longest of views."

"That's correct," said Celine.

"But as you can see, it is now imperative that we return to our homeworld. We cannot activate the Cynth Pedestal remotely. We must be there, directly present, to perform the ceremony."

"I do see this, yes," said Celine. "And now that you have mentioned it, I believe I understand something else West recently told me. First, you should know that her warning against your return to Nibiru included the words, 'until the time is right.' Perhaps that concept was not clear in the memory you saw in my mind. In any case, that brings me to her more recent words. When she spoke to us in Father Greer's home on Mu, she said I would soon recognize the time was right for a fateful journey. I believe she was referring to our fateful journey—*your* fateful journey—back to Nibiru. Back for the pedestal ceremony!"

"Oh, my," said Fianna. "That makes perfect sense."

All the others agreed, and an excited discussion began.

As the planning progressed, Fianna brought up a crucial point. "When we have arrived on Nibiru, and the inevitable welcomings are complete, Vin and I must be wed. As soon as can possibly be arranged. There can be no delay, for the ceremony of the pedestals—its proper name is the Unification Ceremony—cannot be performed until I have a husband."

"This is a matter of grave concern, sister," said Ahimoth. "I do not believe it would be prudent to wait so long; not prudent at all. And yet I see no way to avoid the delay. Not without ignoring the prophesies—which would be even less prudent."

Fianna noticed Celine and Jager's puzzled looks.

"My brother speaks wisely," she said to the young Humans. "You see, it would take weeks to accomplish a wedding, following all the proper protocols and traditions. And I believe you are familiar, Celine, with how strict my parents can be when it comes to protocols and traditions."

"Hmm," said Celine. "I do see what you mean, and you're right. What a dilemma!"

"Tell me," said Jager, "is there anything that would prevent a wedding right here and now, legally speaking? Say, if we had a Mentor to perform the ceremony?"

"Ahhhh!" said Ahimoth, brightening. "You are most wise, young Jager. Clever and crafty, too, in a most positive way."

Jager beamed.

"The answer is no," Ahimoth went on. "Nothing would prevent such a marriage. And with a Mentor to conduct it, no one would contest its validity. Of course, we would still face the challenge of explaining the situation to the king and queen, and securing their blessings. However, though they can be stuffy and strict, they are by no means unreasonable or inflexible. And the safety and security of our people is their supreme concern—that is the highest and most sacred royal tradition of all. Besides, once the Unification Ceremony is complete and the Dragon Homeworlds are safe, they can hold the grandest royal wedding in all our long history! And nothing could be more fitting, I say."

Happy pandemonium followed. And when the cheering and capering had subsided, one and all concurred: Fianna and Vin would be wed the next day; preparations would begin at once; they would recruit the outpost staff to help, and Celine would convince West to perform the ceremony. They set to work at once.

CHAPTER 25

Royal Union

Through much of the night, the Dragons, Celine, Jager, and an enthusiastic bunch of outpost personnel worked to transform the meeting hall into a lovely wedding chapel. The staff had turned up a forgotten supply of decorations, tucked away in a storage room after some long-ago celebration. They used this little trove, whatever else they could scrape together, and a good deal of clever improvisation to create a delightful setting. There were streamers, candles, paper flowers, garlands—even a swath of gorgeous blue and white chiffon fabric to form a glittering background to their improvised altar.

The kitchen staff worked late into the night to prepare a wedding banquet and bake a sumptuous cake. They topped it with a pair of dragons, sculpted from white chocolate and adorned with blue icing. When West came by to see what all the commotion was about, Celine asked if she would perform the wedding. The Mentor happily agreed, and the two retired to a corner of the hall to work out a simple ceremony.

"This is certainly different from the way weddings look back home," said Ahimoth, as the tired crew stood back to admire their handiwork. "All your care and effort are truly appreciated," he said to the group. "They mean so much to Fianna and Vin, as they do to me."

"It's our pleasure," replied Celine and Jager together.

"And ours!" agreed the rest of the workers. They all said their good-nights and headed for their quarters, hoping to catch a few hours' sleep before the happy event.

Next morning, Celine and Jager were the first to reach the hall, eager to begin. Soon the Dragons arrived, along with the few outpost staff who weren't on duty. Everyone smiled cheerily, their lingering sleepiness banished by anticipation. The staff chatted animatedly. A wedding here was a rare event indeed—much less a wedding of Dragons!

When all had arrived, West stepped up to the little altar and raised a hand for attention. The room went silent. Vin entered, made his way up the aisle and stopped before the altar. Lovely processional music began to play, and all eyes turned to the doorway. A sigh went up as Fianna entered, her white neck and head adorned with a simple, elegant sash of shimmering blue and white. She advanced up the aisle, slow and graceful, her smiling eyes set firmly on the handsome, waiting Vin. She reached the altar; the couple joined Dragon-hands and turned to face the faintly glowing Mentor.

The ceremony was brief but beautiful, sealed with the Dragon couple's kiss. Earlier, Celine had asked them if this was a wedding custom of their people. They had admitted it wasn't, but thought it a lovely touch and insisted it be part of the proceedings.

Their kiss concluded, the happy pair turned to face their gathered friends.

"I am honored to present to you," said West, "Albho Fianna Uwatti and Vin Druk Malbaz, Princess and Prince of Nibiru."

The couple bowed, and up went a merry cheer from the whole assembly, Celine and Jager loudest of all. The cheering went on and on as husband and wife made their way down the aisle. Reaching the doorway, they turned again, and one and all flocked to congratulate them—plans for a formal reception line forgotten.

The Dragons had more cause for celebration than anyone. Vin and Fianna were married; with their Companions by their sides, and with Jager wielding the Staff of Malek, they now had the power to shield their world and their people from harm. Or so they sincerely hoped.

During the celebration that followed, Celine and Jager approached the Mentor, who sat in a quiet corner of the refectory observing the festivities. "West," said Celine, "may I ask something?"

"Certainly, my dear. What can I tell you?"

"Not long ago, you said I would know when the time was right to return to Nibiru with the Dragons."

"Yes, that is so," agreed West.

"It seems to me the time has come. Is that right?"

"It has indeed, Celine. Your perceptions, as usual, are correct. Though the journey is still fraught with danger, it must be made. It must be made so that you, Jager, Vin and Fianna may perform the Unification Ceremony. Linking Pax and Nibiru, to extend the shielding force 'round all the Dragon Homeworlds and trebling its power, is now an imperative. You must make the journey within a fortnight; no longer."

"I understand," said Celine. Jager nodded.

"There's something else I feel we must do first, though," said Celine. "If I can arrange it, and make it happen quickly."

Jager turned to look at her, mildly surprised. What's this about, he wondered.

"I see," said West. "It must be important indeed. May I ask what it is?"

Just then, Jager's comm pickup emitted a brief tone, signaling a connection request. "Please excuse me," he said to Celine and West; he reached up and tapped the device to accept the connection. To his delight and amazement—and Celine's— Dino's voice came through, loud and clear.

"Calling Ensign Cornwallis; Major Hadgkiss calling Ensign Jager Cornwallis; do you read me?"

Major Events

Jager leapt to his feet and tapped at his comm pickup. "Major! Major! Oh. Sorry—I mean, Ensign Cornwallis here, sir."

"Jager! Thank the Ancients," came Dino's reply. "Celine—is she with you?"

"Yes, sir. Right here, sir."

"Good. Good. Are you both all right?"

"Yes, sir. We're fine. Celine was pretty well roughed up a few days back, but she's recovering nicely. Right Celine?"

"Yes! Right! Hello, Major!" she called, "We're *so* glad to hear your voice." She leapt up and hugged Jager, grinning from ear to ear. "My father—is he with you?"

Dino had known the question was coming, but he cringed nonetheless. "No, I'm sorry, he's not with me; the commander is, ah, occupied elsewhere at the moment," he said, then quickly changed the subject—not *too* quickly, he hoped. "Where in all the hells *are* you two? And what's going on? It sounds like a party!"

"Well, sir," said Jager, "you're right. There's a wedding

celebration going on. Two of our Dragon friends were married. But we don't know exactly where we are. That is, what planet we're on. All we know is that it's one of the Mentors' hidden outposts. Security, you understand."

"Ah. Okay. At least you're in the best of hands," said Hadgkiss. "Can you get me clearance to come to you?"

Celine turned to West, who had been following the conversation. "Can we?"

"Certainly. I will communicate with the Major on a secure channel from my console, and send him the coordinates."

"Heard that," said Dino. "Please thank the Mentor for me. I'll await her call."

"The Major thanks you, West," said Celine, "and so do I. So very much."

"You are welcome, my dear," said West, and she left for her working station.

"West has gone to her console," said Jager. "We'll be standing by. I hope you don't have far to come."

"No problem there," said the major, "I'll be jump-shifting, then either making a surface landing or transbeaming down. I'll work that out with West. Will see you shortly. Hadgkiss, out."

Celine and Jager hugged, then called for the Dragons' attention to tell them the good news.

It wasn't long before Hadgkiss arrived in *Spitfire*, above the planet that hid the Mentor's outpost beneath its barren surface. Leaving the ship cloaked against unwanted detection, he transbeamed directly to the meeting hall and a warm, warm welcome from Celine, Jager and the Dragons. Celine hugged him with all her might, then stepped back so he and Jager could clasp hands. It was their preferred form of greeting, though no less warm than Celine's. Dino nodded toward Omaja, gripped in Jager's free hand. "Some new equipment, I see. I imagine there's a tale behind it, eh?"

Jager smiled at the staff, then back at his "uncle." "Yes, there surely is. A tale I look forward to sharing." Dino nodded.

The outpost crew in attendance looked on in awe. They routinely worked with the wise and powerful Mentors, but it wasn't often they encountered a high-ranking officer of the Fleet.

Because the major had met only one of the Dragons—Fianna, and she only informally—Celine introduced him to each, guiding him through the formal greeting protocol until he got the hang of it. The Dragons were thrilled and honored, and he was just as pleased to make the acquaintance of such warm and noble people. West arrived just as the introductions were concluding, and greeted the major herself.

With all the formalities complete, the Dragons excused themselves to allow the Humans their privacy, and returned to the wedding celebration.

"I can't tell you how happy I am to see you," said Celine. "There's so much to brief you on, and so much I want to know! I should have asked you before this, but are my mother and Mia okay? Are they safe?"

"Yes. There's quite a lot to tell on that subject, but the short answer is, they're safe."

"Thank you—that's such a relief," Celine replied, and hugged the big man close. "Now, if it's okay with you, I don't want to even try to debrief to you right now, even though I know it's important. It's just that, before you called, I was about to tell West something I think is equally important, and I want to go ahead with that—and tell you, too. You couldn't have arrived at a better time!"

"All right, then. You've got me interested, that's for sure." He snuck a wink at Jager. They both knew very well it would've been useless to object. "Go right ahead. What's this all about?"

"Thank you! I knew you'd understand," the girl said. "It's about something I feel I *must* do. And I'll need your help. A lot of your help, I'm afraid." She turned so she could address West and Jager as well, and began.

"It starts with High Chancellor Jin's daughters," she said. "As far as I know, they're still missing; is that right, Major?"

"Yes, that's correct."

"Okay. And whoever has them is still demanding I be turned over as ransom, right?"

"Correct."

"Right. Then there's still a search-and-rescue operation in progress. I want to join that operation. Jager does too."

"That would be dangerous," said Dino, "but I know better than to try to stop you, if you've set your mind to it. There's a bit of a problem, though: We still have no idea where they're being held. We recently learned that Jin himself took part in having them kidnapped." Celine and Jager gasped at the revelation; Hadgkiss continued. "We were about to arrest him, in part to discover where the girls were being held, but the Brothers got to him first. He's dead."

"That's awful!" said Celine. "Kidnapping his own daughters? How could anyone be so evil? But it may be that his death won't stop us from recovering them."

"Hm! How's that?" asked the major.

"Well, I actually think I know where they are. Not their location, exactly, but how to find them—how to lead a rescue party there. I'm sorry, I know that sounds strange, and it's complicated, but I just know we can get to them."

"Oh!" said Hadgkiss, "That changes the picture considerably. And I believe you can do it, too. You know what you know, and I've seen enough of your capabilities—and Jager's—to respect that."

"Right," agreed Celine. "And thank you. But rescuing Dorte and Bonafede isn't all I want to do."

Again Dino looked surprised. "I see! Go on, then," he said.

"It's like this. Soader's people kidnapped my mom, and Mia and me. Along with a lot of cadets. All girls. And they took us to Soader's compound on Earth, where he already had other captive women and girls—thousands of them. And he's got other prisons just like that one. On a few other planets, and another one on Earth, too, if my information's correct."

"And while we have a rescue operation going, you want to rescue all of *them,* too?" said Dino, only half amazed at the young woman's audacity. Out of the corner of his eye, he could see Jager smiling in proud approval. West still listened quietly.

"Exactly," said Celine, looking at each of the others in turn, her face all grim determination.

"Hmm," said Dino. "That would be quite an undertaking. The logistics alone would be monumental."

"Oh, I know," said Celine. "I thought of that, and nearly gave up on the whole idea. But I truly think we *must* do it anyway. Before the war reaches our sector. From all I've been able to learn, it's nearly arrived already. And once things go hot here, I hate to think what could happen to those girls. Even worse than what they're suffering already."

"You're absolutely right," said Dino. "We can't just leave them there. We couldn't abandon *anyone* to such a situation. And many of them are cadets. As you know very well from your own cadet training, we never leave our own behind."

"I agree as well," said West. "They must be recovered. And here is yet another example of your exceptional character, Celine. I commend you."

"Thank you. Thank you both," said Celine. "But this isn't all my idea. Jager's been in on it, too."

"That comes as no surprise," said West. Hadgkiss nodded agreement, and gave the young man a proud smile.

Celine blushed, suddenly aware of just how much praise was being heaped upon her, from people she respected so highly. "Thank you again," she said. "The problem is—as you said, Major—the logistics. Rescuing so many people, from multiple planets...it's just about overwhelming to think of."

"You're correct. It's quite a challenge," said Dino. "But I believe we can manage it. There are plenty of people who owe me favors, and considering your cause, I know they—and plenty of others—will be glad to assist in any way they can."

"Perfect. Perfect," said Celine. "One thing I really wonder about is where we can take them all once they're free. It's got to be someplace safe, and they're going to need food and housing, and there's sanitation to think about, and I'm sure a lot of them are going to need medical attention, too."

"Correct again," said Dino. "And again I think I have a solution. Quite a good solution, in fact."

"Amazing," said Celine. "I can't imagine what you have in mind, but great. The last trick—as if this needed to be any more impossible—is time. Do you think there's any way we could accomplish it in, say, a week?"

Dino laughed. "You *do* think big, don't you?" he said. "Big, and fast." He laughed again. "A week, eh? Doing it in a month would be more realistic, but we don't have that luxury. Not with the battle zone advancing our way, as you've correctly pointed out. So, yes. Somehow, we'll do it in a week. But why a week?"

"Well," said Celine, "when the rescue project is done, at least to the point where all the girls are someplace safe, Jager and I and our Dragon friends have another urgent, urgent job to do. It really *is* urgent, isn't it, West?"

"Celine is correct, Major. There is a task they must perform, and only they can perform it. It will impact not only the current war, but the future of this universe as well. This universe, and others beyond."

"I see," said Hadgkiss. "Then that settles it. We *will* complete the rescue operation in a week. And shall I bring these two master planners back here when we've finished?"

"That would be ideal, yes," said the Mentor.

"Perfect!" said Celine. "And then we'll travel to Nibiru to do what we must do."

"Nibiru again!" said Dino. "You certainly do get around—and to inaccessible planets, no less."

"I have my methods," teased Celine.

"I'm sure you do," said Dino, shaking his head. "You really do owe me a mega, mega debrief. But we'll get to that in good time. If you have a job to do on Nibiru, so be it. You're obviously the one in charge here. But, if you'll permit me, there's somewhere I want to take you and the ensign, right away. Once there, we can hammer out the details of your grand rescue operation, and get it underway."

He turned to the Mentor. "Pardon me, West. These two are under your protection here. May I take them with me, to plan and then execute the rescue we've discussed? I give you my word, I will do everything in my power to keep them safe and secure."

"Thank you for your considerate request," said West. "In fact, I have been anticipating it. Yes, you may take them. As for keeping them safe and secure, I trust you implicitly."

"Thank you," said Dino with a bow. "I appreciate your faith in me." He turned to Celine and Jager. "Okay, people. Let's move. Grab your kits and then we'll brief your Dragon friends and be on our way."

"Aye, sir!" they said, and off they went. The pair returned to the meeting hall a few minutes later, Jager with his staff and each wearing a bodypack. The Dragons gathered round, wondering what was happening.

Celine addressed them. "Fianna, Ahimoth, Joli, Vin," she said, "we're going away with Major Hadgkiss, to carry out a vital task. Many of our people are in desperate danger, and we must help them. I wish we could take you with us, but it simply isn't possible. Our hearts will be with you every moment, though. We will be gone for a week, maybe a day or two longer. No matter what, we will return to you. And then together we will travel to Nibiru, for the even more vital work awaiting us there."

"Oh," said Fianna, utterly crestfallen. The others clearly shared her upset. "If that is what you must do," she said, "so be it. I will not pretend to like it, but I would far less keep you

from something you know you must do. And I see in your heart that this is just such a thing. We will miss you terribly. And our hearts will be with you as well. Our hearts, and all our support.”

“Thank you, Fianna,” said Celine. “And thank each of you, too,” she said to the others. She turned to Dino. “Shall we go, then?”

“Yes we shall,” replied the major. “We’ll ’beam one at a time, though—*Spitfire* only has room for a small transbeam unit.”

“Just a moment,” said West. “I am sorry to interrupt and to delay your departure, but there is something I wish you to know before you leave. Something all of you should know, Humans and Dragons alike. I believe it will lighten your hearts and bolster your spirits. May I go on?”

All turned to the Mentor, waiting and wondering.

“Thank you,” she said. “You should all know that the Repts known as the Barbdews—the Brothers—are dead.”

The whole assembly stared at her in shock.

Celine broke the silence. “*Dead? Both of them?*”

“Yes, my dear. Dead. Gone. Both.”

“That’s...that’s...wonderful news. Of course. But, how?”

“Good news indeed. For this whole universe, and others besides. A grave scourge and source of unspeakable evil has been obliterated. And in fact, it is you, Celine, and our dear Fianna who are responsible.”

“What?! Us?!” cried the girl and Dragon, in unison.

“Yes! When you broke the hex upon the Nibiru Dragons’ eggs and saved their race, you also sealed the Brothers’ fate. The renewal of Nibiru’s life ushered in the Barbdews’ death.

"You see, the hex they cast so long ago was a terrible weapon—terrible for those it was used against, and potentially terrible for those so despicable as to wield it. For the hex contained a provision: should it ever be broken, the person or persons who cast it would die. Die a painful, inescapable death. The Brothers were even warned of this by the person they forced to assist them in casting it.

"And so, when your counter-spell was complete, their death began. Day by day they declined until at last they perished. As fate would have it, they perished in the presence of the very person who had warned them against the evil, evil deed. She is free now. Just as the universes are free of the vile stain of their presence. Free as *they* shall never be."

There was a long, silent pause as each person present considered what the Mentor had revealed, and what it meant.

And then they all burst into wild, joyful cheering, hugging, dancing and song.

When at last they quieted, Jager passed Omaja to the major, took Celine in his arms, and kissed her long and lovingly.

"All right, you two," said Dino at last. "We have business to attend to."

The couple broke apart and saluted the officer smartly. "Aye-aye, sir!" they said as one. Hadgkiss held out Jager's staff, the young man accepted it, and then, one after the next, the three vanished in the swirl of a transbeam field.

Dreadful Revelation

Once all three were aboard *Spitfire*, Dino gave Celine and Jager a quick tour and a briefing on the essentials of the little ship's operation and equipment. They were about to deploy her in an ambitious mission; the major wanted them familiar with what she could do, and how to make her do it. Both were impressed with the trim, capable vessel.

The briefing complete, all three secured for a jump-shift and Hadgkiss activated the drive.

"Looks like we've arrived," said Jager, scanning the gray-green world that had popped into view on the ship's main display.

"Mm," said Celine, "but where are we, Major?"

"That lovely little planet is known as Remini," Dino replied.

"And Mom and Mia are down there?"

"Yes—but not anyplace you can see on the screen. They're in an under-world beneath the surface. Similar to the one Soader used on Earth." He saw Celine flinch at that last detail, so he quickly added, "But constructed as a safe haven, and maintained that way."

"We seem to be running into a lot of these sub-surface bunkers and under-worlds," observed Jager. "I had no idea they were so common."

"Yes. There was a period when a number of different races were creating such places, for a variety of reasons," explained Dino. "Most for safety and security, but a few for less honorable purposes. The practice has largely died out, though we occasionally learn of a new one under construction."

"Did Soader build the one on Earth?" asked Celine.

"I highly doubt it. He could never have afforded it—they're astronomically expensive to build. More likely he invaded the place, wiped out the original occupants and turned it to his twisted uses."

"That wouldn't surprise me, but I don't suppose it matters now," Celine replied. "Let's get down there and see Mom!" And then, as a guilty afterthought, "And Mia." For all Celine's efforts to be understanding and charitable toward her sister, she still didn't relish encounters with the petulant teen.

"Right," said Hadgkiss, bracing himself for what he must do next. "Before we go, though, there is something I need to brief you about."

A cold chill of dread swept over Celine. It struck Jager nearly as hard, through their shared mental/spiritual bond.

"What?" asked Celine, her tone hard and flat.

"Something I've been avoiding," said Dino, "but I can't put it off any longer."

"Fine," snapped Celine, suddenly irritated for no reason she could have named. "So tell us. Get it over with."

"It's about the commander. Your father."

The chill struck deeper, now soul-numbingly cold. "Tell

me, damn it."

"All right. I'm sorry. Celine, your father is gone. Soader ambushed and murdered him."

For a long moment Celine stood frozen, without expression. Then, "NO!" she screamed. "No, damn you! *Damn Soader!* Damn everyone! Damn the whole sick, vicious, worthless universe!" She stood facing her godfather, face flushed crimson, breath shallow and fast. "No."

"I'm sorry."

Jager, deeply stricken himself, reached to comfort her. She batted him away.

"How? When? Why didn't you TELL me?"

"I'm sorry. Truly sorry. There's been no real chance, no appropriate time."

"Huh. So you say. So, when and how?"

"A little less than two weeks ago, Soader tricked Fleet and your father into believing you were being held on a remote planet in one of the Pleiadean systems. Scobee. Soader knew your value to G.O.D., because of the situation with Jin's daughters."

Celine listened grimly, struggling to keep a grip on her emotions.

"He also knew your father would insist on being the one to come free you. *Asherah* went there, and the commander 'beamed to the planet's surface. A fire team went down to back him up, but he was ambushed the instant he arrived. He killed some of Soader's people in the fight, but in the end Soader shot him, too badly to save. I'm to blame. Should never have let him go without better backup."

Celine dropped her head and stared blankly at the deck.

Jager held back, desperate to comfort her, but knowing it was best to let her grapple with the horrible news on her own, at least for the moment.

At last, the girl uttered an empty, defeated, "Oh."

She collapsed to the deck, face in hands in a vain attempt to contain her own grief. She began to cry, harder than she ever had. She cried for his loss, and for the certain knowledge that he had died trying to rescue *her*. She would never forgive herself for that.

But then, after little more than a minute—and to Dino and Jager's puzzled surprise—she stopped. She hugged her knees, head down and face hidden, but her wracking sobs ceased. She sat up and leaned against a console, wiped her eyes with a sleeve and looked at Jager and Dino.

"All right. I'm okay. Okay for now," she said, in response to their looks of questioning concern. "I have a lot still to do, to process all this. If I ever *can*. It's horrible." Tears welled in her eyes again, but she shook her head and wiped them brusquely away. "It seems almost unreal. But we have too much to do right now. Too many people are depending on us, even if they don't know it."

Jager shook his head. "You," he said, "are an amazing person. You may be the strongest person I know." He helped her to her feet and wrapped his arms around her, gently rocking her from side to side. Dino wrapped his long bionic arms around them both. For a time, the three stood close in quiet thought.

As they stepped apart at last, Jager broke the silence. "Okay. I suppose we ought to go down. Do they even know we're coming?"

"No, they don't," answered Dino. "They're in for quite the

surprise. Brace yourself, Celine. If I know your mother, she won't know whether to cry like a baby, scold like a banshee, or quietly hug you to death. She's likely to do all three."

Celine laughed. "Shush, Major, sir. You'll frighten the ensign. You're talking about his future mother-in-law."

"Forewarned is forearmed," said Jager. Inside, he was thrilled at what she'd said.

"All right," said Dino. "Let's go."

They headed aft toward *Spitfire's* tiny transbeam unit.

CHAPTER 28

Reunion, Recovery and Remembrance

Celine, Jager and Dino emerged from the transbeam less than fifty meters from a group of modest cabins, set on a grassy rise. Jager and Celine scanned the surroundings, quickly recognizing they were in an enormous cavern.

"Big place!" commented Jager.

"It is," said Dino. "Madda's initial survey put it at about a hundred kilometers in diameter. Not perfectly circular, but close. Carved out of native rock. Formed and landscaped to simulate natural terrain. Even has a sort of miniature mountain range, out that way." He pointed toward a line of low, craggy peaks in the far distance. "Lit by that suspended orb up there, as you can see. It's set up to travel from one side of the cavern to the other over an eleven-hour period. Then it goes dark, returns to its starting point and repeats the cycle. Mimics the day-night cycle that occurs on the surface. Climate and ecology artificially established, water cycle and all, but self-sustaining to a surprising extent. Fully automated monitor and support system fills in the gaps as needed."

"Okay, gentlemen," said Celine, "I'm fascinated too, but

we didn't come to admire the engineering, eh?"

"Right," said Dino. "Remi, Mia and the rest are all set up in those cabins. Let's go pay them a visit."

They crossed the expanse of soft, low grass and approached the cabins. "That's it," said Dino, pointing to one of the little structures. They stepped up to the front entrance, and Dino knocked on the white-painted door.

Through the door's small window, Jager could see a middle-aged woman approaching inside—Remi. When she recognized Hadgkiss, her eyes went wide; she rushed forward and swung open the door. "Dino!" she began, "You're..."

And then she saw Celine. "Celine!" she gasped. Bursting out onto the landing, she engulfed her daughter in a desperate embrace. "Oh, Celine. Oh, oh, oh." And then she went quiet and held the girl tight, tears streaming.

"Mom!" said Celine, hugging back just as fiercely. For the moment, that was all the talk she could manage.

A younger woman appeared in the cabin's entry: Mia. "Hi, Dino." she said.

Remi released Celine and moved slightly aside. "And Celine," said Mia, "Hi."

Remi gestured, inviting her elder daughter to join them. The girl came and embraced her mother and sister, sibling animosities forgotten for the moment.

"Mother, Mia," said Celine, when they separated at last, "I think you've met Ensign Cornwallis, yes?

"Yes, we have," said Remi, extending her hand. "I'm pleased to see you again, Ensign."

"The pleasure is mine, ma'am," said Jager, holding her hand firmly but gently and making a polite bow.

Mia held out her hand and gave Jager a smile. "So nice to see you, Ensign," she said. "A pleasure." *He's definitely a handsome one,* she thought.

"It's good to see you again, too, ma'am," he replied, taking her hand and bowing a fraction less deeply than he had to her mother. Perfect protocol, and carefully neutral. Celine had told him enough about her sister to know he'd have to be on his best behavior, or risk unwanted drama.

"How do you two know each other, Celine?" asked Remi. "I don't remember your being present when I met the ensign earlier."

"Oh, we met in school years ago," said Celine, stretching the truth a bit. She didn't mention that "school" referred to the Mentors' secret tutoring, which had begun before either she or Jager could walk. Nor that they had been inseparably close for almost as long—confirmed soulmates, destined to marry.

Remi's motherly perception told her the two were quite a lot closer than they were letting on, but she said nothing. It had always been clear to her that Jager was an exceptional young man. The fact that Dino had taken him under his wing was evidence enough of that. Celine had chosen well. And so had Ensign Cornwallis.

Mia also detected their bond, but reacted with a faint pang of jealousy. She was used to snaring all the male attention. The ensign seemed to appreciate her looks and femininity, but she hadn't triggered any serious interest.

Celine had observed their momentary exchange with a woman's intuitive accuracy. She felt a calm pride at Jager's loyalty—and the briefest hint of satisfaction at the unintended snub he'd just dealt her coquettish sister.

Remi turned to Hadgkiss, her face suddenly serious. "Dino, does Celine know about...?"

"Yes. I told her," he replied. Celine knew exactly what he meant.

Remi turned to her daughter with a look of both anguish and sympathy. They fell together again, but now their shared tears were the more painful kind. Mia rejoined them, then Dino and Jager stepped in to lend their support and what comfort they could.

In a short while, Doc Deggers arrived, fresh from the cabin he'd converted to a makeshift infirmary. He stopped short when he saw the grieving group; though he felt Rafael's loss perhaps as deeply as they, he waited at a respectful distance.

"Doc," said Dino in quiet acknowledgement, when he noticed Deggers's presence. The doctor nodded in reply.

Remi and Mia looked up, and the group separated.

Mia brushed a sleeve across her eyes. "How is he, doctor?" she asked, hopeful.

"Hyatt's better. Considerably," said Deggers. "It will take some time, but he's going to recover."

"Oh! Thank you!" said Mia, and the rest echoed her gratitude.

"Hey, everyone," said Dino, "I think it would be a good idea to have a service for Rafael. It would give us some closure. And you know Raff—he would never want us grieving on and on. He'd expect us to put this aside and get on with our lives. *Asherah's* crew has honored him with a spacer's burial; that's Fleet tradition. And you can be sure Fleet will be in touch with you all as soon as you're back home. This service would be just for us."

"That's a perfect idea," said Remi, dabbing away the last of her tears.

"Yes. Perfect," agreed Celine; Mia nodded her approval.

"All right, then," said Deggers, "As acting chaplain, I will make the arrangements. Would tomorrow morning at 8:00 be agreeable? The light is brightening at that time; quite lovely."

They assured him it would be fine, and he turned to leave.

"Doc," said Celine, "before you go, I'd like your permission to visit Hyatt. I...well, I have some skills that might help him heal more quickly."

Doc cocked an eyebrow, uncertain of what sort of skills she might be referring to.

Mia scowled and began to speak, but Remi cut her off with a look.

"Well..." Deggers began.

Dino caught his eye and gave a single, subtle nod.

"Well, I suppose that would be fine. Of course. You're welcome to visit him. Come with me, I'll show you to the infirmary."

"Thank you, Doc," said Celine, and the doctor led her away.

Little more than an hour later, Celine returned to find Dino, Jager, Remi and Mia in quiet conversation. "Hello," she said as she entered. "Hyatt would like you all to come see him. Doc says it's okay." They rose, and she led them to the temporary infirmary. There they found Hyatt propped up in a bed the doctor had moved into the cabin's main room, a cheerful look on his face. A light blanket covered him from the waist down, but its contours couldn't hide the fact that only one leg lay beneath.

"Hey!" he said. Mia brightened. His color had improved immensely, and she hadn't seen him in such good spirits since the horrible day of the accident. He turned to face her directly, arms spread wide. "Come here, you!"

She went to him and leaned over to accept his embrace—then hugged back just as warmly...with tears of happy relief coursing down her cheeks.

He held her away, looked deep into her eyes, and kissed her, fast but firm. "You see?" he said. "Better and better."

Mia shook her head in amazement; he'd improved so much, so quickly. How...?

Sensing her wonderment, Hyatt piped up. "The doc is a genius. And your sister? She's...I'd have to say she's magical." He flashed Celine a huge smile of gratitude. And respect.

Mia turned to regard her sister.

Celine steeled herself, determined not to react to the nastiness she expected next.

"Yes," said Mia. "Yes, I think 'magical' is the word. And it's wonderful." And she gave Celine the warmest, sincerest smile the girl could ever remember.

"Thank you, Mia," said Celine, in utter shock. "I...well... thank you."

Remi looked on, at least as shocked as Celine. And then the three embraced all over again, tears flowing once more.

"Quite a day, eh?" whispered Jager to Hadgkiss.

"Quite," said the elder man. "You have no idea." A tear rolled down his own hard but handsome cheek.

The next morning, the group met beside the sparkling stream that ran through the meadow below the cabins. The light-orb off to the "east" was gradually brightening toward full daylight, and birds flitted through the trees that grew along the water's edge. Madda was present, still in her hover-chair but near to full recovery. Even Hyatt had come—under his own power, using a pair of crutches Deggers had fashioned for him.

The doctor called for everyone's attention, said a few words, then asked Dino to come forward. The major delivered a simple, moving eulogy for his beloved Rafael—his lifelong friend and revered commander. Once again, tears visited everyone's eyes.

When Dino had finished, all joined hands and bowed their heads in silent reflection.

At last, the doctor spoke. "Thank you, Major. And now, everyone, I should tell you that I've taken the liberty of arranging a special dinner for this evening, in celebration of our dear Rafael's life."

They spent the day in quiet talk. Celine offered Madda assistance with her healing. Madda, very much the engineer and Fleet officer, was skeptical. But she'd seen the dramatic change in Hyatt, so she agreed. The two retired to Madda's cabin.

Dino showed Hyatt his bionics and demonstrated their capabilities. Doc assured the young man the same could be done for him. Hyatt was excited at the prospect; so was Mia, perhaps even more than he.

When Madda and Celine returned from their healing session, one and all could see the change in her. "Ensign," she said to Hyatt, "I won't be needing this hover-chair much longer. You're welcome to it, if you like."

"Thank you, Lieutenant," he said. "But I think I'll tough it out with Doc's crutches. Maybe I won't be needing them for long, though—not if he can arrange to get me fitted for a bionic."

That evening the group gathered for Doc's promised dinner. The mood was quiet and reflective—just what the healing process required at that point. After the meal, they took turns sharing fond memories of Rafael. More than a few tears were shed, but their grief was easing. The pain of loss would always be with them, but its sting and ache would fade.

Toward the end of the evening, Celine moved her chair close to Remi's. "Mother," she said, "we're going to be leaving in the morning—Dino, Jager, Madda and I."

"What? Why?" said Remi. "You just arrived!"

Celine explained her plan to rescue the cadets and other women Soader had imprisoned and enslaved. "There are Baylis and Mia's other friends, still on Earth—and all the rest we saw there. Then there's another whole prison-lab on Earth, and several others, on other planets. I don't even want to think about what's being done to them. You know."

"Yes, I know," said Remi. "But no. You will do nothing of the kind." The air was electric with the tension between them. Everyone turned to watch and listen. "I appreciate your kind intentions, Celine, but others will see to them; it is *not* your concern."

"Yes, I'm afraid it *is* my concern, Mother. I owe some of those people my life. Just as you owe them yours. And Mia's. And I can't just leave them all out there. Not knowing what I know."

"I don't care! You can't just go running off and..."

As Remi went on, Celine stood and squared off, hands on hips. "Mother!" she barked.

Remi stopped mid-sentence. Shocked, she sank back in her chair. Her daughter had never taken such a tone with her. Never. No one had ever dared it—no one but Rafael.

"Look. I understand your concern," said Celine. "I do. But you know that's not how you and Father raised me. Responsibility. Honor. Duty. Knowing what you know and doing what you know you must—what's right. And just what do you think *Father* would have done?"

Remi sat silent. The girl was correct. Knowing it didn't calm her fears one bit, but she knew her daughter spoke the truth, and she knew she had to let her go. Just as she had had to let Rafael go, so many times. It was a price of sharing her life with such wonderful, sterling beings. And she knew in her heart it was a price well worth paying.

"All right," she said. "All right. The thought of it makes me sick with worry, but I can't dispute what you say." She stood, and the two embraced.

The evening went on, and the fiery confrontation was soon forgotten. Or nearly so.

When Remi rose the next morning, Dino, Madda, Jager and her precious daughter were gone.

CHAPTER 29

A Plan for Freedom

Back aboard *Spitfire*, Madda, Dino, Jager and Celine gathered in the ship's galley to plan the upcoming operation.

"Ever since Celine suggested the whole idea, I've been thinking it over quite a bit," said Jager. "If I may, I'd like to show you what I've worked out. From there we can hammer out the details. Even toss the whole thing and start over, if you think we should take a different approach."

"Fair enough," said Dino, intrigued to see what Jager had come up with. He knew the young man had a good head for strategy and tactics—here was an opportunity to see just how good.

"At the risk of boring you with things you may already know, I'd like to begin by reviewing the situation we face," said Jager. There were no objections, so he continued. "It's fairly straightforward. Soader has established five prisons, capable of housing a total of about three thousand females—adults and teens, mostly Humans, all able to bear children. One of his objectives was to breed the prisoners to produce top-grade bodies for soul transfers. Demand for such bodies has been terrifically high, largely due to the declining fertility among the various peoples of the G.O.D.-controlled planets. Bodies of non-Human races can also be used for transfers, but none are as favorable to the process as Humans.

"Most births are the result of artificial insemination, though prison personnel are infamous for their callous 'sport matings,' accounting for some additional births. Cross-racial breedings are not uncommon, or even seriously discouraged, though they rarely result in viable offspring. Even hybrids that are carried to term and survive infancy are typically unsuitable for soul transfers. Still, the practice is tolerated; as long as there are plenty of usable bodies available, no one cares much about how the breeding stock are treated.

"The five prisons are set up on four planets: two on Earth and one each on Shak, Nuh-Ana and Myla. According to the data I have, each currently holds between four and five hundred individuals, for a total of about two thousand two hundred women and girls. They could all hold many more, but reportedly the population has been depleted by heavy demand. Staffs are between fifty and sixty—Soader's usual mix of Repts, Greys and Humans, rough characters all."

"Excuse me, Ensign, but I have a question," said Dino.

"Sir?"

"You've given us considerable detail here."

"Yes, sir. I have quite a bit more, actually. Exact locations, detailed layout of each facility, identities of the people in charge of each, security codes, schedules and so on."

"Impressive!" said Dino.

"Amazing, I'd say," added Celine.

"Indeed," agreed Madda.

"Mmm," said Dino, "And certainly all this is not just posted on the data nets for anyone to find—Soader was light-years more secretive than that. So, could you tell us where it all comes from?"

"From memory, actually," said Jager.

"Excuse me?" said Dino.

"Memory, sir. Soader's memory, to be exact."

Celine brightened, realizing what he meant. Madda and Dino were more perplexed than ever.

"You see, back before the last scuffle we had with him on Earth, he—his soul—had been transferred into my body. This body."

This wasn't getting any clearer for either Dino or Madda. Celine smiled, enjoying the show—though she thought Jager might be enjoying himself a tad too much.

"Soader thought the little minion who performed the transfer had put me—my soul—into a containment vessel during the process. In fact, what went into the vessel was a copy—a quasi-Jager, so to speak, which I had created. I was still in my own body along with Soader, but completely hidden in a sort of mental/spiritual capsule. West had taught me how to create and use one, and how to create a 'quasi-me'.

From within the capsule, I had complete access to Soader's entire mind and the memory records of his whole existence. I could impinge upon him if I chose to, but he had no idea I was there. I realize that's all a bit out of the ordinary. Later on I'll be glad to explain it further if you like, but that's the essence."

"I see," said Dino. "More or less. Mostly less. So yes, I'd be interested in hearing more about it later. But if I understand correctly, you were able to see, or read, or somehow... absorb?...the details of Soader's prison stations. Is that right?"

"Exactly!" said Jager. "The brute's mind was a terrible mess, and he couldn't have recited the details I'm talking about if you'd asked him. But the mental recordings of everything he'd seen, read, heard or experienced were all there, intact and perfect to the last detail."

"Mmm," said Madda.

"All right," said Hadgkiss. "I suppose we'll have to go with that. Fair enough."

"Right," said Jager. "So, now we come to my plan..."

In broad terms, the plan was simple, and broke down into two main phases. First, rounding up the materials, equipment, supplies and personnel needed to house and care for the rescuees, transporting them to a safe location, and then setting everything up for use.

Second, there was the rescue operation itself. There would be four rescue units, each composed of a fast, armed strike ship with a team to free the prisoners, plus one or more transport vessels to ferry the freed women and girls to the safe haven established in phase one.

"We're going to need a lot of housing," Jager said, "and unless one of you knows a safe, secure place that happens to have enough ready-to-occupy housing for a few thousand Humans, we're going to have to set some up, and in a hurry."

"Not a problem," said Madda. "I don't know of any place just standing ready to receive that many people, but I do have some connections who could supply easily erected pre-fab buildings. All we'll require, as well as the personnel to set them up within a day or two."

"That's serious speed," said Jager, "but it's really what we need."

"That's wonderful, but we still have to have a place to put them," observed Celine. "Though it wouldn't surprise me if you had that worked out too, Ensign Cornwallis."

Jager looked a bit sheepish. "Well, no. Not exactly. I was hoping the Major or Lieutenant might know of someplace suitable…" He looked hopefully at Dino, then Madda.

Dino chuckled. "As it happens, I do know of just such a place. Pretty nearly perfect, in fact."

"Great!" said Jager. "Where's that?"

"We just left there," said Dino. "Remini. Its under-world."

Madda smiled.

Celine laughed.

Jager smacked himself in the forehead.

"Uh, yeah. Pretty nearly perfect. That is, if it's okay with the Mentors that we use it. You said they built it, right?"

"That's correct. And I know they will have no objection whatsoever to its use for such a worthy purpose. So that's settled, eh?"

"Yes. And better than I'd hoped," replied the ensign.

He went on to explain they would also need facilities for water, sewage and waste management, and food storage and preparation.

"Yes, and medical facilities," added Celine. "I know from nasty experience the prisoners will have been treated badly. A huge percentage of them will need treatment—physical, mental or spiritual. Probably all three, in most cases. And they've been used as sex slaves and breeding stock, so a lot of them will be pregnant; we'll have to be ready for a lot of births, and baby and child care too."

"Right," said Jager. "Quite a project we've taken on."

"You gauged *that* correctly, Ensign," said Dino. "But a worthier project would be hard to imagine."

Jager beamed. "Thank you, sir. It also occurred to me that many of the women and girls will want to be reunited with their families; probably most of them, actually. We'll have to work that out later, though. For the moment, they will be free and safe—and that's worth a lot, especially with a war approaching."

"Agreed," said Dino. Celine nodded.

"Next," Jager continued, "let me explain how I've envisioned the rescues themselves."

As Jager saw it, each team would jump-shift to the near vicinity of its assigned prison planet, but outside the reach of any defense emplacements, whether on the surface or in orbit. According to Soader's memories there weren't any such emplacements, but Jager wanted to be careful. Next, the strike ship would move into close orbit and make a rapid sweep to locate and neutralize any defenses. He was sure that if they happened to find any, they would be minor— Soader couldn't have afforded anything else.

Once the strike ship was certain the way was clear, its rescue team would transbeam down to the prison station itself, grab its commander, and make him order all personnel to the station's common room for a briefing from Soader, who had supposedly arrived for a surprise inspection. When the crew were all present, the rescue team would lock down the common room and gas everyone, enough to put them out of action for at least a day.

"As I mentioned earlier," said Jager, "each team will have all the info and details they need—locations, schedules, passwords, everything. Contingency plans included. Once they secure the station crew, they'll send an all-clear signal to their transport, which will move into orbit above the prison. The landing party will free all the prisoners and lead them to a pre-determined spot—they're a bit different, station to station. The strike team leader will brief the freed prisoners on what's going on and begin transbeaming them up to the transport vessel.

"Transbeaming is going to take a long time, as there are between four and five hundred prisoners at each station. Fortunately, all but one station keeps an operational shuttle on site. That site used to have one too, but they crashed it and Soader refused to replace it until they paid him an outrageous fee. Anyway, while the 'beaming is going on, two of the landing party will go to the station's shuttle, verify it's operational, then use it to speed up the transfer process.

"Some types of transport ship carry their own shuttlecraft, so Major, if you can round up any of those, so much the better."

"Understood," said Hadgkiss. "And let me say that I'm truly impressed with what you've put together here."

"I concur," said Madda. "Fine work, Ensign."

"Thank you!" said Jager. "Thank you both. I guess you taught me well."

"I think it's wonderful, too," added Celine—and she stepped up and gave him a big kiss.

"Ohhhhh-kay!" said Jager, blushing. "Thank you too, pumpkin!"

Dino and Madda chuckled. "All right," said Hadgkiss,

"let's start hammering out the details. There's a beast of a lot to cover here."

The four spent the next many hours working out the specific tasks to be done, who would carry out each one, and a workable timetable to follow. They knew that no matter how well conceived, their plans would almost surely be disrupted here and there along the way; the potential variables and challenges were just too many to account for. But at least now they had a starting point, a path to follow—and to return to after dealing with unforeseen issues and glitches. And they had well-defined endpoints for each major aspect of the operation.

When the planning session was finished, they took a break for a hasty meal and a couple of hours' rest. Then Dino jumped *Spitfire* back to Erra and slipped into orbit high above the spot where *King Hammurabi* still lay hidden.

Madda and Celine remained aboard while Jager and Hadgkiss transbeamed down to *King*. They immediately inspected every centimeter of the ship. Fortunately, they found no evidence the Brothers had damaged or sabotaged the vessel after Madda's escape, and there was no sign of bugs or trackers.

"We're all clear here—spaceworthy and secure," reported Jager to Madda and Celine. "But before we launch, we're giving her a fast cleaning and disinfection. Enough to handle the worst of the stench left behind by the Brothers and their people. When all this is over and we can get her back to her base, the ground crew can complete the clean-up."

Dino continued the briefing. "Hadgkiss here. We'll be ready for space shortly, but there's no need for you two to wait. Go ahead with your tasks as planned. Keep us briefed; we'll do the same."

"Aye, sir," Madda replied, and she and Celine headed for the first destination on their itinerary. Almost all their tasks involved rounding up the long list of structures, equipment, supplies and personnel they'd need to set up the refuge on Remini. Dino and Jager were responsible for finding and enlisting the required vessels and crews—both the strike ships and the transports that would accompany them. They would also have to arrange for each ship's temporary absence from its regular functions and duties.

For both teams it was a massive undertaking. But Dino and Madda had many loyal, highly capable and well-connected friends. And those friends had friends and so on, in a truly impressive network. They found almost everyone they contacted eager to help. Whether Fleet or civilian, these were people of action. Most had completed preparations for the impending war months before, and had been "on hold" ever since. And that had been driving them crazy. Here was a chance for action—daring action, with a lofty purpose. They jumped at the opportunity and threw themselves into the project. A better task force couldn't have been paid for; not for any amount of mere money.

CHAPTER 30

Rescue

In a few hours shy of three days, the two teams had performed an organizational miracle: They had lined up everything they would need for the mega-rescue.

Two strike ships—both light gunships—were set to join the operation as soon as they received the go signal from Madda. One of these, currently on a routine patrol, would respond to a "distress call." The other, also on patrol assignment, would log the detection of an unauthorized vessel in restricted space and jet off to investigate. The Fleet officers and crew of both ships were fully briefed on what they'd *really* be doing, and all looked forward to the worthy but off-the-books operation with great enthusiasm.

So did the crews of the civilian freighters that would complete the rescue teams, transporting the freed women and girls to Remini. There were two ships assigned to go to Earth, accompanied by Hadgkiss, Jager and Celine aboard *King Hammurabi*, and one freighter each for *Spitfire* and the two other Fleet gunships.

Three of the five freighters were already in action. Under Madda's direction and coordination, they were working flat out, gathering and transporting materials, equipment, supplies and personnel for the rescued women's "village"—more like a small town, in fact—on Remini.

According to the plan, each freighter was to collect its assigned cargo, transport it to Remini and unload. The bulk of its crew would then remain planetside to tackle the herculean task of setting everything up and preparing for operation. There were buildings to erect; utilities to establish, hook up and test, and all the other essentials of daily life.

While the first transports were being unloaded, Madda and Celine met with Mia, Remi and Hyatt to explain the plan and enlist their help. Celine was sure Remi would dive into the project at once, and probably end up managing the whole thing. As expected, her mother took the mammoth project as a worthy challenge, and the best possible tribute to her late, beloved husband.

Celine wasn't sure how Mia would respond, but her expectations were not high. To her happy surprise, after some initial uncertainty and equivocation, her elder sister warmed to the whole idea and engaged wholeheartedly in the work. "It's funny," she later explained to her mother and Celine, "at first I didn't want to have anything to do with it. But then I realized it was a way to actually do something useful with what I learned in all those years at the Academy. I'd never thought I'd do anything with that stuff. I'd just be someone's pretty wife, having babies and going to parties and fashion shows. Soader gave me a little taste of what all those prisoners have gone through, though; it was awful. Now I can help them heal and go back to living happy lives."

With great effort, Celine managed not to blurt, "Where is my sister? And what have you done with her?!" Instead she stood, crossed to Mia's chair, and gave the older girl a hug.

Here we go, thought Hyatt—sisterly tears in three...two... one... And, right on cue, the tears began to flow. Mia's and Celine's, but Remi's too. Along with a few of his own.

Hyatt was eager to pitch in as well. He had a gift for organization and logistics, and immediately came up with several ideas to make the set-up operation more efficient, and simplify operations once the facilities were occupied.

"Lieutenant," he said, addressing Madda, "if your offer of that hover-chair is still open, I might take you up on it. It would make it a lot easier to get around, and even help with some of the physical work." Madda had stopped using the chair the evening before, and was glad to turn it over to the young ensign. She showed him how to use the device, and before long he'd mastered it. He capitalized on its capabilities, using it for towing, lifting, high-reach tasks and more.

Two days after the first transport had unloaded its cargo, everything was nearly ready to welcome the freed prisoners—thanks to the freighter crews' round-the-clock work and Remi and Hyatt's brilliant management.

Dino and Jager arrived to report the strike ships were in place, ready for action. The time had come to begin the rescues.

First, Hadgkiss, Celine and Jager would take *King Hammurabi*, with its superior capabilities, to rescue High Chancellor Jin's daughters, Dorte and Bonafede. Madda would stand by aboard *Spitfire*, ready to lead the larger rescue operation as soon as Dino sent word the Jin girls were safe on Remini. The plan was to keep them there until they could be transferred to a more suitable location, safe from traitors within G.O.D.—traitors like their late and unlamented father.

Back aboard *King*, Celine, Dino and Jager met on the operations deck. "Well, Celine," said the major, "you're calling the shots here. Where do we go to recover Jin's daughters?"

"I believe they never left his ancestral estate on Kahn," she replied.

"Oh!" said Dino. "That makes sense, considering the traitor turns out to have been behind their 'abduction.' And it's the last place one would think to look for his own daughters. But could you tell me how you know they're there?"

"Sure. A few days ago, before I explained how I wanted to mount this whole mission, I'd been having persistent thoughts about the girls. I brushed the thoughts aside at first, but they kept coming back, and they intensified. Then it hit me that I was *picking up* thoughts—Bonafede's. More like fervent hopes than regular thoughts, really. Or perhaps I was 'overhearing' her praying. In any case, it was clear they were being held in a deep dungeon beneath the Jin manor house. I also caught a few stray thoughts and impressions from Dorte; not much more than soft weeping. My guess is they have some latent telepathic capabilities. In any case, I'm certain they're there. Now it's a matter of extracting them."

"I get it," said Dino. "Jager, would I be correct to guess that you've already planned said extraction?"

"Yes you would, sir," he replied. "Not too complex. We jump to Kahn, cloaked, and take up orbit over the Jin estate. The three of us transbeam down to the dungeon level, subdue any guards, liberate the girls and 'beam back up. Done."

"That's simple, all right," said the major, "though I'm sure you're aware it's likely to become more complicated in practice."

"Sure—just like you taught me. And I've surely seen the

truth of it. But I'm still confident we can pull it off."

"Me too," said Celine. "And I can take care of the 'subdue-the-guards' step."

"Blast pistol on stun, or something more creative?" asked Dino.

"You know me well," she laughed. "Something more creative, and less likely to set off a lot of alarms, personnel-suppression gas or other inconveniences."

"Tidy!" said Dino with a chuckle. "All right, then, we'll leave that to you. Now, assuming they're being held in some sort of cell, how do we break them out without hurting them, or triggering the aforementioned inconveniences?"

"Ah, that part you can leave to me," said Jager, raising Omaja a centimeter or two.

"Fine, fine," said Dino. "Just one more question: Do you two need me along at all? Or shall I just wait 'upstairs' in the ship and catch up on some reading?"

"Well, nothing as casual as that," said Jager, "but now that you mention it, it might be best if you were to remain aboard, in case things go south and we need a little outside assistance."

"Fair enough," said Dino. "I'll stand by, then. And we'll set you up with a camera button to wear on your tunic, so I can enjoy the proceedings from here. I believe that covers everything, yes?"

"Yes!" said Jager and Celine at once.

"All right, then. Prepare for jump-shift," said Hadgkiss.

As planned, *King* burst into being above Jin's home planet, fully cloaked. Celine mented Jager her perception of the girls' location; he translated the concept into the necessary coordinates and fed them into the transbeam console. The pair stepped up to the unit's transmission platform, Celine with her incant-baton raised and ready, Jager with Omaja held high. "Activate," he commanded, and the transbeam did its work. In moments, they found themselves in a dimly lit tunnel, apparently bored or burned through solid rock. The light was brighter up the tunnel ahead of them, silhouetting a pair of armed guards.

Jager nodded to Celine and swept his hand toward the guards, as if to say, "They're all yours, m'dear."

With a grim smile in return, she raised her incant-baton, pointed it toward the distant figures, and whispered an incantation. The guards slumped sideways against the tunnel walls, then collapsed into most gratifying heaps—out cold. No alarms, no hiss of paralytic gas. Apparently the way was clear.

The pair stole silently up the tunnel to where the guards lay unconscious, just at the entrance to a wide room. Recessed into the room's far wall was a cell, roughly five meters by five, fronted by thick, black steel bars and poorly lit by a single, wan glow-orb at the center of its ceiling. Celine closed her eyes and, standing just outside the entrance, extended her perceptions to scan the whole room and cell beyond. She detected four video pickups; raising her incant-baton and whispering another brief incantation, she froze each one. The monitors they fed would now continue showing the same unremarkable scene, but nothing later than the moment of their freezing. Celine stepped through the entrance, Jager right behind her.

Inside the cell they could now see two slight figures, facing each other across a small table and engaged in a card game.

"Dorte! Bonafede!" whispered Celine, wary of setting off

any sound-activated alarms.

The girls turned toward her, eyes wide. "Oh..." began Bonafede, the elder of the two.

"Shhhh. Please—quiet," said Celine, still barely above a whisper. "We're here to take you to safety." Pointing toward a corner of the cell, she went on. "If you'll move quietly and casually over there, we'll have you out in short order. No quick motions or loud talk, please. Alarms, you know."

They nodded. Bonafede rose, stretched, and looked absently round the cell. "Huh!" she said, and pointed to the corner Celine had indicated and muttered a few words to her sister, as though she'd noticed something odd. Now Dorte stood. She had been born with a withered leg, and used crutches; sleek, power-assisted crutches, thanks to her father's wealth, but crutches nonetheless. The pair made their way to the corner and pretended to examine something at the base of the stony wall.

Celine stepped away from the cell door. Jager stood tall, pointed the head of his staff at the door's heavy lock mechanism, and silently intended "Open."

At once, but quiet and unhurried, the door's thick locking bolts drew back and disengaged.

Dino, watching from his flight couch hundreds of kilometers above, whistled in appreciation. His protégé had clearly acquired skills well beyond those he'd managed to teach the lad.

Jager and Celine entered the cell and approached the girls, Celine in the lead and wearing a reassuring smile. "Hello. I'm Celine. This is Jager. We're going to take you to our ship, and then to a safe place. Is there anything here you want to take with you?" Both girls shook their heads. "Okay.

We'll transbeam up now."

"Thank you," said Bonefede. "Will our father be there?"

"Yes, will he?" asked Dorte.

"Uh, no—I'm afraid he's not there," said Celine, hedging. "But you'll be okay."

"Oh," said Bonafede. Dorte looked downcast, but nodded.

Celine gave them a reassuring smile, then turned to Jager, looked straight at the camera button on his tunic and gave a thumbs-up. In moments, a transbeam field enveloped the four figures. Dorte and Bonafede were free.

Safe aboard *King Hammurabi*, the girls were dazed at first, not quite ready to believe they were free. They followed quietly as Jager and Celine led them to the ship's galley; when offered seats at a dining table, they complied with numb semi-smiles. They seemed to perk up when Dino entered, though—a Fleet officer!

"Hello Bonafede, Dorte," he said. "I am Major Dino Hadgkiss. This is Ensign Jager Cornwallis..." Jager bowed, "... and Celine Zulak." Celine bowed as well.

"Thank you," said Bonafede. "Thank you for taking us from that prison. Can you tell us where it was? We woke there...um...many days ago. Weeks? We had no idea how we got there, or where it was, or what would happen to us, or anything." A tear appeared at the corner of her eye.

Dorte nodded. "She's right. No one hurt us. We had food and water, and someone must have cleaned when we were sleeping, because it never got messy or smelly. But no one would tell us what was happening, or where we were, or why. They wouldn't talk to us at all." Though nearly a decade younger than her late-teenage sister, Dorte's behavior was mature beyond her years.

"I'm sorry you were put through all that," said Dino. "Truly sorry." He could see they had no idea their father had anything to do with their "kidnapping," and assumed they did not know he'd been murdered, either. He would hold onto that sad news until later, when they'd recovered somewhat. For the moment, they'd been through quite enough.

"You were kidnapped in your sleep and held in an underground prison. On your homeworld, Kahn."

"Oh," said Bonafede. "But why? And does our father know? Mother died almost a year ago, but Father would be out of his mind with worry."

"Your father was informed about your situation, and you're quite right: he was deeply...concerned. Unfortunately, it's not possible to reunite you with him at this time. Right now, other urgent measures are necessary to keep you safe. He'd understand. We're going to take you to a secure location and give you any care you might need. Once we've apprehended your kidnappers and it's certain you're no longer in danger, we'll take you back home."

Growing up as near-royalty, the girls had been briefed on the possibility of such events as this, and how to deal with them should they ever come to pass. That training, plus the sincerity and kind, protective intent their rescuers displayed, put them quickly at ease.

"All right," said Dorte.

"We understand," said Bonafede. "They told us something like this might occur someday, because of Daddy's position and all. I never thought it would actually happen, but here we are. Thank you again for getting us out of that awful place."

"Yes, thank you!" said Dorte.

Bonafede rose, went to Dino, curtseyed, took his bionic

hand in hers and kissed it lightly. Dino did his best to maintain his composure. He was familiar with such customs, but this was the first time he'd been on the receiving end.

Dorte went through the same polite ritual with Jager. Then, one after the other, the girls approached Celine, grasped her shoulders, and kissed her lightly on each cheek. Jager watched, fascinated, as Dorte's powered crutches smoothly assisted the maneuver.

"Thank you," said Dino. Jager and Celine echoed his sentiment. "Celine, would you take these two to the med bay and run a quick check on them? Just to be sure they're not in need of any immediate attention."

"I'll be glad to," said Celine, and she led the sisters aft. She understood the "quick check" should include scanning for and deactivating any locator chips.

"They seem to be fine girls," said Dino to Jager.

"They do!" the younger man agreed. "Growing up with that pompous rat Jin for a father, I more than half expected them to be arrogant little...specimens. Nice to be wrong on that."

"I don't imagine their father was around them much, growing up. Too busy advancing his career—by any means necessary. My guess is that their mother was their chief influencer. Had the pleasure of meeting her once. Lovely woman. Well educated, witty, elegant in an unpretentious way. Can't imagine how she ended up married to Jin. And wouldn't be surprised if he had something to do with her untimely passing." They headed to their flight couches to run some routine scans and systems checks, waiting for the girls to return.

A short while later, the three young women appeared on

the ops deck. "All clear, ready to go," announced Celine.

"Ladies," said Jager, are you familiar with securing your-selves for a jump-shift, or would you like some help?"

"Oh, no problem," replied Bonafede, obviously proud of being a seasoned space traveler. "Just point us to our couch-es. I can help Dorte." She gave Jager a winning smile; the kind that had melted more than one healthy male heart. Celine repressed a chuckle as a flicker of embarrassment escaped Jager's control and dashed across his features. He indicat-ed the couches they should use, and they busied themselves with securing Dorte's crutches and strapping in.

"All secure for jump-shift?" called Dino.

"Aye, Captain!" came their replies.

"Initiating jump-shift," he announced, and ship and occu-pants experienced the brief but mind-and-matter-bending event that was a temporo-spatial passage. And then, bright on the forward viewscreen, appeared the planet Remini.

CHAPTER 31

New Home, New Life

Leaving *King Hammurabi* in orbit, Dino, Celine and Jager brought the Jin girls down to Remini's sub-surface world. They went straight to Remi's cabin, where they were lucky enough to find her home—she had been spending nearly all her time supervising the new settlement's set-up.

Dino introduced Remi to the girls; Remi, in turn, introduced Mia. The four took to each other at once. Though their backgrounds and experience were quite different, they seemed kindred spirits at heart. And Mia, who hadn't quite shed her fascination with glamour and celebrity, was delighted to associate with a High Chancellor's daughters—the closest thing to royalty in the sectors' society.

With the girls in Remi's capable hands, Dino, Jager and Celine returned to *King* for the next phase of the rescue operation.

After settling Dorte and Bonafede into their new quarters, Remi and Mia sat down with them for a cup of teala and a talk. The Jins told the tale of their imprisonment and rescue, then Remi offered to brief them on the broader rescue operation. "Yes, please!" said Dorte, and Bonafede concurred.

After explaining Jager's plan for freeing the prisoners from Soader's five compounds, Remi went into detail about the settlement project. The essentials were now all in place, she explained, and everyone was working flat out on final preparations.

"It's breathtaking!" said Bonafede, "I mean, all you've done, and so fast! Do you think…is there…is there some way I could help? Something I could do to help the women and girls?"

"Me too!" chimed in Dorte. "Don't forget me. I want to help too!"

"You certainly can," said Remi, "Both of you. Let's see…" And they spent the next hour discussing the various functions and duties that would soon have to be covered, and how Dorte and Bonafede could best contribute.

"Oh!" said Dorte at one point, "I can make things for people—things they need. I like to make things. I learned how to sew—I could make clothes, or adjust them for people so they fit more nicely."

"She's right," said Bonafede. "She's quite good at it." She thought for a moment, then whispered in her young sister's ear. Dorte brightened like a Rigelian sunrise.

"Yeah!" she practically crowed. "I can bake, too. Pastries!" She explained how one of their household cooking staff had once invited her to help bake. She had taken to the activity at once, and started showing up in the kitchen almost daily, hoping to give her new friend a hand with the day's baking. "I got really good at making this one kind of pastry," she said, "though Yaneese had to help me get things into and out of the ovens. Anyway, I would make some, and give them to Bona, and the governess, and some of the other staff people.

Mother, too, before she went away. Everyone loved them! Except Father," she added with a frown. "He never had one. He was gone all the time, and if he came home he would only eat things the head chef made."

"Well! I'm definitely keeping *that* in mind," Remi assured Dorte. "I imagine it's been a long, long time since any of our new friends have had anything as nice as a fresh pastry."

Dorte beamed at the acknowledgement, and the prospect of contributing.

Later in the day, when Dorte was napping, Remi asked Bonafede about the younger girl's withered leg.

"The doctors say we must wait until she's older to fix it," Bonafede explained. "Until her body is closer to adult size. I did some research though, and found out they could actually fix it at any time, if they used magic to help. It would grow like anyone's normal leg, and she wouldn't have to go through the rest of her young years as a cripple. But years ago, Father issued an edict forbidding all magical practices in our sector. The news people said he did it to follow the 'shining example of wise and far-thinking governance' of another High Chancellor, called Scabbage." She scowled. "Oh! But you're from Erra, so Scabbage is High Chancellor in your sector, true?"

"Yes, I'm afraid he is," said Remi. "And I'm familiar with his own edict on that subject. And a lot of others besides..." She hesitated to say more—then realized that here in their under-world refuge they were safe from Scabbage's spies and informants. "A lot of others just as senseless. And worse than senseless."

Bonafede nodded sadly. "I think Scabbage forced Father to do it—issue the edict, I mean. I can't really say anything about how I know that, though."

"I understand," said Remi. And then she remembered the magical assistance Celine had rendered Hyatt, and its remarkable effects. "No magic, eh?" she muttered. "Well, we shall see about that. Yes we shall. I'm glad you confided in me."

———— ⚬ ————

BACK ABOARD *KING HAMMURABI*, Dino contacted Madda and gave the go-ahead to launch the operation. "And send my two assigned freighters to meet me at Earth. Any shuttles you can spare, too. They can take up orbit behind that nice big moon it's got, until I call them in to pick up the rescuees."

"Aye-aye, sir!" Madda replied, and she jumped into action. After dispatching Hadgkiss's support vessels and the groups assigned to Shak and Myla, she led her own team to rescue the four hundred twenty-seven girls and women imprisoned on Nuh-Ana.

All five rescues were executed in a just over a day. For the most part, the operations went off like clockwork. Some of the teams—including Madda's—ran into unexpected obstacles, but they managed to work around them and bring their precious cargoes home. In all, the freighters brought more than two thousand two hundred women and girls to Remini's secret under-world—with not a single life lost.

On arrival, those clearly in need of immediate medical attention were taken to one of the settlement's infirmaries. The rest were given a hot meal and all the fresh, pure water they wanted. For most, it was the first they'd had in months; longer, in a few sad cases.

After the meal they were shown to their new quarters, where they bathed and donned clean new clothes. The only thing most of them wanted next was a sound, uninterrupted sleep, in a real bed and a safe space. None had experienced *that* particular luxury since their capture by Soader's thugs. For some, that meant years.

A few were too exhilarated over their sudden freedom to sleep just yet. They gathered on the lawns and under the trees near their new quarters and talked among themselves, some well into the evening.

After breakfast the next morning, they were taken, a group at a time, to the infirmary closest to their new living spaces. Each received a thorough check-up, and treatment or prescriptions to care for less-serious conditions. Malnutrition was the most prevalent, followed by the myriad bruises, cuts and scrapes they'd acquired at the hands of Soader's brutal minions.

Those who evidenced more serious problems were scheduled for further examination and treatment, all to take place within the next day or two. This group included more than three hundred who were clearly pregnant; no surprise, since Soader had been using them as breeding stock.

Everyone who was not obviously with child received a pregnancy test. Once again, it was no surprise that quite a large percentage of the tests read positive. Fortunately for all, preparations for their arrival had included extensive facilities for prenatal care, childbirth, and postnatal care. Starting very soon and for months and months to come, there would be hundreds and hundreds of blessed events, and tiny new mouths to feed.

The evening after the rescuees had arrived, Dino, Remi, Celine and Jager gathered at Remi's cabin for a breather.

"Remi, once again you amaze me. You've gotten everything

rolling already! I wouldn't call it 'smoothly' yet, but…"

"Nor would I!" broke in Remi, with a laugh.

"No, but smoother than many a smaller enterprise I've seen," said Dino. "Admirable. Most admirable."

"Thank you, Major," Remi replied, and she gave him a warm smile.

Celine noticed the warmth with interest. Hm! she thought, and filed the moment away. "It *is* going well," she said aloud; she raised her mug of teala. "A toast to Remi!"

"Hear, hear!" they all agreed, raising their drinks, then sipping.

"It's going so well," Celine went on, "that I think it's time Jager and I got back to our Dragon friends. We've another major task ahead of us, and I feel very uneasy delaying it any longer."

"True," said Jager. "West almost appeared concerned about it. Which is saying a *lot*."

"Oh, Celine!" said Remi. "You know I don't want you to leave, but that will probably always be the case. And I know it's for the best, and what you have to do. It's a mom thing."

Celine gave her a huge hug. "I understand, Mom. And I'm so lucky to have you as a mom. I know it, even if I don't always show it as I ought to."

They hugged again, then Remi let her daughter go. "Off you go, then, before I change my mind!"

Celine, Jager and Dino laughed. They'd heard *that* before! Remi stared at them a moment, confused—and then she saw the humor in it, and laughed along.

"Let's go, then," said Dino. Then, to Remi, "I'll take them to the outpost, then come back here. You've got this operation

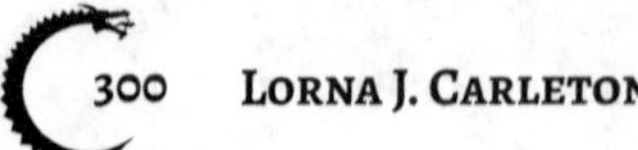

in hand, but anyone can use some backup now and then."

"Roger that!" agreed Remi. "But before you all go, I have an announcement to make." When she had everyone's attention, she went on. "A proposal, really, more than an announcement. It occurred to me that that this settlement we've established should have a name. It's not big enough to be called a city yet, but we've only just started, and I do believe it *will* be one, someday. Therefore, and for other reasons I'm sure will be obvious, I propose that this settlement be known henceforth as Zulak City."

"Perfect!" cried Celine.

"Yes! What could be better than that?!" said Jager.

"Of course," said Dino, somewhat more solemn than the others. "A fitting tribute."

"It's agreed, then," said Remi. "*Now* you may all get going. Please!"

IN THE DAYS THAT FOLLOWED, the staff of Zulak City—temporary, permanent, volunteers and paid staff alike, worked night and day to settle in the new residents. Mia was transformed, working tirelessly to help out in any way she could. Bonafede worked right beside her; the two had become fast friends, and the challenges they faced deepened their bond by the day.

Dorte was as helpful as could be, too, visiting and comforting the youngest girls and finding all sorts of ways to ease the newcomers' transition to their new lives. Each day she made time to visit one of the new city's kitchens, to bake up some of her special pastries. She distributed each day's batch, still fresh and warm, to as many of the new residents as she could.

Word of the wonderful treats spread rapidly, and soon Dorte was faced with a dilemma: She wanted to share with everyone, but how could she possibly do it on her own? She decided she would have to enlist some help, and recruited a few girls to assist her. Then the head baker at one of the dining facilities set aside part of his bakery for the group to use. The girls turned out dozens and dozens of the delectable treats each day, and the food-service people helped distribute them.

One afternoon, Dorte overheard a group of girls chatting about what might be on the day's dinner menu. One of them said, "I *do* hope we get Dortes today," and the others wholeheartedly agreed.

Dorte approached the group. "Excuse me," she said politely to the girl who'd spoken, "but I heard what you said just now, and I'm not sure what you meant."

"Silly!" came the reply, "That's what everyone calls your yummy pastries. Dortes! They're the *best!*"

"Yeah!" the group cheered, and they began to chant, "Dorte! Dor-te! Dor-te!"

Dorte was overwhelmed—so happy she practically floated back to her cabin home.

KNOWING WELL HOW IMPORTANT it was to take care of herself, lest she "burn out" and let everyone down, Remi began taking an hour or so early each morning for a hike. The first couple of days, she explored areas close to Zulak City. On the third morning, she was feeling particularly ambitious, so she borrowed a small, one-person flier from the transport shed and soared off toward the mountain range Dino had pointed out when they'd first arrived. She landed in a likely spot, high in the foothills, and set off up a lovely canyon. After a time, she decided she ought to be getting back. After a last look up the canyon toward the peaks above, she turned around to head back to the flier.

There, standing not a dozen meters away, was a Dragon.

CHAPTER 32

Return to Nibiru

Within the hour, Celine and Jager had packed their gear, said their goodbyes, and transbeamed back aboard *King Hammurabi* with Major Hadgkiss.

"Secured for jump-shift?" asked the major.

"Aye!" the two replied, and in moments they were in orbit over the Mentors' outpost, where four Dragon-friends anxiously awaited their return.

"Good luck to you," said Dino, at the transbeam unit's controls. "From all you've told me, our prospects in the war, and the future of our sectors hinge on what you're about to undertake."

"Oh, all in a day's work," joked Jager. Celine agreed, with mock nonchalance. In truth, both were feeling more than just a twinge of apprehension. What they intended to accomplish would not necessarily be difficult, but *so much* hung in the balance...

Dino smiled, proud of their courage and optimism—and glad each had the skills and competence to warrant them.

When the two were gone from the platform, he sent a

silent "good luck" after them, then returned to the ops deck for the flight back to Remini.

Fianna and Vin were waiting at the platform when their Companions arrived. When the 'beam released Celine and Jager, Humans and Dragons rushed together, greeting each other as though they'd been separated for months, not days. Ahimoth and Joli joined the celebration, sparking another fervent round of hugs, greetings, and excited questions.

Suddenly, Celine went silent, head cocked and hand to chin. "Wait a second," she said to Fianna. "How did you know we were coming? We didn't ment, since the place is thought-shielded. So...?"

"North told us!" explained the Dragon. "She'd set the defense sensor system to alert her the moment *Spitfire* or *King Hammurabi* appeared, so she knew right away when you made orbit. She mented us the good news, and we came running."

"And nearly knocked out part of a doorway in the process," said Vin with a grimace, flexing a bruised wing.

"Ouch!" said Jager. "Look, there's so much to tell you, but here's the instant summary: The rescue operation was a complete success. We freed all Soader's prisoners and took them safely to Remini. High Chancellor Jin's daughters, too—so Celine is no longer a pawn in the traitors' sick ransom scheme."

Fianna heaved a huge sigh at this final bit of news.

"*That* was a worlds-class sigh, my friend!" said Celine. "Good thing you're not a fire breather, or we'd have a conflagration on our hands!" When the group's laughter subsided, she went on. "We'll tell you all the details tomorrow, if that's okay. Right now, we're both weary to the bone. Would you excuse us?"

The Dragons agreed, bid their young friends good night, and retired to their quarters. Jager escorted Celine to her room, gave her a kiss, made his way down the corridor and entered his own space. The bed looked awfully inviting, and he was truly spent, but he felt unsettled; he didn't want to try to sleep that way. Not with something left unresolved, even if he couldn't isolate what that something was. So instead of climbing into bed, he stripped down and headed for the shower—the place he'd always done some of his best thinking. He turned on the water, good and hot, and let it wash over him, eyes closed.

The precise source of his unease failed to present itself, but the feeling gradually faded away. Now he was relaxed, physically, mentally and spiritually. Ready for a sound, productive sleep. He shut off the water and began toweling dry. A chance glimpse of the steam-fogged mirror called up memories of his young life on Earth, before he and his parents had been spirited off to Erra, away from the sinister forces that sought to capture him. Since then, he had become a Fleet junior officer.

Under the Mentors' tutelage, he'd made tremendous strides in his training as a sorcerer. And, after years of only mental contact, he had finally met his soulmate face to face. He thought of how his old friends on Earth would view his present circumstances. He lived on an alien world, served aboard an alien spaceship, had a beautiful, brilliant witch for a girlfriend, and a lifetime bond with a genuine flying *Dragon*. Those old friends would have said it was "totally insane," and meant it in the most admiring way possible. The "old" Jager couldn't have dreamed up such a scenario if he'd tried. And the "new" Jager guessed that if he recorded the tale as a movie or adventure novel, it would top the charts back on Earth.

His concerns banished for the moment, Jager fell grateful into bed, then on down into a restful sleep.

Next morning, rested and refreshed, Celine and Jager joined the Dragons for a light breakfast. The little group could easily have eaten more, but Celine and Fianna advised Jager and Joli—who had never traveled the tube-chute—that they'd almost surely weather the journey more comfortably on empty stomachs.

The meal over, everyone returned to their rooms to prepare for the trip. Celine mented North to let her know they'd soon be ready to go. "Very well," replied the Mentor. "Is half an hour sufficient time?"

"Sure, that should be fine," said Celine.

The group met up with North at the appointed time. She transbeamed them, three at a time, to the Mentor ship orbiting high above, then 'beamed herself to join them. The jump-shift to Earth went smoothly, and there they were—parked in orbit above Scotland and Loch Ness, where the hour was near midnight.

"I wish you good luck and good speed," said North, as she set the transbeam coordinates for the shore of Earth's most famous loch. "What you are soon to do will have effects farther-reaching than you can easily imagine. May the spirit of the Ancients be with you, and their wisdom guide you."

When the transbeam field cleared, Jager found himself standing on the lake's brightly moonlit shore. He stared in wide-eyed amazement at the spectacle before him: the dark waters swarmed with Dragons. Water Dragons, in an array of handsome shades and hues. He could only see their backs,

Katrin Hierl-Steinbauer - age 9

long necks and horned heads, but they were an impressive lot nonetheless. And they were gathered here to assist two Humans and a group of Dragons of a radically different race. In that moment, he was struck by the truth of something Celine had said, not long ago: "No matter a people's race or origin, love and understanding break down all barriers."

Closest to the shore was Nessie; Jager knew her by her brindled blue-and-bronze scales, which Celine had mentioned more than once. She bowed her great neck, to come face to face with the young man. "Greetings, Jager!" she said, in her distinctly feminine Dragon voice, mellow and deep. "Welcome to our home. I have looked forward to our meeting—Celine has told me much about you. She is rather fond of you, you know."

"Thank you!" said Jager. "I am rather fond of her, too—to put it far too mildly. But please, may I address you as Nessie? I am afraid I've neglected to learn the proper protocol for meetings with Water Dragons, especially one so widely esteemed."

"Yes, yes," she replied. "Nessie will do quite nicely, thank you." She turned to Celine. "My, but he is a gallant one, is he not?"

"He is indeed," said Celine. "And quite handsome, too, as Humans judge such things!" She and Nessie shared a laugh; Jager tried to suppress a blush, but failed miserably.

Vin and Joli greeted Nessie, who they had met once before.

And finally, Nessie introduced the group to the scores of her clanspeople who had gathered to take part in the coming ceremony.

"All is in readiness for the calling of the vortex," said Nessie. "Yesterday, North sent word of your impending arrival, so

we were afforded ample time to prepare. We need only wait for the coming of the midnight hour, which is almost upon us."

Fianna thanked her, and the little party of travelers came together to discuss how they would proceed once the vortex appeared. Vin admitted he was apprehensive. His first experience with the tube-chute had been disastrous. And, unlike Celine and Fianna, who had long training and experience, he and Jager had had no chance to train as Dragon and Companion. This tube-chute journey would be their first "flight" together.

It would be Jager's first tube-chute passage, too. He was unsure what to expect, but not especially worried. Celine had assured him he'd have little problem, though he would likely find the experience unpleasant. She couldn't imagine him being frightened by much of anything.

Celine explained how the Water Dragons would call the vortex and where it would appear. She suggested that she and Fianna should enter first, followed by Joli, then Vin and Jager, and finally Ahimoth. Once inside, she explained to the first-timers, they would find it strange in the extreme, and probably quite disorienting. She warned specifically of one particular factor: they would be immersed in what seemed like a liquid, churning and swirling and suffused with air bubbles. Nevertheless, they would be able to breathe adequately, if not quite comfortably. She counselled them to remain as calm as they could, and do their best to remain upright.

She also promised to cast a spell that would envelop each of them in a sort of bubble of calm. Their bubble would make it easier to breath, and to ride along with the chute's strange current. They found her calm, matter-of-fact attitude reassuring. Each had experienced the power of her magic, too, which quieted their apprehensions further. When she was finished, they felt well prepared for the challenge.

As Celine was doing a final check to be sure Vin's handsome new saddle was secure, and that Jager was snugly settled in, they heard Nessie call out. "The time has come, friends!"

The brindled Dragon turned toward her waiting clan, stretched her long neck moonward, and gave a resonant, trumpeting call. The Rite of the Vortex had begun.

The travelers moved to the water's edge and watched in awe as the spectacle unfolded. It was a thing of wonder, even for those among them who had experienced it before. When the vortex itself appeared and opened wide in its dazzlingly beautiful display, Celine called out: "Here we go!" She hunkered down in her saddle; Fianna leapt upward, through the vortex's yawning mouth and into the tube-chute. Just as planned, Joli leapt next, then Vin and Jager, and Ahimoth last of all.

Once inside, Fianna slowed their forward progress through the churning, spinning "fluid" within the chute so Celine could turn in the saddle and watch for their fellow travelers to enter. As each appeared, she thrust forth her incant-baton and called out the incantation that would bring into being a "bubble" of quiet and calm. The bubbles shielded their occupants from the worst of the tube-chute's turmoil, helped them keep oriented, and eased their progress through the time-space wormhole that now bore them toward Nibiru.

The moment he entered, Jager was disoriented, buffeted and spun by the rowdy current. Vin was seized with a moment of panic, reminded of his first awful encounter

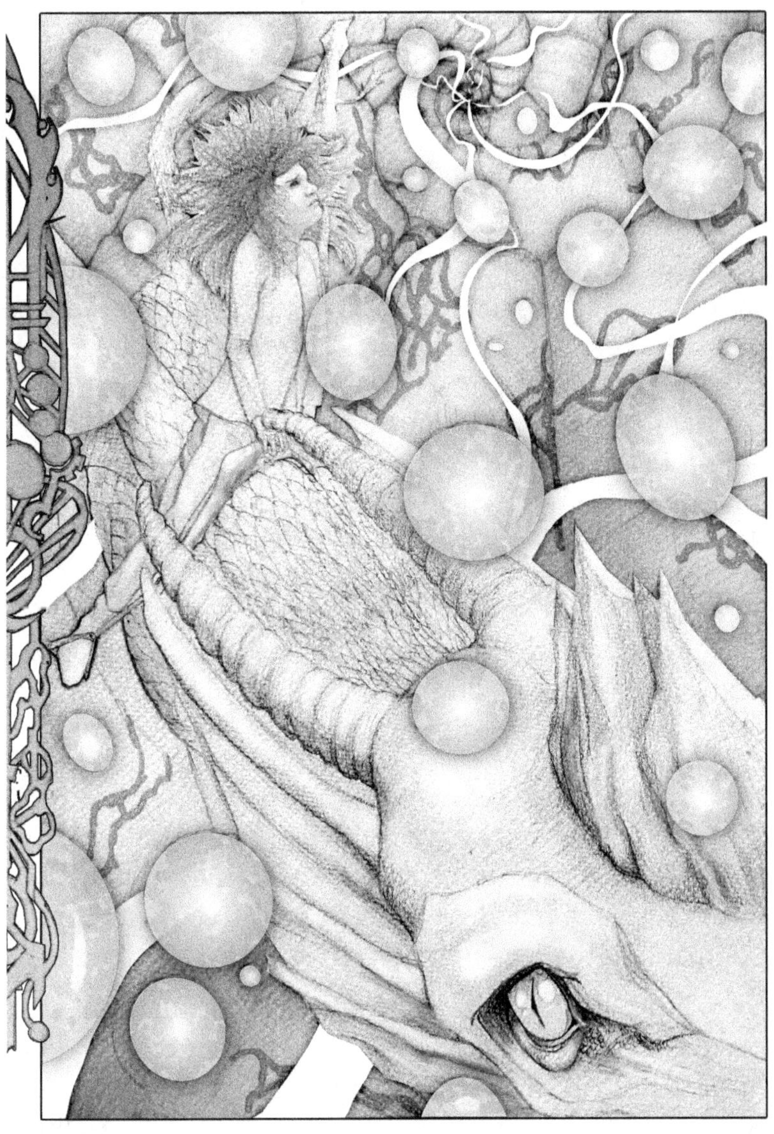

with the chute. Joli had only traveled it as a bodiless spirit, unaffected by the physical turmoil. Like Jager, she was disoriented at first, but Celine's bubble helped. Ahimoth had first been through this with Vin, long ago; he had fared better than his friend, but the experience had been horrendous; he was deeply grateful for Celine's magical help this time around.

Soon the newcomers, buoyed in their bubbles, regained their bearings and caught on to the trick of riding the chute's rushing, roiling current. The experience was still unpleasant; bodies—Human, Dragon or otherwise—reacted oddly to the weird distortions of normal space and time that characterized the tube-chute's "structure." If it could even be *called* a structure in any relatable sense. One thing they all knew for very certain: they would be relieved and glad when the "ride" was over.

And hours later, the ride *was* over.

One moment, they were bumping and jostling along. The next, they were on solid ground—tumbled about the open space surrounding the Cynth Pedestal, safe within the walls of Nibiru's Dragon Hall.

"We're here!" cried Celine.

The Dragons got to their feet as gracefully as they could manage. Fianna and Vin knelt to allow their Human Companions to dismount.

"Whoa," said Jager, hand to tousled head. "That will never make my list of favorite modes of transportation." He slowly turned, studying his surroundings in an effort to get oriented. What he saw impressed him deeply. Dragon Hall was a place of natural splendor. "Ah," he said, spying the Cynth Pedestal. "So like the one on Pax!"

"They are exactly alike, if I recall the lore correctly," said Fianna, "though I have never been to Pax to observe the Talyth Pedestal for myself."

"Oh!" exclaimed Jager. "That reminds me..." He went to Vin's side; "Excuse me, my friend," he said, and he drew Omaja from its sheath in the saddle's glossy leather flank. "Here you are!" he said, addressing the staff and holding it aloft.

The motion drew Celine's attention upward, where she caught a flicker of motion high above. "We have company!" she called to the others, pointing skyward. They all looked up to see a flight of Dragons descending upon the hall. Down and down they came, landing in the broad open area, then quickly stepping aside so others could land. More and more arrived until the hall was filled with Dragons of all their race's handsome colors.

All waited quietly, regarding the six travelers with keen interest. Ahimoth and Fianna recognized many among them. Vin and Joli recognized some too, and even Celine picked out a few familiar faces. No one spoke, though—it was plain they were waiting for something. Then several more Dragons appeared above: old Orgon the Wise and Tamar—Fianna and Ahimoth's uncle and aunt—followed by their parents, King Neal and Queen Dini. Neal was the last to land. He advanced to stand before Fianna and Ahimoth, regarded them for a long, silent moment, while the whole assembly of Dragons waited breathlessly behind and around him. Then he spread his shimmering golden wings high and wide, stretched his noble muzzle skyward, and trumpeted joyfully.

The crowd cheered and stamped, stamped and cheered.

At last the din subsided, and Neal and Dini rushed forward to embrace their beloved children, Dragon-tears flowing. King Neal stepped away from the family group and raised a wing for attention. "My people!" he called out. "Behold, my son has returned! Ahimoth, Prince of Nibiru!"

Though embarrassed by such attention, Ahimoth stood tall and accepted it graciously. His parents and teachers had schooled him well in the public responsibilities and traditions that went with royal blood.

All present knew Fianna and Celine, and welcomed them warmly. The pair were famous throughout Nibiru—not only because Fianna was their princess, and Celine her Companion—but also because they had rescued the Nibiru race from the edge of oblivion.

There followed a formal round of introductions and welcomes: Vin, who had disappeared with Ahimoth in the long-ago days of their youth. Jager, Celine's soulmate. And, much to the astonishment of all who had known her, Joli. She had been killed in the tragic accident that led to Ahimoth and Vin's self-exile to Earth. Yet here she was, alive again! With Fianna and Ahimoth's help, she told the tale of her bodiless flight to Earth and her rebirth there with the loving help of Dagmar, the venerable Dragon-friend.

At Celine's insistence, Joli also told of how she and Ahimoth had rescued Vin from imprisonment and torture at Soader's wicked hands, then borne him half-way across the planet to safety. Joyous tears flowed aplenty throughout the greetings and tales—especially when Vin and Joli were reunited with their parents, who had thought their precious children lost forever.

When the introductions and tales were complete, Fianna stepped forward to stand before her parents. "Father, Mother," she said with a bow, "and dear people of Nibiru," she swept her gaze over the assembled Dragons, "I have a momentous announcement for you all." She motioned Vin to come forward and stand beside her. "I wish to present... my husband: Vin Druk Malbaz!" A collective gasp went up, but nothing more. The assembled Dragons waited respectfully for their king to speak. He was just as shocked as they, perhaps more so, and needed a moment to collect himself. It was Queen Dini who broke the silence, though. She stepped gracefully to her daughter's side and rose up to embrace, then release her.

"Dearest daughter. What a wonderous gift you have brought your people. A new Prince—Prince Vin Druk Malbaz of Nibiru! Welcome to our family!" She embraced her new son-in-law, whose handsome blue face quickly shaded to violet.

Led by King Neal, the crowd broke into a new round of cheering, trumpeting, flapping and stamping. Fianna let them go on for a bit, then rose up to call for attention.

"There is more you must know," she said.

"More? Tell us, princess-daughter!" said the king.

"My own Companion's soulmate, Jager, has bonded with Prince Vin—they are Dragon and Companion!"

The crowd gasped at the revelation.

"Another wonder, dear Fianna," said King Neal. "A second Dragon-Companion pair among us! This redoubles the safety and security you have brought us. A blessing indeed!"

The happy tumult broke out once more, just as exuberant as it was before.

Now Ahimoth fanned his ebon wings for attention.

King Neal laughed aloud. "Will the astonishing revelations never cease?! Go on then, my son—what have you for us now?"

Ahimoth called Joli to come stand beside him. "As some of you know, Joli was the love of my young life. My good friend Vin was also enamored of her. Our rivalry grew until at last we fought a duel to resolve it. During our childish battle, dear Joli was struck by lightning and killed. Thinking myself at fault for her tragic death, I punished myself bitterly. At last I abandoned my family, my home and my people in shame. I set off in search of Joli's spirit—Joli *herself*, that is—in hopes of guiding her to a viable egg, and rebirth. This, to me, was the only worthy reason for my own continued life.

Vin, as crushed as I by Joli's death, joined me in my quest. The tale goes on, and it is a long one. But as Joli herself has explained, we—Joli, Vin and I—were at last reunited. And with that, I am thankful to say, our old rivalry was no more. We were glad to be alive, and wiser for the long and dreadful experience.

Vin and my dear princess-sister have already announced their union. Now I have a similar announcement, which I deem every bit as joyous. It is this: Just as Nibiru has a new prince, it shall soon have a new princess, for Wilda Joli Jonty has agreed to marry with me. On that day, she shall be your princess; she is already mine. And I warrant that you, and all who come after you, will be inspired at how well she embodies her dear name's meaning: She truly *is* an untamed, lovely gift of God.

Now the crowd knew no restraint. They did not wait for their king to have the first word—they burst at once into wild celebration. The king and queen never even noticed the slip in etiquette; they were too busy celebrating themselves.

When at last the cheering died down a bit, Jager mented a quick thought to Fianna and Celine. "Perfect!" Celine mented back.

"Splendid idea!" mented Fianna.

At that, Jager approached Vin and whispered to him; Vin nodded and knelt beside his Companion. Jager clambered up onto Vin's back and raised his arms high, facing the king and queen as though to address them. It took a moment for the Dragons to notice, Jager being so comparatively small— but notice they did. A respectful quiet settled over the crowd.

"Yes, dear Jager. Do you too have something to share? Please, please, tell us!"

"Thank you, Your Highness," said Jager. "Just one moment, please." He reached down and drew Omaja from his clever scabbard, set along the side of Vin's black saddle. He stood again, tall upon Vin's back, then thrust Omaja skyward. The staff burst into a brief but dazzling display of light and color, ending with its head alone illuminated in purest white.

Fianna rose to her full height. "Behold, my people!" she cried, "Omaja, the Staff of Malek!"

The crowd had been respectfully quiet; now their silence was complete—as though their breathing had halted and their hearts' beating ceased. Every last Dragon had heard, from their youngest days, the tales and legends of the first Companion, Malek, first Holder of the Staff of Power: Omaja. They had heard the exploits of the Holders who'd followed, on down to the heroic Schimpel. But there the tales had ended. With the passing of Schimpel, Omaja too had disappeared.

King Neal broke the silence. "I call upon Orgon the Wise. Would you come forward, brother?"

The elderly Dragon approached the king and bowed.

"Noble Orgon," said King Neal, "are we agreed on the

significance of this revelation?"

Knowing precisely what Neal meant, Orgon replied: "We are agreed, my brother."

The two turned to face Jager.

"My son," said the king, speaking loudly enough that all might hear, "you may not be aware of it, but our revered prophesies tell of one such as you who shall come to us, bearing the Staff of Malek after long absence. Coming to aid and protect us in time of direst need."

Jager nodded. "I was not aware of this prophesy, Your Majesty. I thank you for enlightening me."

Orgon spoke: "One question remains, Jager Cornwallis, before we may know with certainty that the prophesy has indeed been fulfilled. Tell us: How did you come by this staff?"

"Well," said Jager, "I *didn't* come by it, really. It would be more accurate to say the staff came by *me*. It revealed itself, as though it had somehow *chosen* me."

The elder Dragons conferred quietly, then turned to Jager once more.

"What you say confirms our conjecture," said Orgon.

"Indeed. There can be no question," said Neal. He turned to scan the crowd all around him with regal regard. "People of Nibiru! Here before you is Jager, Companion to Prince Vin and Holder of the Staff of Malek!"

Celine and Jager braced themselves for the uproar they were certain would now erupt. But instead of wild celebration, every Dragon present lowered his or her head in silent respect.

The King continued, addressing Jager: "The prophesies

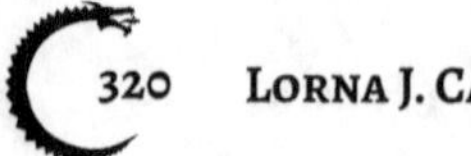

said you would come as our protector. We understand that you may not yet be fully cognizant of the significance and responsibilities of your role, nor of the part you are yet to play. However, we are confident all will be revealed to you, and to us, in due time. For the present, we welcome you. And we pledge to do anything we can to assist you. You need only ask. We—I, my brother Orgon, all Nibiru's people—are at your service, just as we believe you are here to serve us."

At first, Jager was stunned. "Thank you, Your Majesty, and Wise Orgon," he said. And then a certainty settled over him: There was nothing to be stunned about. All this was meant to be. It was a part of the destiny the Mentors had hinted at more than once. It was one of the motivations behind their care and guidance.

He turned to address the gathered Dragons: "And I thank all of you, noble Dragons of Nibiru! I pledge to do everything in my power—and to channel the great power of Omaja—to safeguard and promote your happiness and prosperity, as long as I live."

"Let the celebration continue!" cried King Neal. And so it did.

Celine approached Vin and Jager. The young man leapt from the Dragon's back and embraced her, still holding Omaja high. "This is beyond anything I've ever experienced," he mented. He *had* to ment—the Dragons' happy noise drowned out mere speech.

"It truly is," agreed Celine. "The peoples of our many worlds could learn precious lessons from these Dragon-folk. Lessons of love, kindness, loyalty, courage and forgiveness." She kissed him lightly on the cheek, and they shared a loving smile.

Brianne Robins - age 13

CHAPTER 33

An Endangered Race

Remi froze. The Dragon remained where it was, but cocked its great head to one side, regarding her closely. She couldn't help but feel the look was one of suspicion. Unfriendly suspicion.

As her initial surprise subsided, Remi was struck by the Dragon's beauty; she was near certain it was a female. The body, head and features spoke of feminine grace and power; it was clad in lustrous scales of deep, rich azure, faintly iridescent. The eyes—large, round and golden, with black, vertical pupils—looked out from beneath ridged brows, elegantly curved.

"Who might you be?" the Dragon demanded.

Remi was startled to hear the Dragon speak—a remnant of the humanoid races' ancient concept of Dragons as animals. "My name is Remi. Have I intruded?"

"I shall ask the questions," came the Dragon's brusque reply. "Why are you here?"

"I am taking a walk," she said, "I do this each day, to refresh myself."

"Are you alone?"

Increasingly irritated, Remi struggled to remain civil. She realized this place was likely the Dragon's home, and she herself was the intruder. "Yes, I am. I come from the settlement that lies many kilometers in that direction," she said, pointing. "I mean you no harm, and apologize if I have intruded."

"Hmm," huffed the Dragon, and the suspicious cock of her azure head softened slightly. "Yes, I know of your settlement and your people. You are quite noisy, you know."

Remi chuckled. "Yes, we can be noisy. But, may I ask who you are?"

"I am called Fallon. My name means 'leader.' I am meant to be leader of my people one day, but I have been trapped in this place for what seems like two years or more, separated from them."

"I am sorry to hear that," said Remi. "How did it happen?"

"I was learning to cast spells," she said, her suspicious tone now gone. "I was practicing with fellow students, near our place of learning. Suddenly there was a great sound, like all the thunder in the world at once, and then...nothing. When I became aware again, I was here. Alone. I sense that this place is still part of my homeworld, but somehow inside it—the sky here is not true, merely a cleverly colored roof. Nor is the sun real—it is a contrivance, hung from the false sky. But can you tell me what world this is?"

"My people call it Remini," said Remi, "though you may know it by a different name."

"Oh! Thank you. No, Remini is how we name it as well. So is this place a sort of cave, then?"

"Yes, it is," said Remi. "It was built beneath the surface of

your planet as a safe refuge, by Mentors."

Fallon brightened. "Mentors! Oh! That is wonderful. I have learned of them." She frowned. "But why would Mentors imprison me here?"

"I am certain they did not," replied Remi. "They would never do such a thing. I suspect that your arrival here was an accident."

"I see," said Fallon. She brightened again. "I have been watching your settlement. New people come; some go away. If they can go away, perhaps I can as well. Could you help me go away from here, and return to my people?"

"Perhaps I can!" said Remi. "If you like, you may come to our settlement and speak with our leader. He may be able to help you return to your home."

Fallon rose up. "That would be wonderful. But I am afraid to show myself. You seem friendly, but my people have suffered horribly at the hands of Humans. That is why I was so gruff with you, when you arrived. I am sorry. Would you bring your leader here? Just the leader and you, no others? I will be here tomorrow at this same time. Thank you." Before Remi could respond, the Dragon turned abruptly and disappeared into the dense forest.

"Well!" said Remi aloud. "That was less than polite!" Then she thought better of it. Perhaps that was simply how Dragons behaved. She shrugged and set off toward her waiting flier.

When she arrived back at Zulak City, she sought out Dino and recounted the whole incident. "You hear how exquisite Dragons are," she said, "and the image-captures I've seen do look lovely, but nothing compares to seeing one in person. Magnificent. So, do you think you can help her?"

Dino chuckled. "You seem to have had quite a change of heart since the last time the subject of Dragons came up."

"Yeah, I suppose I have. Meeting and talking to one—finding out they're just people, with the same kind of emotions and hopes and problems as anyone else—that changes everything. You know what? I need to get out more!" They shared a good laugh, then Remi went on. "Anyway, Fallon wants to talk to you. She's trapped down here, and as I said, I suggested you may be able to help her get back home."

"I'll be happy to meet her, sure. You said she wants to meet at the spot where you ran into her today. Can you get us back there?"

"Sure. I remember it well—and even if I didn't, the flier's recorder would know the way. It's just a one-seat model, so we'll have to use a different one. We can transfer the record to my hand-held, though, just in case we get lost. She said she would meet us at mid-day."

Late the next morning, as they flew toward the meeting place, Dino mused about how well Remi seemed to be doing. So soon, too, after learning of Rafael's death. It had taken him quite a time to come out of his deep grief at losing his wife and son. He chatted with her about progress at the settlement, but avoided the subject of her late husband.

"There it is!" said Remi, pointing to the canyon mouth where she'd set down the previous day. Dino landed; they disembarked and settled under a tree to await Fallon's arrival.

Within minutes, the azure Dragon emerged from the foliage. "Greetings," she said. "I thank you for coming. Remi, is this the leader of whom you spoke?"

"Yes, Fallon. Please allow me to introduce Major Dino

Hadgkiss." Remi hoped she had done this properly; she had heard Dragons were quite particular about manners and proper forms and protocols.

"It is my pleasure to make your acquaintance, Major Dino Hadgkiss," said Fallon, dipping her head briefly in a sort of abbreviated bow. "I am Nimu Fallon Roark, daughter of Haco Quade Roark, who is a king among Dragons of our world, called Remini."

"The pleasure is mine, Nimu Fallon Roark," replied Dino, dipping his head in an approximation of Fallon's gesture. "My friend Remi tells me I may be able to assist you. How might I do that?"

Fallon explained her situation, just as she'd told it to Remi—then added that she now had reason to believe her people were in dire danger. She *must* return to help them.

"I understand," said Dino, "and I am sorry to hear of your predicament. I do believe I can help, though. If you will direct me, I should be able to take you home to your people. We will have to use a spaceship, though. Have you traveled in one before?"

"No, I have not. My people do not have such technology," said Fallon, "nor do we have need or desire for it. However, we respect those who possess and use physical technologies, and do not fear their use. I am willing to travel in your ship." In fact, the young Dragon was excited at the prospect, though she felt it would be improper to admit it.

"Very well, then. I will make the necessary arrangements. If you wish, we can make the journey later today."

"That would be wonderful," said Fallon. "I must say that my friend was right in what she said about you. You are a kind and good person."

"Oh! Why, thank you," said Dino. "My I ask what friend told you so?"

"The friend who spoke to me in my dream. Her name is Albho Fianna Uwatti. She lives on Nibiru, a Dragon Homeworld much like ours. She told me you were a kind and *good* Human, and that you would do whatever you could to help me and my people."

"Your friend spoke the truth," said Dino with a chuckle.

Remi shot him a questioning look, as if to say, "What's funny?"

"I'll explain later," he assured her. Fianna! He thought. I wonder if Celine is involved here, too. Turning back to Fallon, he asked, "Have you had trouble with some Humans?"

"Oh, yes," said Fallon. "The Humans here—on Remini, that is—hate Dragons. They hunt and kill us. They poison our waters and drive away our game. They say we are evil, and the source of all that is bad in their lives. We do not know why they think this. To our knowledge, Dragons have never harmed or interfered with Humans. We can only imagine that perhaps some of our distant ancestors did so, long, long ago, and the Humans choose not to forgive it."

"That is sad to hear," said Dino. "I promise you, and all your people, that the Humans who are visiting this under-world will never harm or interfere with Remini's Dragon folk. And you are welcome to call upon us for assistance at any time."

"Thank you, Major Dino Hadgkiss. I look forward to passing on your promise to my father and my people."

The three agreed to meet in three hours, on the bank of the river near the settlement. Dino wanted time to return to Zulak City and explain that a friendly Dragon would soon be visiting, so the residents wouldn't be alarmed when she approached and landed. "Please forgive me for asking, but I know Dragons do not use timekeeping devices. Is there anything we need to do, to make sure we meet at the time we've set?"

"I thank you for asking," said Fallon. "You are a considerate and thoughtful Human. There is no need for concern, though. We Dragons have a fine sense of time, and from my schooling as a youngster, I understand your concept of 'hours.' I shall be punctual." To Dino's surprise, she finished her statement with a smile. He knew certain expressions and gestures were common to many races, but he was always pleased to see that fact in action.

During the flight back, Dino called ahead to Madda, who was busy inspecting construction, installation and equipment-testing projects. "I have a special request," he explained. "I'd like you to take a few techs up to the *King* and set it up to accommodate a Dragon on a short flight."

"Certainly, Captain," said Madda with a laugh. "Just another ordinary day under Major Hadgkiss's command!" She signed off and began rounding up a team to do the job.

At the appointed time, Fallon appeared in the "sky," high above Zulak City. Far below her, she could see thousands of Humans in and around the city, gazing up in sheer amazement at their approaching guest. Few among them had ever seen a living Dragon. She spiraled down and landed neatly beside the river, where Dino and Remi waited.

"Greetings, Fallon!" called Dino. "We thank you for coming."

"Greetings, Major Dino Hadgkiss," she replied. From her repeated glances toward the settlement and all the watching Humans, it was clear the Dragon was not completely at ease.

Dino reassured her that the watchers meant her no harm—they were merely curious. He added that, to Human eyes, she was quite a beautiful sight. "Thank you," Fallon said. "I sense you are correct—there is no hostility among them, only interest. Interest and...admiration! How pleasant. Please tell them I appreciate and thank them."

"I will be pleased to do so," said Dino. "And now, are you prepared for the journey we discussed?"

"Yes, prepared and eager. How will we travel? What must I do?"

"First, we will travel to our spaceship, which is high above Remini. We will go there using a device called a transbeam. It manipulates matter and energy in such a way that we will be transported from here to the ship. It takes only a few moments and is not dangerous or painful, but you may experience unusual sensations and perceptions during the process. Once we are aboard the ship, I will fly us down to the planet's surface—to wherever you direct me."

"Thank you," said Fallon. "I see this will be a completely new experience. An adventure! I am excited, though a little fearful at the same time."

"I understand completely," said Dino. "I think you will enjoy the adventure, and any fear will pass quickly."

"Very well," said Fallon. "May we begin?"

"We may," said Dino; he tapped his comm pickup and asked Madda to 'beam their party aboard.

Moments later, the threesome stood on *King's* transbeam platform. Madda stepped from behind the 'beam console to welcome them. "Greetings!" she said. "Welcome aboard *King Hammurabi.*"

"Oh!" exclaimed Fallon, still a bit shaken by the transbeam

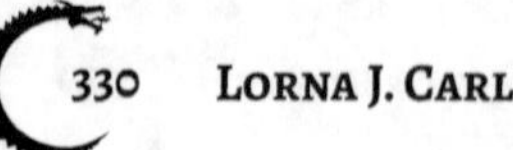

passage. "A Rept! I did not know there were Repts among you, Major Dino Hadgkiss. I have only encountered one other, in all my life."

"I see," said Dino. "Fallon, please allow me to introduce Lieutenant Madda, my second-in-command."

"Greetings to you, Lieutenant Madda," said Fallon.

"I also extend greetings, Fallon" said *King Hammurabi,* "and welcome you aboard. It is a pleasure to serve you."

The Dragon was clearly startled. "Who...who said that?" she asked. "I see no one else here."

"I am sorry, I should have explained in advance," said Dino. That is *King Hammurabi*—the ship herself. Through application of a highly advanced technology, it is—or rather, *she* is—a conscious entity."

"Oh, my," said Fallon. "This truly is an adventure, Major Dino Hadgkiss. A city of friendly Humans, flying through space in an instant, meeting a Rept, and now a living space-ship. Thank you!"

"You are welcome, friend Fallon," he replied. "And now, we must prepare ourselves for the flight to your home. Madda, I will go with Fallon to the hold and then stay there with her, to relay her instructions about where to land."

Madda made her way forward, while Dino led Fallon to the hold and helped her settle into the makeshift flight couch Madda's techs had prepared for her. Then, relaying Fallon's descriptions and directions, Dino talked Madda down toward Fallon's home. A viewscreen had been set up in the hold so he and Fallon could see the surface as they approached.

"There!" cried Fallon, pointing to the screen. "That is the place! That is Pagan Mountain." Madda brought the ship to a gentle halt, roughly a kilometer above the craggy peak Fallon had pointed out. About two hundred meters below the peak swept a broad, level terrace. Several openings could be seen in the steep walls at its mountain-side edge. As they watched, a large Dragon emerged from one of the openings. Spying the craft hovering high above, the Dragon spread his wide, deep-violet wings and roared a warning to his fellows.

"Horvat!" said Fallon. "That is one of our lookouts, Horvat." She turned to Dino. "Major Dino Hadgkiss, I thank you for bringing me home. I am ever in your debt."

"You are welcome, Fallon. I am glad to have been able to assist you. And, if you wish, you are welcome to address me as Dino."

"That is good," said Fallon. "I shall do so, Dino. And now I must ask you to do one more thing. You see, my friend Fianna of Nibiru bid me tell you that you must meet and talk with my people. With my father in particular, because he is a king among us."

"Oh!" said Dino. "I see. That changes my plans somewhat, but I suppose I can do it."

"Good. That is good," said Fallon. "Fianna also told me to say that it is something Celine would want you to do. Celine is a Human, like you. She is Fianna's Companion. That is an important thing," she explained.

Dino laughed. "Well, if Celine would want me to do it, I suppose I have no choice!"

"Good!" said Fallon. "Now, if you will open the door, I will fly down to my home to tell my father you are here to see him." She thought for a moment. "*Is there a door?* We came into the ship using the...what is it called? Oh—using the transbeam machine, so I do not know if there is a door.

How strange."

"Yes, there is a door, Fallon, and I will open it for you. If you think you can arrange the meeting with your father quickly, Madda and I will wait here. Otherwise I will give you a signaling device, and we will fly the ship back up into space to await your call."

"Very good," said Fallon. "I think it will be best if you go back to space. My father is not a hasty person; he may want a few hours to consider a meeting, and to prepare for it."

"All right, then," said Dino. "Wait here for just a minute, while I get you a comm pickup." He left the hold, retrieved a spare comm pickup from an equipment locker, then returned and showed Fallon how to use it. It was rather a trick, since the device was designed for people with smaller bodies, but the clever young Dragon quickly found a way to manipulate its tiny controls with her sharp front claws. She tucked the device under one of the larger scales below her throat, and indicated she was ready to depart.

"Excellent," said Dino. "The ship's largest door is right here at the back of the hold." He gave the ship a command to open the hold's hatchway, and the broad, tall door began sliding back into a recess between the outer and inner hulls. A gust of bracing cold air burst into the hold.

"Ahhhh!" cried Fallon. "Open air! Mountain air! How I've missed it!" She stepped to the hatchway, then turned once more to Dino.

"Thank you, Major D...oh, no...thank you, Dino. I will communicate with you soon. I am excited that you will meet with my father. I must warn you he can be gruff. And although he does not love Humans, having known only those who have persecuted us, I believe he will like you."

"Thank you, Fallon. I look forward to meeting him. Because he has raised such a fine daughter, I trust he is a sterling person himself."

"Again you are kind," the Dragon replied. "I leave you now. Fly well and fly safe." She crouched at the edge of the hatchway, then sprang straight outward and away from the ship, wings held tight to her body. She plunged downward for several seconds, then spread her wings wide, caught the air and banked into a tight, steep spiral toward the terrace below.

Dino watched her go, then shut the hatch and headed for the ops deck. "Quite a youngster, eh Madda?" he said, settling into his flight couch.

"She certainly is. I imagine her father is a formidable character, too."

"Must be. Well, I'll be finding out directly. Take us back to orbit, would you?"

Madda nodded, and the ship leapt spaceward at her command.

When they reached orbit, Dino retired to his cabin and attempted to contact Celine, then Jager, with no response from either. Next he called West; to his great relief, the Mentor replied at once.

"Celine, Jager and their Dragon friends have gone to Nibiru," she explained. "That is why you were unable to reach them."

"Ah. Nibiru," said Dino. "That's right. To perform the crucial task you mentioned. Is there anything I could do to assist them?"

"At the moment, no. But I believe that at some point, an opportunity to do so may present itself."

"Thank you, West. I'll be watching for one."

"Before they left for Nibiru," West went on, "they briefed me on the rescue operation Celine and Jager conceived, and which you were instrumental in executing. Have you any news for me on that subject?"

"I do," said Dino. He gave the Mentor a brief update on activities at Zulak City, then described Remi's encounter with Fallon, their efforts to return the Dragon to her people, his upcoming meeting with the Remini Dragon king, and Celine and Fianna's involvement in all that had transpired.

"This is excellent news, Major. I trust your encounter with King Quade will be an interesting one—perhaps even challenging—and that great good will come of it. Please tell Quade I send my regards."

ARRIVING WHOLLY UNEXPECTED AT the Dragons' Pagan Mountain stronghold, Fallon was greeted with astonishment, wild enthusiasm, and enormous relief. Her people had thought her lost forever, and their grief at her loss had lingered long. Her father, a stern and stalwart leader, wept tears of joy at their reunion. His wife, Fallon's mother, had been lost a year before Fallon's disappearance, murdered by a Human assassin. With Fallon gone too, King Quade had become sullen, sometimes morose, and more fiercely hateful of Humans than ever. The light of his daughter's return banished much of the darkness that had haunted his recent life.

When their joyful tears had abated, Fallon explained to her father what had happened, where she had been, and how she had managed to come back to him. When he learned there had been Humans involved in her return, he would not at first believe her. Kind, honest, helpful Humans? Not possible. Not on Remini! But she gently repeated her account, emphasizing her dream-time messages from the princess Fianna, and how true the Nibiru Dragon's assurances had proven to be. At last the Dragon King agreed to meet this Human, Major Dino Hadgkiss—if that was what the Nibiru princess and his princess-daughter advised.

"Thank you, Father. I promise that you will not be disappointed."

The king marshalled his people to prepare for the meeting, while Fallon returned to the terrace to call Dino.

"My father has agreed to meet with you," she said. "Please come to the terrace below the peak when the sun is highest in the sky. About two hours from now."

"Thank you, Fallon," said Dino. "I will be there. I will use the transbeam; you may want to explain it to anyone who will be present, so they are not startled when I appear."

"That is kind advice; I shall follow it," she replied, and broke the connection.

Two hours later, the transbeam deposited Dino on the rocky terrace, just as agreed. He was met by a score of Dragons, many of them larger than any he'd seen before, all glaring at him with frank suspicion. Scanning the area, he noted several more looking down from the heights: sentries, just as big as those in the group before him. *They grow them big on Remini,* he thought. *Or maybe this is the biggest and toughest of the lot, chosen to make a point. Or a sort of honor guard. We'll see.* He smiled his most confident smile and bowed politely.

Fallon came forward through the line of hulking Dragons, who stepped aside in obvious deference. She made a bow to Dino in the Dragon fashion, and he returned it in the Human way.

Then the line of Dragons parted further, and another, the largest yet, came forth. He was as azure-blue as Fallon. Lines of deeper blue—nearly black—accented the contours of his muscular form and reinforced his air of power and command. He stopped several meters from Hadgkiss, raised his horned head high, and gazed down upon the Human visitor.

Fallon drew herself up and spoke: "Father, allow me to introduce Dino Hadgkiss, who is called Major, the Human of whom Princess Fianna of Nibiru has spoken. As I have explained, he is leader of a band of Humans newly come to the under-world where I was trapped until today. It is he who freed me and brought me home. Princess Fianna says it is possible he can help us, in the way that you and I have discussed this day."

"Hmmm," the imposing Dragon rumbled, with a sound like a rising earthquake. He nodded to Fallon, then turned back to Dino. "Greetings, Major Dino Hadgkiss, friend of Nibiru. I am Haco Quade Roark, leader of this fold, called the Fold of Mount Pagan. And last living king of the Dragons of Remini. For returning my daughter—our princess—I thank you. I thank you from the depths of my heart and from my living soul. Please accept my gratitude, and that of all our world's Dragon-folk."

"I am honored to meet you, King Haco Quade Roark, and grateful for the opportunity to assist your charming daughter. I am advised I may be able to further assist you and your people. If you believe this is so, shall we proceed to discuss the matter?"

Quade nodded twice, turned to look at his daughter, swept his gaze up and down the honor guard of Dragons behind him, then turned again to Dino. The regal Dragon raised a forefoot and held it poised, gave a resounding snort, stamped the raised foot twice upon the ground, then resumed his original stance, looking calmly down at Dino.

Having no idea what the proper response might be—if indeed there was one—Dino nodded and smiled. "Thank you," he ventured.

Quade frowned, then repeated the snorting and stamping sequence.

Still at a loss and beginning to sweat, Dino looked to Fallon, hoping for a hint. Diplomacy and ritual had never been his strong suits, and now he wished he'd studied them more carefully.

The young Dragon repeated her father's actions, though her snort was dainty by comparison.

No help there, thought Dino; he looked again at Quade, with a smile he hoped didn't look too helpless.

For the third time, the Dragon king went through the brief ritual, a trifle more slowly and with a distinct air of insistence.

Oh! By the Ancients! Dino thought. What they're doing—it's a ritual! Hoping to the heavens he was right, Dino raised his right knee, paused, snorted—as close as he could manage to the king's tone and volume—then stamped twice, calling on the power of his bionics to make the stamping admirably authoritative.

"Excellent," rumbled Quade. "Yes. Let us proceed."

Dino nearly fainted with relief.

The Dragon king gestured toward his right, motioning for Dino to follow, and marched toward a large, raised elliptical

slab—a natural dais, perhaps twenty meters across its long axis. Dino followed, as did Fallon, the honor guard, and dozens more Dragons who Dino hadn't even noticed arriving. When the procession reached the dais, Quade mounted it and seated himself at its center. An elder Dragon followed and sat to his right. Then came Fallon, who sat at his left. Finally, the honor guard lined up several Dragon-paces behind their king.

Fallon pointed to a spot several meters in front of Quade and addressed the major: "You may stand there and face the king." Dino did so, while the newly arrived Dragons ranged themselves on the terrace below the front of the dais, eager to witness whatever would follow.

Looking at Dino, Quade cocked his head, then gestured to someone off to his left and made a brief, guttural sound. A Dragon nodded and rushed away; he returned a few moments later, rolling a wheel of stone before him, about a meter in diameter and a bit less than a meter thick. He hefted it up and onto the dais, rolled it close to Dino, then tipped it sideways. It thudded to the rocky floor, raising a puff of dust. Quade gestured toward the stone; clearly Dino was meant to use it as a seat. He bowed to Quade and sat upon the wheel's edge.

In the conference that followed, King Quade explained that Dragons and Humans had once lived in harmonious cooperation upon Remini. Then, a few generations ago, a leader had risen among the Humans and somehow convinced them that Dragons were to blame for any and all misfortunes that befell them—floods, famines, plagues, strife among their various tribes—the Dragons were behind it all, he maintained.

The Dragons had attempted to reason with the leader and

his people, and offered to help them in times of trouble, but to no avail. The Humans' suspicion grew to anger and finally hatred. They began ambushing Dragons and killing them, poisoning their favored game animals and waterways, and wreaking havoc in any way they could.

The Dragons fought back, but the Humans had acquired powerful weapons—from what source, no one knew. The Humans of Remini were not a technologically advanced people, but with the mysterious new weapons they could easily overpower any individual Dragon, and even repel massed Dragon attacks.

"Seeing we were no longer a match for the hostile Humans," Quade explained, "we retreated, then retreated again, hoping that by distancing ourselves from them, they would no longer feel threatened and would leave us alone. This worked for a while, but in recent years they have begun hunting us again, destroying our homes, defiling our lands and devastating our sources of food and water.

"We have learned that they plan a final, massive assault, to exterminate us utterly. The last of us—the four hundred of our race who remain—are gathered in the high valley that lies below and to the south of this peak. We have prepared to defend ourselves, but without serious hope of survival. Not until Fianna of Nibiru learned of our peril—we know not how—and, only two evenings past, invited us to come to Nibiru to live. Fianna communicated her invitation to Fallon"—he nodded toward his daughter, with a proud smile—"and this day Fallon has relayed the princess's generous offer to me."

"But...that's wonderful!" said Dino.

"Indeed it is," said Quade. "Fianna further explained that because of a foul curse which ravaged the Nibiru race for

ages, there are now regions of their world which are unoccupied. Regions which she and her people welcome us to settle. We may practice our own customs and traditions. We may engage and interact with her people as much or as little as we like, though she hopes we will forge strong bonds between us, to the greater benefit of all.

"Fallon expressed her deepest gratitude to Fianna, but deep fears as well: First, she herself was trapped in the under-world in which you found her, and therefore unable to tell us of Fianna's kind offer. Second, even if Fallon were able to reach us, she knew of no means by which our people could journey to Nibiru. Fianna counseled her not to worry—that she should seek you out, and that you would help us to reach Nibiru."

"I see," said Dino, astonished. "So...you want me to help you get to Nibiru. All of you."

"That is correct," replied Quade.

"Damn!" said Dino, to himself.

"What was that?" said Quade, "I could not hear you just now."

"Oh—I'm sorry. I was just thinking to myself. But Fianna may be right. I may be able to help you. If you will excuse me, I will return to my ship to confer with someone and examine potential solutions."

"Certainly. You are free to come and go as you wish."

"How many of your people did you say there are?"

"Four hundred. Four hundred and twelve, to be precise. Thirty-seven of our eggs, as well—when they must be moved, they are kept safe in special containers."

"All right. And have you belongings you'll wish to take

along?"

"Very few. Some precious relics, some ceremonial items, some tools, but little else. We are a simple people." He did not mention the Remini Dragon's rich treasure hoard, safe where none but Dragons would ever find it. On Remini it would remain, while his people guarded the secret of its existence.

"Thank you," said Dino. "I think that is all I need to know for the moment." He bowed deeply to Quade, then to the elder Dragon beside him, and finally to Fallon. "I'll go now, and return as soon as I'm able. Perhaps a few hours. Should I return to this same place?"

"Yes. That would be best. If I am elsewhere when you return, another will be here to greet you, and to bring you to me."

"Thank you, King Quade." With that, he tapped his comm pickup and spoke to Madda. Moments later, a transbeam field whisked him away.

"Well!" said Madda, as Hadgkiss stepped from the transbeam platform, "Nothing charred, no obvious damage—may I assume you were well received?"

"Well enough. And wow, have I brought back a project!"

Dino explained the Dragons' plight, and the two considered ways they might solve it. They would need transport ships, of course, but that didn't present much of a problem. The freighters that had just taken part in the massive rescue operation had all offered their services, should they ever be needed again. Well, they would soon learn that "ever again" had come quickly. Hopefully at least some would be able to oblige.

At this point, though, the planning ran into a solid wall: The objective was to deliver the Dragons and their few belongings to Nibiru—the location of which, *no one knew.* Even more discouraging, the planet was said to be impenetrably shielded. So even if they managed to get the Dragons *to* Nibiru, would they then be able to land them on its surface?

"I'm going to have to contact West," said Dino. "She encouraged me to visit the Remini people, so she must have anticipated their need, and the problems it would present."

"We can hope so!" said Madda.

"Take them to Earth," said West, when Dino had explained the situation.

"Earth? Forgive me—I don't mean to doubt you, but why Earth?"

"There is a time-space wormhole with a terminus on Earth and another on Nibiru. The Dragons call it the tube-chute. They have used it for centuries to visit Earth and return safely home. Now the Remini Dragons can use it to reach Nibiru. The transit is perilous, especially for young Dragons, but my sisters and I may be able to devise a way to mitigate the danger, at least for the passage of the few young ones among the Remini fold. Even taking the Dragons to Earth at all is dangerous at this time, but their situation is dire, and for the moment I see no other alternative."

"Brilliant," said Dino. "Thank you, West. Madda and I will arrange for transport vessels and move the Dragons to Earth as quickly as possible. I'll keep you abreast of our progress. There's no time to lose; as I think I mentioned, the Dragons expect an overwhelming assault just three days from now."

A few hours later, Dino and Madda had worked out the

necessary details. Madda took *Spitfire* and went straight to work to re-recruit the necessary freighters, while Dino returned to Pagan Mountain to brief the Dragons.

"I have conferred with friends, and I believe we have a workable plan to transport your people," he told Quade.

"Mm! You must have powerful friends!"

"Yes—some capable and resourceful Human and Rept friends, in this case. And a Mentor as well."

Quade's eyes went wide. "A Mentor! A powerful friend indeed!"

"That's for certain," said Dino. "The Mentor West, to be precise. In fact, she asked me to relay her regards. Please forgive my not doing so sooner."

"Ahhh! West! Yes. The mere mention of her name fills my heart with hope."

"And your hope is well founded," said Dino. "I'll return to my ship now, to make preparations."

"Very well," said Quade. "And I shall prepare my people."

CHAPTER 34

Preparations, Revelations and a Swim

Late into the evening, Dragon Hall echoed with the joyful noise of celebration. The time was approaching midnight when Fianna, engaged in a lively discussion with one of her childhood friends, felt a sudden wave of fatigue. *Odd,* she thought. *Until now, I haven't been feeling at all tired.* And then a suspicion struck her. "Forgive me for interrupting," she said to her friend, "but would you excuse me for just a moment?"

"Oh, yes, Princess, certainly."

Fianna smiled, then scanned the scene around her until she spotted Celine—struggling to stifle a yawn as she and Jager chatted with Vin, Joli and Ahimoth. The yawn won the struggle, and Celine blushed faintly with embarrassment. *Ah!* thought the Dragon. *Time to get my Little One home for some rest.* She turned back to her friend, and guided their conversation to a cordial close.

"It's been wonderful to talk with you, Fianna. Congratulations once again on your wedding. May your lives together be long, full and supremely happy."

"Thank you so much, Jenifee," replied Fianna. "May you

and your fine husband enjoy the same—and all the young ones to come, as well!" The two embraced affectionately, then parted company.

"Sister!" boomed Ahimoth, as Fianna approached the little group, "Are you enjoying the evening?"

"Yes, truly," she replied, "but I think it best that we take our leave. It has been a long, long day." She glanced at Celine with a fleeting wink.

"Thank you for rescuing me," mented the girl. "This is all wonderful, but I'm exhausted!"

"Mmm, I believe you are correct," said Vin. "I am ready for a solid rest. Wormhole riding takes its toll, does it not?"

"Achh!" agreed Ahimoth, "So it does!" The rest nodded their wholehearted agreement.

"This brings up a somewhat delicate matter," said Vin. "What are the lodging arrangements to be?"

"Well, I...I am not...you see..." began Fianna.

Ahimoth jumped in to rescue his stuttering sister. "Oh, it need not be complicated," he said. "Vin, earlier I heard your father mention that the spacious cave-home you occupied back in our younger days is still vacant..."

"Ah! Quite so," said Vin. "And yes, that would be an ideal retreat for gentlepersons such as you and I."

"Splendid," said Ahimoth. "My thought precisely."

"And my riverside home in the valley to the east would suit we ladies handsomely," said Fianna, "though Joli may prefer to stay with her parents—at least until her wedding day arrives."

"Thank you for the kind offer, Fianna," said Joli. "I would love to stay with you and Celine—we have grown so close in such a short time. I do think it best if I visit with my parents, though. We have been separated so very long, and they are growing old, as you have seen tonight. I believe I shall remain behind here, and accompany them home when the night's festivities are over."

"I understand completely," said Fianna. "But please know that you are welcome to visit at any time. In fact, I dearly hope you will. I treasure your company."

"As do I," added Celine.

"Thank you. Thank you both," said Joli. "I promise to take you up on that offer. After all, we are all soon to be family!"

"And what about you, Jager?" asked Vin. "Will you join Ahimoth and I, or do you prefer to go with Celine?"

"To be honest, I'm torn," said Jager. "But, much as I'd love to come along with you two, I believe I should go with Celine and Fianna. We have work to do in preparation for the Unification Ceremony, and much of it will best be done together."

"Very well," said Ahimoth. "All is arranged. Shall we thank our host and hostess, then, and be on our way?"

They all agreed, and after expressing their thanks to the king and queen, they departed.

"Oh!" said Fianna, as they gathered on the broad landing ledge just outside Dragon Hall, "This will be your first flight together, Vin and Jager! How exciting!"

"At least I've had plenty of practice getting into and out of the saddle," said Jager, "and we've done plenty of 'dry run' take-offs, flight maneuvers and landings, under your kind guidance."

"I know you'll perform admirably," said Celine. "Most

important of all, though: enjoy the experience. Nothing can compare to it!"

Jager checked to ensure all the saddle's fastenings were secure, then climbed aboard and prepared himself for flight, his heart racing. "Ready, my friend!" he called to Vin.

"Let's go!" called Celine, snug in Fianna's saddle.

Fianna crouched, then sprang into the air.

Vin followed, his powerful body and wings finding the unaccustomed weight of Jager and the saddle little more than a pleasant pressure. Jager himself was exhilarated; Celine was so right—nothing could compare to this!

As soon as Vin and Jager were clear of the ledge, Ahimoth launched himself, and in moments the happy group were winging through the moonlit sky. Jager and Celine whooped and cheered; then the three Dragons joined the aerial celebration in a jubilant Dragon-trumpet trio. The joyful noise of it echoed up and down the river valley. Those still celebrating in Dragon Hall went momentarily silent when the sound reached them—then, realizing what they were hearing, they all joined in as well.

The group flew on up the valley and came to ground at last on the broad greensward before Fianna's cave. Jager climbed down from the saddle and embraced Vin, thanking him for the fabulous experience.

"You are welcome, my Companion!" said the blue Dragon. "I believe I enjoyed it as much as you. And be assured, it was but the first of many, many flights to come." He arched his great neck round to nudge the young man with his snout, playfully rough. With that, the two male Dragons said their goodbyes and departed for Vin's cave-home.

Next morning, after a quick breakfast, Fianna bid Celine

and Jager a happy and productive day, and flew off to visit with her parents at their home near Dragon Hall. During the evening's celebration, she and Ahimoth had agreed to spend this day with them.

Once Fianna had departed, Celine dove eagerly into her work. First, she unwrapped the ancient grimoires, *The Book of Atlantis* and *The Book of Mu*, which Orgon had retrieved for her from their safe and secret repository.

Celine paused a few moments to admire the venerable volumes—and she couldn't help but reflect on all she and her friends had gone through to recover them from their ages-long hiding place on Earth. She re-wrapped the books loosely, then carried them out of the cave and across the lawn to an old tree beside the river—the spot she and Fianna considered their favorite in all the worlds. There she spread out the wrapping cloth, set the books side by side, and opened them to address the task before her. She must locate, decipher and carefully rehearse the enchantment that would extend Nibiru's shielding to shroud and safeguard distant Pax, and the Dragon Homeworlds that lay between: the Unification Ceremony.

She had just begun her search when Jager approached. "I see you've started," he said. "I won't distract you further; just wanted to let you know I'm going to be studying those cave-wall paintings you've told me so much about. I have a feeling there's something there I'm *meant* to find."

"I've the same feeling," said Celine. "Good luck!" She blew him a kiss—an Earth gesture he'd taught her (she'd deemed it "adorable")—and turned back to her studies.

Jager returned to Fianna's cave-home, lit up a light-orb, proceeded to the cave's rearmost recess, and began inspecting the largest, oldest and most elaborate of the paintings that adorned its walls. It was just as Celine had described it, and he found it fascinating. The central feature was a pair of young Humans: a fair-haired, blue-eyed boy and a green-eyed girl with chestnut tresses, just like he and Celine.

As he moved closer to examine a detail, he felt a movement of air to his right and heard a faint *whoosh*. He turned to see what had moved—and gasped. The motion he'd perceived had been the cave wall itself: it had opened inward and back, to reveal a whole new chamber, extending deep into the rocky hillside. There was no light within, so he rushed to a basket near the cave's entrance and grabbed a couple of the light-orbs stored there. Returning to the newly revealed chamber, he held the orbs aloft and gasped again. The walls were covered with paintings, and at first glance they appeared as rich in detail as the one he'd just been examining. He spent the next two hours and more in rapt wonder, studying his new discoveries.

At last he stepped away, took a moment to reflect on what he'd seen, then headed out of the cave to tell Celine of his miraculous find. Seeing that she was still completely absorbed in her own studies, he mented to Vin instead.

"That is wonderful, my Companion!" said the Dragon, when Jager had described his discoveries. "I did not know you were interested in our paintings. You must come to my cave-home soon, for many such works are to be found here as well."

"Oh!" said Jager. "I would like to do that—and soon. Celine is still searching for the proper ritual and incantations for the Unification Ceremony, but once she's found and deciphered them, she says there will be things for me to learn and practice."

"I see," said Vin. "I will come to fetch you later today, if

you like." I am enjoying a restful day, but I could use a good flight—and your company will be welcome, too."

"Okay," said Jager. "Shall I expect you this afternoon, then?"

"Yes—I will arrive there when the sun is an hour past its peak."

"Cheers," mented Jager. And, after a snack, he returned to examine more of the cave paintings. After a rapid survey of the newly revealed works, he returned to the ones that had been visible before the additional chamber had opened. There was one in particular he wanted to review, one which Celine had mentioned more than once as troubling, even frightening. It featured several red Kerr Dragons brutalizing Humans—decapitating two, and burning one at the stake. The scene was horrifying; could it be historically accurate?

Shifting his position to catch a better view, he noticed something he hadn't seen before. Near the top of the painting, partially obscured by a rock protruding from the cave's ceiling, were depicted a young man and woman. He felt certain they were the same as those shown in the large painting he'd examined earlier. Huddled beside an open fire, they had books spread before them—books he recognized: *The Book of Atlantis* and *The Book of Mu!* Examining two other scenes near the first, he saw they featured the same pair of Humans; in one, they wielded incant-batons. The second showed people of several different races gathered around the two, cheering and waving.

"Celine!" he called out and mented.

"Yes, Jager! I'm here. Is everything all right?"

"Yes, yes. Better than all right. Come quickly, if you can. There's something here you must see."

Celine carefully covered the grimoires, set a spell of protection over them, then ran to the cave to join Jager. Since she was a few centimeters shorter than he, Jager had to cup his hands to form a stirrup, then boost Celine up high enough to closely examine the scenes he'd found.

"Oh, my!" she said, awed at what the images implied. "If these mean what I think they do, you and I may be able to have a much larger effect on the wars than I ever imagined. Maybe even more than the Mentors have imagined." She hopped back down to the cave floor.

"Based on all I've learned, I have to agree," Jager replied, dusting off his hands. "Seems there's quite a future ahead of us."

"Yes. Almost overwhelming to think of it," Celine agreed.

"Which, I believe, makes this the perfect time..." he paused, looking thoughtful.

"Yes...?" encouraged Celine.

"For a swim! Race you to the river!" he laughed, and dashed toward the cave entrance.

"You...*augh!!*" she cried, racing after him. "You're impossible! Can't you ever be serious?!"

He reached the riverbank ahead of her, stripped down and dove into the cool, lazy current. She followed, just seconds behind, caught up to him and wrapped him in her arms. "I asked you a question, you goof!" she laughed.

"I heard you, I heard you," he said, "and the answer is yes. I *can* be serious." And with that he kissed her passionately. "See?"

"Yes. I *do* see!" She returned his kiss, with matching passion.

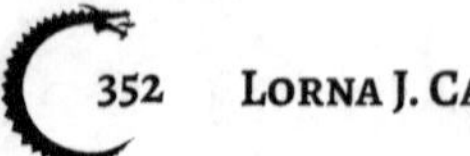

"Now listen," she said. "You won the last race, but only because you caught me by surprise. Now we're going to have a *fair* race. First one to that tree on the other bank and back to this spot wins. On three. One, two, *three!*"

Both struck out for the far bank, angling slightly against the current. Jager was a powerful swimmer, but Celine had had more practice, and her sleek form made her an absolute seal in the water. When they reached the appointed spot on the far shore, she was ahead by a length, and her lightning-quick turn extended her lead. By the time they'd returned to their starting point, Jager had nearly caught her, but still she managed to win.

They stood in the shallows, puffing and panting too hard to laugh.

"The winner!" Jager cried, grasping her wrist and raising her arm high. And then they kissed again—but with a few breaks in the action; they still hadn't entirely caught their breaths.

"Okay," Celine said at last. "Study break's over. It's back to the books for me."

"There you go, being practical again," Jager joked. "But you're right. And it's back to the walls for me." He paused. "Oh! No, it's get dressed and be ready for a Dragon flight." He told Celine about his appointment with Vin, who would be arriving in less than an hour.

"Wow! I wish I could go along," said Celine. "I'd love to see those paintings. In fact, I really *need* to see them at some point. But I can't afford the time today. The ceremony is set for tomorrow night, and I've got to be ready, obviously. I think I have the right spell, and it's quite similar to one I've used before—but I have to make sure, and then decipher it fully. And practice, too.”

“Sounds like you’re making decent progress,” said Jager, “but I understand about the time crunch. Tell you what—when I get back from Vin’s cave, which I think will be shortly after sundown, maybe I can help you.”

“That would be wonderful,” said Celine. “By that time I should be at the stage where your help would be invaluable. And you’re going to have to learn and practice your own part in the whole thing, too. So don’t be late, eh?”

“No, ma’am—I mean, pumpkin!” He gave her a peck on the cheek, snatched up his clothes and headed for the cave. Celine slipped back into her outfit and returned to her studies in earnest.

Vin arrived a short while later. Jager emerged from the cave, Omaja in hand, to see Vin spiraling down from high above and coming in for a dramatically showy landing. Jager ran to greet his friend, holding his right hand up before him, palm out. Vin laughed, raised his right forefoot, and—carefully!—slapped it against Jager’s hand in the Earther greeting the young man had taught him. Celine, watching the ritual from her study spot, laughed and shook her head. Men can be *so* silly, she thought. Earthers in particular.

“Happy studies!” Jager called to her as he clambered up into the saddle and secured his staff for the flight ahead. He gave Vin a friendly smack on the shoulder; the Dragon jumped upward, his wings pumping mightily. Once airborne, Vin circled the cave site, banking steeply. “Later!” called Jager to Celine, and the Dragon sped off toward his cave-home.

In the hours that followed, Celine verified that she’d found the correct incantation and ritual. She had it about half deciphered when Jager returned, just as the sun dipped behind a mountain range far to the west.

After warm greetings all around, Vin took his leave of the young Humans and flew homeward.

"The paintings—they're a marvel!" said Jager. "But more on those later on; how did your studies go? Where do we stand with the ceremony?"

"It's all gone smoothly," said Celine. "Better than I'd expected, really. I verified I've got the correct incantation, and it's about half deciphered now. Is your offer of help still good?"

"Of course, m'lady!" said Jager with an elaborate bow. "Let's get to work, shall we?"

The pair spent the next hour completing the deciphering process. The time flew by, and in the end they had the deciphered spell fully laid out, ready for rehearsal. They were happy to discover that Celine had all the materials they'd require, already on hand—the proper candles, salts, crystals, botanicals and so on.

"So!" she said when the work was finished, and she'd carefully stored the grimoires away, "Let's have a bit of dinner, and you can tell me about Vin's marvelous paintings."

Over a simple meal, Jager described the paintings he'd seen. He had only had time to scan them rapidly—Vin's dwelling place was more a cavern complex than a simple cave, and there were scores of paintings to be seen. One intriguing detail had caught his eye and interest, though. "One of the paintings included a little conference between the figures we assume to be ourselves—we show up a lot, as you'll see—and a couple of men. I could swear they're supposed to be Major Hadgkiss and your father. And we—the blonde male and brunette female figures—appear somehow more mature than in other paintings. It was almost as though the scene was one that hasn't happened yet. That wouldn't be too surprising, since Fianna and Orgon already explained many of the paintings are meant to show the future. But depicting Commander Zulak in the future—well, unfortunately that doesn't add up. So I figure my idea of who's being shown in that scene isn't right. I guess someday we'll find out who it really is."

"I guess so," said Celine, saddened by the reminder of her adoptive father, now lost to Soader's treachery.

"Once the ceremony's done, we should have some time to study all the paintings carefully. The ones here and the ones in Vin's cave, too. And hey, maybe Orgon knows where there are even more!"

Celine brightened at the prospect. "Adventures ahead," she said. "That's exciting. Especially if they show us how we can fend off the horrible war."

"*Especially* that," Jager agreed.

Their dinner and their day complete, they each shared a happy ment-conversation with their companion-Dragons, who were still visiting their parents. Then the pair retired to their beds and curled up for a good night's sleep. They wanted to be well, well rested for the momentous events the next day held in store.

Unification

Early on the day appointed for the Unification Ceremony, Ahimoth and Fianna sat with their parents in pleasant conversation. They had spent the previous day in much the same way.

"I would like to bring up a matter we have not touched upon," said Fianna. "It has been on my mind, but I have hesitated to mention it, for fear of spoiling our pleasant time. Now I feel I must, so that everything may be right between us before tonight's ceremony."

"Go on, daughter," said her father, "we are ever willing to hear your thoughts."

"Yes, by all means, dear," encouraged her mother.

"I thank you both," said Fianna. "The matter is simply this: I wish to apologize for marrying without your prior approval. I realize my action was a severe violation of our venerated traditions; particularly egregious because, as a member of the royal family, I should set the highest possible examples of proper conduct, for all our people. And I fear I have embarrassed you terribly! I am so deeply sorry."

"Mmm, yes," began King Neal, pausing to share a look

with Queen Dini. "It is true, we were deeply embarrassed when you presented your new husband at a public gathering, and without prior communication. It was only by your mother's quick thinking and action that we avoided an unpleasant spectacle."

"I thank you again, and hope you will accept my sincere apology," said Fianna.

"We do accept it," said Neal.

"Yes, Fianna, certainly," agreed Dini.

"Nonetheless," scolded the king, "your apology and our acceptance does not alter the fact that you have broken radically from cherished tradition. It is our traditions that bind us as a race."

Fianna straightened, ruffled herself and sighed—a mild Dragon display of dominance.

"I acknowledge the truth of what you say, Father, but I also ask that you consider these points: First, the prophesies handed down to us say that when circumstances have become sufficiently dire as to necessitate extension of Nibiru's shield to all the Dragon Homeworlds, a Dragon princess *and her spouse* shall perform the Unification Ceremony—with their *Companions* at their sides. I dare say the current threat to our worlds could scarcely be more dire; there can be no doubt we must raise the shield with all speed. Even the Mentors have proclaimed it so, and they have done and risked much to make it possible.

"It seemed clear to me that if Vin and I were to marry in the traditional way—with your consent and with the weeks of preparation that custom demands before a royal wedding, the delay would have been intolerable—potentially fatal. I consulted Vin and Ahimoth on the matter, and each agreed. We acted in the knowledge that you might not approve, and that you would have just cause to be offended and angry—but in the belief that the fate of all Dragon peoples and their homeworlds hung in the balance.

"We also agreed that, with your approval, there should still be a traditional royal wedding once the Unification Ceremony had been performed, and the imminent danger averted. To do so would honor tradition, and strengthen good will among our people. Please consider these things before censuring us further."

"Mmm," said the king. "Allow your mother and me a moment, please." Neal and Dini touched their heads together, menting privately.

"Thank you, daughter," said King Neal at last. "We have discussed the facts you present, and the reasoning you followed. Now that we understand your choice more fully, we could not be prouder of the quality of your character, and Vin's. Clearly, clearly, it reflects your deep concern for your people and your willingness to risk censure, shame and perhaps worse on their behalf, to do what you believe must be done. We commend you, and thank you from the depths of our hearts."

"Thank you, Father. And you, Mother. That is precisely how I viewed the matter; sacred and precious though our traditions may be, the lives and safety of our people come first above all. I was concerned you might not see it that way, and perhaps think me unfit to lead the people of Nibiru when the day of succession comes, as it one day must."

King Neal's ridged eyebrows shot up in surprise. "Excuse me, Daughter, but what do you mean? Ahimoth is to succeed to the throne; that has always been the plan. In fact, your mother and I have just recently brought the matter of succession before the Council, and all are agreed: we are to step down within a fortnight, passing the reign to your brother."

"I see!" said Fianna. She looked to Ahimoth. He nodded and turned to the king.

"And I see as well," he said. "I had not known you intended the succession should take place so soon. Regardless, I must tell you this: I have no wish to assume the throne."

"What?" asked Neal, the word little more than an astonished whisper. He shook his golden head and began to pace, agitated. Dini watched, anxious and at a loss for words.

"Please allow me to explain," said Ahimoth. "It has become clear to me—and I believe you will agree, when you have heard me out—that Fianna would and will be a superior leader. I have been away from our world for many long years. She has been here through all that time, living among our people, sharing their concerns, seeing their needs. Your own brother Orgon has taught and advised her at great length, while acting as Steward during your captivity on Earth. Time and time again, she has demonstrated admirable responsibility, courage, and leadership.

"Further, Fianna has a Companion; I do not. Vin, her husband-to-be, is bonded with a Companion as well. In fact, their Companions will also soon be mated. A more potent and qualified alliance for leadership I cannot imagine. I believe I may best serve our world in other ways, ways to which I am more uniquely suited."

The elder Uwattis were quiet, contemplating their son's words. Again they mented between themselves, weighing what Ahimoth had said and discussing their views, concerns and conclusions. At last they turned to their children.

"The points you have made are keenly observed and wisely considered. One among them is of particular note, when it comes to the matter of tradition: Our prophesies say that a great leader shall rise among us. That leader will rescue us all from oblivion, safeguard us against evil, outworld forces ranged against us, and lead us to great happiness and prosperity. That leader, it is said, will be bound with a Companion. Fianna and her Companion have *already* rescued us—our whole Nibiru race—from oblivion, by breaking the hex upon our precious eggs. Further, with the ceremony they are to perform this night, they will safeguard us against just such evil forces as the prophesies describe. Clearly, Fianna is the great leader of which the prophets spoke.

"To deny or ignore what is so plain would be the most foolish and foulest disregard of tradition imaginable! And so the queen and I accept what you have said, and shall proclaim and acclaim it to the Council and to all our people. None of sound mine and good will could refute it. In truth, I dare say all shall be overjoyed."

The old king bowed in deference to his son, then went to Fianna and touched each of her ivory cheeks gently with his own of burnished gold. "Daughter, forgive an old Dragon's scolding. I respect and support your decisions, and the courage it took to stand by them in the face of tradition and more. You are and shall be a legendary leader of our people."

"Thank you, Father. It is not a role I would have chosen, but my sacred responsibility in the matter is clear. I shall do everything in my power to discharge that responsibility with wisdom and courage."

The four royal Dragons gathered together in silent communion, necks entwined and Ahimoth's night-black wings wrapped far around.

When they had separated, Ahimoth broke the contemplative mood. "On a rather lighter note, I should like to make a suggestion."

Neal nodded. "Yes, my son?"

"In a few days shy of a fortnight, if I guess correctly, we shall be treated to a joyous event—the wedding of my dear sister and my stalwart comrade, Prince Vin. I suggest that we make the occasion even grander by holding a *double* wedding—by including myself and my darling bride-to-be, Joli. What say you to that?"

"I say that is *precisely* what shall be done!" cried Dini. "And I will brook no argument in the matter."

"Well, then!" said Neal, laughing. "Since there would be no use whatsoever in my objecting—and since I *have* no objection, not even the slightest—so it shall be!"

Ahimoth startled them all, and many a Dragon for kilometers around, with a joyful trumpeting.

The four royals were busily sketching out wedding plans when Celine, Jager, Joli and Vin arrived. The newcomers were moved and thrilled to learn of the momentous decisions that had been made, and a happy chatter ensued.

After a while, Celine interjected: "We have some exciting news as well." She and Jager told of the newly revealed paintings in Fianna's cave, and the significant details Jager had spotted in Vin's murals.

"Wonderful. Wonderful," said Dini. "So much is happening, so much has been revealed. For all the perils we face, these are yet exciting times." Everyone heartily agreed.

"Not to change the subject too radically, but if I may, I'd like to ask a couple of questions," said Jager.

"Yes, yes," said the king. "Please do."

"Thanks," said Jager. "They're just things that I've wondered about in the course of studying the paintings and so on. First, I understand Dragons—here on Nibiru, at least—are marvelously diligent about gathering and storing treasure. Mainly gold and silver, and a few other precious metals and gems."

"Quite so," said King Neal. The other Dragons nodded.

"Yet, as a people, you don't seem concerned with wealth. Not in the way most other societies are. Your lives appear peaceful and pastoral, with little of the competition and commerce common to worlds such as Earth and Erra, and none of the avarice. So what prompts your interest in treasure?"

"I would be glad to explain," offered Vin, "if the others here will jump in and correct me, should I stray from the facts." The other Dragons murmured agreement.

"Thank you, my friends. Now, it is my understanding that we collect and store treasure not because it represents wealth, in the sense of an abundance of means of exchange and acquisition, but rather because of the resonant properties of certain metals—chiefly gold and silver—and certain mineral crystals.

"In societies where wealth is measured in quantities of these same metals, they are referred to as 'precious,' while the crystals are called 'gems' or 'precious stones.' To be fair, we Dragons consider them precious as well, but we do not covet them. We simply collect them from wherever they may be found or acquired, and store them all together in large repositories. Treasuries, you would call them. And these treasuries are regarded as the property of all—our society as a whole—rather than of individuals.

"As I mentioned, we value these materials for their resonant properties: the ways in which each interacts with various wavelengths of energy, and also with each other when in the *presence* of such energies. Our distant ancestors discovered that their own mental and spiritual powers—powers often referred to as 'magical' or 'mystical' in more materialistic societies—could be channeled, focused, modulated and—most important of all—greatly amplified, when directed toward or through such materials. It is this which makes them precious to us. Our treasure stores enable us to control the Cynth Pedestal, for example. And to call upon the tube-chute vortex, and maintain the shielding which surrounds, penetrates and protects our world."

"Fascinating!" said Jager and Celine in unison.

"It all makes sense now," continued Jager. "I remember learning about those properties of metals and crystals. Like the crystals they use in timepieces back on Earth. Ha! Turns out to be more important and useful than I'd ever imagined! That must be how the Staff of Malek fits into the picture—I'm guessing that it resonates with the Dragon treasures too, so its Human Holder can amplify, channel and manipulate spiritual energies just as you Dragons do."

"Precisely," grinned Ahimoth.

"Hey, if that's the case, I want a staff too!" said Celine, only half joking.

"Little One," said Fianna, "it is my belief that you are unique, with regard to need of a staff such as Omaja."

"Oh? How so?"

"I believe—indeed, I have observed—that your native spiritual gifts are of such range and power that you need no

staff to work great wonders."

"And I say she's right about that," added Jager. "My skills are considerable, and I'm eternally grateful for them. But I've always stood in awe of your vision, skills and abilities, Celine. And judging from our many years of experience with the Mentors—nurturing, tutoring and coaching us—I believe they too recognize how exceptional you are."

Celine blushed deeply. "Oh. Oh, my," she said. "I...well... thank you! I suppose that might be so. I...I'll have to talk to West about this. It's an awful lot to wrap my wits around. But again, thank you."

"You know, this also explains a lot about the Unification Ceremony," said Jager, changing the subject only slightly. "It must take almost unthinkable energies to extend the shielding from Nibiru all the way to Pax. That's why the extension ceremony requires such an extraordinary consortium of power. Think of it: a Human sorceress of exceptional native power, the Dragon to whom she is bonded in Companionship, a Human sorcerer who is Holder of the Staff of Malek, and his Companion-Dragon as well—all calling upon and channeling the power of the Cynth Pedestal."

"And, as you will see," said Fianna, "all the Dragon-folk present will contribute as well."

"Oh! Even better," said Jager. He continued: "Considerable power is also required at the 'receiving end' of the process—Pax—though not as much as is needed here on Nibiru. On Pax, Jaecar's power as a sorcerer, aided by the power of the Staff he wields and Pax's Talyth Pedestal, are sufficient to receive the shielding and complete the connection."

"It is a wonder, surely," agreed Dini. "But Jager, you said you had two questions to ask of us. What was the second?"

"This one is less important, I'm sure," said Jager, "but I'm curious. You see, growing up on Earth, I sometimes heard stories of Dragons who were said to breathe fire. Studying the paintings in Fianna and Vin's caves, I noticed some Dragons depicted spouting fire from their mouths. Because it was in your paintings, and I've been told they are all either historic or prophetic, I assume there really are, or were, Dragons able to do this. Is that correct?"

"Yes, the paintings are accurate in that regard," said Ahimoth. "And in fact, both Vin and I have the ability."

"Oh! Then I've asked the right people," laughed Jager. "But my real question is, how do they—or rather, how do *you*—do it?"

"Our breath weapon is not a matter of magic, though some have thought it so," began Ahimoth. "Instead, it is the product of biology and evolution. First, I am sure you are aware that most carbon-based bodies such as yours and ours produce methane gas, as a byproduct of digestion."

"Yes," said Jager. "Sometimes I'm embarrassingly aware of that." Celine rolled her eyes. *He can be such a kid sometimes,* she thought.

"Very good," said Ahimoth. "And as you suggested just now, the gas may be released at either end of the digestive tract. As it happens, some Dragons—usually larger males— have a pair of special pouches or reservoirs situated above the digestive organs and within the rib cage. In these they can store methane and release it through the mouth, at will. There is also a gland in the roof of the mouth which contains phosphor. We are able to expel small amounts of phosphor from this gland, also at will."

"Remarkable!" said Jager. "I think I see how this works,

then. May I tell you, to see if I have it right?"

"Certainly," said Ahimoth.

"So, you store up methane in the reservoirs. When you want to make a flame, you release a burst of methane through the mouth, and simultaneously expel a bit of phosphor. Or perhaps you expel the phosphor a second or two before the methane, so it has a chance to come in contact with air before the methane arrives. Anyway, since phosphor combusts on contact with air, it would ignite the passing jet of methane, and you'd have a gout of flame."

"Exactly so," said Ahimoth. "I am impressed."

"As am I!" added Vin. "Dragons who have this capability, and anticipate reason to use it, also undergo training to sharpen their skill at producing flames. With practice, we can control the intensity of the flame, modulate the size of the burst—making it broad and diffuse or quite narrow and focused—and a few other aspects."

"Yes," said Ahimoth, "and by selectively eating certain things, we can even choose the color of the flames. This can make for some impressive displays, as I am sure you can imagine."

"I can!" said Jager.

"A related fact of interest is that when a Dragon is undernourished to the point of near-starvation, the fire-breath mechanism ceases to function. This is why Dragons held in captivity are often cruelly underfed. Soader occasionally did this to both Vin and me, during our captivity on Earth."

"Fascinating," said Jager. "Thank you both for explaining all this."

"You are welcome, my friend," said Ahimoth.

"Yes! Or, as I believe you might say it, 'you bet,'" said Vin, smiling.

"Brother, I had not known you could be such a fine instructor," said Fianna. "I am impressed."

Ahimoth made a dramatic bow, and the whole group shared a laugh.

"Come to think of it," said Jager, "the painting I saw in Vin's cave—the one depicting the Unification Ceremony—included a couple of Dragons doing some impressive fire-spouting, or breathing, or whatever it's properly called. Is that part of your role in tonight's ritual?" he asked Vin and Ahimoth.

"Yes, it is," said Ahimoth. "In fact, though we had breakfast not long ago, Vin and I are obliged to take our leave of you all, for a little while. We have some selective eating to do, for that very purpose. Quite a lot, actually!"

"You are excused, of course. Your devotion to duty is ever so admirable," said Fianna, with a wry smile. The rest agreed, laughing.

"I believe we all have matters to attend to," she continued, "in connection with the ceremony. Shall we go our ways now, and gather again this evening for a final rehearsal of our various parts?"

All agreed, and departed. All except Vin, who told Ahimoth he wished to speak with Fianna, and would catch up with him shortly to discharge their selective dining duties. When Ahimoth had gone, Vin spoke to his bride. "Beloved, I sense you are troubled by something. Can you tell me about it?"

"You are quite right, my dear. For some time, I have been growing increasingly sad about the prospect of separation from my Companion. Celine and I have become so incomparably close, you see. We have spent nearly all of our time together for more than a year now. Having passed through so many intense and harrowing challenges—as well as delights and triumphs—has reinforced our bond, making the thought of separation even more painful. And though she has not mentioned it outright, I believe Celine has similar concerns.

"Once you and I have been traditionally wed here on Nibiru, we will naturally begin to spend much time away from others, including our Companions. When Celine and Jager are married, they will wish to do the same. And they shall no doubt return to their lives and duties beyond Nibiru, at least for considerable periods. There is nothing inherently bad or wrong in this—it is natural and proper. Nonetheless, it will mean far less of the closeness I have become accustomed to—the physical proximity and the shared experience alike.

"You have been bonded with Jager for only a short time—but it is plain to see that your bond is beautifully close and strong. And so I fear that you too will be saddened at separation from him. I hate to be one who worries, for worry is neither productive nor effective. Yet I worry still, and know not what to do."

"I understand completely," said Vin, "and I must admit the thought of distance from Jager has troubled me as well, young though our Companionship may be. There is so much to explore between us, so much to learn and to do. And so I have thought on this, and believe I may have a solution—one that could work for you and me both, and for our Companions."

"Oh! That is wonderful," said Fianna. "What is it?"

"Quite simply this: When you and I have made a home

together, and Celine and Jager have wed, we should make a pact between us: whenever we are all on Nibiru—or all together visiting Earth or perhaps other worlds—we will make time each day to commune, each with our Companion-person, and hold that custom inviolable. I believe this custom would evolve naturally in any case, but I think it important to make an outright declaration of it, and solemn agreements."

"That seems quite sensible and proper," said Fianna, "and I believe it will alleviate the difficulty to some extent—though not fully. There still must be times of physical closeness, don't you think?"

"Indeed I do," said Vin, "which brings me to the second part of my suggested solution. I believe we should plan regular and frequent visits and activities—again, when we are all together on a planet. Some activities with all four together, others in Companion-pairs, separate. And we should make this custom similarly inviolable among us. Study and learning together, flight training and practice, hunting and dining, journeys to favorite places and exploring others we have never seen, gatherings with family and mutual friends, acts of service to our communities. And just as important as any of those activities, there should be times—days or even weeks—without specific plan or purpose beyond Companion-company and communion.

"Not all such sharing times would necessarily be preplanned; some, even many, might be spontaneous. In any case, with a solid foundation of agreement among us, I believe we will evolve a workable system or pattern to guarantee sufficient Companion-time to nurture and deepen our precious connections, to our own benefits and to the benefit of our peoples. In the case of the latter—that is, benefit to our peoples—I believe that as Companion-pairs we bear a sacred responsibility to share the spiritual wealth our connections make possible."

Fianna remained silent, regarding her mate with loving admiration. "How beautifully devised and expressed," she said at last. "Simple as it is, I know in my soul that the plan you suggest will succeed. And I know in my soul that I am truly blessed to have you as a friend and life-mate. Thank you, my dear." She embraced him, kissed him gently on the cheek, then held him, close and quiet, for a long, warm time.

Celine, who had gone to Dragon Hall to make final preparations for the coming ceremony, mented to Fianna. "When you are ready, we can begin our rehearsal," she said. "I've finished my inventory of the items we'll need. It's lucky I did—I discovered my supply of one of the essential herbs had lost its full potency. I was absolutely distraught! Seriously—I was in tears over it when I went to ask Tamar and Orgon if they knew where I might find more. Pretty embarrassing. But they calmed me down, and dear Tamar assured me she knew where a fresh supply could be had. And even offered to bring me some. So kind of her! So, I have everything together now. I'll review the incantation and practice it a bit more until you arrive. Oh—Jager, Vin and Ahimoth have parts to play as well, but it will be an hour or so before we need them for rehearsal. I promised I would ment Jager when the time comes, and he will tell Ahimoth and Vin."

"Thank you, Little One. I will join you momentarily. Vin and I have had a most productive chat, and now I am anxious to rehearse. I confess I have the...what is it you say? The jinners? No, jitters! It is such a momentous event, and I am determined to play my part perfectly."

"You will! I don't have a worry in the world about that,"

said Celine. "See you soon, then!" And she opened her notes, careful and detailed, to review the ceremony—for perhaps the twentieth time.

Minutes later, Fianna arrived. Celine jumped up to greet her, and they discussed how they would proceed. Fianna retired to a corner to review and rehearse her portions of the incantation. Meanwhile, Celine meticulously swept the area, beginning at the Cynth Pedestal and moving outward and outward in a great spiral that eventually embraced the entirety of the hall. She did this not so much to clean it—it was already nearly immaculate—but to commune with the space and further ground and align herself in its energy fields and flows.

Vin, Jager and Ahimoth arrived at the appointed time, and Celine supervised their final rehearsal, with Fianna performing her role as well. In response to a question from Jager, Celine explained that before she had left the Mentor outpost, West had briefed Jaecar, on Pax, on their plans. He knew the appointed date and time—expressed in terms of local time on Pax—and how to prepare for his own role in the proceedings.

West had assured Celine that when the time came, Jaecar would be in position at the Talyth Pedestal, Zulema in hand and thoroughly coached and practiced in his role. "You and your fellows on Nibiru will know the ceremony is a success," the Mentor had explained, "when Jaecar greets you all, across the light-years that lie between your worlds. A moment you shall never forget, I assure you!"

Now the hour was nearly upon them, and all was in readiness. Jager was surprised to find himself a trifle nervous. He had never participated in anything like this, nor had he ever had to perform in *any* way before hundreds of Dragons!

Celine ran him through his role once more, and his jitters subsided—though he had an inkling that the sudden calming may have had something to do with the faint, faint, lulling vibration and almost imperceptible emerald glow Omaja had begun emitting, part-way through the final rehearsal. "Hm!" he said aloud, "Thank you, Omaja. I think!" A fleeting, sky-blue twinkle from the tip of the staff's head confirmed his suspicion. The staff *was* helping him. The Staff of Malek was, in fact, his partner.

Earlier, Celine had used colored salt and sand to mark out a broad circle. The Cynth Pedestal was situated near the "back" of the circle—the portion closest to what was considered the rear wall of Dragon Hall's open-air meeting space. Several meters in front of the pedestal, beneath a burnished metal tripod nearly a meter in height, a ceremonial fire burned bright. Fueled by aged, oil-infused wood of particularly high density, its flames could be counted upon to continue for hours—more than enough time to complete the ceremony.

The five participants seated themselves at pre-assigned positions within the circle to await the midnight hour in quiet meditation. Soon the Dragon-folk began to arrive. In silent respect, they ranged themselves all 'round, outside the ceremonial circle, until the entirety of Dragon Hall was filled to overflowing. Only Celine and her four fellow participants would occupy the circle-space until the ceremony's conclusion.

Late arrivals, seeing no room on the floor of the hall, settled into niches and ledges in the surrounding craggy walls. They had traveled far to take part in the historic event, and take part they would!

When the hour of midnight was some fifteen minutes

away, Fianna called out for attention. The hundreds of gathered Dragons were silent at once, and stone-still—save for those few shifting this way and that for a better view.

"The hour is upon us!" Fianna announced. "Let the Unification Ceremony begin!" She turned away from the crowd to give Celine her undivided attention.

Celine walked gracefully to the center of the circle and set down her bodypack beside the fire. She opened the pack and drew out a length of shimmering fabric, loaned her by West, and draped it round her shoulders in the manner of a long, elegant shawl. Reaching nearly to her ankles, it gently billowed and flowed with her every movement, as though it were a living part of her.

She stood, turned to face Fianna, and nodded. The Dragon princess began a low, rhythmic chant, quickly taken up by all the watching Dragons.

Turning back to her pack, Celine withdrew a lengthy series of items—one at a time, careful and deliberate. She regarded each for a moment and turned it in her hands, as if to acknowledge its existence and importance before laying it neatly aside.

From among the arrayed items she selected a dozen candles of varied sizes and colors, then crossed to where Jager stood, a few meters away and to the left of the fire. After bowing to him, she distributed the candles in a circle around the young man, lighting each as she went. She returned to the fireside, selected another dozen candles and distributed them in a matching circle, at the same distance from the fire as Jager's, but to its right. Finally, she made a third candle-circle, twice as wide as the first two, around the fire itself.

All the while, the Dragons' chant rose gradually in tone

and intensity, and resonated throughout the stone-walled Hall.

Next, Celine picked out a leather water-sack and a small metal cauldron from among the remaining array of objects. Placing the cauldron next to the fire, she filled it from the sack, then set it in the ring at the apex of the fire-tripod—a perfect fit.

As the water heated, she took up a tiny satchel of dried herbs and placed a few pinches of its contents in a shallow bowl. She did the same with another satchel, then another and another, until the bowl contained more than a dozen different herbs, leaves and flower petals—some rare, some quite common and familiar. Thyme, frankincense, rosemary, myrrh, golden turmeric and more. Each had been known from antiquity for its remarkable qualities; now they intermixed to produce a powerful synergy found nowhere in the natural world.

With the tip of her incant-baton she stirred the herbal mixture, careful and slow, murmuring an incantation all the while. Finally, she sprinkled a generous amount of the powdery compound into the steaming cauldron, then shook the bowl around and about the fire to scatter the remainder into the flames. Smoke and steam arose from fire and cauldron, filling the hall with a heady scent.

Celine turned to face the wall beyond the Cynth Pedestal. Taking a wide stance, she raised her incant-baton toward a spot a few meters above its base. Her high, clear young voice rang out with a seven-word phrase in the tongue of ancient Mu. A tremor rocked the Hall, but the Dragons continued their chant without missing a beat. When the tremor had passed, a circular opening appeared, like a tiny, black eye, precisely at the spot Celine had indicated with her incant-baton. The aperture grew, upward and outward, until it was some fifteen meters across and a dozen high. Whatever lay beyond the opening was shrouded in darkest shadow.

Then dozens of light-orbs scattered within burst to life, revealing a smooth-walled, hemispherical cavern. Heaped from front to back and side to side were masses, mountains and mounds of treasure. Chiefly gold and silver, but scattered with other metals and with gems of all sizes, colors and kinds, it was an unimaginably dazzling display. Though many of the Dragons carried on the chanting, many more could not help themselves: at the sight of the vast trove, they gasped or cried out. Then, quickly recovering themselves, they rejoined the chant.

Celine turned to face the gathering once more. She raised her hands before her, palms together, the incant-baton pressed between them and pointing skyward. Closing her eyes, she bowed her head for a long moment, then looked serenely up again. It was time to begin the final incantation.

"Please quiet them now, dear friend," she mented to Fianna.

The Dragon spread her white wings briefly for attention. Then, with her forelegs and claws, she motioned to her assembled people in a gesture familiar to any Dragon: "quiet, quiet." At the same time, she reduced her own chanting to a hum.

Those who'd immediately grasped what she wanted began to hum too; soon everyone had gotten the idea, and only humming could be heard in Dragon Hall. The rhythm and intonation were the same, but words were absent and the sound soft and low.

Now Celine began her incantation, paced and intoned so the Dragons' humming served as a complement, a perfect background.

Gods and Goddesses of the light
Righteous rulers of day and night
True protectors of Dragons and Men
From time's beginning unto its end
Bless their families and all their friends
Unite their souls and bless their gens
Bless my words and make them strong
Join the Homeworlds with this song

North and East and South and West
Four who keep and guard us best
Sisters four to bless our lives
And see that life here e'er survives
Strengthen our bonds and guard our homes
Link our hearts wherever they roam
Link our worlds and all our souls
Help us succeed and gain our goals
Spirit of Light, Spirit of Dark
Worlds are scattered, fallen apart
Our lives are broken our homes unsafe
Save us please, as you might a waif

Dragons of this, and Homeworlds far
Angels of wisdom, powers of the stars
Vanquish hatred, empower love
Keep us safe from evils above

Pausing a moment before moving on to the next portion of the incantation, Celine added a new element: her skill of forging a mental image so complete that it gradually became manifest in the physical universe. The image she created was the ceremony's ultimate objective—an impenetrable shield-barrier stretching from Nibiru to Pax. Her pause was also a cue, both for Fianna and for Jager.

Fianna's part was now to form a mental image—to see it in her mind's eye—matching the one Celine had created. Once she had done so, she reached out to all the Dragons present, urging them to join with her: to see the vivid image in their own minds' eyes.

Jager turned to face the Cynth Pedestal, feet wide apart, and held Omaja at arm's length, straight before him and shoulder high. When Celine began the chant again, he added his voice to the rite, and shared in Celine's visualization of the transworld shield.

We cast three circles close about
To keep all evil spirits out
And chant our spell anew this time
With words and music joined sublime
To bring together worlds, and shield
Against all those who swords would wield

Great Pax, Nibiru, lands between
Save all our people and kings and queens
Goddesses of Love, Gods of War
Unite our spirits, permit them soar
Bind all together in love of light
Pax to Nibiru, day to night

As Jager and Celine chanted in unison—and to the amazement of one and all—a spiral of glowing gems and flashing metal discs emerged along Omaja's full length, pulsing in rhythm with the chant. Then, at the end of one phrase, a burst of blue-white light flashed from the great staff's head. As if in answer, a glow arose from the massed treasures within the gaping cavern, pulsing in perfect synchrony.

Like a symphony, thought Jager, a fantastic symphony of sight, sound, energy and spirit.

The incantation flowed onward.

We have a bond which shall not bend
Our loved ones cherished to the end
Guardians of life and love and spirit
Gird our souls that we may ne'er fear it

Let our future be ever fast united
Filled with love, with no hopes blighted
Cast out all hatred, send it far
With power of planets, moons and stars

Bind tightly now our worlds in love
Confound all who'd strike from above
Let our eternal love and affection
Empower this shielding, life's protection

Bless our families, comrades, friends
Unite our souls and all our gens
Now bless my words and make them strong
Join all our worlds with this, my song

When she perceived that all present held the crucial image firmly and vividly in place, Celine sang out the rite's final phrase.

At the sound of it, three events occurred at once.

Ahimoth and Vin stretched skyward, opened their great jaws, and sent towering blasts of red-yellow flame toward the stars.

At the same moment, Jager struck the stone floor with Omaja's base; a bolt of blue-white energy leapt from the staff's head to join the Dragons' flames.

From the Cynth Pedestal, a blazing beam of golden light flashed skyward, intertwining with the others.

The four shafts of energy, now joined as one, activated Nibiru's vortex, opening the wormhole—or "tube-chute," as the Dragons called it: in an interplanetary link, from Nibiru to Pax, that transcended "normal" physical space and time.

On far-off Pax, Jager's twin Jaecar stood beside his world's own Pedestal of Power, Talyth. He raised his staff, Zulema—a

mirror-image of Omaja—toward the heavens, and sang out the same phrase Celine had just uttered. Bolts of energy burst at once from Zulema's head and from Talyth, melding together to form a single energy-shaft, flaring skyward.

A high, piercing, warbling sound filled the plaza around the Talyth Pedestal. Jaecar shook his head at the shock of it, but still held Zulema high. Then, for a fleeting moment, it seemed to Jaecar as though the universe itself had disappeared. There was only black, dead-silent nothing, and less than nothing.

When the world reappeared, all seemed just as it had been. But then Jaecar looked up to behold what appeared to be a swirling, scintillating disc of liquid light and color, some seven meters above him. It was the mouth of the vortex—and into it poured the energy still streaming from his staff's head and from the pedestal at his side.

From out of the vortex came a second shaft of energy—all the way from Nibiru via the tube-chute—to intertwine and unite with the bolt Jaecar had conjured. The energies comingled for a long moment, and then another and another, until, with a deceptively tiny *"pop!"* and the merest blink of bright white, they were one: a single energy beam stretching—in "normal" physical space now—from Pax to Nibiru.

Then, in an instant, the beam began to expand outward, as though it were a sort of tube or pipe formed of energy, growing and growing in diameter. It expanded slowly at first, then faster and faster until it encompassed all of the Talyth Pedestal's plaza upon Pax, and the whole of Dragon Hall on Nibiru.

But the expansion did not stop there. It continued on and on, out and out, until it extended for thousands of kilometers around both planets. As it crossed the vast gulf of space between them, it bulged to far, far greater diameters, until it was precisely wide enough at its center point to enclose all the Dragon Homeworlds, strung through space like brilliant beads, between Pax and Nibiru. This was the Shield: the goal and object of the Unification Ceremony.

On Pax, Jaecar looked up to see that the vortex's mouth had transformed utterly: What had been a bewildering-beautiful whirlpool of liquid light and color was now a simple, circular window. And through that window he could see, as though they were in an adjoining room, Jager, Celine, and…Dragons. Many, *many* Dragons.

In Dragon Hall, the events had been the same: the union of the energy shafts, the forming of the shield, and the transformation of the vortex from wonder-thing to window.

"Greetings, Brother!" came Jaecar's voice from the vortex-window. "Greetings, Celine! And greetings to all of you good Dragon-folk as well!"

"Greetings!" shouted Jager and Celine.

The pair turned to the watching Dragons. Shouting to be heard by all, Jager said, "Dragons of Nibiru! You see before you, within the vortex-window, my brother Jaecar—Holder of the staff Zulema and regent of the planet Pax. It is only with his help, and that of the power invested in Zulema and the Talyth Pedestal, that we—all of us here, yourselves included—have raised the Shield. Nibiru is now more powerfully protected than ever. Pax now falls within that protection as well—as do *all* the Dragon Homeworlds. Would you extend your greetings to my dear brother, who is your friend?"

"GREETINGS!" the Dragons roared, with a noise that shook the Hall and rolled like thunder across all the country around.

"Thank you, dear friends!" called Jaecar. "We are now well protected. And I say that from this day forward we shall conceive and perform great works together, Dragons and Humans alike, to the benefit of all."

"Let it be so!" shouted Celine and Jager.

"Let it be so!" roared Princess Fianna and Prince Vin.

"Let it be so!" roared Prince Ahimoth and the beautiful Joli.

"Let it be so!" roared King Neal and Queen Dini.

"LET IT BE SO!" roared all the Dragons of Nibiru, and the Hall and hills shook once more.

Knowing the vortex could vanish at any moment, Celine and Jager hastened to thank Jaecar. They promised to visit him again on Pax, as soon as they possibly could. He was in the midst of acknowledging them when the vortex winked out of existence.

Ah, well, Jaecar thought to himself, I'm sure I'll be seeing them soon. The Talyth Pedestal was quiet and cool now, as though nothing unusual had occurred. He gingerly tapped Zulema's polished head, but she too was cool. Amazing, he thought, recalling the torrents of raw energy that had streamed from pedestal and staff just minutes before. With a smile, he turned toward his residence and strolled casually home, his customary entourage close behind.

When the vortex vanished, Jager and Celine shared a look, then turned to watch the spectacle around them. The Dragons were cheering and trumpeting, stamping and dancing in elation and gratitude.

The young Humans feared the sheer volume of it would

bring the high, stony walls down upon them all. Thankfully, Dragon Hall was up to the sonic buffeting of its jubilant people. It simply echoed their joy and sent it on up to the skies.

Later, someone asserted the happy din that night could be heard across all the light-years to Pax, and on the Homeworlds between. The story was repeated, and soon took its place among Nibiru's cherished folk tales. From time to time, some scholarly Dragon or other would point out—almost apologetically—that such a thing was physically impossible. But still the tale was told, retold, and retold again, on down the centuries. The Dragon peoples love their legends and lore.

CHAPTER 36

Moving Day

Quade had made good his promise to prepare his people. They were ready—the Dragons themselves, and the few indispensable, cherished, or sacred items they intended to take along to their new home.

As all Dragon peoples do, the Remini tribes had amassed great troves of treasure through the centuries. These they would leave behind on their beloved homeworld. This was not a matter of concern for the Dragons, though. Their treasuries were both physically hidden and spiritually shrouded—so thoroughly that they could not be located by any means Remini's Humans possessed. Further, the planet was not "on anyone's charts" as a potential treasure source. In fact, Remini was so obscure and technologically backward as to be almost completely unknown to anyone off-world. The Dragons rightly felt their stores would be safe until they could return to retrieve them.

Early the next day, Madda returned in *Spitfire*, with a freighter close behind. After a briefing from Madda, the freighter crew jumped to the task of making their cargo holds as safe and comfortable as possible for the Dragon passengers soon to arrive. Meanwhile, Madda contacted Dino aboard *King Hammurabi* and briefed him on the results of her trip.

"I brought one freighter back, and they're now preparing to take on Dragon passengers. The bad news is, only one other ship is available—and it won't arrive until roughly twenty-four hours from now. Its capacity is only a bit better than the one that came with me."

"Hells, it's practically a miracle you were able to get any ships at all," said Dino, "but with only two, we've got a serious situation. Even with both ships, there's nowhere near enough room to take everyone to Earth at once. We'll have to make multiple trips. And the transbeaming at both ends—loading here and unloading at Earth—adds a whole lot of time. I can't see any way we're going to be able to get everyone off this planet before the Humans launch their assault. We'll just have to go as fast as we can, and hope for the best."

They exchanged a look. Both knew that without some sort of miraculous intervention, some of Remini's Dragons would not reach safety before the Humans' attack.

"Maybe I could bring in some firepower," mused the major.

Madda looked dubious.

"No, I know what you're thinking, and you're right," said Dino. "That would make it a Fleet action, requiring Fleet's cooperation, and they would never agree. And I can't just secretly 'borrow' some gunships and munitions. Every Fleet vessel's movements are automatically recorded in detail—and so is every use of its weaponry. Everyone involved would be toast, no matter how noble the cause might be. We're dangerously close to being toast already—we've been pushing

   Lorna J. Carleton

the envelope to the limit. And beyond."

"That's the truth," said Madda, worried.

"Okay, so we're back to 'go as fast as we can and hope for the best,'" said Dino. "And who knows? Maybe something else will turn up."

Madda called the freighter's captain for an update, and the two worked out the details of the onboarding process. Meanwhile, Dino transbeamed down to the Dragons' mountain stronghold to supervise the operation there.

Within an hour, the freighter's captain reported to Madda that her ship and crew were ready to accept passengers. After praising the captain's quick work, Madda called Dino to relay the news; she was mid-sentence when suddenly everything went...*weird*.

Madda was in total, soundless darkness, utterly numb. She had no perception of her own body, the ship that bore her, nothing. And then, after what seemed like a few moments—or was it hours? days?—and just as suddenly as it had begun, the eerie blankness ended. All her perceptions returned, and everything seemed just as it had been. A faint hiss told her the comm-link connection to Dino was live. "Major?" she said.

"I'm here," he replied. "Did you feel that?"

"Yes, sir," she said. "Most unusual."

"That's putting it mildly. I've got a bunch of bewildered Dragons down here; whatever it was seems to have affected them too. Any idea what happened?"

"None, sir. I'm running a systems analysis, but so far there's nothing to see. Not even a gap in the time record. It's as though everything stopped, including time, then restarted. There's not even any way to tell how long the...the interruption? Well, whatever it was, I don't know how long it lasted. It *seemed* just momentary."

"Right. But of course that's totally subjective—a matter of what we felt or thought we experienced. Well, no sense worrying about it now. Everything seems okay, so let's just get on with the mission. What were you saying?"

Madda continued her report. "Standing by to begin trans-beaming passengers on your order," she concluded.

Hours later, the first contingent of Dragons was aboard, and the freighter's crew was busy making sure they were all secure and as comfortable as possible, ready for the jump-shift to Earth. The strange "interruption" hadn't repeated.

"Major," Madda said over the comm link, "the freighter captain reports ready for jump-shift."

"Excellent," said Dino. "Please relay my compliments and thanks. Tell her to proceed, and..." he paused. The comm link was blinking purple, signaling an urgent call incoming. "Just a moment, Madda," he said. "I've got an urgent call incoming. No idea what it's about. Stand by, please."

"Aye, sir." She broke the connection.

Dino addressed the comm link: "Accept." The purple light flicked to green. "Hadgkiss."

"Major, this is Ensign Cornwallis."

"Jager! Where are you?"

"On Nibiru, sir. What a relief. Wasn't sure I'd be able to reach you with just a comm pickup. I assume you're on Remini—is that correct?"

"Yes I am. But if you're on Nibiru, how can you have gotten through to me *at all?*"

"I'll explain, sir. But first I have some excellent news."

"Go ahead."

"Yes, sir. It's this: the Dragon Homeworlds are now all shrouded and shielded. Just like Nibiru. In fact, they're all inside the same shield—we extended Nibiru's shielding to cover them all."

"That's an interesting development," said the major. "Later I'll let you explain how you managed that, but first tell me: would Remini happen to be one of these 'Dragon Homeworlds' you're talking about?"

"Yes, sir. Nibiru, Remini, one called Kerr and several more—I'm not sure how many, or what they're all called."

"Hm! That must explain why you could reach me. Normally our comms wouldn't work with you inside Nibiru's shielding."

"Exactly, sir."

"One more thing: When did this extension of the shielding happen?"

"Just a few hours ago."

"Ah! That might explain something extremely odd that happened here, about that same time. I can't even explain it well in words. It was as though the universe...well, disappeared. Everything went black, and time was suspended. Maybe it was an effect of the shield going up."

"That sounds odd all right," said Jager. "Maybe West can explain it later."

"Yes, maybe so. But listen, Ensign, this might solve a nasty problem. We're currently loading Dragons into a transport vessel, to take them to Earth. From there they're supposed to travel through that wormhole 'conduit' phenomenon to Nibiru. Your friend Fianna invited them—the whole blasted population."

"Yes, she told us about that. Great to know it's happening—and I'm not at all surprised to learn you're involved. She didn't tell us that part!"

Dino laughed. "These Dragons certainly keep things close to their chests, don't they? But here's my thought: If Remini is now inside the shield, couldn't we make a direct jump-shift, Remini to Nibiru?"

"I don't know why you couldn't," said Jager. "That would be fantastic—it would mean the Dragons wouldn't have to go through the chute. We've been worried sick about that. It's an awful experience, and it can be extremely dangerous for young Dragons."

"Well, that's good," said Dino. "It occurs to me we've still got a huge problem, though. We only have one ship of any size, and more than four hundred Dragons to transport. Another freighter arrives here tomorrow, but if Remini is now shielded, they won't be able to find the place. And even if they could, how would they take Dragons aboard? If regular comms can't get through the shielding, the transbeam won't work either. So essentially the second ship will be useless. And if we can only use one ship, there's no way we can get everyone off planet within the time we have left. Anyone we can't bring aboard will be slaughtered."

"Slaughtered?!" cried Jager.

"That's right," said Dino, and he quickly sketched out the situation they faced—the impending attack, which he was in no position to repel.

"Understood, Major," said Jager. "I see the urgency."

"If only there were some way to bypass this shielding," said Dino.

"Come to think of it," replied Jager, "I believe there may be a way to do exactly that."

"Oh! Tell me," said Dino.

"In learning how to extend the shield using Omaja—the... well, I guess you'd say 'magical' staff I recently acquired—there was a mention of also using it to manipulate the shield in a localized area. I'll have to go look at the materials I studied to get the exact details, but if I understood correctly, I ought to be able to create a small opening in the shielding field—just big enough for a ship to pass through. That would mean we could let your second freighter through the shield, load it up on Remini, then fly it here."

"All right," said Dino. "And since no one knows where 'there' is—Nibiru's location—I'll have to home on your comm pickup signal to navigate, and escort the freighter."

"Right," said Jager. "Madda should be able to do the same, escorting the first ship. You can both shuttle back and forth between Remini and Nibiru for as many runs as it takes to get all the Dragons to safety. Once they're all here, we pay the freighter crews handsomely—I'm certain Fianna will be more than willing to take care of that—swear them to secrecy, thank them for their service, open the shield again and send them on their way."

"That sounds quite workable," said Dino. "It's still going to be much tighter than I even like to think about, but I don't see any way to make it faster."

"Understood," said Jager. "If I think of anything at all, I'll call at once. In any case, there's one more element to deal with. Security. They're going to be flying to Nibiru, which means their nav computers and ship's logs will end up with records of its location."

"Correct," said Dino. "I'm pleased you thought of that."

"Well trained," said Jager. "By you, Fleet Academy, and West too."

"And what's your solution in this case?" asked Hadgkiss.

"Once the operation is complete and we're ready to release the freighters, you and Madda board them and wipe all record of the Dragon flights from their systems."

"Very good, Ensign," said Dino. "Anything else?"

"Hmm. Yes. Before each ship begins its first Remini-Nibiru transit, I would install some code to prevent anyone aboard from accessing or copying any coordinates or route information *during* the operation, too.

"And when the job is done and we're ready to send the freighters on their way, we wipe their records as I said before, but we also program their nav systems ourselves, so they're jump-shifted to some neutral location. In the end, even if one of the freighter people wanted to break their oath of silence, it would be impossible to find their way back to Nibiru, or tell anyone else how to get here."

"Well conceived," said Dino. "We'll have to wipe the records aboard *King* and *Spitfire,* too."

"Roger that," said Jager. "Now, can you tell me how soon the first 'shipment' will be ready to send?"

"They're ready now," said Dino. "In fact, I was half a second from sending them to Earth when you called me."

"Whew! That was close," said Jager. "Glad I got to you in time. I'm guessing it will take me a good while to verify I can open the shield for that second ship. But you mentioned they won't arrive at Remini until tomorrow, so that shouldn't be a problem. Meanwhile, Madda could board the first ship and install that security code, then escort them on the first transfer run."

"All right," said Dino. "I'll get her onto it. You'll need to establish a comm connection with her too, so she can home on your comm pickup."

"Roger that," said Jager. "I'll do so right away. Then I'd better go tell the Dragons here they're about to have company. After that, I've got some fast studying to do!"

The jump from Remini to Nibiru went smoothly, though many of the Dragon passengers would have disagreed. None had ever experienced the wholly alien sensations and disorientations of the jump-shift drive in action.

Once *Spitfire* and the freighter were safely in orbit above Nibiru, Madda called to Jager. "We've arrived, Ensign, and we'll be ready to begin passenger transfer to the surface within the hour. Where shall we send them?"

Fianna had arranged for temporary shelter near Dragon Hall for all the newcomers; Jager sent Madda the coordinates, then mented Celine, Fianna and Vin with the good news.

"Thank the Ancients!" replied Celine.

"Indeed," said Fianna. "It is a miracle."

Soon the transfer process began. The Dragons were transbeamed down a few at a time, owing to their great size and the limited capacity of the transbeam equipment. Fianna, Ahimoth, Vin, Joli and a host of others were there to welcome them. They kept their welcome calm and gentle—the newcomers had been through month after dreadful month of fear, violence and loss on their homeworld. All but a few had been forced from their homes there. Many had lost loved ones to the marauding Humans. Many more had been injured. Nearly all were malnourished, dehydrated or both. Every last one was heartbroken at being driven from their beloved Remini.

As the transfer progressed, the freighter's crew grabbed any opportunity they could to catch a glimpse of the forbidden planet below, on monitors or from the ship's few small viewports. Other than Celine and Jager, they were the only off-worlders to look upon Nibiru since centuries past.

Each arriving Dragon was given individual care, and attention to their most immediate needs. There was plenty of nourishing food and fresh, clean water for all. The ill and injured were given medical care. The grieving and heartsick had sympathetic listeners to lend an ear and offer comfort.

Once any pressing needs had been met, they were led to shelter, safe, warm and dry. The local community had opened their hearts and homes to welcome the refugees and ease the transition to life in a new world. Space had been made for them in cave-homes along the river valley, upriver and down from Dragon Hall, and in the surrounding hills and valleys. When all the Reminis had arrived and had a chance to rest and recover, they would be moved to homes of their own in a peaceful, verdant river valley less than a half-day's flight away.

The following morning, Jager received a call from Dino, aboard *King Hammurabi*. The second freighter had arrived; earlier than expected, to the major's great relief. However, the presence of the shield presented a knotty new problem. Hadgkiss could see outward through the shielding, and his instruments could detect the freighter—but its captain and crew couldn't detect *him*, or the planet they'd been told was their destination. To make matters worse, there was no way for them to contact the major, and no way for him to reach them and explain. The freighter's people were perplexed. Was this all a hoax or trap of some sort? Had they been given the wrong coordinates, or made an error in navigation?

Dino sketched out the situation; Jager grasped it at once. "That's a rough one," he said. "But fortunately I finished up my studies and worked out how to manipulate the shield. With a lot of help from Celine, Fianna and old Orgon, I should add. It's easiest if I'm positioned at the Cynth Pedestal here to make it work. I'll explain what that is later on. Anyway, I'm at the pedestal now—been here since last night, in case you called."

"Excellent work, Ensign," said Dino, proud of his young protégé. "Now, how fast can you open the shield? I don't want these people to give up and jump-shift out of here before I can tell them they've come to the right place."

"Give me two minutes," said Jager. "I've gotten myself into position while we've been talking, Omaja is awake and ready, and the incantation is a short one."

"Standing by," said the major.

Holding Omaja high, Jager assumed the proper position near the Cynth Pedestal, and chanted the shield-manipulation spell. Bursts of light and arcs of raw energy leapt from pedestal to staff, then staff to pedestal; a deep, deep hum, at the very lower limit of Human hearing, filled Dragon Hall. Jager continued to chant, advancing from one point to the next in a five-pointed pattern around the pedestal.

When the chant reached its climax, Omaja's head flashed brilliant white and was answered at once by a matching flash from the pedestal. Then the flashing display ceased; only the deep hum remained, emanating from staff and pedestal.

"Major," Jager called, still holding Omaja high, "the shield in close proximity to Remini should now be open. I can only hold it for a few minutes, though, so I'm afraid you'll have to get through in a hurry. Over to you."

"Roger that!" answered Hadgkiss. Moments later, his voice came through again. "I've contacted the freighter. That's one surprised captain and crew, I can assure you. One moment they were in what seemed like empty space. The next, boom! There was Remini, and *King Hammurabi* too!"

Jager laughed. "You can tell them there will be no charge for the show," he said. "It's all courtesy of Ensign Cornwallis."

"Right," said Dino. "Now, if you'll excuse me, I'll direct them through the shield opening and into a proper orbit. I'll let you know when they're inside so you can close the door behind them."

"Understood," said Jager. "Standing by."

The second freighter, captained by a Rept and former Fleet spacer, moved off toward the planet. Dino signaled Jager when it was well inside the shield's zone of protection, then braced himself, anticipating another "interruption" like the one he'd experienced when the shield was raised the day before. To his relief, the phenomenon didn't repeat. All he felt was a momentary unsteadiness, as though he'd stood up too quickly after a deep sleep.

He followed the freighter into orbit above Remini, then transbeamed aboard to advise and assist with preparations for the passengers who were soon to arrive. With that operation well underway, Hadgkiss returned to *King,* briefed Jager on where everything stood, then transbeamed down to the surface.

He brought Quade and Fallon up to date, assured them the first group of passengers had arrived safely on Nibiru, and briefed them on how the operation would proceed to its conclusion. He explained that he and Madda would not return to Remini's surface again, unless some emergency made it necessary. Instead, they would be escorting the freighters to and from Nibiru.

Quade explained to Dino that although his people had made quite a clamor, insisting he, as king, should travel to Nibiru in the first group—or the second, at the very least— he had insisted on remaining on Remini until the last. He was their king, he'd told them, responsible for *all* his people. He would not leave before everyone in the final group was safely aboard their transport vessel. He had also assigned Fallon to travel with the second group—the one now trans-beaming up. She would represent the royal family on Nibiru until he arrived, and assume the monarchy if anything should happen to him.

The major heartily approved of the king's reasoning and plan, and told the big Dragon so. We're forming a strong bond, Quade and I, thought Dino.

And, as if he had "overheard" the major's thought, Quade addressed him: "Though we have only just met, I perceive us to have more in common than I would have imagined, Major Dino Hadgkiss. More, in truth, than I would have thought possible with any Human. I believe you have taught me a lesson of great value; I thank you."

"You are most welcome, King Quade. You have taught me much as well, in your turn—for which I thank *you*." He bowed to the Dragon, and the king echoed the gesture in Dragon fashion.

In the end, it took seven trips to transfer all Remini's Dragons and their possessions to Nibiru—four runs by the first freighter, three by the second. The final refugees had been transbeamed to safety less than a quarter-hour before the Remini Humans launched their assault on Quade's mountain stronghold. Against all odds, the Dragons had escaped calamity.

When the last shipload arrived at Nibiru and its passengers were safe on the surface, Fianna and her parents—using Jager to relay their message—invited the two freighter captains to transbeam down themselves, so they could be properly thanked and rewarded in person.

For the captains, it was the opportunity of a lifetime. Of ten lifetimes! To have seen the fabled planet at all was one thing, but to set foot on its surface, to meet some of its Dragon-folk face to face? Utterly unheard of. In fact, they doubted anyone would ever believe them, even if they were at liberty to tell the tale.

Still, at the back of the two captains' minds was a niggling worry: what if this were a trap? What if the Dragons meant to eliminate them and destroy their ships and crews, now that they had visited the forbidden world? That would certainly end any chance of their revealing Nibiru's whereabouts, or what they had done on the Dragons' behalf. But in no time at all, both tossed their worries aside. The opportunity was well, well worth the risk. They gratefully accepted the offer and transbeamed down to the coordinates Jager provided.

When the transbeam field cleared, the freighter captains found themselves at the center of Dragon Hall. Dragons by the hundreds surrounded them, on the hall's stony floor and perched on ledges above. Directly before them, some fifteen meters away, were their official hosts—Fianna and Vin, with Celine and Jager at their sides; King Neal and Queen Dini, Ahimoth and Joli.

Though they had also been invited to attend, Quade and

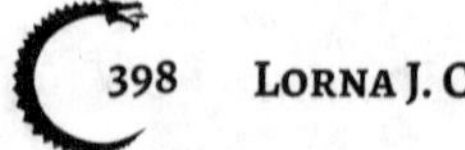

Fallon had elected to stay with their people, looking after the immediate needs of those most traumatized by recent events.

Ranged just behind and to either side of the official welcoming group were a dozen of the most imposing Dragons Ahimoth had been able to muster. Half were natives of Nibiru, the rest—and the biggest and burliest of the lot—represented the Reminis. Fianna and Ahimoth had agreed: the "welcoming committee" should make it clear as finest crystal to the freighter captains that the Dragon peoples were not to be trifled with.

It took the captains nearly a minute to take in the overwhelming tableau and regain a bit of composure. The committee, wearing pleasant but not-*too*-friendly smiles, waited patiently.

"Welcome, esteemed captains!" said King Neal, when the visitors seemed to be over their initial shock. "I am Neal Tawni Uwatti, King of Nibiru." He introduced the rest of the committee, Humans included, then turned the proceedings over to Princess Fianna, heiress to his throne.

"On behalf of all our people—the Dragons of Nibiru, and those of Remini whom you have brought here out of dire peril—I thank you once again. Our debt to you cannot ever truly be repaid. Nevertheless, we wish to present you and your fine crews with these tokens of our eternal gratitude." She looked off to her left and gave a nod. The crowd parted and out from behind them marched two pairs of handsome young Dragons, each pair bearing a stout, iron-bound wooden chest between them. Placing the chests before the captains, they bowed briefly and withdrew.

Fianna advanced to the chests and removed their heavy lids, revealing the contents: treasure. Dragon treasure. Gold, silver and other fine metals, some in the form of gleaming ingots and coins, some in raw, native nuggets. Among the metals were diamonds, sapphires and other precious stones from a host of worlds. The captains gasped and gaped. Here were greater riches than they'd ever dreamed of seeing all in one place—much less *owning*. They were speechless.

"Yours," said Fianna. "To distribute as you see fit among your brave and skillful crews. I know you will be fair in this. Just as I know that you and your people shall ever be steadfast in honoring your word, your promise to us: to reveal nothing, to anyone, at any time, of what you have seen and done this day."

The captains bowed deeply—hoping this was the proper response—first to Fianna, then to the committee behind her, and finally, turning and bowing, turning and bowing to acknowledge the Dragons all around them.

"We thank you, gracious Princess," said the Human captain, bowing a final time.

"And *all* your noble people!" said the Rept, raising his arms high and turning another full circle.

Celine and Jager stepped forward from their places beside Fianna and Vin.

"Good captains," said Celine, "you and your crews have just contributed, more profoundly than you may ever know, to the futures of all good people in our sectors of the galaxy. And to such people throughout this universe, and, no doubt, in others beyond."

"Indeed you have," said Jager; then he advanced to within a pace or two of the captains and spoke quietly, so that only they could hear. "And just one final reminder, mates. Keep your mouths ever so tightly shut, and do all you can to ensure

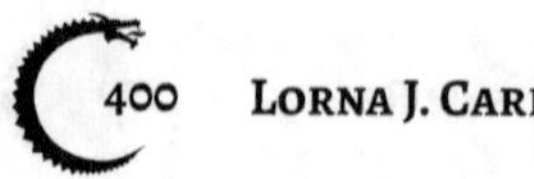

your crews do the same. Understand?"

The captains nodded.

"Excellent. And here's why. For one thing, you don't want to upset these Dragons. Or me. I know right where to find you, and they'll know too."

"Understood," said the Human captain.

"Clearly!" agreed the Rept captain. "But, if I may ask," he added, "just now you said, 'for one thing.' Is there a second thing?"

Jager grinned. "Why yes, there is. You see, the Dragons may one day have further need of your services. So you'll want to be quite sure to remain in their good graces."

"Jager is correct," said Fianna, who had stepped forward to join the little conference. "As the societies on this and the other Dragon Homeworlds develop, we may have need of outer-world goods or services from time to time. Not much need, most likely. We are happy as we are, and greatly prefer to live our lives simply. But if such a need should arise, you two would be the natural choices to call upon for assistance—and to reward."

"And you now know just how generous Dragon rewards can be, eh?" said Jager.

"Aye!" said one captain.

"Oh, we surely do!" said the other.

"But only if you have kept faith and abided by your promises," added Fianna.

"Of course," said both captains.

Fianna bowed a final time and turned to rejoin the committee.

"Again, thank you, my friends," said Jager. "Now I'm going to have you transbeamed back to your ships. Once aboard, you'll have fifteen minutes to secure your ship and crew for jump-shift. While I re-open the planetary shield-wall, the Fleet officers who escorted you will 'beam aboard to program your navs for departure. They'll then return to their ships and activate your jump-shift drives remotely. You'll end up back outside the shielding, each in a different, randomly chosen location. From there you're free to go about your business. Any questions?"

There were none, so Jager tapped his comm pickup and signaled Madda to 'beam the captains—and their rewards—back to their ships. In just over fifteen minutes, Madda and Dino had done their work, and the freighters vanished into jump-shift.

ON REMINI, HORDES OF battle-crazed Humans launched their attack on the Dragons' last mountain stronghold. Like a living tsunami, they surged toward the low outer walls, screaming, cursing and waving their weapons, mad with lust for Dragon blood. Over the stony walls they swarmed, to find...nothing.

Nothing but a single stray rat, raised up on its hind legs, nose and whiskers twitching, curious at the commotion. The first ranks of marauders came crashing to a halt, staring, mouths agape. Those just behind collided with the first in a swearing, angry jumble.

Satisfied that the noise was nothing important, the rat dropped to all fours and waddled casually toward the Dragons' newly vacant caves, sniffing here and there as he went.

Furious with frustration, one of the raiders swore bitterly and fired his weapon at the departing rodent.

And missed.

CHAPTER 37

Into the Future

When the freighters had gone and Jager had closed the shield behind them, King Neal asked Celine to invite Dino and Madda to Dragon Hall, "So that we may properly express our gratitude for all they have done."

Hadgkiss and Madda arrived to the enthused Dragon-applause of the "committee" that had greeted the freighter captains less than an hour before. Quade and Fallon were present as well, just returned from tending to their people. The Fleet officers graciously received the Dragons' thanks: the Nibiru Dragons, and the Dragons of Remini who would now share the fabled planet.

In their turn, Dino and Madda thanked their hosts for the opportunity to contribute to the Dragons' noble cause, and—understanding what an exceedingly rare privilege it was—for being permitted to visit their homeworld.

"Where will you go now, Major?" asked Fianna, when the formal greetings had concluded.

"Yes!" said Jager and Celine, "Where?"

"We will return to the new settlement in Remini's under-world," explained Hadgkiss, "now called Zulak City, in honor of a great leader among us. I'm guessing it will take us a few days at least, maybe a week, to ensure all is secure and in order. Then we've got to return to our Fleet ship, *Asherah*. Though it's been for the worthiest of causes, we've been away from our posts and our crew far longer than is prudent—especially in time of impending war."

A while later, Celine, Fianna, Jager, Vin, Ahimoth and Joli took Dino and Madda on a tour of Dragon Hall and the countryside near about. Their tour included the Glade of Linglu, where Celine and Fianna had cast off the Brothers' centuries-old hex upon the Nibiru Dragons. Though the two spacers were not versed in the ways of magic, they were deeply moved by the account. And equally moved to realize what unique and unimaginably important and powerful people they were privileged to know, in Celine, Jager and their Dragon companions and friends. For a fleeting moment, Dino's military mindset had him regarding them as assets. He pushed that view aside at once, almost ashamed to have taken such a narrow view. In a sense they *were* assets, he had to admit, but they were much, much more than that.

When the tour was complete, the party returned to the Glade of Linglu, where a pleasant meal had been prepared for them. They jumped at the chance for a few moments respite from weighty responsibility and perilous action. Even so, the talk strayed inexorably to recent events, and speculation on what they all might face in the days and months ahead. At a lull in the conversation, Celine took Dino aside for a few minutes' private talk. She gave him messages to relay to her mother and sister. And, knowing he planned to leave the shielded zone soon to resume Fleet duties, she promised to contact him the moment she and Jager were back outside the Homeworlds Shield, as the new barrier had been christened.

"When do you expect that will be?" asked Dino.

"I really don't know. We'll stay here on Nibiru for a couple of weeks at least—it will be that long before the double wedding can be held. That's Ahimoth and Joli, and Fianna and Vin, you know. The Dragons are quite serious and meticulous about their traditions, and royal weddings¬—well! From what I've heard, they're *really* over the top.

"After the weddings, though, I'm not certain. I do know Jager should get back to his post aboard *Queen Asherah*. Scabbage is still out there somewhere, too—we've *got* to track him down, terminate his insane scheme to steal Jager's body and bring him to justice. Not to mention ferreting out and neutralizing the lunatic's criminal network. And then there's the war!"

"Yes, there's certainly that," said Dino. "The war is my primary concern at the moment, naturally. What will you two do between now and the weddings?"

"We'll start with a bit of rest, I think. It seems 'soft' to even consider it, but reality is reality: We've been going so hard for so long, we've got to take at least a day or two to recharge. And reflect on all that's happened, and what we should do next."

"I'm glad to hear you say it," said Dino. "I know precisely what you mean about that 'soft' consideration, but in the longer view, seizing the chance to get back to battery physically, mentally and spiritually is prudent. I salute your wisdom."

"Thank you!" said Celine. "That makes it easier to get over the 'soft' business. I'll relay what you've said to Jager. I have a feeling he's going to resist taking a rest even worse than I. You know how he can be."

"Oh, yeah!" laughed Dino. "I'm pretty sure you'll make him see sense, but if it becomes necessary, you can tell him his captain ordered it—and ordered you to monitor and report on his compliance." They shared a laugh at the idea, but Celine knew her godfather was serious. And that it might prove necessary to play the "Captain's orders" card he'd just dealt her.

"Once we've rested up a little," she went on, "we'll be diving into a lot of study and practice. We both stand to increase our value to the war effort by advancing our magical knowledge and skills. And although they won't be able to spend a whole lot of time at it, Jager and Vin have got to learn to fly and fight together. Who knows when another combat-ready Dragon-Companion pair might be crucial to operations?"

"I never would have thought of that," admitted Dino, "but in light of what you and Fianna have done as a fighting unit, I have to agree! If it weren't for you two, Soader would still be at large."

Their private talk complete, Celine and Dino rejoined the others. The whole group made their way to Dragon Hall, where they were ushered into the presence of King Neal and Queen Dini.

The king announced that plans were under way to hold a grand celebration for the newcomers from Remini, and Dini formally invited Dino and Madda to attend. Neal explained that the festivities would take place after their Remini brethren had had a little time to settle, rest and recover from their recent ordeal—most likely two or three days hence.

Dino and Madda thanked the royal couple for the kind invitation, but explained that they must return to their ships and duties.

"We do understand," said the king. "We appreciate your dedication to your work—and we are eternally thankful for all you have done to defend and protect our people."

"Since *King* and *Spitfire* are inside the shielded zone," said Jager, "you'll be able to fly back to Remini. When you've finished your business there, give me a call and I'll open the shield to let you out. Then I'll close it again. Once it's closed, I believe it should remain sealed, except in extreme need. Like when it's time to transport the evacuees who want to go home, or when Remi, Mia and Hyatt are ready to leave. The Mentors and the Dragons themselves are quite correct in their supreme concern for the safety and security of these worlds, and every time we open the shield, there's an element of risk."

"Agreed!" said all the Dragons present: King Neal and Queen Dini, Princess Fianna and Prince Ahimoth, Prince Vin and Princess-to-be Joli—the Royal House of Nibiru.

The officers paid their final respects, then transbeamed back to their ships: Dino to *King Hammurabi* and Madda to *Spitfire*.

Two days later—after abundant rest, good food, attention to their most recent bumps, bruises and batterings, and several invigorating swims—Celine and Jager were eager to get back to work.

Celine turned to her grimoires, seeking out, deciphering and practicing spells to employ in the battles that might lie ahead.

Jager honed his magical skills as well, but spent the greater portion of his time inspecting the paintings in Fianna's cave, and in the galleries discovered in Vin's cave complex.

Each day he briefed Celine on what he had found, and several times took her to inspect a painting in person. Fianna and Vin were happy to fly their friends between caves whenever the need arose. On two occasions, the pair called upon old Orgon to help interpret a scene, and to consult with him on what it might portend for the future: the future of the Dragons themselves, and of the peoples, worlds and universes beyond the Dragon Homeworlds.

After breakfast on the fifth day, Celine cheerily announced she wanted a break from the books.

"Good. You've earned one," said Jager. "What would you like to do instead?"

"Could we go together to Vin's cave and study paintings?"

"Some break!" laughed Jager. "Taking time off from your studies, to study some more!"

"It's not the same," Celine said with a dramatic pout, then swatted him playfully.

"I know, I know. Just kidding. And sure, I'd love to study some together. There are a few I've already seen and want to show you, but plenty of new ones to explore too."

Half an hour later, they entered Vin's cave. "I love doing this," said Jager. "I loved exploring caves back home, but never figured I'd be doing it on another planet. It's like a super-holiday!"

"Ha!" laughed Celine. "There you go again. How do you do it? You can always find something positive about a situation."

"Must be in my genes," he said, and they trotted, laughing and light-orbs bobbing, deeper into the cavern network.

After pointing out a few items of interest from his previous day's viewing, Jager announced, "Here's where I left off.

How about if you look this one over while I do the one on the opposite wall, and we just work our way down the tunnel."

"Sounds good to me," she said, and they went to work.

Celine noticed some of the images were similar to those in Fianna's cave; others were more elaborate and of much better quality. Quite artistic, she thought. She took notes as she went, and even drew a few sketches. It quickly became clear why Jager was so intrigued by the paintings. They were amazing in themselves, just as art works—but they carried so much meaning! Many depicted events and circumstances on worlds beyond Nibiru. She found it all utterly fascinating, until she came to a depiction of several angry Kerr Dragons. She shuddered at the memories it stirred; the recent desperate battles with Soader and his two-headed Kerr were all too red and raw in her mind.

Completing her inspection of one painting, she advanced to the next—and gasped at what she saw.

"Jager, come look at this!" she called; he joined her. "Look," she said, pointing, "there's you, and me, and you're holding Omaja."

"Right. And those Dragons—it's Ahimoth, Fianna, Vin...

"And that's got to be Major Hadgkiss over to the left there," said Celine. "And those look like Mentors behind him. And right there is what I really wanted you to see. That person next to the major can only be my father."

"Hm! I think you're right," said Jager. He examined the image more closely. "Yes. That's Commander Zulak. This is the second time one of these has seemed to show him with us, in the future. We've never all been together like that in the past."

"No, we haven't," she agreed, frowning. "Something's

really odd here. Hey, let's see what all this script is, down below. Funny, it's laid out like a poem." She lowered her light-orb, bent down to see the neatly lettered inscription more clearly, and began reading aloud.

The princess and the boy
The princess and the boy
Where have they gone
The princess and the boy?

Some say together, some say not
Some say lovers, some say lost
The princess and the Dragon
The princess and the Dragon

Where have they gone
The princess and the Dragon?
Some say white, some say black
Some say for good some say for bad

The princess and the prince
The princess and the prince
Where have they gone
The princess and the prince?

Some say up, some say down

Some say back, some say now

Her and he
Him and she
They and them
Where are they now?
Where could they be?

"I can't believe it," she said when she came to the end. "Have you heard that before?"

"No," said Jager. "Have you?"

"Yes. Many times. It's a song from my childhood. I sang it to Fianna when we first met. How can it be *here*, though? And written in Pleiadean?"

"Good question. *Very* good question," said Jager. "But I would bet anything it's a lot more than just a song for kids."

They moved closer to examine the image's details more closely. There could be no mistake: Commander Zulak was clearly depicted, as was Dino. Celine brushed away a tear and shook her head, bewildered. "This is definitely not something that's already happened. We know many of the paintings foretell the future, but this is the second one doesn't make sense that way."

"Maybe they only tell of *possible* futures," suggested Jager. "And maybe they can be mistaken, and show things that never happened or never will."

"I don't know," said Celine. "Maybe Fianna can explain it. Or Orgon. All I know right now is I've had enough for today. All right if we end off and go back?"

"Sure," said Jager. "Let's go." He took her hand and gave it a reassuring squeeze.

Celine remained silent, deep in thought, as they walked back toward the cave entrance. Then she spoke up: "Sweetie, I know we already had a funeral for my father, but at some point we really should give him a proper burial."

"Uh, hold on," said Jager. "*Burial?* What do you mean?"

"You know—a burial. Lay Father's body to rest. The major says he's still got it. Hidden, and safe in a stasis tube."

"*WHAT??*" said Jager, nearly shouting. The word echoed down the stony passageway, deep into the mountain. "But Fleet gave him a space burial!"

"Yes, the major mentioned that," said Celine, "but it must have been an empty-coffin ceremony."

"Oh, oh, oh, *oh!*" cried Jager, head held tight between up-raised hands.

"What?" said Celine. "What is it?"

"*Lazarus!*"

"Lazarus? The spell you devised?"

"Yes! I've used it to bring back people who've left their bodies—to bring them back and help them re-animate the body, if they're willing to."

"Yes, but Father was killed weeks ago."

"Right. But if the major has his body in a stasis tube, it won't have deteriorated at all. If I can find the commander—your father himself, the living being—I could help him back to life. It's never failed before, so..."

"Oh! Oh, my," said Celine, her thoughts racing. "That would change *everything*. The whole future. It would be...it could be just as that painting shows!"

For a long moment, she stared at her soulmate, open-mouthed, incredulous.

"*OH!*" she cried, and engulfed him in the tightest embrace she'd ever mustered.

They parted, beaming—then joined hands to dance and dance and cheer and cheer, streaming tears of new hope and joy.

ABOUT THE AUTHOR

Lorna J. Carleton makes her home in Vernon, British Columbia. A BC native, Lorna is a Safety Advisor for a major utility, while also working toward a university degree. She's dreamed of being an author since childhood, and made several attempts at novel writing. *Dragons of Remini* is her third published work, and the third book in the Dragons of Nibiru series. She drew inspiration for the series from observations of life over the years; chief among them were clashes among diverse cultures, and the struggles of former cult members to get on with their lives and find happiness. While continuing the book series, Lorna is also planning a vacation trip to the Pleiades Cluster—providing she can find suitable transport (technological or otherwise).

www.lornajcarleton.com